Also by Cour

HOLIDAY NOVELS
A Cross-Country Christmas
Merry Ex-Mas
My Phony Valentine

STAND-ALONE NOVELS
The Happy Life of Isadora Bentley
Things Left Unsaid
Hometown Girl

NANTUCKET
If For Any Reason
Is it Any Wonder
A Match Made at Christmas
What Matters Most

HARBOR POINTE
Just Look Up
Just Let Go
Just One Kiss
Just Like Home

LOVES PARK, COLORADO
Paper Hearts
Change of Heart

SWEETHAVEN

A Sweethaven Summer

A Sweethaven Homecoming

A Sweethaven Christmas

A Sweethaven Romance (a novella)

A Cross-Country Wedding

a novel

COURTNEY WALSH

Sweethaven
Press

For everyone who loves when friends become more.
You are my people.

Prologue

Text Exchange between Maddie Rogers and her best friend,
Lauren Richmond, 1 a.m., Christmas Eve

LAUREN

Maddie! <bride emoji><heart emoji><groom emoji><ring emoji>

MADDIE

WHAT!!??

LAUREN

!!!

MADDIE

I knew it! I knew he was going to propose! Captain America for the win!

Tell me everything!

LAUREN

I have to tell you the whole story in person.

I wanted you to be the first to know!

MADDIE

<dancing woman emoji><dancing woman emoji><dancing woman emoji>

LAUREN

And you'll be my maid of honor?

MADDIE

Are you kidding!? If you'd asked anyone else, I would've disowned you.

Hey! You know what you should do!?

LAUREN

Uh oh. Something crazy? <crying laughing emoji>

MADDIE

I think you mean something FUN!

LAUREN

I forgot in your world those two things are the same thing.

<tilted laughing emoji>

MADDIE

You know you love me.

LAUREN

Yeah. I do.

Tell me the idea!

MADDIE

You two fell for each other on a cross-country trip, right?

LAUREN

We did.

MADDIE

It makes sense to get married the same way.
. .

A cross-country wedding!

LAUREN

I'm intrigued. . .How would that work?

MADDIE

<shrugging woman emoji>

Get married in little bits at a time as you
repeat the road trip where you fell in love.

LAUREN

I actually kind of love this idea.

You're a genius.

MADDIE

That's what I keep telling people.

LAUREN

<crying laughing emoji>

MADDIE

When's the wedding?

LAUREN

July. After baseball season ends.

MADDIE

But. . .that's only seven months.

LAUREN

Yep.

MADDIE

Can we plan an on-the-road wedding in seven months?

LAUREN

We're brilliant. We can do anything.

MADDIE

Ha. I'm just here to make some noise and have a good time.

<tilted laughing emoji>

LAUREN

Go to bed, will you?

MADDIE

Are you kidding? I'm going out!

LAUREN

<shocked emoji> Go to bed! And Merry Christmas!

MADDIE

<Santa emoji> <Christmas tree emoji> <present emoji>

Chapter One

Simon

Six months later

There's a hammer in the background of my dream, but that's not quite right.

Pounding. Knocking?

Knocking. Frantic. Incessant.

I peel my eyes open and roll over. I do that middle-of-the-night listening thing where I tilt my ears toward the sound, forcing my wide-open eyes to blink, adjusting to the darkness.

Neighbors? Maybe neighbors. They like to drink on Friday nights. Sometimes they stumble in late. Or into the bushes.

I stupidly thought graduating college and moving into a building with mostly professionals would mean the days of overhearing drunken people loudly debate whether cereal is soup were over.

No such luck.

Pound, pound, pound!

"Simon?" A muffled voice from outside.

Maddie.

I whip off the covers, fully awake now.

Why is my knee-jerk reaction always to jump to her rescue?

I know Maddie well enough to know she's not going away until she gets through the door.

It's a familiar scenario.

And I can guess why she's here.

The first time she showed up I was so worried someone had died. She'd had puffy eyes, cheeks stained with mascaraed tears, and she was nearly inconsolable. I quickly learned that Maddie was the personification of melodrama. Apparently, break-ups caused big emotions.

And she'd been through a lot of them over the past ten years.

I pull open the door and find her standing there, looking like a disheveled French pauper who sings in the rain about being on her own. The familiar trails of black makeup have snaked down her cheeks, and her long, wavy, blond hair has fallen in an uneven lump onto her shoulders.

Slowly, she lifts her chin and meets my eyes.

Ah, great. She's got me now for sure. If someone glanced at Maddie's little finger, they'd see me wrapped around it like a vine on a trellis.

No matter how many times she shows up like this, I'll never turn her away.

"What happened?" I pull her into my apartment, into my arms, and hold her as her body shakes with sobs.

She buries her face in my chest, and I inhale her—deeply— just for a breath, while simultaneously hoping that I don't smell like sleep. I've memorized her scent over the years—it's the scent of sunshine. Citrusy and sweet.

I really hate how much I like having her in my arms. However, I've been placed squarely in the friend zone for so long I've sunk a well and staked a claim to a plot of land there.

Another breath.

She pulls away and looks up at me. "He broke up with me."

I'm not sarcastic by nature, but a few things pop into my mind. Things like "Shocker," or, "You don't say. . ." or, "Given his three burner phones, I'm surprised it took this long."

Maddie's love life was not unlike holding a cute porcelain cup, kiln-glazed and beautiful—and then filling it with gasoline and tossing it in a bonfire. The combination of her personality and her terrible taste in men pretty much ensured that pounding on my door at 2 a.m. would always be the end result.

I love her personality. I love that she loves with her whole heart. I love that she throws herself into every relationship with no net, no parachute, no safety line. Her choice of guys, on the other hand, I don't love.

I never have. They never measure up.

She shifts and sniffs. "Why? *Why?*"

"Why what?"

"Why can't I find a nice guy?" She throws up her hands as she says this.

I try not to be offended.

She steps away, and I'm thankful her question seems to be rhetorical.

She tries to hang her purse on the hooks by my front door and completely misses; it lands with a leather *thud* on the floor. She hangs her head down, shaking it slightly and seemingly defeated, but then looks at me with a glint in her wet eyes and a smirk on her face.

I can't help it. I look away and press my lips together to stifle a laugh.

"Oh *yeah*," she says, ruefully. "That's just about how my love life is going. Missed it by *that* much."

She heaves a sigh and moves through my apartment like she

owns the place. Like she belongs here. The thought—and the ones that follow—are the kind I routinely have to squash.

She plops in a pile at the end of my couch, in "her spot," as she calls it, tucking her feet under the pillows.

I run a hand through my already messed-up hair. "So, this guy, uh, what's his name. . .again. . .? Orlando? Columbus?"

"*Austin*," she says, kicking a pillow at me.

I know his name. I know *all* of their names.

"Right, I *knew* it was some kind of city." I pause, hoping to keep it light. "He's no good, then?" I don't ask this because I need clarification.

Over the years, Maddie has woken me up for a number of reasons. There was the time she thought she hit a dog on the interstate (it turned out to be a bag of garbage someone had tossed out into the street). Then there was the time she insisted she left her phone in an Uber and needed help to track down the driver (she eventually found it in her inner coat pocket). Or the time she showed up with a kitten she'd found in the alley behind whatever bar she'd been at that night.

I'm allergic to cats, so I had to kick her out that time. Plus, cats are the devil.

Ninety-seven percent of the time when Maddie shows up like this, it's because of some guy. Seeing her like this is its own kind of pitiful. Maddie is usually sunshine and unicorns. If she had a color, it would be bright yellow. But when she has her heart trampled on, which is often, she turns into a very different version of herself.

No one besides her best friend Lauren and I ever see this side of her.

So, in spite of my friend zone relocation hopes, I tolerate these late-night visits. Honestly, I'd probably spend my entire life rushing to her aid if she'd let me.

I'm Maddie's perpetual shoulder to cry on. Pathetic?

Maybe. It's also the nicest thing I can think of to do for her. Good old, reliable Simon Collier. Her *friend*.

I've made my peace with that.

Mostly.

And somewhere, in my head, I know I need to move on, I need to look elsewhere, that it's a lost cause. I *know* that.

It's just not that easy when she shows up like this at my door.

I tuck in to the other end of the couch, letting out a stretchy, sleepy sigh. "What happened with Boston?"

She shakes her head at me as if she's gearing up for a fight. "*Austin.*"

"Right, right." I hold my hands up in mock surrender. "Sorry."

I don't really want the play-by-play. I know exactly how these relationships go. And since Maddie insists on dating carbon copies of the same guy over and over again, the details never really change.

"He broke up with me." She sniffles.

"So you said."

She frowns. "I really liked him."

"I'm sorry." I only half-mean it. "Can I get you something to drink?"

Another sniff. "Hot chocolate?"

"Hot choc. . ." I stop mid-word. "It's summer."

She raises her eyebrows at me as if to ask, *Your point is. . .?*

"Yes, ma'am. One hot chocolate, coming up."

I stand and walk over to the kitchen, then fumble around with the kettle and the packet of hot chocolate while Maddie's sniffling continues. I glance up and see that she's now fully laying down. No way she's going home tonight. Which means I'm not going to get much sleep.

Because how can I sleep with Maddie in my apartment?

"Do you want to talk about it?" I ask gingerly, knowing that in order for her to move on, like all of the others, she's going to have to tell her side of it.

And, like all of the others, I'll pretend to want to hear the story.

"No," she says. "It's too humiliating."

I pull a bottle of water out of the refrigerator for me and wait for the kettle to whistle for her hot chocolate. I know in another few moments she'll lay down her defenses and. . .

"It's just another guy who's decided he's not looking for a relationship, or if he *is* looking for a relationship, he wants to have it with the nineteen-year-old intern at his office. Or maybe he decided I was too *much* for him. Not serious enough. Too flighty."

. . .and there it is.

I move to stand behind the couch where she's laying. "I just wish you could understand that the problem isn't you."

She sits up and looks at me.

Uh oh. Shoot. I didn't mean to say that. Exactly.

"What do you mean?"

"Austin wasn't the guy, Maddie," I say this with more authority than I should have since I have no idea what kind of guy Austin is.

"He could've been."

"He couldn't have been."

"How do you know?"

"Because *Austin* was too stupid to realize what a good thing he had."

She narrows her eyes for a split second, then sinks back into the couch. "That was really nice," she says, feigning grumpiness.

I turn back to the kitchen so she can't see me smile. "I think you deserve a bit of nice."

What these guys don't see in Maddie, I'll never understand. And the fact that their stupidity makes her think something is wrong with her irritates me.

She was always *too extra* or *not serious enough* or *too immature.*

But to me, she wasn't *too* anything. To me, she's perfect. Well, nearly perfect. I do wish she was a little less of a slob.

If things were different—if Maddie and I weren't *just friends*—I could show her that she is worth having around. That she'd be my reason for getting out of bed every day.

But things aren't different. They just aren't. Maddie and I *are* just friends. And it's not the most terrible thing. But existing in a world where I want something I can never have has its limits.

How do I tell her I'm considering moving away? I think as I hand her a steaming mug of hot chocolate.

She takes it, then looks up at me, her doe-eyes big and bright and bluer than any pair of eyes should have the right to be. "Do you have any marshmallows?"

I stare at her for a few long seconds until she flutters her eyelashes at me.

"Oh my gosh, you are so high maintenance," I mutter.

She smiles, holding her cup up to cover her face except her eyes. "That's why you love me."

I turn back toward the kitchen.

That and so many other reasons.

Chapter Two

Simon

I t wasn't a dream hammer that woke me this time—but Maddie's frantic exclamation.

"Oh! No!" She practically shouted it from the couch, and all at once I'm out of the chair I dozed off in, eyes bleary, assuming a drunken kung-fu stance.

"What! Where? What is it?" I shake my brain awake and try to focus. *Maybe if I grab that lamp I could fight off the intruder and...*

Maddie is sitting up straight, on the couch, eyes wide and it's still the middle of the night.

"What's wrong?" My heart is pounding.

"Lauren's wedding." Her face is filled with panic.

I notice the awkward fighting stance I'm in and drop it immediately. "What about it?"

"Austin was supposed to be my date."

It takes a moment for me to register that.

Last night, before we fell asleep, we talked long into the night. About Austin, about love, about life.

There's nothing like those soft and dark conversations when it's too late to be awake.

"Wait. You were going to take this guy on a cross-country road trip?"

"Yeah."

"To a wedding."

"Yeah. What's the big deal?"

I stare at her.

"I can feel you judging me."

"I'm not judging you."

She stares at me.

"Okay, yes, I'm judging you."

"Simon! This is a crisis!"

Like I said—*dramatic.*

"I'm sure you'll find another date." I sit back down in the chair and lean my head back on the headrest, eyes closed.

"It's next week, Simon."

"Then go solo."

"I can't go solo," she says. "Talk about a third wheel. It would make them uncomfortable, and as the maid of honor, that is not okay. My whole function during this trip is to make Lauren happy."

"Don't drive." I hold one hand up and give a half-wave goodbye, eyes still closed. "Just fly."

She frowns. "I promised Lauren I'd do this with her. It was my idea, for cryin' in a bucket."

The adrenaline of being shocked awake has started to wear off, and I can feel my eyelids beginning to form a union to petition my brain to stay closed.

A pause. "Simon?"

I know that tone. . .she's about to ask for something.

"Do you think. . ."

I open my eyes.

She shakes her head. "No. Never mind. . ."

Maddie, you could ask me to scale that building across the street, and I'd figure out a way to do it.

I lean my head forward. "What is it?"

"Do you think. . .you could be my date?"

I sit.

I look at her.

I go to sit again, but realize I'm already sitting.

"Me?"

"Sure," she says, genuinely. "You and Lauren are friends, and you were invited, right?"

"Yeah, we are, and yeah, I was, but. . ." My train of thought is still boarding at the station. "You want me to go with you? On the road trip? I was going to wait for their reception here, when they get back."

"You *could* do that," she says. "Or you could come with me!" She sits forward a bit more. "It could be really fun, Simon. Plus, you're uptight; it would be good for you."

"I'm not uptight," I say.

She laughs.

I'm not uptight. I just like things to be a certain way. Things in their place. Predictable. Understandable. Even-keeled.

Unfortunately, a quick glance at Maddie's purse still in a clump on the floor by the hooks tells me that she has a unique way of upsetting my apple cart.

I frown, more focused and awake now that she's asked me to be her date. "How is this even going to work? I don't know anyone who's gotten married on the road."

"I'll pretend not to be annoyed that you don't remember our conversation about this," she says. When I don't respond, she continues. "The wedding is in Illinois, but they're going to say their vows in pieces on the road, at all the different spots that are meaningful to them."

I'm puzzled. "Why would they do that?" I ask, half to myself.

"What do you mean 'why'?" She frowns back. "Because it's romantic?"

"It is?"

"You're *so* literal." She shakes her head. "Romance isn't literal. It's a feeling."

There are a ton of feelings battling for my attention right now—but there's no way I'll let her know that.

"So. . .what do you think?"

"About their cross-country wedding?"

"No, you nerd, about going with me."

She looks expectantly at me.

"I. . ."

She scrunches up her shoulders and nods in anticipation of my answer.

"I. . .have work."

She slumps slightly. "But, it travels, right? You can work remotely?"

I turn away. "I don't know, Maddie, I just started my business and. . ."

"Come on, Simon! How long's it been since you took a vacation?"

"Last month. I didn't work for a week."

"You had the flu!"

"Right, but I was still off. It was like a stay-cation."

"Ugh, come on." She moves over to me, sitting on her heels and putting her hands on the armrest of the chair I'm sitting in.

"Please? It's just a week," she says, having no concept of how much work I have to do in that period of time. "And we'll make sure you can still do all the things you need to do. You'll have Wi-Fi. You'll have a phone. It'll be great. Perfect. Awesome." She kneels up. "And the best part is," she holds her arms out wide, "that you'll be with me."

She has no idea how right she is.

I scrunch up my face and look at her.

She gives me a goofy smile and reaches out clasped hands.

"Please, m'lord," she says, affecting an eerily perfect Irish accent. "Aye, I beg, accompany me on dis 'ere foine adventure!"

I snuffle out a laugh and say, "Good grief, fine, I'll go. Just get off the floor. And don't speak Irish at me."

She laughs, clambers to her feet and claps her hands together. "You will?"

I tilt my head. "Yes. I will."

"Oh my gosh!" She grabs my hands, pulls me to my feet, and hugs me full. I can feel her body against me and mine instantly reacts. I stand there for a moment, then reach my arms up and return the hug.

"You're the best!"

I pull back and stare at her, and after a moment, I point to the dark smudge under her eye. "You look like a raccoon."

She rolls her eyes. "I don't even care. I have a date. A good one, too. Gosh, why didn't I think of this before? No pressure, no feelings, just friends! It's perfect!" She holds up a fist and I go to high five it—and then she tries to switch to a high five as I switch to a fist bump.

It's a metaphor for this whole relationship. My timing is just a bit off.

"We'll work on that," she says. "I'm going to wash my face."

I nod and she turns, and then I'm alone.

And I wonder—for a long moment—what in the world I just agreed to.

Chapter Three

Maddie

Sometimes, when I least expect it, friendship with Simon feels different.

Not different "bad." Or even different "odd."

Different "nice." Different "safe."

With Simon, there are no expectations.

He's the person who's always there, despite my many, many shortcomings. He's never made me feel bad for being a literal disaster. I know he knows I'm a mess, but for as long as I've known him, he's kept his thoughts on the subject to himself.

I'm sure that's what great friends do, but Simon is literally the best at it.

When Austin broke up with me, I wasn't sad about losing him. Not really. It wasn't actually *Austin* that had upset me, but knowing that I was too much or not enough or just not right for yet another guy.

And not for lack of trying. I put my heart out there all the time. One would think I'd learn some kind of lesson by now.

So, I go to Simon's. After the inevitable crash and burn I need someone who doesn't judge me or try to fix me.

Simon is that someone. Always has been. For ten years, he's been my best friend. Steady. Stable. Dependable. He's the iron pipe I tether myself to when the tornado is bearing down on me, Bill Paxton, Helen Hunt, and the barn.

A bright moon cuts through the darkness of Simon's living room. He went to bed over an hour ago and is probably fast asleep. I, unfortunately, am the elusive kind of tired that keeps sleep just out of reach.

When I close my eyes, my mind spins. Feelings of *not good enough* swirl. I'm usually pretty good at letting rejections roll off my back, but for some reason, this one is sticking with me.

Maybe I'm just tired of the whole thing. Dating apps and first dates and butterflies and rejections. It's exhausting.

I roll over, the light of the moon hitting me right in the eyes.

I sit up. I lay back down. I turn. I fuss with the pillow.

It's simultaneously too bright and too dark. It's quiet but not exactly silent.

I start to think about the upcoming trip. The wedding, the vows, and Simon—once again—saving me in a pinch.

My body instantly starts to relax, sinking a bit deeper into the couch cushions.

I start to imagine how much more fun it will be with a great friend instead of someone I barely know. Someone who doesn't keep a record of wrongs, someone who isn't constantly judging me, someone who. . .

Light. Brightness.

The next morning, it takes me a few seconds to orient myself. Before I open my eyes, I draw in a breath—met by the scent of coffee and pine trees and. . .vinegar?

I look around. I'm on a couch. That's right, I'm at Simon's.

I go to move, but my whole left arm is completely numb. I must've fallen asleep in a weird position and cut off the circulation to it.

I sit up, and with my right hand, take my dead left arm and lift it, letting it slump lifelessly on my lap. I do it again, higher this time.

It feels so weird.

I take it with my right hand again and waggle it in the air, trying to get the feeling back in it. I stifle a giggle, thinking *"dead arm."* I shrug my left shoulder at the coffee table to flop my thick arm onto a pile of books, where it lands with a meaty *thump.* I spurt out another laugh. I have no idea why this is so hilarious to me.

I take it once more with my right hand and start thwacking it against the backrest of the couch.

"Whatcha doing there, Maddie?"

I stop cold. Normal people would feel totally embarrassed, but I don't.

It's Simon.

I burst out laughing. "Oh my gosh, Simon, my whole arm is asleep, look!" I try to put a coffee table book in my left hand and my fat-feeling fingers fail to close and the book hits the floor.

With all this action, my capillaries finally get with the program and turn my arm and hand into slow-moving pins and needles.

I turn with a grin. "Thank goodness it's not permanent."

He's standing in the kitchen, looking bemused. "I'm going to wait to hand you your coffee."

I jump up, squeezing my left hand in and out of a fist, shaking it back to life. "Thanks for letting me sleep here."

"'Course." He raises his eyebrows in a question as he slides a cup toward me.

I look at my left hand, feeling almost returned, and give him a smirky nod.

"And for coming with me on the road trip."

He glances at me over the top of his mug. "Like you were going to take no for an answer."

I smile. He's fun to spar with, especially when anything is out of place. Me being on his couch means that his entire day will be out of place. Because Simon likes routine, and I've messed his up. I know that, and I feel a twinge of guilt about it.

But just a twinge.

Sometimes I wish Simon were as open with his feelings as I am with mine. Most days, I'm trying to get him to relax, to have a little more fun, to live in the moment. Most days, I fail.

Teasing him is about the only way I've found to do that, but sometimes honesty works too.

I wonder if I know Simon half as well as he knows me.

"I'll pay you back, I promise. I'll do your laundry for a month," I say, in my brightest tone.

He opens the fridge and pulls out caramel creamer. I hesitate briefly—that's my favorite, and I know he doesn't drink it.

"Please don't. I don't want to end up with pink undershirts."

"Hey. I resent that," I say.

"You know I'm right." He takes a sip of his coffee and leans against the counter.

I pour cream into my hot mug and stir it. "Fine, then what can I do for you? How can I repay you?"

Our eyes meet, and he holds my gaze. He's wearing his glasses, which he hardly ever does anymore, and I'm reminded of the Simon I knew back in the day. Back before he grew up and got a real job. Back when he was a dorky college kid obsessed with his grades. And *Star Trek*.

He is basically the same now as he was then. An old soul.

He wears wool socks in the winter and full-on pajamas year-round. He listens to jazz music and does puzzle books and has a piano in his apartment that, as far as I know, he doesn't even know how to play.

There are a few fundamental differences to the grown-up version of the boy I'd known all those years ago, though. For instance, that boy was skinny. Scrawny even. The version I'm staring at isn't skinny. He's filled out. A few years ago, he started lifting weights, and it shows.

I've teased him about it more than once. You'd never know he's hiding a six pack under his work suits.

Finally, after apparently running through a mental laundry list of possibilities, he says, "You don't have to repay me."

I frown. "Are you sure?"

"I'm sure. Just fold the blanket you used last night and we're even."

"Done."

We sit in a moment of silence. It's not uncomfortable—it's easy. Safe. Content, even.

"You've really gotten your life together, Simon," I muse, looking around his apartment. "It's admirable."

"Was there a time you were concerned I wouldn't have my life together?" One of his eyebrows quirks ever-so-slightly.

I shrug. "No, I pretty much always knew you'd be a crazy success."

He holds up his cup in a fake toast. "Nerdy guys often are."

"You aren't really a nerd," I say, even though he absolutely is. "I mean, you used to be, but then you met me. Your coolness factor grew by at least five hundred points."

"Uh-huh."

Just then, a jangle of keys in the lock and the door of his apartment opens.

"Simon! I hope you're up. And please tell me you're decent."

I know that voice. This isn't going to look good.

"We've got to discuss the pitch for—" At the sight of us in Simon's kitchen, his sister, Bea, stops talking and stares.

"What the heck is going on here?!"

I cringe a smile and lift my cup. "Um. . .want some coffee?"

Chapter Four

Maddie

Bea doesn't like me.

I'm not sure Bea likes anyone, but she especially doesn't like me.

She seems to have the wrong idea about my relationship with Simon, and she's been very vocal about it. She's made it clear that she thinks I take advantage of him.

"What am I looking at here?" Bea drops her bags onto Simon's couch and crosses her arms over her chest.

"Uh, I'd say you're looking at two people having coffee?" Simon's grumpiness increases whenever his sister is around. It drives Bea nuts, but I think it's funny.

"Wait. Did you two. . ."

Simon and I swing a look to each other, shocked, then back at her.

Simultaneously and overlapping, "No!" "Are you kidding?" "What in the world?" from the both of us.

"Are you nuts? Simon's my best friend. How could you even think that?"

I briefly notice Simon doesn't say anything after that.

She narrows her eyes. A perfect indicator for me to find the exit. "I should go." I stand. "Travel mug?"

Simon nods and takes my coffee mug from me. It's become part of our ritual, a to-go order, normal after my pre-dawn hysterics.

I walk past Bea and grab my bag from the hook by the door. Simon must've hung it up before he went to bed because, last I remember, it was in a heap on the floor.

"I want this mug back," Simon says as he walks the travel mug over. "It's my favorite one."

"Have I ever not returned something I borrowed?" I ask as I take the mug from him.

"Do you really want me to answer that?"

"I'll bring it back, I promise." I grin. "Thanks for the coffee. And for. . .everything." I might've said that last part a little suggestively on purpose.

Behind him, Bea is practically fuming. Is that steam coming out of her ears?

I flash her a smile. "It was lovely to see you again, Bea."

In lieu of responding, Simon's sister turns and walks into the kitchen.

"She loves me," I whisper.

He shakes his head. "She loves everyone."

I touch his arm. "You're the best, Simon."

"Yeah, yeah."

I lower my voice and give his arm a hard squeeze. "And my hand works now!"

"Ow! Will you get out of here?"

I laugh as he practically pushes me out the door, and as it closes behind me, I hear Bea say, "All right, Simon. Spill it. What happened with you two last night?"

Text exchange between Maddie and Lauren

MADDIE

Hey, change of plans. I'm not bringing Austin on the trip anymore.

LAUREN

You're not? What happened?

MADDIE

He dumped me. <broken heart emoji>

LAUREN

Oh, Maddie, I'm so sorry. But you're better off without him!

He's a jerkface and we can't stand him. You'll be fine on the trip alone!

Or would you rather not go?

MADDIE

Are you kidding? I wouldn't miss this for the world!

And I won't be alone.

LAUREN

You won't? That was quick.

MADDIE

Hey now.

It's not a date, it's Simon.

LAUREN

Wait. Simon?

MADDIE

Yes! I asked him last night to go as friends!

It actually makes WAY more sense.

LAUREN

Simon?

On a road trip?

MADDIE

It'll be good for him. <laughing face emoji>

LAUREN

The things that man puts himself through for you. . .

MADDIE

He needs a vacation! I hardly had to do any arm-twisting at all.

LAUREN

No, I'm sure you didn't. I hope he's not miserable.

MADDIE

I'll make sure it's fun!

LAUREN

Pretty sure you and Simon have different ideas of "fun."

MADDIE

It'll be great! Promise! I've got work. We'll talk later.

Chapter Five

Simon

Ten years ago

Group projects should be optional.

Either that or outlawed.

That's what I'm thinking as I nervously make my way across campus to the dorm room of a girl named Lauren who mercifully asked if I wanted to join her group.

She was obviously the kind of person to take pity on shy kids. Or maybe she was guessing that I'd do all the work.

Either way, she'd saved me. I owe her.

As I pull open the door to the residence hall, I'm cursing Professor Hansen's name. Why anyone thought a group project was a good idea I'd never understand. Being forced to socialize, to share ideas, to *converse*—I don't even like getting my hair cut because of the small talk. It makes me want to crawl out of my skin.

I make my way up the stairs to the fourth floor, thinking this would be the first time in my life that I'd been in a girl's room.

And—go figure—it's to study.

I'm trying to figure out a way to avoid the public speaking aspect of this project when I step out of the stairwell and onto the fourth floor. I'm instantly accosted by the sound of a Sara Bareilles song blaring from the end of the hallway.

I'm thankful I live in the honors' dorm where there are strict rules about noise.

Girls dart in and out of their rooms, most of them carrying caddies full of bathroom supplies. I step back against the wall to try and avoid questions, but I quickly realize this makes me look a little like a creep. I keep my head down and start off in the direction of Room 432.

The music is getting louder the farther down the hall I go. As I reach Lauren's room, I'm assaulted by the very loud, very off-key singing of a girl doing her best to drown out the music. I double check the room number and note that the sign on the front of the open door says *Maddie & Lauren*.

I feel even more like a creep now, standing outside the door, peering inside the very pink room, but once my eyes latch on to the girl with the offensive voice, I can't seem to look away. She's wearing shorts and a tank top under an open button-down, and her wild blond hair falls in loose waves past her shoulders. Her skin looks like it's been baked in the sun, and I can't be sure, but there seems to be a bright white light all the way around her.

She's the most beautiful girl I've ever seen. The kind of girl I barely look at, let alone speak to.

I'm frozen in place, my feet two giant blocks of ice. I give a perfunctory glance around the small room. Lauren's not here. None of the members of the study group are here. It's just me and this. . .tone-deaf angel.

Sara flawlessly hits a high note, and the blonde does her best to match pitch. She fails, but A for effort—she's really throwing herself into this performance.

I know I should walk away or knock on the door or do anything other than what I'm doing now—gaping at her from outside her room—but I can't. I've never seen anyone like her. She seems to have zero inhibitions. She can't sing, but she doesn't seem to care, and somehow, she looks like she's having the time of her life. Alone in her dorm room.

My nights alone in my dorm room are usually spent with cold pizza and *Star Trek* reruns and are never nearly as entertaining as this.

"Oh." The girl drops her hairbrush microphone to her side and hops off the bed. "I didn't know I had an audience." She fakes a low bow, as if on stage.

"Sorry, your door was open."

"Oh my gosh, don't apologize. I love having an audience." She grins. "You're here for Lauren?"

I nod dumbly because I'm great at talking to beautiful girls.

"Come on in. She went to grab snacks."

I do as I'm told, certain she's cast some sort of strange spell on me. I'm in a trance, hypnotized by the combination of her beauty, her free spirit, and the smell of oranges and grapefruit.

She walks over to a mirror hanging on the wall and picks up a tube of lip gloss. Her eyes find me in the reflection, and I realize I'm staring.

She smiles in spite of that. "You can sit."

Dorm rooms are ridiculously small, but this one has a nice-sized sitting area with a futon and a small armchair. Both face Lauren's roommate, so no matter where I sit, I'm still going to be helpless to pull my attention from her.

She walks over to her closet and pulls off her button-down. I look away, but not before I catch a glimpse of the simple, tight, thin-strapped white tank top she's wearing underneath. I can hear her sliding hangers around in the closet, and when I dare

29

another glance, I see she's settled on a brightly colored sleeveless top.

She's like something out of the sixties—all she's missing is a flower for her hair.

She looks at me again, and my throat closes. I beg myself not to make a complete idiot of myself, which is usually what happens when I get nervous.

She picks up an earring and as she puts it on, she says, "Group project?"

"Uh, yeah," I croak out my answer.

"You should blow it off and come out to the frats tonight."

I genuinely laugh, a bit too loud. I look at her and see confusion on her face.

"Oh. You're serious."

"Yeah. It'll be fun!"

"Uh, pass."

She laughs and picks up the other earring. "Have you ever been?"

"To a frat party? No."

She narrows her eyes. "I'm sensing judgment."

"Hey, if you want to waste your time with a bunch of drunk morons, be my guest. I have better things to do." I keep my tone light, but she was right to sense judgment. I've done a poor job of hiding it.

"Like studying."

"Exactly."

"Well, you look like you could use some fun." She turns back to the mirror. "When was the last time you went out?"

I'm dying on the inside. I don't want to tell her I've never actually gone out socially, but in addition to being stunning, she also seems to be psychic.

She turns to face me. "Have you *ever* gone out?"

"Yeah, uh, sure. . ." I trail off, grasping for the next sentence like a blindfolded mountain climber. "But I have to keep my grades up."

"Please, how hard is that for you to do? I bet you don't even have to try to make A's."

She isn't completely wrong, which she clearly realizes in my silence.

"There's more to life than school, you know." She grins and gives me a once-over as Lauren rushes in the door.

"Oh! Simon!" She looks at me, and the undeniable look of pity crosses her face. "You're here. I'm so sorry I'm late." Her eyes dart to Maddie.

"Last chance for you guys to ditch the boring homework and come out with me!"

Lauren laughs her off, dropping her bag on the desk chair. "You'll have enough fun for all of us."

"You know I will." Maddie wags her eyebrows. "Have fun studying!"

And with that, she's gone, and I think maybe group projects aren't so bad after all.

Chapter Six

Simon

Present day

"Alright, Simon, spill it." Bea is glaring at me. "What happened with you two last night?"

I turn to the refrigerator and pull out a carton of eggs.

"Did she *sleep* here?"

"She sleeps here sometimes, Bea," I say. "She was on the couch. It's not a big deal."

I hear the pointed scoff as my sister moves into the kitchen. If she's this mad about Maddie sleeping over, I wonder how she's going to react when I tell her I'm leaving with her for a week.

"Look, Simon, I'm not trying to tell you how to live your life, but—"

My laugh cuts her off. "Bea, that's what you do. You tell me how to live my life." I crack an egg in a buttered pan. "But you forget that you and I are different."

"Oh, no, I know we're different," she's waving a hand at me, bossy big sister on full display. "I'm different because I can tell when someone is taking advantage of me."

"Here we go again." I crack another egg.

Bea puts both hands down on the counter, leans in and glares at me. "I don't know when you'll ever learn."

"If I'm not learning, maybe it's because the teacher won't stop yelling at me."

"Oh, for Pete's sake, you sound like a twelve-year-old boy."

I roll my eyes and grab the bread from the cupboard, dropping two slices into the toaster. "I'm going to, um. . ." I wince, anticipating her response. ". . .be gone for a few days."

"When? And for what?" She's still glaring. I'm beginning to think it's her resting face. "And don't think I didn't notice the change of subject. We're not done talking about Maddie."

I shake my head. "Next week. And for a. . .road trip."

"A *road trip*?" She says the words like a swear.

"Yes." I turn and face her.

"For how long?"

"Like a week."

Her eyes go wide. "A *week*? Simon, you can't leave for a whole week!"

I fake-wince. "I can actually. I own the business."

"A very new, not-yet-off-its-feet business." She frowns at me. "What are you *thinking*?"

"I'm thinking that. . .I have a chance to see some of the country. And I want to go."

"This is so irresponsible," she says, turning away and beginning to pace. "You have three meetings this week with potential clients. We aren't exactly in a position to risk screwing those up." She returns and sits down on a stool on the opposite side of the counter.

I groan. "You're really bossy." I pour her a cup of coffee, hoping it will soothe the savage beast.

When I slide it across the counter, she narrows her eyes. "Don't think you can make this better with your locally sourced, organic, freshly ground coffee."

I hide my smile behind my own mug. "You know you can't resist it."

She rolls her eyes, pours a splash of cream into the steaming mug, and takes a drink. I know she relies on me for her coffee fix, but when she sets the mug back down, she's still got a salty look on her face, albeit a bit calmer. "You asked me to help you with your business, Simon. This is me helping."

"That's not how I remember it." I hold up a finger. "I think you ordered me to let you help. Something about needing to find purpose in your life?" Ever since Bea became a mother, she'd been floundering. My business gave her something to do to help her feel like she was something other than "just a mom."

Her words.

"If you don't need my help, I can go," she says, standing and moving as if to leave.

"No, no, stop." I reach out a hand and she sits back down. "I *do* need your help. You're the most organized person I know."

She softens. "Thank you."

"Plus, you're working for free, so that makes you kind of irreplaceable at the moment."

She gives me a half-cocked smile, clearly annoyed. "Have you even thought this through?"

"Yes, of course," I say, trying not to be offended that she doesn't think I have. "Don't you know me at all? I'm going to keep all three appointments online, so don't worry. We'll land them all."

At least I hope I will. I really—really—need the business.

LUNA, my web design and brand-building business, started off strong, but I've seen the projections. I need to bring in more business to give myself a cushion, the goal to eventually replace the salary I was making at Smith and Beatty.

This living paycheck-to-paycheck thing is not how I want to live my life.

How does Maddie do it? Doesn't she wish she had a little more security?

"I don't get it. Why are you up and leaving at the drop of a —" she stops short, as if she's just put it together. "Simon. Tell me this trip isn't about Maddie."

I take a drink of my coffee. "This trip isn't about Maddie."

It's not exactly a lie.

"You're lying."

I make a face.

"I'm just doing what you ordered me to."

She shakes her head at me. "So, what happened, did her flavor of the month dump her, and she asked you to be her fill-in boyfriend?"

It's eerie how Bea nailed that. I shovel eggs into my mouth.

"Uh-huh. That's what I thought. And, once again, you're dropping everything to come to her rescue," Bea says. "Does she even realize what you're putting on hold so you can drive across the country with her?"

"I'm not coming to her rescue, and I'm not putting anything on hold."

Those are also not exactly lies.

She eyes me. "Be honest. Did something happen between you two? Is that why you won't let go of this ridiculous infatuation?"

I bristle a bit at this—not because I'm angry, but because Bea's making it sound like my feelings for her are on par with a middle school crush.

The truth is—and I won't admit to this, even if I'm hooked up to a lie detector at gunpoint with the fate of the world resting on my shoulders—I love her. I think I've loved her since the day I met her, singing off-key in her dorm room.

"Maddie is one of my best friends," I say flatly.

"Who slept here last night."

"On the couch."

"Her choice or yours?"

Sisters can be astute and annoying, and Bea has mastered the art of being both simultaneously.

"Both. It's not like that. Two adults can sleep in the same apartment without anything happening," I say.

"Oh, yeah, I know," she says. "But not because you didn't want it to."

I roll my eyes. "Will you stop?"

"I think she knows how you feel about her."

The thought tightens my stomach, and I hope my reaction doesn't show on my face. She better not.

"She knows, and she likes it," she says, matter-of-factly. "So she takes advantage of you."

I set my cup down harder than I mean to, porcelain on granite. "Enough. She does not," I say. "She doesn't ask me to do anything I'm not willing to do anyway. It's what friends do." I pause, leaning in slightly. "And you're not my mother."

I can tell by the look on her face that I made my point—and hopefully she'll back off.

There's a slight lull between us, and Bea sighs and tilts her head. "You're right, Simon. I'm not. But I *am* someone who loves you and wants what's best for you." She's studying me now, and I don't like it. "Even if you don't have a clue what that is," she quips.

"I don't have a clue, but you do?" I chortle. "Okay, go ahead. Tell me what's good for me."

She clicks her phone open, taps it, and turns it around to

face me, the logo for one of those ridiculous dating apps twinkling back at me.

"I don't care about the app." I groan.

She reaches around the front of her phone and, without turning it around to see it or missing a beat, she flicks through pictures with stats and matching interests and says, "How are you ever going to meet the great love of your life if you never put yourself out there?"

I'm pretty sure I've already met the great love of my life, but I know better than to say so.

I reach gently and take her phone and click the side button to turn it off. "Bea, I work in technology, so you know I'm a fan. Honestly, I am. But there is no way I'm going to meet the love of my life," I hand the phone back to her, "on a dating app."

"Because of Maddie."

Astute and annoying. "I need to shower."

I pick up my coffee and start toward my bedroom, but Bea stops me with a question. "Did you tell her about Seattle?"

"No," I say, shoulders slumping with a sigh. "Not yet. I don't even know for sure if I'm moving."

"Look," she comes over to me, turning me around. I'm like a child who wants to leave the room but Mom isn't finished reprimanding yet. "You know I don't say this to hurt you, but you're making it worse. It's going to be harder to leave if you don't just rip off the Band-Aid and walk away."

I don't want to point out that there's absolutely no way my sister can relate. She met her husband Tom her junior year of high school, and they've been together ever since. They have two kids and a big house in the suburbs, and in a couple of months, they're moving to Seattle.

And I'm considering going with her.

Fresh start. New opportunities. Clean slate.

My reasons have less to do with Maddie and more to do

with restlessness. Ever since I made the switch from employee to entrepreneur, I've felt an itch to take advantage of my new-found freedom. I never realized how much I didn't like working for someone else until that someone else wasn't there anymore.

As far as my sister is concerned, the only thing that really matters is that Maddie doesn't have such easy access to me. She thinks *that* will make me forget about her.

As if that's even remotely a possibility.

"Simon, if something was going to happen between you and Maddie, it would've happened by now. It's been ten years."

I look up at the ceiling. I don't need this reminder.

"You know I'm right."

"Well, then it's a good thing I don't want something to happen between me and Maddie."

She steps back from me, hands on hips. "You know you're not fooling anyone, right?"

I'm not so sure. I've fooled Maddie for years.

Right?

"Maybe this trip is a good thing," she says. "Maybe this is what you need to get some closure. To make a decision."

"I don't follow."

She moves about the room, as if pitching in a boardroom. "You go on this trip. Seven days with Maddie. You talk, you spend time with her, you," she stops and looks directly at me, *"be honest with yourself*—and if nothing changes," she shrugs a *welp, there you go* shrug. "If she doesn't come to her senses and realize she'll never be able to do better than you—then you can finally move on."

I purse my lips. "Move on. You mean move away."

"Either. Or both." She watches me. "Look, if you see things the way everyone else sees them, maybe then you can pull the trigger on Seattle. Go on a few more dates. Entertain the idea that the world doesn't actually revolve around Maddie Rogers."

Crossroads. This trip is literal *and* metaphorical.

I don't want to admit it, but my sister has a point. This road trip *is* an opportunity. What if I use the trip as a chance to test the waters with Maddie?

I have no idea how to do that.

I'm a smart guy. I can figure it out.

Even though Bea is still talking, I'm having my own silent conversation. A personal persuasive argument.

I'm going to do it. I'm going to let Maddie know how I feel.

Good grief, am I actually deciding this?

"Simon, you're wasting the best years of your life." Bea's forehead draws downward, carving a single vertical line between her eyes. "It's time to let her go."

Unless. . .it's time to go for it.

Chapter Seven

Maddie

Road Trip Day One

I'm in the middle of an *excellent* dream. I'm standing in a situation room, all eyes on me, waiting for me to make a decision that will turn the tide of a huge battle.

And for some reason the Avengers are there. And Thor is super short.

I'm caught off guard by how short he is, but he's still hot, and in the dreamy mist of my mind I wonder if society would frown upon our relationship, and then all of a sudden someone behind me starts knocking on the door.

Wee Chris Hemsworth holds my gaze, then quirks a brow. "Are you going to get that?"

I shake my head.

"Maddie. The door."

The knocking gets more intense.

"Maddie. Get the door!" He raises his voice. I know if he gets too upset, he might bring the lightning, and part of me kind of wants that to happen.

Weird.

"Maddie!?"

My eyes shoot open. I blink them hard, trying to focus, but still seeing the image of a tiny Asguardian holding a hammer that's bigger than him. *Pound, pound, pound.*

"Maddie??!"

The knocking and the calling of my name—those were real.

I gasp, remembering what day it is. "The alarm!" It didn't go off. And now I'm late.

I throw back the covers, absently wondering if this is how Simon reacts when I knock on his door in the middle of the night. I run to the door and fling it open to reveal Simon, wearing khaki shorts and a vintage wash red T-shirt.

"Did you just wake up?" His frown deepens. "We're meeting Will and Lauren in twenty minutes. You're supposed to be on the curb, ready to go." He glances down for a second, then back up at my eyes.

Oh my gosh. I'm not wearing a bra.

I immediately spin on my heel and pull my shirt away from my chest, moving quickly into my bedroom, leaving him standing in the doorway. "My alarm didn't go off!" Or maybe I forgot to set it. It doesn't matter—I'm late. "I just have to throw some things together, and I'll be ready before you know it. I'll be quick!"

He closes the door and steps inside. "You haven't packed?"

"I'm a light packer," I call back, ignoring the judgment in his voice. "Totally low maintenance."

"We both know that's not true."

I simultaneously shimmy out of my pajama bottoms and pull my hair on top of my head in a messy bun. I rush to the bathroom and grab my toothbrush, shoving it in my mouth as I pull on jean shorts and a cropped pink T-shirt. I race back to

41

the bedroom, fling open drawers, and start tossing clothes onto the bed.

I turn to see Simon standing in the doorway of my bedroom, surveying the messy pile of clothes. "Don't you need stuff for the actual wedding ceremony? Like a dress or something?"

"Lauren shipped it to Will's house," I say through my toothbrush. "His sisters are taking care of most of the details."

"Probably smart."

My eyes flick to his. "Why?"

He simply indicates to the whole room.

"Hey. I resent that," I say, chucking a zip-up hoodie onto the bed. "As if I'd forget to bring my bridesmaid's dress."

Toothpaste mixed with drool is starting to run down my chin. I can feel it. I half wipe it and rush back into the bathroom.

"Right, that would be hard to believe."

I spit. "Want something to drink?" I ask. "I don't have anything locally sourced, but there's probably a bottled water in the fridge."

"Maddie. We're late."

I stop moving and look at him. "This is making you crazy, isn't it?" I grin. Ruffling his feathers is one of my favorite pastimes.

"You know I don't like to be late."

I start to move in slow motion on purpose, reaching for a pair of jeans. "I. . .seem. . .to. . .be. . .caught. . .in. . .a. . .*time*. . *.freeze. . .*"

Big sigh from him. Another point for me.

"You could come help me, you know."

He muses. "Was this your plan all along? Sucker me into helping you pack?"

"No, but it would've been *genius* of me if it was," I say.

"Also, you can come in. You don't have to stand at the doorway."

"I don't want to catch a fungus."

"Ha. Ha." I roll my eyes.

He walks in and picks up one of the mugs I made. There's a collection of them on my dresser. I turn away. It's hard to watch people study my work, even if I'm proud of those mugs.

"This is cool," he says from behind me.

"Yeah?" I turn back to face him. The compliment sparks something inside me.

"Yeah, why have I never seen these?"

I flinch, mainly because I don't know why I've never shown him. I grab a duffle bag from under the bed and start to shove clothes in it.

"Oh, you know, they're just kind of silly projects, not a big deal," I lie.

I glance over long enough to see him turn to face me. "They're amazing. You should sell these. They're kind of masculine without being too in-your-face."

"Wow, thanks."

Simon is the kindest person I know, so there's no way he'd say anything rude about my

work, but I still cling to the words, starved for attention like a middle-aged former beauty queen, trying to live her life vicariously through her daughter at the local beauty pageant.

I blow a strand of hair off my forehead as he turns the mug around in his hands. This one is a deep, beautiful navy blue color with a gray base. I honestly might've been thinking of Simon when I made it. It's masculine, like he said, but with an elegance that few men could pull off without seeming snobby.

Simon is smart. Successful. Polished. But he's also self-deprecating and dry.

"You can have it," I say. "If you want."

His eyes dart to mine. "Uh, no, I'll absolutely pay you for this."

"It's a gift," I say. "A thank you for coming on this trip with me."

He shakes his head. "No, I want you to owe me for that for a little while." He pauses, and looks up at me and smiles.

I gape. Simon made a joke.

"How much for the mug?"

I roll my eyes. "I've told you a million times, you're not paying for my pottery."

"Okay, so then we'll settle it when we get back," he says, ignoring me.

I walk across the room and stop in front of him. He's still holding the mug, and I put my hands over his. He doesn't look at me right away, and I don't speak until I have his attention.

"Simon," I say, "it would make me so happy if you would take this mug and drink your fancy Peruvian coffee filtered through Far East bamboo paper with your organic goat's milk while you build your empire and make your first million." I force myself not to smile, because *oh, the cleverness of me.*

"It's Columbian, actually. Not Peruvian."

Completely straight-faced. He's better at this than me. I stifle a laugh.

"You really should sell it, you know." He says this matter-of-factly.

I return to balling up my clothes in the duffle bag. "I told you, it's a hobby."

"But it could be more," he says. "And you've got a whole studio full of this kind of stuff."

Whenever he talks like this, I almost—*almost*—believe that it's possible.

It's a Someday Dream, one that I've never talked about with anyone, and yet, Simon knows.

Simon always knows.

"Aren't we in a hurry?" I take the mug and set it down on the dresser next to the others. "I'll save it here for you."

He reaches past me and straightens the mug slightly, so it perfectly matches face with the others on the shelf.

I wonder if he's the kind of person who would straighten a crooked picture in a random hotel room. I don't wonder long, because *of course he is*, and I absolutely know that for a fact.

Simon and I have been friends for nearly ten years. He'd helped me move into this apartment, but I can count on one hand the number of times he'd been in my bedroom. While I freely visit his place, he seems almost allergic to mine.

It could be because he can't stand that everything doesn't have a place. Or that my bedroom seems to have been decorated by a teenager.

"Your room is very. . .bright," he says.

A fluffy pink rug covers the original wide-planked wood floors, and my Anthropologie knock-off, brightly colored, patterned bedspread and curtains are the perfect Boho style that make the room cheerful without even trying.

"It's *happy*."

I open my dresser drawers and pull out a few pairs of shorts, a swimsuit, a couple of tank tops, a stack of clean underwear, a few lacy bras and toss them all on the bed in a clump.

Then, I look at Simon. "Can you put this stuff in the duffle bag while I grab shoes?"

I notice he's not looking at me, but at the pile I just threw down.

I bet I could stow all my stuff in the frown lines in his forehead. "How are you going to fit all of that?"

I smile. "That's why you're here."

He looks confused.

"You like puzzles," I say. "You can Tetris everything in there."

"Maddie." His tone reminds me of a disapproving teacher.

Instead of verbally sparring, he takes the duffle bag and holds it upside down, dumping all of the clothes out on the bed.

"Hey! What. . .!"

He holds up one finger to shush me, then picks up a pair of my shorts, shows them to me, lays them down, rolls them up, and gently puts them inside the duffle bag.

He ends this display with a *there, you see* gesture with both hands.

"What are you doing?"

"Packing your clothes." He rolls another pair.

"Why are you rolling them?"

"Keeps them from wrinkling," he says, not looking at me. It's obvious by his nonchalance that he thinks this is normal. When he looks up and finds me staring, his expression changes.

"What?" Again, completely like this is what everyone should do. Roll clothes.

"You really don't have to roll up my clothes. I'll wear them wrinkled."

"Oh, I know," he winces. "Do you have toiletries or anything?"

"Uh, yeah." I walk into the bathroom dumbly. "I'll grab those."

Through the crack in the door, I catch a glimpse of him, carefully rolling up each item of clothing and tucking them neatly inside.

"I could've brought you an extra suitcase," he says, without looking up. "Bea bought me a whole set for college graduation that I hardly ever use."

"I'm okay with the duffle bag." And I'm struck by how he handles my things. It's so. . .*Simon.*

"Has the mess set off your inner Mr. Clean?" I ask, walking back into the room. I look over his shoulder at his handiwork. "I hope you're color coding those clothes," I joke.

"Your books are next," he says dryly, pointing without looking up. "I tripped over a stack on my way in here. They're a fire hazard."

I would laugh, but I think he's serious.

He zips up the bag easily, everything fitting, and stands.

"You're finished?"

He breathes in through his nose, hands on hips, surveying the scene and nodding, as if he's just completed an architectural project. "Yes."

"You're a very efficient packer."

He turns and smiles. "Thanks."

"One of your very best qualities." I grin. "You'll make someone a great wife someday."

He lets out a genuine shocked laugh. Another point for me.

So fun.

I flip the light switch and start to walk out of the bedroom, then stop a few steps into the hallway.

"Hey!" I turn and face him. "I just realized we've never been on a trip together before!"

"This will be our first."

"I can't think of a single trip you've been on the entire time I've known you."

He shrugs, looking slightly embarrassed. "Yeah, I'm not much of a traveler."

"It's a bit outside your comfort zone, huh?"

"A bit, yeah."

"Because you like to be in control of your surroundings," I say.

"Because I've been working."

"And because you like to be in control of your surroundings."

"Are you going to be like this the entire trip?"

I grin. "Yep."

I start toward the front door, doing a quick check of my little apartment to make sure I didn't forget anything.

I'm about to open the door when Simon stops near the sun porch. "Did you rearrange your studio?"

"I love that you call it that," I laugh. "*Studio*. So posh."

He frowns. "What? It's where you work, right?"

"No, Simon," I say. "It's where I do my *hobby*." Even as the words escape, I want to take them back. They feel false, like I'm not giving enough respect to what actually happens in there. That sun porch is my favorite spot in the whole world—a place where I can take off the mask and let my guard down.

The clay never asks me to cheer it up. It just lets me be.

"I love when you underestimate yourself." Simon slings the duffle bag up over his shoulder and looks at me. "It's my favorite."

"Sarcasm doesn't look good on you." I roll my eyes and push him toward the door. "Besides, you're going to make us late."

He scoffs as I grab my sunglasses and purse, stepping out into the hallway and locking the door behind me.

Chapter Eight

Maddie

We walk downstairs and outside to his car. Simon unlocks the doors and stuffs my duffle bag into the back seat with very little effort.

I peer past him to see his small black suitcase behind the driver's seat and a garment bag hanging in the window. A cooler sits on the floor.

He packed a cooler. Of course he did. I'm betting he had a whole checklist of items to bring on this trip.

I brought zero snacks and zero drinks. If it weren't for Simon, I'd still be asleep. The fact that I'm a walking disaster isn't lost on me. He's an adult, doing adult things.

I should aspire to do a few adult things myself, but it just doesn't seem like very much fun.

I hop in the front seat and notice how clean his car is. He'd probably detailed it yesterday, and his woodsy, masculine scent mixes with the undeniable clean car odor that I'd never had in my own beat-up Corolla. My backseat is a disaster, but hey, if someone ever needed a soda-sticky hair tie from a year ago, I'm the girl to call.

He gets in the car and buckles his seatbelt, then looks at me. "Buckle."

I yank the seatbelt over my shoulder and fasten it. "Do you know where we're going?"

He shoots me a sideways glance and pulls out into the street. "Haven't you been reading the group chat?"

My face—and my mind—both go blank.

"Will and Lauren have given us all the details via text. I have the whole itinerary."

I wave him off. "I don't really need a play-by-play."

He shakes his head. "How have you managed to stay alive all these years?"

I grin over at him. "I have you."

There's a lull, and then I say, "I hope we don't want to kill each other after this trip."

He taps his thumb on the steering wheel. "Why would we want to kill each other?"

"It's practically a given—people, in close quarters, who are fundamentally different in every way end up hating each other," I say. "It's a wonder it hasn't happened already."

"We're not so different," he says.

I laugh. "After spending five minutes in my apartment, I can't believe you can say that with a straight face."

"Because you're a slob?"

"Hey!"

He shrugs as if to say *well, it's true.*

"Okay, fine, I'm a little. . .loose. . .in my domestic. . .duties."

He chuckles.

"But you have to admit you're a neat freak," I say. "Plus, you live your whole life by a schedule."

"I do. It's better."

"It's stuffy."

"It's structured."

"It's stupid." I immediately give him an open-mouthed smile and point. *Got him.*

He shakes his head, then after a pause, mutters, *"You're* stupid."

I whip around and look at him full on, mouth agape. He scrunches his shoulders and puts his head down, stifling a laugh, like he just ripped off the wittiest comment in the fifth grade that got the whole class laughing.

"Wow. Good one." I smirk.

This trip might turn out to be the best week of my life.

"I am so glad," I say, settling into my seat, "we decided to become friends in the first place."

A slight pause, a shift, then a smile. "Yeah. Me too."

"Your life would be so boring without me." I'm projecting a bit.

"I think you mean 'peaceful.'"

I turn sideways in my seat and find him grinning. I fix a serious expression on my face. "This trip means no breaks from each other. You might realize you don't want to be friends with me at all. That I'm *too extra.*"

He glances at me. "I might. And. . .you might think I'm—"

"Too uptight?"

The look on Simon's face splinters for the quickest beat. Is he afraid I'd actually think that? I instinctively say, "Come on. Who would make me hot chocolate if you ditched me?"

His face settles and almost looks relieved. It's odd—I feel like his feelings are hurt somehow. But why?

"Good point." He smiles softly.

I try to compliment him. Maybe that will help? "I'd be lost without you and your late-night pep talks."

"You would," he agrees.

"And your life would be a complete snooze-fest without me."

"You say snooze-fest," he says, finally looking back to normal. "I say a tranquil and lovely existence."

"Uh-huh," I say.

There are moments when my teasing lands differently. I feel like that was one of them. I make a mental note to tread softly. The last thing I'd ever want to do is hurt the best person I know.

We drive toward the Santa Monica Pier, the beginning (or end, depending on where you're starting) of the historic route we'd be following all the way to Illinois.

I start to get an idea of what this road trip is going to be like and decide it's far too quiet. I shift around in my seat, aware that beside me, Simon seems perfectly content.

"You're not going to make me listen to NPR or something, are you?"

He quirks a brow. "I might."

"Or one of those boring business podcasts?"

"You might like it."

"I won't."

"You don't know that."

"I do."

"Could give you some insight when you start your pottery business."

I blow out a puff of air. "Funny."

He lets the subject drop (thankfully) and I shift again in my seat. "Sorry I made us late."

"We're not late," he says, pulling onto the freeway. "I told you to be ready an hour before we needed to leave."

I stare in disbelief at this revelation.

"You what? Why?"

He glances my direction, a bit caught. "Oh. . .you know. Just in case."

"Just in case what?"

He shrugs. "The Maddie Contingency."

My jaw goes slack. "There's a Maddie Contingency?"

"Yeah," he says, like it's no big deal.

"This is a thing? Is it capitalized?!"

"In my head it is." He pauses, then admits, "I know you're not big on details, so I plan accordingly. I allow more time in case you're running late. Or still asleep, that sort of thing."

He's not wrong. I've spent most of my life being flaky.

But lately, maybe because it seems like all my friends are doing grown-up things, I've started to wonder if it's time to make some changes.

Maybe it's time for me to grow up too.

Although. . .I'd probably need to move away and start over. Nobody that knows me would ever take me seriously. Not when I'm the kind of person with a contingency named after me. And I don't know how to change anyone's opinion of me.

It's not the easiest when you discover you've been living down to everyone's expectations.

Chapter Nine

Simon

"I'm so glad we decided to become friends in the first place."

The words are repeating in my head as I drive.

The decision in my own head to broach the subject I've been avoiding for the better part of my adult life seemed so easy back in my apartment, but now I see I've got my work cut out for me.

We've just started the trip, and I know I've got time—so why does it feel like there's an invisible ticking clock in this car with us?

It's stressing me out.

I don't need to ask her why she doesn't think of me as more than a friend. I already know. Comments like the ones about me being uptight make it obvious.

We're different.

And yet, I believe our differences could make us great together. They already do. If we could add a little kissing, our relationship would be perfect.

That thought is like a jumpstart to my pulse, and I inadvertently jerk the wheel slightly.

Maddie puts a hand on the car door, instinctively bracing herself, being overly melodramatic. "Whoa, partner! You okay?"

"Yeah, totally, just. . ." I indicate vaguely to the windshield, "there was—I thought there was something in the road."

I can feel her amused stare.

She reaches up and takes hold of the grab handle above her door. "Am I good? Do I need to hold onto the Jesus bar?"

She constantly pokes fun at me. I love that she feels comfortable enough to treat me like she treats everyone else— but I don't want to be everyone else. I want to experience everything with Maddie, but telling her that risks our friendship. A friendship that I value more than any other relationship in my life.

Am I really ready to do that?

Maddie turns around and opens my cooler. "This is cute. You brought snacks."

I nod. "Yeah, you know, I just wanted to. . ."

She finishes my sentence, ". . .wanted to be prepared, I know. I love it. I didn't bring anything." She holds up my bag of Sea Salt Avocado Crisps and shakes it. "What the heck are these things?"

"Those are amazing, and super healthy. Gluten-free, vegan. . ."

She cuts me off. "Wait. Vegan? You're a vegan?"

"No, totally not, just saying those are healthy."

She dramatically breathes a sigh of relief. "Phew! Thank goodness. I once dated a guy who was vegan, or a pescatarian, or something. Wouldn't eat anything with a face."

"How did that go?"

She turns and smiles. "I ordered steak."

I chuckle. I don't like hearing about her ex-boyfriends, but I sure like hearing how they didn't work out.

"I know you have a sensitive stomach," she says.

I love that she knows me.

I toss her a sideways glance. "Are you making fun?"

"No! Honestly! I think it's part of your charm." She laughs, and I hear my spot in the friend zone firmly sealed in cement.

I need a plan. A road map.

This whole trip metaphor is just getting better and better.

I need to think of "getting out of the friend zone" like any other project. Problems always arise, and I have to figure out how to tackle them. And I'm good at that. It's my specialty.

This is no different.

Right?

"Can we stop for coffee?" Maddie's question—thankfully—pulls me from my thoughts. "There's a Starbucks up here." She glances at my travel mug in the drink holder. "You brought your own coffee, didn't you? Did you grind the beans yourself? Did Juan Valdez bring an eco-friendly sack to your apartment?"

"I make no apologies," I say. "And Starbucks is gross. They purposely burn their beans. Do you know how bad commercially processed coffee is for you?"

"I only know how *good it tastes, mmm. . .*" she says with a gravelly growl and a grin. She turns and stares out the window, and I grab my travel mug and take a long drink. After a moment, she quips, "I wish I could've seen you roll up my panties."

I cough, spraying a fine mist of coffee on my steering wheel. Shock is Maddie's favorite form of teasing. I don't talk about certain topics. Maddie talks about *everything*. She sent me to the store once for tampons, and I've never been the same.

Through my reaction, I struggle to set my mug back in the cup holder and sputter a "...What?"

She just sits and smiles.

I flounder. "You call them *panties*?" It feels weird just saying it.

"What do you call them?" she asks.

"I don't call them anything!" I say, louder than I want. "Besides, I didn't see any—" I shudder as I say this—"*of those things* in the pile of random clothing you tossed on the bed."

Her eyes shoot to mine. "Simon. There was a whole stack. Tell me you packed them."

"I feel like I would've remembered folding your. . .under. . .unmentionables."

She laughs big. "My under unmentionables? What, are you a 65-year-old woman?"

A wince.

"Simon," she says flatly. "You really didn't see them?"

"No. There weren't any on the bed."

She groans. "That's so not cool! We're going to have to stop and get some. I can't be on the road for a whole week with no clean panties."

"For the love of all that is holy, stop saying 'panties.'"

"This is an actual emergency," she says.

"An emergency? Really?"

"Yes."

"An underwear emergency."

"Yes." A pause. "A *panty predicament.*"

I shoot a glance and see the *yes, and* glint in her eye. I know what she's doing, because it's something we've been doing since we met.

Something unfortunate will happen, and she'll alliterate the event—and prompt me to come up with another one, and back and forth.

It started when she accidentally locked her keys in her car and I said, "That's unfortunate."

She said, "Unfortunate?! It's horrible! It's a. . .car catastrophe!"

I responded with, "What, like an automobile abomination?"

Then came "DMV debacle," "Toyota tragedy," and "motor meltdown."

I won with "Ford Fiasco."

And now, her prompting with *panty predicament* leads me to blurt the only thing that popped into my head.

"It's a crotch crisis."

"Oh my GOSH SIMON!" She laughs a real, deep laugh, the kind that makes her have to clear her throat for the next hour. I only manage to get these kinds of laughs once in a great while.

I love it.

She's glaring at me, but I keep my eyes on the road until I can't stifle the smile for another moment.

"You're totally lying!" She smacks my arm. "You totally rolled my panties!"

I chuckle to myself. "I really like the Mickey Mouse ones. Bold move to walk around with Mickey's face on your butt all day long."

This back-and-forth with Maddie is the stuff dreams are made of. I'm not comfortable with other women, but Maddie has always put me at ease. That is, when she's not turning my whole world upside down.

That's the part she doesn't understand. No matter how bad of a day I've had, the second she walks in the room, everything's fine. My stress level decreases. She might as well be a shot of serotonin.

She's done laughing, but her eyes are still tearing up. She

reaches for my mug to take a drink.

She won't like it.

She makes a face as she returns the mug to the cup holder. "Yuck."

"You know I drink my coffee black."

"I thought I could handle it," she sputters, making a face like a person does when they've just smelled a skunk. "Do you have something against cream and sugar?"

"Seems extra."

"I can make you a better one than this. This is an affront to coffee drinkers everywhere."

"I like it black. It's healthier that way."

"I have serious concerns about your taste preferences."

We reach the pier, and just as I park, Maddie jumps out of the car. She races over to Lauren, who is standing next to Will's Jeep, two disposable cups of coffee in hand.

In typical Maddie fashion, she throws her arms around Lauren and squeezes her so hard, Lauren looks like she might burst. I've never been that free with my affection. For anyone. If it weren't for Maddie, it's likely I'd never touch another human being, and I only touch her when she initiates contact.

I suppose I'm what you'd call stoic. Or what Maddie would call "serious."

Serious Simon.

Maddie, on the other hand, seems to not have much use for anything *but* emotions. Probably why her apartment looks like it'd been decorated by woodland fairies.

"You're getting *married!*" Maddie reaches into her giant, slouchy, brown leather bag and pulls out a headband with a white veil attached to it. She sticks it on Lauren's head. "You have to wear this the entire trip."

Lauren laughs and hands Maddie a cup of coffee. Maddie turns to me and grins, "cheering" the cup in the air and wiggling her hips, as if this is proof that the caffeine gods have her back even when she oversleeps.

"Sorry we're late," I say, ignoring her. "Someone wasn't awake when I got to her place."

Lauren laughs. "Oh, Maddie, I love you."

Yeah. And she's not the only one.

Chapter Ten

Maddie

Ten years ago

"I don't think this is a good idea," I say into the phone as I clomp down the sidewalk toward the off-campus restaurant I've been to a thousand times.

"Why not?" Lauren asks.

"Blind dates," I say. "Just, ugh."

"I promise this guy is different," Lauren says. "He's nice. And you could use a nice guy."

"If he's so nice, you should save him for yourself," I say.

"Yeah, I'm not dating right now," Lauren says.

"Right." I groan. "Brother's best friend fallout. You know it's time to get over that." I run across the street as the stop light turns red and a guy in a red car honks at me. I lift my hand in a wave, as he speeds off.

"He's such a sweet guy, Mads. Give him a chance."

The restaurant comes into view. "Lo, I don't date 'sweet guys.'"

"And how well is that working out for you?"

I roll my eyes.

"I can hear you rolling your eyes at me through the phone," Lauren says. "You've had a string of losers, try something new for a change."

"Sounds boring."

"Yeah, a guy who treats you like a princess is utterly dull."

"I'm not a princess, Lo," I say. "Don't need a prince. Or a white horse. I can take care of myself." But even as I say it, I hear the lie hiding inside that notion. I want the freedom to be able to take care of myself, but I also want someone to treat me like a princess.

Can't both things be true?

I know Lauren has a point. I'm starting to wonder if I'm a jerk-magnet. Most of the guys I've dated this year seemed to want nothing but a good time. I'm beginning to wonder if any other kind of guy exists.

I step inside the noisy bar and look around. Near the back wall, I spot a guy who sort of looks like the photo Lauren showed me. He's wearing a preppy black sweater and jeans, and looking as out of place in this restaurant/bar as a priest in a brothel.

"Are you there?" Lauren asks in my ear. "It just got louder."

I turn away as the bartender catches my eye and waves. "Lauren, this guy looks smart."

"He *is* smart."

"I don't date smart guys."

"It's amazing that you've totally read that whole book by looking at its cover," she says.

Touché. "You know what I mean."

"So, based on what you've said, you date dumb, rude guys," Lauren says. "Sounds about right."

"No, that's not what I—" I stop, feeling uncharacteristically self-conscious. "He's never going to take me seriously."

"You don't know that."

I do know that. I don't even take myself seriously.

I know how people see me because it's exactly how I want them to see me. Even *nice* guys. What's the point in trying to pretend otherwise?

"Look, I know him. Yes, he's a bit of a brain, but I also know that he needs to have a little fun." She pauses. "You're fun, Mads. You're the most fun person I know."

I look across the bar again, trying to size him up.

"Thanks for the compliment."

She goes on. "You need to see that nice guys really do exist —it's a win-win."

I groan and turn back to the table just in time to see Mr. Nice Guy checking his watch. I'm late, and I feel bad about that, but I'm dreading this. He's not bad-looking, and usually when I'm around guys like this, it takes 0.3 seconds for me to say something stupid.

Why would anyone like him want to date someone like me?

"Just give him a chance," Lauren says in my ear. "He's nothing like the other guys you've been out with since you got to school. I promise."

The guy's gaze lands on me from across the room. There's something vaguely familiar about him. He lifts a hand in a wave, and I lamely wave back. No ducking out now.

"You owe me, Lauren," I say.

"No, you're going to owe me." I can hear the smile in my best friend's voice. "When he offers to pay, let him. When he holds the door open for you, thank him. When he—"

"I know, I know."

"I wasn't sure you'd recognize a gentleman," Lauren teases.

"Hanging up now."

"Call me after!"

"Yeah, yeah. Bye." I click the phone off and tuck it in my

purse, then make my way through the crowd to the back of the bar. When I reach the table, he stands.

I feel my eyebrows pull. Lauren wasn't kidding. Nobody I've dated has ever stood when I've shown up beside a table.

"Hey," he says. "Maddie." His eyes drift to the table, then back to me, then somewhere off in the distance like he's not quite sure where to focus. Probably regretting saying yes to this date.

"Yeah." I smile. "Simon?"

He nods and motions for me to sit. "You're late—is everything okay?"

"Yeah, sorry," I say. "I'm pretty much always late."

"Like on purpose?"

I hear something in his voice. Something like judgment.

When are you going to grow up, Maddie?

I sit down and silence the voice at the back of my mind and bring my eyes to Simon's. Cute in a nerdy way. A little scrawny.

But not my type.

Too clean-cut. Too well-groomed. The kind of guy my father would set me up with. And probably doesn't have a single tattoo.

What was Lauren thinking?

"You look familiar," I say.

He nods. "We've actually met."

He doesn't elaborate, so I try to place his face, but I come up empty. I half-laugh. "I meet a lot of people."

"It was a few months ago," I say. "You were belting out a Sara Bareilles song before study group with Lauren."

I lean in. "How'd I sound?"

"Uh. . ." He looks nervous.

"I'm kidding, I know I can't sing," I say.

He looks surprised. "But you still do it?"

"Sure, you don't have to be good at something to enjoy it."

His eyes narrow so slightly I almost miss it. "But you might enjoy it more if you're good at it."

"Ah." I lean back in the booth.

His brow furrows. "Ah?"

"I think I just figured you out."

"Already?"

"I'm good at reading people."

"Okay." He doesn't look away. "What is it you know about me?"

"I'm guessing. . .perfectionist," I say. "You don't like failing, which is why you never really do. You only try things you're really good at, and. . .you're hard to know."

Now, his gaze drifts down to the table. "Wow."

"Am I close?"

He brings his eyes back to mine. "You're way off base."

I laugh. I know better. This guy is so easy to read, he might as well have come with an instruction book.

And because I know this, I can say, with absolute certainty, that he and I are not a good fit. And I'm not about to pretend like we are.

Chapter Eleven

Maddie

Present day

The waitress is staring.

I don't blame her. I'm also staring because Simon is taking for-EV-er to order his meal. I'm partially sympathetic because of his stomach, but I'm also noticing I'm feeling a little protective because I don't want anyone else to be irritated with him.

Socially, that is. I'm socially protective of him.

It takes a while to get to see through his quirks and get to the good stuff. And there really is a lot of good stuff.

I lean toward Simon. "Bacon and eggs? No gluten in that."

"My body doesn't respond well to bacon," he says quietly.

"An omelet, maybe?"

Simon glances over at me, then up at Will and Lauren. "Actually, that sounds great."

He's not one of those people who puts people out because he's entitled or rude. The truth is, he hates to be a bother.

"Perfect," I say. "Glad I could help."

Simon turns to the waitress. "Could I get cheese and vegetables? American cheese with a little mozzarella?"

The waitress scribbles in her pad. "Toast?"

"Gluten free, if that's okay," he says. "Crispy but not burnt, and I'll take the butter on the side."

"Potatoes?"

So many choices! By comparison, my order is going to be so much easier.

"Hash browns. Could you have them cook them in light butter instead of heavy oil?"

The waitress's eyes dart to Simon, and she doesn't even try to hide her annoyance.

"He's particular," I say, patting him gently on the shoulder.

Simon looks at me.

"What? You are!" I glance across the table. "Isn't he?"

Lauren and Will shrug.

"You are," I say, turning back to Simon. "You already know this. You like things a certain way." I turn to the waitress. "He just likes things a certain way."

"Uh-huh." She's acting like it's hour eleven of her eight-hour shift.

"You just know what you want, man," Will says. "That's a good trait."

"Yeah, it's great," the waitress says, looking at me. "What can I get you?"

"The tall stack of pancakes, crispy bacon, and a milkshake."

I notice Simon is shaking his head. If he's disapproving now, just wait until dessert.

"What?"

"You're going to make yourself sick."

"I'll be fine," adding with emphasis, "*Dad.*"

"Someone needs to watch out for your arteries."

This makes the waitress laugh to herself, and her expression shifts. Simon has a way of disarming people without even realizing it.

He leans in to the table and half-whispers, "Why is she laughing?"

Lauren and Will share a *classic Simon* look between them, but neither responds. Instead, Lauren beams over at us. "I'm so glad you're both coming with us."

"Thanks for letting me join at the last minute," Simon says.

"Are you kidding?" Lauren's eyes are wide. "This is perfect! More than perfect. Exactly how it should've been all along." She shoots me a look as she says this, and I don't need clarification to understand it. Lauren is convinced (and has been for years) that Simon is my soulmate.

And she's not quiet about it—especially if I'm dating someone. The second she hears about a new relationship, she's back on the Simon train. It's almost comical how someone who knows me *so well* could be so far off.

Lauren continues. "We can't wait to show you our favorite places. Big Mom's Wigwams, Pop's Diner. So many cool vintage gas stations and—"

The waitress brings our drinks. I accept my milkshake with both hands, exuding all the excitement of a kid at Disney reaching for a Dole Whip.

I take a big drink and swoosh all around the inside of my mouth. I turn to Simon, and with half the shake still in my mouth, I say, "Want some?"

Simon shakes his head.

"You *do* want some." I stir the whipped cream from the top into the shake. "This is killing you, isn't it?"

"Actually, I think it's killing you," he says.

"Wait till you see how much syrup I put on my pancakes." I grin.

"Lauren, should we start planning her memorial service now?" Simon asks.

"The heck with that. I don't want a memorial service," I say. "I want a party."

"And a party you will have," Lauren says. "But not today. We've got things to do!"

At that, I squeal. "You're getting married!"

Lauren looks at Will. Will looks at Lauren. He brushes hair away from her face, and I pull out my phone to snap a photo.

When they notice, Lauren's cheeks turn pink.

"I'm going to document this trip for you," I tell them. "Long, lingering looks and all."

Will drapes an arm around Lauren, and I'm struck by how easily they seem to go together. They're so comfortable with each other. I'm zapped with a flicker of envy. Not the jealous kind of envy, just a twinge of that "missing out" feeling.

"Is the itinerary the same as what we talked about?" Simon asks.

"Pretty much," Will says. "We're going to stop in Flagstaff to camp tonight. Thought that would be a great way to spend our first night—sleeping under the stars." He reaches over and takes Lauren's hand.

"But not *really* under the stars," Simon says. "I mean, we'll have tents, right?"

Will grins. "Where would be the fun in that?"

Simon scrunches up his face. I'm no lover of nature, but I can sleep anywhere. I could fall asleep in a gas station bathroom if I had to. Simon needs high-thread-count sheets and his pitch-black bedroom to fall asleep.

The waitress sets our plates down in front of us, pausing with Simon's.

"That look okay, sweetie?"

Sweetie? Wasn't she grump city ten minutes ago? If there's

a Maddie Contingency, then there is also the Simon Effect. He has this quality that endears people to him.

Simon looks up, deadpan, and says, "Yes, this looks perfect. You've done amazing. My compliments to the chef."

The waitress laughs a bit too long, and says, "I'll tell him. Enjoy!"

I slow turn to Simon, who has started cutting up his omelet into neat little squares. He takes a bite, thinks for a moment, nods as if to say *"Ah yes, this is acceptable,"* then sees me staring. He swallows, wipes his mouth with his napkin, and says, "What?"

I simply shake my head at him. Part of me loves it that he has no clue that his particular nature sometimes makes him more endearing.

I take a breath and grab the syrup as Will and Lauren fill us in on the plans.

They first took this road trip over Christmas, and to hear them tell it, that was when they fell in love. But since then, they've driven from California to Illinois and back again several times.

"We've racked up a lot of memories—and miles—on these road trips," Lauren says. "So, we want to make sure to stop off in some of our favorite places."

"But also leave some things open."

"Absolutely. The best things happened to us in the times we didn't plan," Lauren says.

"Like El Muérdago." Will smiles.

"Yes! The torchlight parade. . ." Lauren sighs the words, as if she were saying "aww. . ."

"That's where you started to fall for me," Will says.

"No." Lauren's expression turns shy. "I started to fall for you when I was ten years old, the day you showed up at my house with Spencer."

I knew about El Muérdago and the torchlight parade and even the fact that Lauren had a crush on her brother Spencer's best friend that pre-dated her braces. Their history was rich and full and wonderful—and now I get to be a part of their story.

I set my fork down and look away.

"Mads? What's wrong?" Lauren reaches across the table and takes my hand.

I shake my head, trying not to cry. *Why am I crying? What the heck?* "Nothing, I'm fine."

Simon shifts in the seat next to me. I know he doesn't do well with emotions, but as I look up at him, I can practically feel concern radiating off of him.

Weird.

"I just think it's so beautiful," I say. "The way you guys look at each other. All the history you have. The special places. This life you're building." A lump at the back of my throat silences me, and after a second, I choke out, "It's really beautiful."

"So this is you being sappy," Simon says. "Nothing is actually wrong?"

"I can't help it," I say. "I'm just really lucky to be here with you guys." Then, to try and lighten the mood, I add, "Even if your PDA is nauseating."

We all laugh, except for Simon, who says, "It is a little," which makes us laugh harder, which makes him more confused, and the tension I've caused dissipates.

"I'm not sorry." Lauren smiles up at Will. "This is what it's like to be in love." He leans in and kisses her, and I look away.

Her words hang over the table like a neon sign. This is what it's like to be in love. Would I ever experience that for myself? If I put any of my past relationships up against Will and Lauren's, it's very clear that so far, the answer is no. I've never been in love.

I'm almost thirty, and I've never really, truly, been in love.

Oh, I've been infatuated plenty of times. Lust a handful. Crushed a bunch and fallen hard for a few.

In the starkness of 20/20 hindsight, it's pretty obvious that's all they've ever been.

And it's not like I don't try. I *love* to try. And I've got a pretty short memory. I throw myself into every relationship like the last one never happened, but so far, none of them have ever resulted in anything more than a few months of fun dates.

If I were smart, I really would swear off dating forever, but even I know that proclamation wouldn't last long. I don't like to be alone. And I very much want to find that person who looks at me the way Will looks at Lauren.

I glance up and find Lauren watching me. She's wearing a hint of a frown, silently asking if I'm okay.

I nod slightly. *All good here, sister.*

I'm Maddie Rogers. I'm always okay.

And I'm not going to drag anyone down on this trip because I'm beginning to have a crisis about the state of my life.

I smile across the table, refusing to be the source of Lauren's worry. This trip is not about me.

"I'm really glad we get to come with you," I say. "Thank you again for inviting us along."

It's clear by the look on Lauren's face she's not really buying my put-on mood, but she must decide it's okay to drop the subject.

"Your emotions are such a wild rollercoaster, Mads," she'd said to me once, very early on in our friendship. "The highs are so high, and you're fun and happy. . .but I worry about the lows."

She's silly to worry. I'm the happy one. The fun one. A little introspection isn't going to change that.

"You're going to love it." Lauren smiles over at me. "I'm so glad you're here."

I clear my throat and tell myself the time for reflection is over. My only job on this trip is to make sure Lauren has an amazing time. And to bring my usual brand of happiness. Shouldn't be too hard.

I pick up my milkshake and hold it in the air. "So, we'll stop in all these places and hear your sappy love stories and Simon and I will grin and bear witness the truest love of the century. And once you're pronounced man and wife, we'll send you off to live happily ever after to have all of the shagging with none of the shame!"

"Maddie! Oh my gosh!" Lauren turns beet red, which was my goal, and Will bursts out laughing.

I giggle to myself, then bump my shoulder into Simon's, motioning for him to lift his glass.

Lauren and Will lift their glasses and clink them against mine. Simon simply sits with his held in the air.

"Hey, space cadet," I wave my hand in front of Simon's face. "I just made a toast. You have to clink," I say.

"That was a toast?" He lamely leans his glass and touches it to mine.

"Yes, that was a toast." I use my most exasperated tone.

"I hope you've got something better for the wedding."

Lauren giggles across the table, and I roll my eyes.

"So, this trip is sort of like, you're taking the honeymoon before the wedding?" Simon asks as I continue the assault on my pancakes.

"No," Will says. "We are *definitely* taking a real honeymoon. Hawaii."

"Wait." Simon glances at Lauren. "Don't you hate to fly?"

"More than anything," Lauren says.

It was sweet—and a little surprising—that Simon remembered that.

"So, how are you. . .?"

73

"Drugs," Will says, with a smile. "Good ones."

Will and Lauren go back to gazing at each other.

"You guys are ridiculously cute," I say, a little more food in my mouth than I realized. I swallow, stand, and call out, "My friends are getting married!"

The chatter in the restaurant heightens, and someone starts applauding. I laugh as Lauren covers her face with her hands. I stick my fingers in my mouth and whistle, and the entire diner erupts in cheers.

A woman near the window picks up her glass and starts clinking it with her fork, and Will and Lauren both grin. He turns toward her, takes her face in his hands, and kisses her so sweetly my heart nearly explodes.

More cheering.

I applaud, feeling like I might burst with happiness because even though I'm a little envious of this love, the fact is, Lauren deserves to be happy more than anyone else in the world. Maybe one day I'll find someone to love me the way Will loves her.

I'm still clapping when my gaze falls to Simon, who is half-heartedly applauding, but completely focused on me, smiling just a little.

He's probably embarrassed that I've made a scene, but he's been around long enough to know that this is my way. I make a goofy face at him, and he shakes his head in that familiar way back at me—and I wonder if he thinks he's made a mistake riding with me for a week.

For crying out loud, we haven't even left the pier.

Chapter Twelve

Maddie

After breakfast, Lauren and I go to the restroom. I'm standing at the mirror scrounging for a lipstick in my bag when Lauren emerges from the stall.

"Okay," Lauren says. "When did Simon get so. . .hot?"

I freeze. "I'm sorry, what?"

"And funny? What the heck?" Lauren flips on the faucet and sticks her hands under the stream of water. "Don't pretend you haven't noticed."

"Lauren, it's Simon."

Simon. My friend. The guy who rolls clothes.

Lauren smiles as she rinses the soap off of her hands. "You're thinking about it, I can tell."

"I promise I'm not."

"You should be," Lauren says.

"You do this every time I break up with somebody," I say.

"Do what?"

"In fact, you do this every time I'm dating somebody. You try and convince me I should date Simon." I give up on finding lipstick. "I hate to break it to you—again—but there is not now, nor will there ever be, anything romantic between me and Simon." I look at Lauren through the reflection in the mirror. "We're friends. Great ones, in fact. He's terrific, but so, so wrong for me."

Lauren turns off the sink, brows knit together. "But have you seen the way he looks at you? It's an actual smolder. And now that he's grown into his looks and everything—" She comically leans on the sink, fanning herself and blowing out a breath on a "Phew!" Then, she says, "I mean, he's a man now. And talk about a glow-up! Don't even pretend you haven't noticed."

"You're crazy," I say. "Simon couldn't *smolder* if he was sitting on a campfire."

Lauren grabs a paper towel from the dispenser, then turns to me with a smug look on her face. "Something happened to your *friend* when you weren't looking, Maddie. He went ahead and changed from a nerdy guy in my study group to a hot, successful businessman."

I shake my head. "What is wrong with you? Have you lost your mind with all this wedding talk?" I laugh. "You're seeing romance everywhere. It's like couples who are trying to have kids and all they see walking around are pregnant people."

Lauren tilts her head at me, seemingly waiting for me to finish.

I press on, turning back to the mirror. "Simon and I have zero sparks. Battery is dead. No voltage. We're completely platonic."

Lauren turns me to face her, but I don't look right at her. Instead, I huff like a kid being shown her messy room. "You deserve someone kind. And smart." She leans in, forcing my gaze. "*And* wonderful."

I laugh, mainly because I don't believe I'm quite there yet. It all seems too serious to me.

However. . .and I've never thought this before, maybe it's time to be a little more serious.

"Even if that were true—which it's not—Simon wouldn't be the guy."

"Maddie," Lauren says, "he always has been the guy."

"Enough already. He's not. Here we are, ten years later, still *just friends.* Plus," I add, "he's a next-level perfectionist." I turn off the water. "You should've seen the way he packed my bag."

"Wait. *Simon* packed your bag?"

I grimace. "I might've. . .overslept. A bit."

"Simon packed your bag." A statement this time.

"Yeah, and it was crazy efficient," I say. "He was so careful with rolling every article of clothing."

"Maddie, that's so sweet." Lauren does that *awww* thing as she says it. Like folding my clothing was a romantic gesture or something.

"What is?"

Lauren waves a hand to indicate my general existence. "This. You. Simon. Isn't it refreshing to think about being with someone who is so much nicer than all your other boyfriends?"

"You always like my boyfriends."

Lauren looks caught.

"Wait. You haven't liked my boyfriends?" I frown. "What about Dylan? You liked Dylan."

Lauren scrunches her nose and shakes her head.

"Lawrence? He was. . ."

She winces.

"Good grief. Kyle? David? Matt?" All of the names elicit the same response, like Lauren just accidentally ate expired mayonnaise. On the last name, I pause and add, "Yeah, you're right, Matt was a tool."

"I'd just really like to see you give a nice guy a chance. Give you some stability, that's all I'm saying."

"You think my life needs stability?"

She shrugs and shifts her purse to the other shoulder. "I also think he'd do just about anything for you."

That, I don't doubt. Simon had dropped everything more than once to come to my rescue. Had I returned that favor? Gosh, I hope so.

"Maybe you'll discover it's great having an efficient packer in your life."

"Out of context that could sound really weird," I joke, hoping she'll drop it.

She laughs. "You know what I mean, Mads."

I feel my forehead pull. "I really have never thought of him like that."

"Never?" Lauren crosses her arms over her chest and leans back against the sink.

My mind spins back to the night Austin broke up with me. It was exactly like so many nights before—me crying. Running to Simon. Simon consoling me. Me falling asleep at his place.

I look up and find Lauren studying me. "Did something happen?"

I shake my head. "No, of course not."

"You'd tell me if something happened."

"Yes, I would definitely tell you." And then, because I can't lie to Lauren, I say, "I might've slept at his place one night last week."

"Okay, but you've done that before."

"Yeah, I know. I was on the couch. It wasn't any different. But. . ." I trail off, a twinge of revelation slowly coming over my mind.

He's there for me. He's always there. Friends do that.

Have I done that? For him?

I look at Lauren.

"Lo. Am I. . .selfish?"

I, for some reason, feel incredibly worried that I've done something wrong to Simon. I've never even given this a thought before. Even knowing Bea thinks I take advantage, still, I blew that off like it was impossible.

Lauren takes me by the arms, looks at me, and lets her hands slide down to mine, taking them in hers.

"No. You're not. You're a great friend, and probably exactly what Simon needs in his life."

"You sure?"

Lauren pats my arm. "You know, you and I aren't exactly alike, either—but you're an amazing friend, and I adore you."

She moves toward the door and reaches for the handle. "And maybe you and Simon could be perfect together."

"Oh my *gosh*, Lo, we aren't *together*."

Opening the door, she says, "I just hope you don't wait too long to figure this out."

I frown. "Why?"

Lauren shrugs. "He had a date last week." She moves to leave the bathroom, but I stop her.

"He did? He didn't tell me he had a date."

"He didn't tell me either," Lauren says. "He told Will."

"He told Will?" I toss my paper towel in the garbage can. "I didn't realize they were close."

Lauren shrugs. "You know Will. He's never met a stranger. He's like you that way." She starts to walk back to the table.

I don't realize it, but I let the door shut with me still in the bathroom. I'm just standing there.

Simon had a date. And he didn't tell me.

That hits me sideways, and I can't help but wonder. . .am I. . .*jealous?*

Chapter Thirteen

Maddie

I finally follow Lauren out of the bathroom, brushing off the unwanted feelings that follow *me* out of the bathroom.

Lauren is love-blind. Too lost in her own perfect fairytale to think clearly. She should know by now that there's nothing between me and Simon.

Even if I am a little jealous he had a date and didn't tell me. Whatever.

That's normal, right? I'm not jealous that he had a date. I'm jealous he didn't tell me. Yes. That's it. Jealous of not being in the know.

And who is this girl anyway?

As we reach the table, I see Simon, and he's doing that thing where he stares at me.

He's not just *watching*. He's studying. He's enjoying. Is he. . .smoldering?

I make a weird face at him and look away. From his perspective it probably seems like I'm having a stroke.

This is unproductive thinking. And ridiculous. Simon

doesn't smolder. Flynn Rider smolders. This isn't Disney, and I'm not a princess.

I don't need saving.

Though, simply by joining me for this road trip, he *is* saving me, isn't he?

He's saved me a lot over the years. Big things and little things. He's my biggest fan, and I'm not sure why. Most guys like Simon—smart, successful, reliable—see me for what I am and don't expect much. I'm the fun one. I'm the good time. I'm not what Simon needs—not romantically, anyway.

I'm not sure what I did to deserve having him in my life, but there's no way I would ever risk ruining it.

I am selfish, aren't I?

As I reach the table, the waitress appears and hands out our checks. Will and Lauren take theirs to the cash register as Simon slides out of the booth.

"All good?" he asks.

"Yep." I smile at him.

"You were in there a long time."

"I was."

"It was the syrup, wasn't it?"

I would normally laugh, but my mind doesn't feel funny right now.

"Everything's fine." Why do I suddenly feel nervous? It's not like he knows what Lauren said. And it's not like it's the first time she's said it.

Nothing's changed. Absolutely nothing. So why does everything feel different?

I spin around in time to see Simon get behind Will and Lauren in the line, waiting to pay.

This is nonsense. It's Simon.

My *friend*. My very particular, perfectionist, serious, living-out-his-ten-year-plan *friend*.

I start toward the others, searching my bag until I find my wallet—more of a coin purse, really, with a single credit card and a wad of dollar bills shoved inside.

"We'll meet you in the parking lot," Will tells us after he pays. "I need to shift a few things around in the Jeep."

Simon steps aside and motions for me to go in front of him.

"No, go ahead, I've got. . .to find. . .my. . ." I shake my head, still fussing with the insides of my bag hoping to find both my card and the words to end my sentence.

He hands his card over to the cashier, his shoulder brushing up against mine as he does.

I step aside and touch my arm, my skin slightly warm, as if it had been pressed against a hot pane of glass. I search my mind for something benign to say, something that would erase the thoughts pinballing around in my head after my bathroom conversation with Lauren. "Uh. . .hey."

He turns to me briefly, a strange look on his face. "Hey."

"Hey there, you. How, uh. . ." I'm scrambling. "How was your food?"

"It was. . .good," he says slowly, like he's assessing someone with a concussion. The cashier hands back his card.

"And you're ready for this trip?" I ask, still making unnatural small talk.

"Sure, why wouldn't I be?"

"I don't know," I say. "I know you like things. . ." I sock him in the arm, then pat it, then brush it—what the heck am I doing?! *Tidy.*

He looks at his arm, where I'm still patting, then back at me. "Tidy?"

"Yeah," I say, forcing my hand to quit. "Like, you pretty much live the same day over and over again, right?"

He frowns a smile. "I've never lived a day like this."

"Well," I smile at him—a put-on for sure. "That's because

you. . ." I poke him, "don't spend enough time with me. I'll shake things up for you, guaranteed."

He signs the receipt and hands it back to the cashier as I give him my credit card. "You usually do." He smiles as he slips his wallet into his back pocket. "You're being super weird. I'll meet you outside."

I nod as he walks away, and I pray the stunted awkwardness goes along with him.

"Sorry, miss, your card's been declined." The cashier's voice pulls me back to reality. He slides the card back to me as my heart sinks straight to my toes. Heat rushes to my face as I pretend to search my bag for another card which absolutely does not exist.

"Do you have another card?" the man asks.

"Um. . ." *Unwrapped tampon. Wad of gum in tissue. The tube of lipstick I'd been searching for in the bathroom.*

"There it is!" I exclaim, pulling out the lipstick.

The cashier is still staring at me.

"Oh. Right. Hang on."

I find a lone dollar bill at the bottom of the bag and pull it out, laying it flat on the counter. Then, I unzip the front pocket of the wallet, coming up with about six more dollars. I open the interior pocket of the bag and fish out a few more dollars in quarters, knowing that while I may be able to scrape together enough for my meal, I most certainly will not have enough for a tip.

I look at the pile of crumpled bills and coins on the counter, aware of the line forming behind me. My face flushes hot, and my heart rate spikes.

How embarrassing.

"Will that cover it?" I ask, having lost count during my little treasure hunt.

The cashier shoots me a look. "Let me just count all of

these *coins* for you," he says, tone dripping sarcasm.

"I'm sorry," I say. "I forgot to deposit my paycheck." It's not true, but I'm too flustered to tell the truth.

Without looking up, the cashier says, "You're short a quarter."

"Oh." I dive back into my purse, knowing full well there is no more money inside. After a second of searching, a woman behind me sets a quarter on the counter.

"Oh, gosh, thank you." My pulse is racing.

The woman nods, as if to say "no big deal." But it's a huge deal to me.

The cashier hands over my receipt.

"Thank you." I take it and step out of the line, feeling that hot flush of embarrassment, like I just got called out by a teacher.

Through the window, I catch a glimpse of Simon, standing in the parking lot with Lauren and Will, all prepped and ready for a full week on the road.

A full week. And I have no money and a maxed-out credit card.

How did this happen?

No sense asking that question. I knew how it happened. I'd been too afraid to check the bank because I didn't want to face it. As if denial could deposit money into my account.

This is my way. Pretend everything is fine, and it will be. Obviously, my way is faulty.

And this is why my *Someday Dream* remains firmly in the background. Why I'll always be a barista or a waitress or a clerk in a vintage record store, living paycheck to paycheck.

Simon glances back toward the door of the restaurant, probably wondering what's taking me so long. And all I can think is I have absolutely no idea how I'm going to pay for a week-long road trip with an unopened sewing kit and a pack of gum.

Chapter Fourteen

Simon

Ten years ago

In a fit of either bravery or insanity, I asked Lauren to set me up with her roommate.

At the time, I had no idea what having Maddie's undivided attention would do to me.

Now, halfway through our date, I'm seeing that it makes me sweaty and impairs brain function—specifically the part of the brain that affects speech and cognitive thought.

I'm aware that it's not going well.

I arrived early to make sure we had a seat, and when I saw her come in, I stood up to welcome her to the table. It's what you do on a date.

I offered to take her coat, and pulled out her chair for her, then spent a good portion of the pre-meal conversation slightly arranging the silverware and the salt and pepper shakers.

Now that we have our food, there's actually a reason for extended periods of not talking—instead of the earlier reason, which is my inability to put two coherent words together.

She's *so* pretty.

Maddie smiles politely from across the table. She takes a bite of her burger, and I mentally scramble for something to say. I'm not great in these kinds of settings. I struggle with small talk, and when I'm in the presence of a woman—especially a beautiful one—I turn into the social equivalent of a large potato.

Driving to the bar, plus the entire time I sat here waiting for her, I came up with a list of topics I could bring up. At the moment, the mental paper I wrote it down on is blank.

"Where are you from?" I stammer, hoping I didn't ask that already.

"Chicago," she says. "That's how I met Lauren. We're both from Illinois, and at freshman orientation, we just sort of clicked."

"It's kind of surprising."

"What is?"

"You and Lauren being friends."

She sets her burger down and frowns over at me. "Why?"

I shrug. "You seem really different. She seems more serious."

Maddie laughs, and I swear the lights got a bit brighter in the room. "You've got her pegged! And I'm not? Super serious?"

"No, you're not. You seem like you don't care about rules or deadlines or listening to people tell you what to do," I blurt.

She shakes her head in disbelief. "Simon, that might be the nicest thing anyone has ever said to me." A smile lights up her face.

I respond flatly, "Then people should say nicer things."

She laughs again, and I'm not sure why. Is this going well? Is this a good date?

I realize I don't know Lauren well, but I've studied with her enough times to know she *is* a serious student. And a little Type A. I don't know Maddie well either, but so far, I'm not getting any of those things from her.

Maybe that's part of why I'm so taken.

A guy stops by our table. "No way. Mad-e-LINE!"

She glances up, then over to me. "Hey, Chip."

Chip? I wonder if he knows the other two guys who've already stopped at our table "just to say hi."

"You gonna be out later? It's not a party unless you're there." He puts a hand on her shoulder.

Maddie half-laughs, shrugging it off subtly. "Ha. Yeah. Oh, I don't know. Maybe?" She nods at me. "This is Simon."

The guy looks at me like he's only just now noticed there's another person at the table. "Hey, you Maddie's brother or cousin or something?"

I start to respond, but Maddie cuts me off. "I'll talk to you later, Chip."

"Hope so, babe." He gives that frat boy up-nod and walks away.

She adjusts her seat, looking down at the table.

"Friend of yours?"

Maddie's laugh is nervous. "He's just a guy I know." She takes another bite, chews, swallows, and brings her eyes back to mine. "It's weird, isn't it?"

"What's weird?"

"Blind dates," she says. "How'd Lauren convince you to do this?"

"She didn't. I. . ." I feel sudden heat in my cheeks.

Maddie looks at me, eyes sparkling. "You what?"

At least Lauren hadn't sold me out. No way I was going to confess I'd asked her roommate to set this up.

"I. . .didn't have anything going on, so. . ."

"Ah, I get it. There was nothing better to do," she says.

"Oh my goodness! No, I wasn't. . .I didn't. . ."

I flounder, and she giggles. The pilot of this conversation has issued a mayday; it's going down in flames.

She waves me off. "I'm just kidding, Simon. Loosen up."

Right. *How do I do that again?*

"Do you go on a lot of blind dates?" she asks.

"Me? No." I awkwardly push lettuce around my salad plate with my fork. "This is the first one. And I almost. . ." I stop myself.

She sets down her food again and looks at me. "Almost what?"

I take a breath and blurt, "I almost canceled—twice. I'm so sorry, I'm just really nervous."

I glance up and see her shoulders relax and her head tilt, a soft smile with a tinge of pity in her eyes.

Just what I was going for. Pity. *Solid first date material, Simon, way to go.* Maybe I should've planned this out better. Taken her somewhere really impressive, or romantic, or expensive.

But those things don't come easily to me. *None* of this comes easily to me. I'm sure she'd rather be sitting here with Chip or anyone other than me. Someone that had the sort of confidence women respond to.

I'm confident about some things—academics, computers, *Star Trek* trivia—I'm definitely lacking in the romance department.

"Maybe we should take the pressure off," Maddie says, breaking up my inner monologue and the silence.

"What do you mean?" If she has a solution for the nausea I'm feeling, I'm all ears.

She sits back in her chair. "First date pressure. It's hard enough as it is, and there's this unspoken pressure of trying to impress, picking the right things to say, wondering what the other person is thinking."

"Yeah," I say. "Yeah, absolutely."

"You probably had a whole list of things you were going to talk about, didn't you?"

I start. "I. . .did. How did you know that?"

"The truth is, Simon, I'm not really looking for a relationship right now, and you seem like a relationship kind of guy. Am I right?"

I shrug. I don't know what kind of guy I am—not when it comes to dating. "I'm not sure. What does a relationship kind of guy seem like?"

She smiles. "Well, for starters, someone who shows up early."

"I'm just punctual."

"And second, someone who makes a list. And holds the door. And pulls out my chair."

I just thought I was being nice. Was that not the right thing to do?

"And those things are really, really sweet." She pauses briefly. "It's. . .nice, actually. I don't know if anyone has ever done those things for me." She gathers herself. "But I'm right. It's, you know—" she waves a hand in my general direction—"pretty obvious."

"Obvious how?"

"The same way it's obvious to you that Lauren and I are different," she says.

"I didn't mean that as an insult," I say, wondering if I'd offended her.

"No, I know," she says. "We *are* different. You nailed it. I can't even tell you what classes I'm in without checking my phone. On the flipside, Lauren is a high honor roll, still owns a

Trapper Keeper, color-coded notebooks for each class kind of student."

I'm not going to go into all of my reasons that red notebooks can only be for English and blue notebooks are for math. And anyone who uses green notebooks for either of those subjects is a psychopath.

"But she was right about you." She picks up her glass. "You're a really nice guy."

Nice. The kiss of death. Girls don't want to date the *nice* guy.

"I'm just not really a relationship kind of girl, Simon." She leans back in the booth. "I like to go out, have fun, meet people. I'm not really looking for a serious boyfriend."

"Do you think I'm looking for a serious girlfriend?"

She shrugs. "I can't be, you know, 100% sure, but if you are, I think you can do a lot better than me."

I take a drink of my water, then say, "What makes you say that?"

She pulls her legs up underneath her, sitting cross-wise in her chair. "What's your major?"

"I'm double majoring in business and computer science."

"I don't have one yet." She holds up a finger as if that is *strike one.* "When you get back to your dorm room, where do you put your keys?"

"On a hook by the door," I say, not following.

"Does it have a label?"

"Well, yeah, or else I'd confuse it with other keys."

"Typically, I toss mine in some random place and have to call my RA to let me in the next time I get locked out." She holds up another finger, *strike two.* "How many times has your RA had to let you back into your room?"

"Um, never."

She raises her eyebrows, as if this proves her point. "How many nights a week do you go out?"

I don't want to say.

"One? Maybe two?" she asks, probably sensing my hesitation.

"Sometimes. Or sometimes not at all," I say. "I would much prefer to stay in than get lost in the mess of drunk college kids at the bars every weekend."

She pauses, and says, "Actually, that's a fair point. But listen. I'm out almost every single night." She holds up another finger. "Three solid reasons why you can find someone better suited for a long-term relationship than me." She pops the last bit of burger into her mouth, and half-chewing, says, "I'm doing you a huge favor right now."

I can't figure out how this is a favor to me.

"This isn't an indictment on you," she says. "This is all me. It's pretty clear that *I'm* the disaster at this table."

"Plus, you talk with your mouth full." I meet her eyes and silently count to three before smiling.

She laughs. "That was funny."

"I am funny."

"Lauren didn't tell me you're funny."

"What did she tell you?"

She leans forward in her chair, as if loving the volley. "She said you're totally nice, super sweet, smart, and I'd better stick with you because you're going to own a big company and be super rich one day."

I'm taken aback. "She. . .said that about me?"

"Yeah. Every word. And you and I could not be more different, and I am *definitely* the wrong girl for you. Period. End of story."

I disagree. "So, since we're so different, that must mean you're mean, super bitter, dumb, and I'd better run from this place because you're going to be fired from every job and live in your parents' basement."

Maddie's mouth drops, and I instantly regret every word I said. My attempts at humor often fall flat, and I wish I could take it back, *and I should just go crawl in a hole, and. . .*

But then she smiles, laughing so loud people at other tables look over to see what is happening. She reaches over and smacks me on the shoulder.

"That. Was. EPIC! Oh my gosh, Simon!"

My whole body breathes a sigh of relief. Maybe she would make a good friend.

She wipes tears from her eyes, still laughing.

"So, what now?" I ask after a pause.

She tilts her head and looks at me, like she's in an art museum, trying to make sense of a single black line on a white canvas. "Now, we absolutely become friends."

"Friends."

"Best of friends. I need you in my life, Simon Collier." She sticks her hand out, as if we're striking some sort of deal.

I reach across the table and take it. "Best of friends."

"A guy friend." She grins. "Just what I've always wanted."

"And. . .just what I've always wanted to be."

Chapter Fifteen

Maddie

Present day

I slide into the passenger seat of Simon's car, my mind reeling.

How could I let this happen?

My pulse races, and beads of sweat gather above my upper lip. How am I going to spend the next seven days on the road? Simon, Lauren, and Will are all responsible adults, all with stable, serious jobs, all able to function in society without overdrawing their checking accounts.

What is the matter with me?

Why can't I get it together!?

"You okay?" Simon starts the car, but we sit for a moment, waiting for Will to pull out and lead the way. He's watching me, and if I'm not careful, he'll figure out exactly what's going on. And I can't let that happen. I can't reinforce the idea that I'm a total screw-up, and I can't let him swoop in and save the day.

I've already been enough of a burden on my friends.

"I'm fine," I lie.

"You look like you want to throw up," he says. "Probably the milkshake. . ."

"It's not the milkshake."

"But it is something." A statement, not a question.

"No, it's not. It's fine. I promise. Everything's fine." I force a smile, but even I know it's not believable. Inside, I'm freaking out.

Will closes the back of his Jeep Grand Cherokee, and Simon messes with the temperature control in the car.

This is bad. Really bad. I've got one job on this trip—be there for Lauren. That's it. That's all I have to do, and now I'm wondering if I can even do that. How do I make sure Lauren has fun if I can't even pay for a hotel room?

I think back on the last few weeks. The bridesmaid's dress had been expensive. I'd worked fewer hours at the coffee shop, which, in hindsight, probably wasn't the smartest decision. I needed all the hours I could get. Why had I scheduled myself off three of my normal shifts?

I know why. I'd been lost in my little love bubble with Austin. My priorities were so far out of whack they needed a chiropractor.

The worst part is, I still have to pay rent this month. I'm going to lose my apartment—I'm still behind from last month.

Turns out I suck at adulting.

Panic washes over me. Things are starting to stack. I'm usually pretty good at keeping each issue in its own tidy internal box, but now everything is getting mentally dumped into one huge pile.

In addition to the rent, my credit card is maxed. The car payment comes out in a week (I think? I can never remember the date), and what happens if I miss one of those? No car? Collections?

My thoughts start spiraling. I love my apartment. It keeps me sane. Next to Simon's place, that little space is the only place in the world where I don't have to pretend.

The sunroom is where I relax and recharge. Sitting at my pottery wheel, surrounded by windows, high enough above the street for it to feel like a private escape, I feel like myself. Not the version of myself that feels the need to entertain, but the real me. The clay never asks me to smile.

It lets me rest. Take off the mask. Stop pretending.

How will I survive if I don't have that?

Will gets out of his Jeep and runs back to Simon's car.

"Just want to give you a quick rundown of the route," he says. "In case we get separated."

I barely listen, hugging my big purse to my chest as Simon and Will chat through the open window. I hear Will say something about this not being the fastest or easiest or straightest way to go, but it is "the most scenic, which matters more."

After that, I tune them both out.

The knot of humiliation pulses inside me, making it impossible to concentrate.

Okay, think. I've been in worse spots.

Though, at the moment, I can't think of a single one.

One whole week of meals and coffees and hotel rooms I won't be able to pay for. Should I bail now? Fake an illness? Go home and try to figure out a way to get myself to Illinois without the built-in vacation?

I can't do that to Lauren. This trip is too important.

I push my hands through my hair. What a disaster.

"We'll follow you, but I've got the directions," Simon says as I tune back in. Will nods, then runs back to his Jeep.

As he pulls away, Lauren waves furiously, first-day-of-vacation-excitement exploding on her face.

I wave back, faking excitement the way only I can do. I drop the facade as soon as Will turns out of the parking lot.

I'm going to ruin everything.

Simon looks at me. He's wearing sunglasses—aviators. Shockingly, he pulls them off. For a brief moment, I see the Simon that Lauren had described.

He is *attractive.*

I'd never really noticed it before. To me, he's always just been *Simon.* The nerdy guy who put up with me, despite the fact that I most likely made him want to pull his hair out.

"You ready for this adventure?" he asks.

I'm in a crisis here. Distracting myself by debating Simon's attractiveness is not helping. I feel nauseous, and the car has barely started moving. "Yep."

"You seem. . .not yourself." Simon follows Will and Lauren out onto the freeway.

No turning back now.

"Maddie, what's wrong?"

The details of this are too much to focus on right now, and I know if I don't pull it together, Simon is going to stop the car and force me to tell him the truth. "I'm fine."

We drive for a few minutes in complete silence until Simon says, "You don't seem fine."

"I am." I press my lips together wishing he'd let it go, but knowing that's not his way.

"You forget how well I know you." He reaches over and takes my hand, giving it a little squeeze. "Your light went out."

The words almost make me cry. I blame the unwanted emotion on the stress of my current situation, but it's more than that, and I know it. I glance down at Simon's strong, protective hand wrapped around mine. I know I could unload everything on him, and he'd carry it for me. He'd offer to pay for everything and wouldn't let me pay him back.

Which is exactly why I can't tell him. For once, maybe for the first time since we met, I'm not going to take advantage of his kindness.

I'm not going to let his sister be right about me. And I'm not going to prove to him that I'm as flighty and unreliable as everyone thinks I am.

This time, I need to figure things out for myself.

I put my other hand on his and give it a few pats. "You don't have to worry about me. I promise."

"I don't believe you, but I know better than to push." He pulls his hand back, and I miss the comfort of his touch instantly. As if somehow, just knowing he's there puts my nerves at ease.

We drive in silence, which I hate, but I can't muster the energy to talk. I'm too busy trying to think of ways to make some fast cash. So far, I've only come up with things that are illegal or morally inappropriate. I might be the "fun one," but I still have standards.

To distract myself—and Simon—I ask, "When did you get those sunglasses?"

He turns back to the road. "They were a gift."

I watch as the muscle in his jaw tightens. I don't need to ask to know who'd gotten them for him.

Hannah. His ex-girlfriend. They'd broken up a few months ago, but it still seems like a sore subject, so I don't ask any more questions. I didn't pretend to be sad when he told me they'd broken up. I was appropriately empathetic, but they weren't good together.

Hannah seemed intent on changing just about everything about Simon. Every time I saw him while they were dating, he'd show up wearing something new. New jeans. New sweaters. New haircut. New facial hair. Apparently, new sunglasses. Sure, Hannah had made Simon look trendy, but had she made him feel like who he was wasn't enough in the process?

That thought makes me angry.

As if Simon would ever *not* be enough. As if he isn't perfect exactly as he is.

Chapter Sixteen

Simon

Maddie's gone quiet again. Even with Michael Jackson's "Billie Jean" blaring through the speakers.

We've been switching off picking songs, which is kind of like allowing one another into a secret room with our most personal collections. Sometimes your whole outlook about someone is changed by seeing what's on their playlist.

I picked this song because I was sure she'd sing along.

But she isn't singing.

She isn't even tapping her foot.

She's just staring out the window.

It's rare that I don't know exactly how Maddie is feeling. I know how to tell the difference between genuine happiness and fake happiness. She doesn't usually pretend with me.

Most of the time, Maddie is the life of the party, but there's a side of her that few people see—a side that's more like when soda goes flat, all the bubbles gone after being left out too long.

What's happening now isn't that. She's not pretending to be happy, but she also won't tell me what's bothering her.

"You want to talk?" I ask.

"I told you, I'm fine."

"But you're lying."

She turns, playfully saying, "Only a little."

I start to speak, but she cuts me off. "It's fine, Simon. Really. Nothing huge, just something I'm working through."

I frown. I don't like not knowing.

"Can I help at all?"

"You can help by getting rid of that face you make when you feel helpless to fix my problems."

"But if I can—"

She cuts me off again. "Lauren said you went on a date last week."

"On second thought, maybe let's not talk."

She turns in her seat and gasps. Uh oh. She's interested now.

"Stop it! Was it fun? What did you do? What was she like?"

"There's. . .uh. . .nothing to say, really." The muscle in my jaw twitches. It feels weird, talking to Maddie about my date. I'm good at listening to her and her dating misadventures, but talking about mine? Not nearly as good at that.

"You told Will," she says. "Am I not as important as Will?"

I glance at her, then back to the road. "Are you jealous?"

"Of you and Will's budding bromance?" Maddie laughs. "Maybe."

"You were in crisis mode," I lift my hands off the steering wheel to gesture, "because of what's-his-name. I didn't want to bug you."

"Simon," she leans her back against the passenger side door and my hand instinctively jerks to the lock button. "This is a big deal. You haven't been out with anyone in months. Not since Hannah."

I wince at her name.

Hannah had been a mistake. Our break-up still gnaws at me. It's not that I'm in mourning or anything. It's just that Hannah had spoken out loud everything I already knew. I never really let her know me, and yet, she saw straight through me.

I don't like that.

She's part of the reason I know I need to make a move or move on. But Maddie doesn't know any of that.

"Aw, friend," Maddie says playfully, patting my shoulder. "Are we still not mentioning her by name?"

I shoot her a look, and mid-perturbed eye-roll I realize something.

"Are you upset that I went on a date?"

"Pshh! *No*," she brushes it off like it's the dumbest thing in the world. "Of course not."

I take my eyes completely off the road and look right at her, eyebrows raised.

"Quit it, you dork, watch the road." She socks me on the arm. "I just don't understand why you didn't tell me."

"Fine," I say, settling back, looking ahead. "What do you want to know?"

She sits for a moment, rubbing her hands briefly, as if she's choosing which sordid question to ask first. "Okay. Where'd you take her?"

"A Lakers game," I say.

"Really?" She scrunches her face.

"What's wrong with that?" Simon asks.

"I hate basketball."

"Well, Tessa likes it."

"*Tessa*," Maddie repeats, as if trying to deduce something about this woman from just her name. "Okay. Where'd you meet her?"

"Dating app."

She gasps. "You're on a *dating app*?"

"No," I correct her. "My *sister* is on a dating app with my name and information on the profile. All communication goes directly to her."

Maddie laughs heartily. "Of *course* it does. She does love to be in charge, doesn't she?"

I nod knowingly. "She practically ordered me to take this girl out. Said she was perfect for me."

"Perfect for you?" I don't need to look at Maddie to know she's grinning at me. "What does 'perfect for Simon' look like?"

Like you.

I groan. "Do we really have to do this?"

"Seven days alone together in this car. We have to talk to each other, might as well make it juicy." She stretches her arms up, settling her hands behind her head and arching her back. In my periphery I can see her figure, and I unintentionally step harder on the accelerator.

Thankfully she seems not to notice the engine—or my heart rate—revving.

"Besides," she continues, "this is all stuff you already should've told me."

"Like I said. . .there's not much to say," I say. "We went to the game. We had good seats that I got a great deal on."

She nods, "Of course, of course."

"And then. . .we both said we should do it again sometime."

She leans in. "Did you mean it?"

I screw up my face. "I don't think either of us meant it. But it got my sister off my case."

"That was it?"

"That was it."

"No sordid details?"

"What, you want to know if we kissed?"

102

She gasps like a teenager. "*Did you?!*"

I focus on the road, wondering if anyone would notice if I, oh I don't know, drove off a cliff.

I take a breath.

"Yes."

"You. . .did?" I notice a slight change in her voice—but maybe I imagined it.

"Yes."

"And?"

"And what?"

"How was it?"

"Maddie, haven't we been friends long enough for you to know that guys don't do this?"

She smiles, feigning innocence. "Do what?"

"Stop it. You know exactly what you're doing."

"I have no idea what you're talking about."

I glance over, and she's holding in a smile by tucking both her lips in between her teeth, her eyes doing that sparkle thing.

"This whole 'girl talk' thing you're trying to do," I say.

"It's not girl talk." She shifts again, this time to face the road. "It's friend talk. Friends tell each other these things."

"Well, I don't," I say. "It's not. . .polite." And it's awkward. I've dated several women over the years, and I've never been comfortable talking to her about any of them.

None of it has to do with politeness.

"Kissed on the first date," she says to herself. "You dog."

"Are you mocking me?"

"I'm impressed," she says. Then, after a beat, she adds quietly, "You should. . .you know. . . call her again."

"Should I?" I glance over and find her looking down. Why am I getting the feeling that neither of us wants me to call her again?

Why does Maddie care?

She looks up at me and holds my gaze for seconds that feel like minutes, then smiles. "Well, yeah. I mean, if you had fun, and she's. . .you know, nice and everything. Of course you should."

I drag my eyes back to the road. "Nah."

"Why not?"

"I don't like basketball either."

The car fills with her trademark laugh and subsequent slug on the arm, and both always make me smile. I will never tire of hearing her laugh.

I absently think, *If I do move to Seattle, I won't hear that anymore.*

Outside, the faceless miles pass by, and I don't like where my mind is spinning, so I ask, "You said you hate basketball, so. . .what's your idea of a *good* date?"

"Oh my gosh, the flower market," she says, without hesitation. "Totally. Walking around all morning, then eating chocolate croissants and coffee from that French pastry shop on the corner. We'd talk straight through lunch, and by the end of the day, we'd know everything there is to know about each other." She draws her legs up onto the seat, arms wrapped around her knees.

She looks at me. "No one's ever asked me that before."

"Really?"

She smiles. "Usually guys do the standard dinner and a movie, or worse, they try to get me to come to their place. I don't know how many times I've had to announce that I'm not into casual hook-ups."

I'm relieved to know she's not. She was—and is—a social butterfly, ever since I met her in college, and I know guys would often get the wrong impression.

Yet another side of her that no one else sees.

"Flowers. Huh."

She starts to pick the ends of her hair. "What's wrong with flowers?"

"Oh, nothing," I say, "I just would've thought you'd prefer something more adventurous. Skydiving or rock climbing or something."

She smiles. "Well, maybe there are things about me you don't know yet. Even after all these years."

Maybe there are.

My phone buzzes from where it's mounted on the dashboard, saving me from blurting out that my dream date already happened years ago in college at a little restaurant/bar populated by college kids. "It's a client. I need to—"

"Sure, take it."

I answer the phone. It's a newer client wanting to discuss the changes he'd sent over via email that morning.

"I'm in the car at the moment, Mr. Rice, but as soon as I get to where I'm going, I'll take a look and we can discuss." Mr. Rice asks me a few more questions, and I'm slightly worried about keeping up with business while I'm driving across the country.

It's not like I'm focused on my job at the moment. After a few more minutes, some technical talk, and a cordial goodbye, Spotify comes back on as I tap out of the phone app.

Love Will Keep Us Together by Captain & Tennille. Ironic.

"Your stress line is back," she says.

"My what?"

She reaches over and taps my forehead. "This."

I involuntarily twitch back at her touch, which is electric. I try to play it off like I was annoyed, hoping she didn't see my true reaction.

"It's a barely detectable line that appears right there when you're stressed out," then she coyly adds, "so pretty much always."

I glance in her direction, heart beating a bit faster now. "You don't have to worry about me."

"Someone has to," she says. Then, after a pause, she adds, "There's more to life than work, Simon."

Before I can respond, I see Will's turn signal is on. "Must need to stop for something."

"It's probably Lauren. She has the bladder the size of a dime," she says.

I chuckle at the imagery as I follow Will off the exit, pulling into the parking lot of a vintage gas station.

Maddie and Lauren both jump out as soon as the cars are parked, and I watch through the windshield as Maddie's bright, happy-go-lucky personality returns. Whatever had been bothering her seems to have faded.

This is her way. She's not fake, but she seems to think it's her job to bring the mood up. I'm confused why she feels the need to pretend.

I open the door and get out as Maddie turns to me, beaming. "This place is amazing! Reminds me of the movie *Cars*!"

The building is covered with vintage metal road signs and gas station logos, and the faded red gas pumps look like something straight out of the 1940s. There's a small general store, and behind it, a restaurant, in a matching building that looks like a big barn.

I haven't traveled much. It's one of those things on my bucket list that I never actually make time for. So, standing here, in front of this antiquated landmark, I take a moment. After all, who knows when I'll have this opportunity again?

Maddie launches into a story, making Lauren laugh, and I marvel at how she seems to slip on a happier, lighter, freer skin. Just like that.

I take a few steps closer, assuming my normal position just outside the conversation.

"How are you two getting along in this tiny car?" Lauren asks, smiling.

"He's letting me pick half the music, so I'm happy at least fifty percent of the time," Maddie says.

Lauren laughs. "Oh, Simon, I feel so sorry for you. How did you survive the One Direction songs?"

"I actually like most of her list," I say.

"What?" Maddie raises a brow. "You always complain about my music."

"You finally seem to have some musical taste," I say. "I must be rubbing off on you."

"Not a chance, old man," she says. "Frank Sinatra didn't make it on my list."

"Give it time."

"Never happening."

"We'll see."

We stand, half smiling and staring each other down, and I'm enjoying the moment.

"So. . ." Lauren breaks the link, and I look over, suddenly realizing that I'd forgotten she was still standing there.

"Lunch?" Lauren asks.

Maddie sticks out her stomach and rubs it with both hands, with no concern for social graces. "I'm still full from breakfast," she says, deepening her voice.

Lauren grins wide. "I swear you were dropped on your head as a child."

Maddie continues unabated, adding a Southern drawl. "Ah did have ah milkshake, an' now I'm-a *stuffed*."

Lauren looks at me with pitiful eyes. "Just know I'm praying for your sanity."

"It's okay," I answer, "she doesn't know I installed an ejector seat on the passenger side."

Maddie saunters over, as if wearing imaginary horse-spurred boots *ka-chinging* at every step, and reaches down to her sides, ready for a quick draw.

"Them's fightin' words, partner."

"You're so weird," I say with a laugh.

She then holds two fingers at her eyes, flips them around in a point at me, and then throws her arm around Lauren's shoulder and the two of them walk off, leaving Will and me behind.

He takes a few steps to stand beside me, and the two of us watch them leave.

"You ever going to tell her?" Will asks, without looking at me.

I glance at him and frown. "Tell who what?"

In lieu of responding, Will simply drags his gaze toward Lauren and Maddie. "Dude," he pats my shoulder, "you are so gone."

In the months since Lauren and Will had been dating, I've gotten to know him pretty well. So much so, I'd call him a friend, which is odd because he's not the kind of guy I normally hang out with. If we'd gone to high school together, his crowd probably would've made fun of me.

But Will is outgoing and easy to talk to. In spite of that, I've never told him how I feel about Maddie. I've never told *anyone* how I feel about Maddie. Bea only knows because she bullied it out of me years ago.

"We're just friends," I say.

Will starts off in the direction of the diner. "Yeah. Uh-huh." He looks at me. "Why is that?"

Because she *just wants to be friends.*

"I mean. . .Maddie and I are different," I say. "Complete opposites."

"If only there was some saying. . .about opposites attracting. . .," he says, feigning forgetfulness.

I stick my hands in my pockets. "Funny."

"Lauren thinks you guys are perfect for each other." Will pulls open the door to the restaurant, a kitschy place called *Big Mom's Wigwams*.

It's only at that moment I notice the logo.

"Wait. Is that a. . ."

"Large old woman's rear-end sticking out of a teepee?" He pauses. "Yep."

I go to step through the door, and then it registers what Will said.

"Wait. Lauren thinks what?"

Will nods, placing a hand on my shoulder and ushering me through the doorway. "She has a whole theory on why you two haven't gotten together yet."

"Oh, there's no theory," I say. "Maddie made it pretty clear that she will only ever think of me as a friend."

"Well," he says, "maybe we can change that."

He says this like getting out of a ten-year friend zone is easy.

"We're better off as friends," I say, even though I know it's not at all how I feel. "We have nothing in common. We'd drive each other crazy."

Will claps his hand on my shoulder a few times. "Keep telling yourself that, buddy."

I do tell myself that, Will.

Every single day.

Chapter Seventeen

Text exchange between Maddie and Lauren

Ten years ago

LAUREN

Hey, you up?

It's after midnight.

Did this date go better than even I could've expected?

MADDIE

I'm still out, but the date ended at 10 p.m.

We agreed to be friends.

LAUREN

Still out? Where?

And friends? You don't have guy friends.

MADDIE

You didn't seriously think I'd date him, did you?

We couldn't be more different.

I bet he's a morning person.

LAUREN

He's the nicest guy.

<prince emoji> <heart eyes emoji> <man & woman emoji>

MADDIE

Nice guys make great friends.

LAUREN

You're never going to see him again, are you?

MADDIE

<shrugging emoji>

I gotta go! My song is up. Come karaoke with me!

LAUREN

I'm going to bed.

MADDIE

<grandma emoji> You should date Simon.

You two have a lot in common.

Chapter Eighteen

Simon

Will's words hang in the air with me.

He strolls off in the direction of the booth where Maddie and Lauren are sitting, and I follow, albeit a bit slower and lost in thought. I stop after just a few steps.

I *am* trying to fool myself, but I'm failing. I don't believe for a second that Maddie and I are too different. I happen to think our differences might be good for each other.

Will slides into the booth next to Lauren with an ease that makes me a bit jealous. Maddie and I are comfortable together, but it's a different kind of comfortable.

I'm not free to touch her the way Will is with Lauren. Casual, kind, carefree touches that communicate love and familiarity at the same time.

I'm not ready to give up. Not quite yet. And I know I can't move to Seattle without telling her exactly how I feel. That might be selfish, telling her that and then leaving, but I feel like if I don't do it now, it will never happen.

First, I have to change the way she sees me.

But how?

Maddie glances up with a quizzical look, and I realize I'm still standing, just inside the door, staring. She motions for me to come over, making a mocking dazed face at me as I start to move.

As I reach the table, Lauren is telling Maddie about their first visit to this restaurant, and I'm thankful for the distraction.

"Will thought I'd be embarrassed by the logo for this place," Lauren says, "but on our way home from that trip, I bought a Big Mom's T-shirt."

"Which you wear proudly," Maddie says. "It's the greatest logo in the history of logos."

Lauren smiles over at Will, and he grins back, and then, just as they have many times, they get lost in their own world for a few seconds.

Are they aware they're losing time when they enter these trance-like states? I doubt it.

But even I can recognize love when I see it.

Beside me, Maddie shifts. She presses her shoulder against mine, leans closer and says, "Should we make googly eyes at each other so we feel like we fit in at this table?" Her playful smirk teases.

And because I'm sometimes not sure how to respond to her teasing, even after all these years, I say, "I don't make *googly* eyes," and open my menu.

"Shame," she says. "I do an *excellent* googly eye."

I try to concentrate on the list of food options and not the fact that her thigh is pressed into mine.

My plan to change the way she sees me has my stomach in knots, and it's hard to concentrate on anything else.

I glance over at Maddie, who is scrolling her phone, her unopened menu on the table in front of her.

"Are you really not eating?" I ask.

"I'm really not hungry. Besides, I can live off of my fat storage for way more than a week." She laughs as she says this, but doesn't look up from her phone.

I test the waters a bit, hoping I don't drown in the shallow end. "Would be a shame to lose those curves though," I say, without looking at her, heart pounding.

I feel—not see—everyone at the table stop. It seems the whole restaurant goes silent.

Oh crap. I went too far, I said the wrong thing, I...

"Excuse me, my what?" There's amusement in her tone. "Are you commenting on my curves?"

I didn't know I'd get this far in the conversation. I have no idea what to say next.

I glance at her. "Um. . .yes. I. . .they're. . .you have. . .excellent curves." I look down at the menu, not reading anything.

"You've never commented on my curves before," she says, now fully facing me.

"Not commenting on them is not the same as not noticing them," I say, clarifying.

Her eyes go wide. "You notice?"

The waters I've tested are now starting to crest up over my head. "Not that I. . .I mean. . .I don't stare or anything, but yeah, I've. . ." I clear my throat, "um. . .noticed." I crane my neck away from her. "I wonder where our waitress is? Is she on a break, or. . .?"

"Well, well, well." She strikes a pose. "Mr. Collier likes my curves. Who knew?"

Lauren grins, and Will looks like he's biting back an *I told you so.*

"What else do you like about me, Simon?" She announces the question to the table and nudges me with her elbow.

I flip a page in my menu and force a smile, wondering where on my list I should start.

I don't usually flirt with Maddie, and honestly, I'm not sure why I crossed that line now, but the way I feel makes me wonder if I should make it a part of my plan.

The plan I have yet to formulate.

I realize I've been in my head for the last few moments, and Maddie says, "Okay, fine. Keep your secrets." She looks at Lauren as if this is the funniest thing in the world.

I look over, and without thinking, I nudge her with my elbow.

She looks over and smacks me on the arm.

"Hey, I really hope you can order in less than five minutes this time," Maddie says, bringing me back to the present.

"And I'm hoping you will eat something other than junk." I return my attention to the menu. It's in focus now.

"It's cute you think you can change this about her," Lauren says. "You know she eats like a twelve-year-old boy."

"I do love a good Pop-Tart." Maddie does a pronounced chef's kiss.

I smile, but I am genuinely concerned for her health.

She must sense my disapproval, because she says, "You need to loosen up, Collier."

I glance at Will. "She's always trying to get me to 'loosen up.' I don't even know what that means."

"You know, get loose. Chill out. Take a breather." Maddie's upper body turns into spaghetti and she shakes everything out. "Less stress. Stop worrying. You're wound so tight, and stress is bad for your heart."

"Being focused and driven is not the same thing as being tightly wound," I say, feeling defensive at this unwanted reminder of how fundamentally different Maddie and I are. Because, while I believe our differences can be good, I'm not sure Maddie agrees.

"That's true," Lauren says, clearly my only ally at this table. "Being driven is a very different thing."

"But it's not the only thing." Maddie takes a sip of water. "You could stand to have some fun."

"My work *is* fun," I say. "I like it. There's nothing like the satisfaction of doing a good job."

"He's got a point," Lauren says.

"Why am I not surprised you agree?" Maddie laughs. "You were a total workaholic until you met Will." Then, she elbows me lightly. "Maybe you just need to fall in love, Simon."

I drag my eyes back to the menu, aware that both Will and Lauren are now looking at me.

Maddie, thankfully, has gone back to her phone.

If I'm not careful, those two are going to out me before I've enacted my plan.

That's the plan that, of course, I just haven't put it in motion yet.

Chapter Nineteen

Maddie

I didn't order anything—but it smelled *so* good.

Lauren gave me half her plate and I tried not to devour it. I can't let on how embarrassed I feel, or that I can't afford this trip anymore.

After practically licking Lauren's plate clean, Simon quipped, "Guess you were hungry after all, huh."

I'm praying he doesn't figure it out. Or ask.

And what was with the curves comment?

Was Simon flirting with me? What the heck?

I try to play it off over the next short leg of the trip with small talk and banter about my 90s music choices.

I hop out of the car as soon as Simon pulls it to a stop in the parking lot of the campground in Flagstaff.

Maybe I'm anxious to get away from him after my performance at lunch and his analytical brain trying to work out the truth. As if I'm going to be able to skip every meal between here and Illinois.

Never mind that he obviously has his own stress to keep

him occupied. Mine shows up in the form of a negative bank balance, but his shows up dressed as work.

Or when faced with camping. Which is what we're doing.

He can't hide that line of worry in his forehead—but it's not like he needs to worry about failure with his new business. The guy is practically a genius.

I stand just outside Simon's car and draw in a deep breath. I try to place myself here, at this campsite, in the moment. I'm usually pretty good at this, drinking things in, mentally capturing events and smells and feels so I can live in them later—but I'm really struggling to not worry about my finances.

I inhale and exhale, looking out across the distance where the mountains meet a bright blue, cloudless sky, and for a long moment, I try to put my troubles aside and bask in the peacefulness.

It works for about three seconds.

I don't know how any of this is going to work out. There's a genuine fear bubbling inside of me. My eyes fall to Will and Lauren, and then to Simon's car.

I'm here, with the people I love most in the world, and in *this* moment, everything's okay.

And that's something.

I squint at Simon's car, trying to see inside against the glare. He hasn't gotten out yet, and a niggle of guilt tugs at me.

He's going to hate camping. I just know it.

And he's only here because of me.

I make my way over to the car as he opens the door. "You're not okay with this, are you?"

"I'm great," he says. "This will be fun." He says it like he's fallen off a ladder, breaking his leg, but still insistent that he's still got *"one good leg that works fine, see?"*

I cross my arms over my chest and give him a very pointed

once-over. "Uh-huh. I think you'd rather have your wisdom teeth pulled by tying them to a horse."

"That's funny."

"I'm funny."

"I promise I'm laughing on the inside." He pauses. "What makes you think I won't like this?" He closes the car door and opens a protein bar.

I briefly wonder if he'd notice if I dipped into his stash of snacks. "The look on your face, mostly, but also the fact that I know you." I narrow my eyes. "Or at least, I thought I did."

He grins. "That's driving you nuts, isn't it? The idea that you don't have me all figured out?"

"No," I say, coolly, even though it absolutely is. He'd said it like he had a secret in mind. Like there were things he'd purposely kept from me. The dating app was a bit of a shocker, but is there more than that? Does he have a secret baby somewhere or is he the heir to a fortune or something?

I glance up and find him smiling. The line of stress is gone.

I dig my heels in, returning the volley and ready for his backhand. "I've seen no evidence that there is one single thing I don't know about you."

He pulls a backpack from the back seat of his car, then closes the door. He faces me, amusement in his expression. "You're probably right, Mads."

"Aren't I?"

He pauses, as if he's making a decision. Then, he puts a hand on my shoulder and gives it a gentle squeeze. "If you say so," then walks away.

He just hit an ace right past me.

"Are you messing with me? When did you get so good at messing with me?" I trail after him like the small kid wanting to get picked for the team.

He *is* messing with me, and I don't like it. In our relationship, I'm the one who does the teasing. Not him. Plus, I have the distinct impression he's doing it on purpose.

He stops and turns, standing in front of me, with an out-of-character casual look on his face.

I raise a brow, working hard to grab the reins on this conversation. "I just don't think there's anything you could say or do that would surprise me."

His gaze falls to my lips, and for a quick beat, my heart stops.

"That right?"

What is happening?

I turn away, flushed.

First, his flirty comment about my curves and now a lingering look at my lips. . .I don't even recognize this guy. And more importantly, I don't hate it.

Simon walks over to where Will and Lauren are standing, and I dumbly follow.

Was Lauren right about him?

I pull out my phone, speechless for maybe the second time in my life, and start searching for a fun place to eat. I scroll through the different restaurant options when. . .*Bingo.*

"I think we should go here," I say, holding up the screen to the other three.

Will squints. "Are those. . .stuffed animals?"

"Mounted, actually," I say, holding the phone closer. "Look at the name of the place!"

They all lean forward, and in unison, read out, "*The Road-kill Café.*"

I'm way too excited about this. "It's a taxidermy shop that was turned into a country and western bar, and they have line dancing." I look up with my brightest smile. I feel like I've dropped the ball on being the fun one on this trip today, and I need to restore order. "I *love* line dancing!"

"A. . .taxidermy shop?" Simon sounds disgusted.

"Yeah, isn't it wild? It'll be totally unique."

"And horrifying."

Lauren laughs. "We can always count on you to make things interesting, Mads."

"Right?" I say. "We *need* to go to this place! If for nothing else but the pictures we're gonna take!" I meet Simon's eyes and try to will him to agree with me.

"I'm game," Lauren says. "Will?"

"Whatever you want," he says. "As long as you promise not to run off with a cowboy."

"I make no promises," Lauren teases.

"It's done then!" I exclaim, trying to get a read on Simon. The flirty side is totally gone, and the crease in his forehead is back.

I'll show you, my friend. You'll finally *learn how to have a good time.*

Will shows us all how to set up the tents, and once our site is ready, we hop in Will's Jeep and drive toward the restaurant, a large log cabin seemingly in the middle of nowhere.

"The Roadkill Café." Simon stares out the window in the back seat of Will's Jeep. "And we're really eating here."

"What's wrong?" I ask. "I thought you liked stuffing."

He rolls his eyes.

"I'm sure it's fine," Lauren says, though even she looks a little unsteady.

I don't have to worry about the cleanliness of the place since I'm not planning to eat anything.

"It'll be an adventure." Will parks the car and turns off the engine.

"Yes!" I say, loudly. "Finally, an adventure! Besides, we're just here for the line dancing."

121

"Because that's so much better," Simon says under his breath, looking slightly seasick.

"Don't look so panicked. They show you the moves."

"Oh, I'm not panicked," he says. "I have no intention of dancing."

I clap a hand on his knee. "Loosen up, Collier." But he does the opposite of loosen up. His muscles seem to tense. I pull my hand away.

We get out of the car and walk into the restaurant, where we're struck by an off-key version of "Stand By Your Man," gifted to us by a heavy-set woman wearing a cowboy hat, red boots, and a denim dress.

"This doesn't look like line dancing," Lauren says.

I pull my phone out, tapping around on the bar's website. "Oh, wait. It's not line dancing night. It's karaoke night!" I raise my arms in the air and let out a little cheer. "I love karaoke!"

"Did you do this on purpose?" Lauren asks dryly.

I hold up my hand, as if swearing on an imaginary Bible. "I promise I didn't."

She raises an eyebrow, as if to say she doesn't believe me. "You're always trying to force karaoke on me."

"Yeah, because you're the best singer I know."

"Don't know a lot of singers, huh?" Lauren says.

"We'll do a duet," I tell her. "It'll be obnoxious."

We make our way over to a table in the corner as the woman on stage finishes her song with a flourish that I'm pretty sure the original writers didn't intend to ever be performed. A man at a table in the front stands and cheers, clapping furiously, but nobody else seems to notice.

"Let's go put our names on the list," I say.

Lauren groans. "You're going to make me do this, aren't you?"

I grab her hands and give her a tug. "You know I am!" Then I look at Simon. "We can't have two no-shows at our table!"

He winces, and I flash him my best smile.

Minutes later, Lauren and I take the stage, flanked by a stuffed owl holding a snake and a coyote on its hind legs. As the opening notes of Abba's "Dancing Queen" begin to play, I lift the microphone to my mouth and glance over at the table where Will and Simon sit, talking.

I've never had stage fright in my life. I love to be the center of attention.

But standing here, on a stage in a room full of strangers, I realize there's only one person's attention I want.

And I have no idea how to process that.

Chapter Twenty

Simon

The bar is loud and full of people—two things I don't love.

Despite those, however, I'm determined not to be the stick-in-the-mud Maddie expects me to be. It's not lost on me that while she lives to go out and have fun, I would much prefer to be in bed right now with a good book.

I'd also prefer not to sleep on the ground in a tent, but I'm not about to say that out loud.

A waitress sets our drinks down, and I pick up my Diet Coke and take a drink, admiring a row of stuffed badgers, frozen in what looks like "hear no evil, see no evil, speak no evil" poses.

"Do you want Lauren and I to make ourselves scarce?" Will's question interrupts me trying to picture the madman (or genius?) who set these animals up this way.

"What? Why? Are you not having a good time?"

He chuckles and *clinks* his glass on mine. "So you can make your move."

I sigh a deep breath. "Will. It's not like that. I told you."

He leans back in his chair, watching Lauren and Maddie dancing and jiving and having the time of their lives up on the stage. "Yeah, I know what you told me," he nods in their direction, "but I also know you're full of crap."

I shake my head. "I don't have moves." I glance up at the stage where Maddie is singing her heart out, quite badly. My mind flashes to the first time I saw her—then immediately to our blind date where she held out her hand, striking the deal that sealed my fate as her forever friend.

"Besides. It's a hopeless cause."

"Things change." Will takes a swig of his beer.

"I know the kind of guys Maddie dates. I know because I've been there when they break up with her." I look away, right into the eyes of a mounted bison head wearing a hat that says *Kiss Me, I'm Irish.*

"My favorite one was that scuba instructor who was on that pro-seaweed diet," Will says. "Or that big, hairy dude with the motorcycle."

"I think that guy called himself 'Croc.'"

Will laughs.

I add, "What about the rock climber who called everyone— even Maddie—'dude'?"

Then, Will says, "Dude, you've gotta see the gash I got climbing this weekend. It's still wide open—dude, you can see the bone." His impersonation is spot-on.

I chuckle, shaking my head. "She does seem to like the thrill seekers, doesn't she?" I think of how she knocked on my door in the middle of the afternoon, soaked from the rain, crying because the rock climber broke up with her right before their three-month anniversary.

Who celebrates a three-month anniversary?

"In all my years of knowing her, I've never known her to date. . ." I almost blurt out *someone like me* but catch myself, ". .

125

.a, you know, a professional. Someone who actually likes to keep his car clean."

There's a pause, long enough to hear the off-putting harmony coming from the mics. As I watch Maddie for a long moment, having a blast, laughing, pointing to the crowd, she catches my eye.

She seems shocked and exhilarated when our eyes lock. She stumbles on the words, and seems to run out of breath. Then, she gathers herself and puts a hand on her hip, arches her back and indicates up and down her body while mouthing LOOK AT MY CURVES, BABY and comically shimmying.

Without thinking, I point two fingers at my eyes, then whip my hand around and point at her.

"Oh yeah," Will says, amused. "You two are SO wrong for one another."

I return my attention to him and clear my throat. "Believe me, I know the odds are stacked against me when it comes to Maddie. I'm not. . ." I wave my hand aimlessly over the table. ". . .her typical. . .guy."

"Simon, she deserves more than her 'typical guy.'"

I put my head down and stare at the table. I notice that the menu for this place is actually lacquered in the top, and some of the items include "Road-Tisserie Chicken," "Steak Tire Tire," and "Skid Mark Stew."

Then, after a beat, I tentatively add, "I actually made this trip a deadline."

He frowns. "What kind of deadline?"

A deep breath. I'm unsure why this is so hard to admit out loud. I look up. "I'm thinking about moving."

His eyebrows raise. "Moving? When? And to where?"

"Seattle." I sigh. "New company, new start." Another breath, and I decide to admit the thing that he already knows.

"I. . .like Maddie. A lot. But she doesn't see me as more than just a friend. She just doesn't."

He sits and listens. Now that I opened the tap, it's time to twist it open a bit more.

"I think I've known that since I first saw her in college. She's so amazing, and fun, and funny, and beautiful, and basically all the things that I'm not."

"Simon. . ."

"No, let me finish. I see all the guys she dates, and I see what she's attracted to and I'm not it. I'm not the guy." I sigh again, resigned. "It's pretty pathetic that I'd have to move to a different state to get her out of my mind, but that's where I'm at."

"Oh, buddy," Will says.

"It's stupid, and it doesn't make sense, but I think as long as she's in my life, I'm never going to be able to move on. Not here."

He nods.

"This all probably sounds pretty pathetic to you," I say. "I mean, it's my own fault she sees me as the guy who picks up the pieces when *other guys* make her feel bad about herself."

"So, you need to change the way she sees you." Will says it so simply, like it was easy.

"I know," I say, having just had that revelation myself. "But how?"

"You need a plan," Will says.

I shake my head and groan. "I have a plan. It's just not formulated yet."

He pulls a napkin out of the holder at the center of the table, then flags down our waitress. "Hi! Can I borrow your pen?"

She hands it over, and Will scribbles something on the napkin.

"What are you doing?"

"Making a plan," he says. "Way more likely to happen if we write it down."

All at once, I feel like I have a partner in this. A wingman. And when it comes to Maddie, that's something I've never had before.

"Step one," Will says. "Change your attitude about yourself."

I raise a brow, questioning.

"You act like being a nice guy is a bad thing," Will says. "Maddie would be lucky to have someone like you."

"I don't know about that."

"Trust me."

I think on that for a moment. "I've always thought if she gave me a chance, a date, a dinner, something—that then maybe I could show her she's been settling for less than she deserves for far too long."

"Right," he says. "Not sure why girls have this attraction to jerks."

"Exactly! Finally, someone else who gets it!"

"It's not just me," he says. "Lauren is firmly Team Simon."

I glance back up at the stage. They've moved on to their encore, "I Will Survive," and Lauren seems to have warmed up to the mic. "She is?"

"Yep," Will says. "She rants about it. Every time Maddie gets dumped, in fact. According to my future wife, 'Simon is smart, he's successful—*and* he's figured out how to make his facial hair work for him.'" Will lifts his beer bottle as if to "cheer" Simon. "Not many men our age can say that." He takes a drink.

"She said that?"

Will nods, swallowing. "She's very passionate on the subject."

"She doesn't think Maddie and I are a wrong fit? We are complete opposites."

"Lauren and I are complete opposites." Will shrugs. "I think that's part of why we work so well." He goes back to writing.

"What next?"

"Step two. Flirt with her." Then, he looks up, pointing the pen at me. "Which, actually, I think you've already started doing."

Heat rushes to the back of my neck, and I feel uncomfortable.

If Will's noticed, then maybe Maddie has too?

"It's not bad, actually. I'm no expert on the subject, but what I've seen between you two is pretty fun to watch."

I feel like out-of-touch Steve Carell in "Crazy, Stupid Love," taking dating advice from the much savvier Ryan Gosling. Am I really this pathetic? Is he going to toss out my jeans or force me to get a haircut?

I grimace, not believing him.

"Okay, step three." Will smiles as he writes, like he's just gotten the greatest idea ever. "Surprise her." Then, after a pause, he lifts his head in a Eureka moment. "You should sing."

I half-laugh, knee-jerking a "forget it" reaction. "I don't sing in public. Ever."

"But you *do* sing," Will says.

"Yeah, when I'm alone." Maddie thinks my piano is part of the decor, but the truth is, it keeps me sane.

Will only knows about this because he'd come by my apartment unannounced a few months ago to go over some changes I'd made to his team's website. He wanted to set up a recruitment page, so he asked me to help, and I'd done it as a favor. Then, after I started LUNA, the college reached out to me to revamp their entire website, and they became my first client as a business owner.

I have Will to thank for that.

Still. . .singing? In public? At a bar?

I'm going to need something stronger than a Diet Coke to make that happen.

"You're good, man. I heard you through the door." Will leans back in his seat and admires Lauren from afar. "I mean, it's not scuba diving, but no one—especially Maddie—would expect it." Will takes another drink.

"I'm not sure karaoke is the answer," I say, mostly because I don't want it to be the answer.

"You're trying to change how she sees you, show her she doesn't have you all figured out. Show her you can surprise her." Then, after a beat, "Or you could just move on to step four."

I frown. "What's step four?"

"Tell her how you feel."

I groan. "Let's not get ahead of ourselves."

"That's why it's step four." He leans an elbow on the table. "Don't overthink it. But don't try to go slow, either. It's like jumping into the ocean—it's gonna be cold, but you just have to squeeze your cheeks and plunge in."

"I know we haven't known each other long, but do I seem like the kind of guy to 'jump in'?" I ask.

"No," Will says. "In fact, I think you're the least spontaneous person I know."

I turn away, knowing it's true. The stuffed raccoon holding a miniature shotgun, propped up in a standing position at the end of the bar, offers no solace.

"I've heard Maddie say this a few times, even on this trip—and I mean it in the best way possible—you've got to 'loosen up, Collier.'" Will smiles. "Besides, what've you got to lose?"

He slides the napkin across the table and I stare at the four simple steps he's written out in dark black ink.

The song ends and Maddie lifts both her hands above her head in a loud, ear-piercing cheer, and all I can think is, *everything*.

I have everything to lose.

Chapter Twenty-One

Maddie

I s it possible to be a third wheel if there are four people in your party?

After two duets, Lauren and I return to the table, out of breath and a bit sweaty. We slide into our seats, and Will welcomes his fiancé with a kiss.

Yep. Yep, it sure is possible.

Surely all this wedding romance is the reason my sensors are misfiring where Simon is concerned.

That has to be it.

After all, in ten years, I'd never had this problem before. My impression of Simon is rock solid. Nothing has changed.

So why did I feel the twinge of nervousness as I slid into the seat next to him?

I take a long drink of water, my shoulder brushing against Simon's as I do. See? That's not the kind of thing I'm supposed to notice. I've brushed against Simon's shoulder lots of times. It's never caught my breath. But now, here I am, forcing myself to inhale on a count of three to try and calm myself down.

Why am I suddenly so keenly aware of Simon?

I don't like these runaway thoughts, so I do what I always do and fill the silence. "I think we should do another one."

"After we eat," Lauren says. "I'm starving."

The waitress, a woman named Trish, appears with a tray of food.

"We ordered," Will says.

Trish hands out plates, setting a burger and fries down in front of me.

"Oh, I wasn't going to get anything."

Simon frowns over at me. "But you didn't eat lunch. Unless you count what you stole from everyone else. I figured you'd want your own meal this time."

My pulse races. I'd put him off, but he hadn't forgotten. Simon never forgot. "You know what, I don't think I brought my wallet. I left it in my backpack, back at the campground."

"I've got it," he says, as if it's no big deal. But given my current circumstances, it's a very big deal.

"I'll pay you back," I say quietly, overwhelmed with gratitude for the meal. As if on cue, my stomach growls.

He looks over at me, and I feel caught. I'm not good at hiding the truth from Simon. "No," he says. "Please. Let this be my treat."

I glance across the table and find Lauren watching me. Her eyes dart from me to Simon, then back to me, and then she widens them as if to communicate, *such a sweet guy!*

Knowing my lovesick best friend, she is, without a doubt, reading into this kind gesture. But I don't need to be convinced that Simon is sweet. I already know he is. It's one of the things I admire most about him. While I have to work not to be too self-ish, Simon would give you the coat off his back in an ice storm if you needed it—whether he knew you or not.

Still, this isn't new.

What *is* new, however, is realizing that I crave his attention.

The whole time I was up on that stage, I wanted him to look at me. I wanted him to smile. And when he did, and when I saw, I darn near forgot my name.

This is crazy. All of this. I need to snap out of it.

"Thank you for the dinner," I say, my voice low.

"It wasn't an altruistic move." He looks over at me and smiles. "I'm hungry, and I don't want to share."

I look at him and notice a smile playing at the edges of his mouth.

And just like that, the shame drifts away.

Simon has no idea the favor he'd done me. And somehow, he's done it without making me feel like a charity case.

I don't deserve his kindness.

Between the two of us, I am definitely getting more out of our friendship.

"Was it hard for you to relinquish your control of that microphone?" Simon asks, picking up a fry from his "Fender Tenders" chicken platter.

"Are you implying that I was hogging the spotlight?" I feign innocence as I say this, desperately wanting everything to feel normal between him and me. "It was simply my time to shine."

"Even though you were off-key?" Simon takes a drink and smiles.

I gasp in mock horror. "I was not."

"Yes," Lauren says. "You were."

"Lauren mostly covered it," Simon says.

At that moment, a thin man with a tiny mustache belts out the high note in "Take On Me."

"At least I'm not the worst one performing tonight," I say. "Yikes. Besides, it's easy for you to mock from your safe spot at the table."

"Yeah, Simon," Lauren says. "I don't see you up there making a fool of yourself."

I laugh. "Simon would never. . ."

Beside me, Simon has gone stiff. He glances up at Will, whose eyebrow raises so subtly I almost miss it.

At that, Simon clears his throat and stands. "I'll, uh. . .be right back." He walks off in the direction of the bathroom.

That was weird.

I dunk a couple of fries into my ketchup. "Where's he going?"

Lauren turns to Will, and he half shrugs. She sets her fork down and turns to him with a look.

"What? I don't know what he's doing."

Her eyes narrow. "You guys are plotting something." Lauren picks up her Coke and tips it slightly at him. "I know it."

Will feigns innocence. "I have no idea what you're talking about."

"And I'll bet," she continues, "that it has something to do with Maddie."

Will holds up one hand. "I cannot confirm or deny that statement."

Lauren turns to me, eyes wide, mouth in an *ohhh. . .!* shape.

I look at Will. "Will you please get control of your fiancée? She's lost her ever-lovin' mind."

Will holds up his hands. "I'm staying out of this."

"Staying out of it?" Lauren smacks him across the arm. "You told me in the car they seem good together."

I stop chewing. "Wait. You said what?"

They're not paying attention to me.

"Yeah, but I know when it's time to butt out." Will gives me a nod in solidarity, but Lauren won't be deterred.

"I don't believe in butting out," Lauren says. "Not when my best friend can't see what's right in front of her face."

"I'm *right here*. I can *literally* hear you," I say, but it doesn't seem to matter.

Lauren turns to me. "Do you want me to make you a pro/con list so you can see all the ways you and Simon are perfect together?"

I groan. "Do not make a pro/con list about me and Simon."

"Pro/con lists are Lauren's love language," Will states, pointing a fork at me.

"Some people are just. . .meant to be friends," I say.

"I don't think men and women can be friends," Will says.

"Why?" I ask.

"Because Billy Crystal said so," Lauren says, in an irritated tone. "I made him watch *When Harry Met Sally* with me, and he quotes it now." She rolls her eyes. "So annoying."

I eat another fry. "So, you agree with Billy that the sex part gets in the way."

Will nods and shrugs at the same time.

"But look at me and Simon," I say. "We've been friends for over ten years, and it isn't a problem for us."

"It isn't a problem for *you*." Will raises his eyebrows, like he'd just made a point.

My whole body says uhh. . .*what*.

I calmly wipe my hands on my napkin. "Are you saying," I straighten the silverware on either side of my plate, "that Simon wants to sleep with me?"

"No," Will says.

"Good," I say.

"He'll want to put a ring on it first," he quips.

"Will!" Lauren snaps, elbowing him in the ribs. She turns to me, as if apologizing for her unruly child who just threw a rock through my window. "He wants to date you. Then. . .the *other* things. *For as long as you both shall live.*"

"What? Where is this coming from?" I ask. "It's *Simon*."

A voice in my mind replies, *Yeah. It is. Start paying attention.*

I shake off the thought. "First you corner me in the bathroom, and now you're both ganging up on me? It's crazy. Is this because you're getting married? You think everyone else needs to dive right in?"

Lauren leans forward. "Maddie."

I level her gaze. "Lauren."

"He's handsome."

"He's okay," I admit.

"He's charming."

"He vacuums out his glove box."

"It's endearing."

"Lo, he stacks his coffee table books alphabetically."

"He's smart. Accomplished. *Adorable.*"

"He orders special coffee online at a specific time of day because he knows how long the order takes to go in, which ensures he gets the freshest delivery. He has 'house shoes' so he doesn't track any dirt into his apartment. He has two alarms on his phone, one for waking up and one for bedtime. He switched deodorant because I commented once that it smelled like this guy I knew from high school. He sleeps with one earplug because he's a side sleeper and it bugs him, and. . ." I look up and notice both of them staring at me.

"What?"

Will raises his eyebrows in a shrug. "You seem to know an awful lot about a guy who's 'just a friend.'"

I laugh and sit back. "Come *on,* guys. You know me. Do you really think I could ever spend my life with someone who's planned out his entire existence from now until the day he dies? There isn't a single ounce of surprise in that guy—and I like to go with the flow. I could never live my life without spontaneity."

At least that's what I've always told myself. Now, I'm not so sure I've been prioritizing the right things.

Lauren looks past me toward the stage, and her face lights into a bright smile. "You're right, Maddie. Simon doesn't seem like the kind of guy who could ever surprise you."

"*Thank* you," I say. "You're finally listening to reason."

"Like, he'd never, I don't know, perform in front of a bar full of strangers."

"Never," I say, matter-of-factly. "I've tried to get him to come sing karaoke with me. He always refuses."

When Lauren doesn't respond, I glance up to find that she and Will have both shifted their chairs slightly toward the stage. I follow their gaze and see a man wheeling a piano out while Simon picks up the microphone stand and sets it next to the instrument.

"What the heck—?" I drop my burger onto the plate.

The man pushing the piano nods at Simon, then walks off the stage. Simon sits down on the piano bench, adjusts the microphone, then looks out at the audience.

"What is he doing?" I whisper a hiss at Lauren. "He doesn't even play the piano."

"Maybe he does," Lauren says.

I shake my head. *I would know.*

Someone in the crowd yells, "Do 'Piano Man'!"

Simon smiles, and *holy fireworks,* even from where I sit, something about it sizzles.

He sits with his profile to the audience, and I pause to admire it for a moment. It's a strong profile. And as he sits for a moment, a quiet confidence comes over him.

Oh no. It's kind of sexy.

Simon runs his hands across the keys, a quick warm-up.

"What the. . .? Simon plays the piano?" I look at Lauren. "How did we not know this?"

Simon had always said the piano in his apartment was for show. I'd never questioned it. Why would he lie? A thought hits me.

I wonder if this is to him what my pottery is to me.

An escape.

The thing that keeps him sane.

"I knew," Will says.

"What?" Lauren and I say in unison.

Will tosses a fry in his mouth. "I'm good at keeping secrets."

I look back at the stage. *But I'm good with Simon.*

"Good evening, everyone," Simon says into the microphone. "It's been a long time since I've done this, so I'm just going to pretend none of you are here."

The crowd laughs, and I feel my shoulders loosen. Simon Collier is on the stage. Behind a piano. Behind a microphone.

And darn it, he looks good.

"He doesn't even sing in the car," I say to no one in particular, without taking my eyes off of him.

Simon adjusts his seat and the noisy, rambunctious bar goes quiet.

I hold my breath. And Simon starts playing. Not some boring ballad. Not a slow, churning, repetitious pop song.

This tune is jazzy. Funky. Something that makes your head bob and your feet move. I don't know music or playing the piano that well, but I know talent when I see it. Immediately the bar starts snapping and clapping along, with whistles and whoops scattered throughout.

He shifts, positioning the microphone in front of him like a man who'd done this a thousand times. But as far as I know, Simon has never done this. Not in front of me anyway.

After the intro, he begins to sing the first phrase of a song I don't know, and it shatters every idea I have of my friend.

If you'd asked me yesterday if Simon could sing or play the

piano, I would've scoffed and said, "No way." Not like this. *Especially* not like this. I would've guessed that if he sang, his voice would've sounded a little like it belonged in an opera. Or maybe a choir. Something stuffy and buttoned-up—something, well, like Simon.

His gravelly, soulful voice fills the bar. It's completely unique and familiar at the same time, like the brother/sister duo Lawrence, or that time when Robert Downey Jr. sang on Ally McBeal.

I'm stunned, along with everyone else in the room.

As I watch Simon, I see there's no hesitation. No wavering, no stage fright, no cracks or off-key notes. It's straightforward, as if he'd done what he said he was going to and forgot anyone else was there.

The Simon I know—the intelligent, stable, slightly awkward Simon—is gone.

In his place is a confident, soulful performer who somehow knows exactly how to connect with an entire room of strangers.

This from a man who struggles to have a conversation with a clerk at the grocery store.

I know that not all performers want to be in the limelight. Not everyone who's good on stage is extroverted or good with people. Still, I never would've dreamed I'd see the day when Simon—*my Simon*—would get up in front of everyone and sing like this.

Huh. "My" Simon.

I feel like I'm on a candid TikTok video with the caption "Singing in front of my best friend for the first time." I give a cursory glance around the room just to make sure nobody is filming me, but not a single eye is turned in my direction.

Everyone is watching Simon, totally captivated.

I pull out my phone and start filming.

"What is this song?" I ask, without looking at Will and Lauren. I can't pull my eyes away from the stage.

"I've never heard it before," Lauren says.

"It's really catchy," I say. "I kind of love it."

"Love the song or the man singing the song?" Lauren teases.

"I. . .I don't know. . ." I absently answer, forgetting I'm filming.

On the stage, he is now half-standing, hands working over the keys, the rhythm of the song taking over, and then he hits the chorus again. This time, the crowd has caught on to the lyrics, and has even started trying to sing along.

I bet he's good with his hands. The thought stops me.

Shut. That. Down.

The voice of reason screams at me, but I don't want to listen. I want to imagine what could happen if Simon and I *weren't* just friends.

My cheeks are flaming hot at this realization, and I take a drink of water to try and cool myself off.

"Kind of messes with your impression of him, doesn't it?" Will says smugly.

"Does it mess with *your* impression of him, Will?" I ask, trying desperately to play this off like no big deal. "You think he's sexy now, too?"

Will quirks a brow. "He's got mad skills."

Lauren whips around to face me. "Wait, did *you* just say you think Simon is sexy?"

I realize I'm still filming and I click it off before my answer is recorded. "That is *not* what I said." But even I know it would be foolish to try and pretend. I lean back in my chair and watch. Simon is good—not just good—he's incredible. The song is unique and clever and catchy.

I want it on my playlist so I can listen to it on repeat.

The chorus is on repeat in my head.

Now I don't wanna jump to conclusions, no
But your hands seem to have a hard time letting go
Can we go back to the time when we lost all track of time
The beginning, when we were more than just friends

Maybe he'd been more in love with Hannah than I thought.

"That was awesome." Will holds out his fist, and Simon awkwardly gives it a high-five.

"I had no idea you had that in you," Lauren says. "That was amazing."

Simon looks at me, expectant. "Are you. . .surprised?"

What was it I'd been saying before he took the stage? That it would be impossible for Simon to surprise me or something like that?

Before I can respond, Trish shimmies over and slides a napkin and a drink toward Simon. "Courtesy of the four women at the bar."

She nods to her left, where a group of women ogle Simon like they've been in the desert for a week and he's a Dasani. Ironic that there's a stuffed cougar right behind them.

He instantly flushes red, laughs to himself, then looks away. "Thanks, but you can tell them I'm just passing through." He slides the napkin back to Trish.

"All right, sugar," Trish says. "But I have a feeling you could drink all weekend for free after that performance." She saunters off.

"You're going to break their hearts," I say.

He shrugs. "Better to disappoint someone I don't know than someone I do."

I sit with that for a moment.

"All these years. . ." I shake my head in disbelief. "You *are* full of surprises."

Another shrug. "I told you not to assume you knew everything about me."

"I guess so," I say.

And as Will begins drilling Simon about his music, I find it hard to concentrate over the resounding question banging around in my mind.

What else don't I know?

Chapter Twenty-Two

Simon

Nine years, six months ago

The little coffee shop a few blocks from campus wasn't my first choice.

Or my second. Or third.

Even with a full academic scholarship, I have expenses, which means I need a job. And Mo's was the first (and only) place to reply to my application.

Jobs in the food service industry are common among my peers, but most of my peers didn't have an innate aversion to people like I do.

On the morning of my first day, I walk into the bustling coffee shop—and nearly turn around and walk out. It's busy, and loud, and everyone's in a hurry. College kids have classes to get to. Young professionals are late for work. Everyone wants everything *right now*, and my personality is hardly the eye of any storm.

I stand just inside the door, staring at the counter, wondering how I will ever get used to this atmosphere, knowing that I'm much better suited to a desk job. Alone. Maybe the university library would hire me and I could earn my money shelving books.

A man in a suit pulls open the door behind me, letting in a warm breeze. "You in line or what?"

"Me?" I glance at him, reading annoyance on his face. "Oh, no, sorry." I shift out of the way.

The guy side-steps me and gets in the line. The entire scene nearly sends me back out onto the sidewalk and into the ranks of unemployed college kids.

But then, a door behind the counter swings open, and Maddie walks out.

Maddie. The girl I had a single date with and have never talked to again, despite our promise to become friends.

It seems the universe has a sense of irony.

The door swings closed behind her, and she steps behind the counter with the confident swagger that drew me to her in the first place. She smiles at a customer as she ties a black apron around her waist.

The entire room brightens.

Her long, blond hair is tied back in a messy knot at the base of her neck, tucked under a black *Mo's* baseball cap.

In a flash, one sentence reverberates through my mind.

She is beautiful.

"Gloria! How's the ankle?" She grins at an older woman in a black power suit. "Let me guess, caramel latte?"

It's like this is her stage and these people are her captive audience.

"Nonfat," the woman calls back, with a smile in her voice. "And it's getting better, thanks. How you remember that is beyond me."

"Court today?"

Gloria nods. "So maybe give me a double shot of espresso."

"You got it." Maddie dances around to the music as she makes the drink. It's almost as if she thrives in this low-paying, thankless job.

"Every Little Thing She Does is Magic" by The Police comes on over the speakers, the perfect soundtrack for the scene in front of me.

Had everything just turned to slow motion or am I imagining it?

"Collier!"

The shout pulls me from my daydream, drawing my attention to the tall, bulky guy standing behind the counter next to Maddie. Logan is one of the guys I met at my interview, and I'm less than thrilled he's here today.

Maddie glances over to where I stand, gawking, her gaze silencing The Police like the scratch of a record.

She stops moving, a quizzical look on her face.

"Are you here to work or stare at Maddie like a stalker?" Logan laughs.

This was a huge mistake.

But I need the money. I'm not sure how to make this job bearable when I'm off to such a terrible start.

Maddie did say we should be friends. Hopefully she meant it.

Never mind that being "just friends" with her might actually be its own special kind of hell.

Logan waves me back, and I follow, harvesting dread like it grows in fields, sheathed by the plow of a tractor in late October.

"Employees come in the *back door*," Logan says, putting deliberate emphasis on the last two words.

"Got it," I say.

Maddie hands Gloria her drink. "Good luck in court."

Gloria winks at her. "Opposing counsel needs the luck today."

Maddie throws a fist in the air. "That's what I like to hear! Go get 'em Glo!"

She moves on to the next customer, chatting him up the same way she had Gloria. She calls him by name (Jerry) and flashes him that smile that could defrock a priest.

Unfortunately for me, Logan's smile isn't as charming. He's the manager, so he's assigned to training me—not Maddie. Also unfortunately, Logan isn't interested in teaching me anything.

I try to pay attention to the few instructions I'm given, but mostly, I'm struggling to concentrate with Maddie so close.

At one point, Logan sticks his hand right in my face and snaps his fingers. "You don't want to zone out here, buddy, you'll be totally lost."

"I'm listening, I promise." It's a lie. I'm not listening. I'm not even half-listening.

Logan inches back. "Okay, let's see how much you've learned. You can make the next drink."

"Me?"

Maddie's eyes flick from the espresso machine to me, and I want to hide.

"Oh, I don't think—"

But Logan cuts me off. "It's not rocket science." He scoffs. "Aren't you supposed to be a genius or something?"

I wish my GPA wasn't at the top of my resumé, but employers—even coffee shop owners—like serious students. Clearly Logan had seen it.

"Come on, *genius*." Logan glances up at the man standing on the opposite side of the counter, waiting for someone to make his drink. He doesn't look like he has time for a newbie barista to fumble around back here.

I knew this job was a mistake. I hate being put on the spot.

I walk over to the man. "Okay, what was your drink?"

He looks up from his phone, a single eyebrow quirked in annoyance. "An Americano with caramel cream."

I glance at Logan, who leans against the back counter, making it clear that he is a "sink or swim" kind of teacher.

At his side, Maddie straightens.

I freeze.

She nods toward the cup. I reach for it, turning it over and trying to remember the ten-minute lesson Logan had given me on the different machines.

I have no idea what goes into an Americano with caramel cream. Espresso? Coffee? Cream? But with so many gadgets staring at me, I'm not sure where to start.

I take a step toward one of the machines, but catch the slight shake of Maddie's head. I move to the next one and she gives a subtle nod. I stare at it.

I *am* a smart guy. How hard could this be?

I place the cup down on the machine, fumble with the buttons, and when it finally comes on, milk shoots out all over my shirt.

Behind me, Logan snickers. In front of me, the customer rolls his eyes.

And beside me, like a bright, shining angel from heaven, is Maddie. She pushes Logan out of the way. "You're such a jerk." She steps forward and takes the cup from me. "Here. Let me show you."

She glances up at the customer. "This'll be on the house, Mark."

At that, the man's face softens. If given the chance, this girl could diffuse two world superpowers with a mocha and a smile.

Maddie walks me through the steps of making the drink, and it makes perfect sense to me. Easy. Straightforward. When she finishes, she hands it to me to put the cap on. I give her a pleadingly thankful nod, then hand the drink to Mark. "I'm so sorry, sir."

Mark looks at Maddie, who gives him a wink and a nod, and he chuckles. Then, to me, he says, "No worries. I get that it's your first day. We all gotta start somewhere, right?"

He walks off, leaving me and my now-slowing pulse behind. I turn and see Maddie wiping down the machine—essentially cleaning up my mess.

"Thanks," I offer.

"You'll get the hang of it," she says.

I look over at Logan, who has now moved on to one of the other employees, pointing at a display and looking condescending.

I'm not sure she's right about getting the hang of it, but I don't say so. At the moment, I'm weighing my employment options, and I'm pretty sure she's the only thing keeping me on this job.

Maddie calls over to Logan, who has his arms folded, overlooking a young guy who is rearranging things on the counter. "That wasn't cool."

Logan leans back on the counter. "I was just joking around." Then, to me: "You know I was kidding, right? Little bit of hazing the new guy."

I start to answer, but Maddie steps between me and him. "What the heck, Logan? He isn't one of your fraternity pledges."

She turns away, and he reaches for her hand. She stiffens and glares up at him.

He looks appropriately apologetic, lips pursed in a mock pout, but it's clearly an act. And not a very believable one. "I'm sorry, Maddie."

She pulls her hand away and folds her arms, tossing a

glance in my direction. "It's not me you should be apologizing to."

Logan's shoulders drop. "Seriously?"

Maddie's only response is a raised brow.

Logan groans as he turns toward me. "Fine. Sorry. I was just playing, man, no hard feelings." He holds out a fist for some reason.

"It's fine," I say, reaching out and awkwardly high-fiving his fist. Maddie laughs, but I have no idea why. Logan looks put off, like I offended him somehow.

Logan shakes his head and turns to Maddie. "Happy?"

Still, she doesn't respond, and in her silence, he takes a step toward her, invading her personal space in a way that could probably get him sued. He reaches for the tie of her apron and unties it, then uses it to pull her closer, wrapping an arm around her waist. He digs his face into her neck until finally, she relents, pushing him away with a laugh.

"We're *working*," she says.

"I know, save it for later," he croons, making my skin crawl a little.

He turns to me. "You good?"

I give him a thumbs up.

He lets go of Maddie's waist and claps me on the shoulder. Old buds now, apparently. "Great. Wipe down the counters and follow Maddie. She'll whip you into shape in no time."

I turn away, grabbing a nearby rag and wiping down the counter like my life depends on it.

Follow Maddie.

Got it.

Chapter Twenty-Three

Simon

I sink into my sleeping bag, still feeling the lights of the stage on my face. In my mind, I replay Maddie standing up and cheering for me when the song ended.

I surprised her.

I'm holding the napkin that Will had jotted the four steps on earlier that night. It's too dark for me to fully make out the writing, but I go over the steps again in my head.

Four simple steps.

Simple. Right.

Beside me, Will sleeps peacefully, a man clearly used to camping. I can't deny I'd felt conflicted when Lauren announced she and Will weren't spending nights together on this trip. I have no idea if this is a wedding week thing or how they choose to live, but a part of me had sighed in relief. I never would have been able to sleep in a two-person tent next to Maddie.

At the same time, my imagination had run a little wild at the prospect of falling asleep so close to her.

Our friendship has involved a lot of overnights, always

with Maddie on my couch and me in my bedroom. *As it should be.* Plus, she was usually either slightly intoxicated or overly emotional when she showed up at my place late at night.

I stare at the ceiling of the tent, adrenaline still high after my performance, and I realize it's going to be a while before I fall asleep. I sit up, then inch my way out of the tent as quietly as possible so I don't wake Will.

I crawl out into the open air, and when I look up, I see Maddie, wrapped in a plaid blanket, sitting next to a dying fire.

She looks at me and frowns. "Simon! What are you doing?" she shout-whispers.

I feel like an idiot, still on all fours, so I quickly stand and brush myself off. "Can't sleep. What are you doing?"

She's quiet for a few seconds before responding. "Thinking."

The warm orange glow of the fire highlights her face. I'm not used to seeing her like this. Pensive. Worried, even.

I know her emotions are big and complicated. And I also know I can't just dive straight in with questions—she'll shut down. As emotional as she is, she often doesn't know *why* she feels the way she feels. Usually she figures it out in bits and pieces, and I've learned not to rush her.

I've also learned that I'm one of two people in the world who ever see this side of her. To most people, Maddie is the life of the party. Always on. Always entertaining. She loves to be the center of attention. She loves to make people happy.

But there's so much more to her than that.

Most people don't stick around to see it.

"Do you want to be alone?" I ask. "I can go in the car."

She shakes her head. "Don't be dumb."

"I could never be dumb," I say.

She rolls her eyes. "Yeah, yeah, I get it—you're smart."

Then, she smiles over at me, and I take a moment to appreciate how it makes me feel warmer than the fire.

I sit down on the log next to her and she drapes the blanket over my legs, moving closer to me so we're both covered in the fleece throw.

"Wish we had some Reese's peanut butter cups," she sighs. "I could kill some s'mores right now."

I frown. "There are no Reese's peanut butter cups in s'mores."

"There are in my s'mores."

I laugh quietly. "Always gotta improve perfection." I stare at the fire for a few seconds. "Hang on, that isn't going to last much longer." I stand and pick up some branches from the little stack we'd gathered earlier and toss them onto the flames.

The fire sparks and sizzles, and I sit back down, this time an inch closer.

Will she notice?

I pull the blanket back over my legs, then hold my hands out to absorb the warmth of the fire.

Step One: Change your attitude about yourself.

I don't know how to do that.

I could tell her everything—jump straight to step four. I could tell her about Seattle, and Bea, and the real reason I started LUNA in the first place. I could explain that while she's been out getting her heart broken, I've been wishing for a chance to glue the pieces back together.

I could. But I won't. I can't.

She bumps her shoulder into mine. "So, that was some performance."

I make a face. "It was fine. We don't have to talk about it."

"Oh," she says. "We're talking about it."

"Okay. . .but there's not much to discuss."

"You don't think the fact that you can do *that*. . ." she looks around, maybe realizing that her voice has gotten a bit louder, then continues, leaning in to me, "and never breathed a word over all these years doesn't warrant a conversation?"

I try not to let the fact I can feel her breath on me affect my thinking. "I. . .just. . .didn't think anyone would ever hear it. It's. . .for me, you know? Not. . ." I vaguely wave, "for other people."

After a moment she says, "Yeah. Yeah, I kind of get that."

Another moment.

"Besides," I fill the space, "I can't think of a more boring topic."

"Really? You really think being an amazing musician is boring?"

"No," I say matter-of-factly, "but talking about me is."

She chuckles and leans into me. "You're rapidly becoming the least boring person I know."

She leaned in, and she has not moved. She's still against me. *What do I do??*

"I can think of lots of things more boring than you," she continues to rib. "Dryer lint, for example. Very boring. Documentaries about chess? Snooze-fest. Turtles? Completely bor—"

"Actually," I cut her off, not being able to help myself. "Did you know the sex of sea turtles is determined by the temperature of the nest?"

As soon as it's out of my mouth I know I've set myself up.

She leans away. Amusement plays at the corners of her mouth. "Is that right?"

Well, I'm in it now.

"Yes, colder sand produces male turtles and warmer sand produces female turtles," I explain as I rub my hands together for warmth. "So. . .that's. . .you know, not—" I look around— "not boring."

She laughs. "You're such a nerd."

Step one.

"But. . .that's okay," I venture. "Right?"

She tilts her face to look at me, softly lit by the firelight and looking more beautiful than I could ever remember.

"You'd also be an excellent partner at Trivia Night, that's for sure."

Not the response I was hoping for, but then. . .

"And yeah. It's okay."

There's a lull then. And in the silence, I search for something to say. Or, I suppose, more accurately, I try to decide if I want to say what I'm thinking. But, in the spirit of "just going for it," I clear my throat, keep my eyes on the flickering flames, and say, "You don't. . . have to pretend." I look at her briefly, then back at the fire. "You know?"

She scoffs to herself. "I'm not pretending. Pretending about what?"

"I don't know, just. . ." I don't want to say the wrong thing here. "Every time you smiled today it seemed like you were pretending." I tuck my hands under the blanket. "Just a little."

"Oh, that," she says, nonchalant. "I'm just out of my natural habitat."

I wait in silence, and she goes still. "I think you're searching for something that isn't there."

There's a haze around us, a slight fogginess that stings my eyes. And still I wait.

"I'm fine," she says, but I notice a slight waver in her voice. "I swear."

She looks away. I angle my body toward hers, and our knees touch under the blanket.

"Maddie. . .what is it?"

She pauses long enough to make me think she might actually open up, but then, she shakes her head and looks away.

"This trip is about Will and Lauren. Not about me." She takes a deep breath. "I'm genuinely happy for them."

"I'm genuinely happy for them too," I say.

"Good."

"But you're dodging the question."

Her eyes flick to mine, and I dare her not to look away. "Come on, Maddie, we tell each other everything."

She gives me an *oh, come on* look. "How can you even say that after tonight?"

I chuckle. "That's fair."

She goes silent. Just the soft crackle of cold sticks piled in the embers.

She breaks the silence. "I wasn't pretending at the bar."

"Right. When you were onstage."

She waits for me to look at her, then says, "No, when you were onstage."

Maybe I'm simply seeing a reflection of the fire, but is there a flicker of something in her eyes? I hold her gaze for three seconds that feel like an eternity, then finally look away.

This is unfamiliar, like wading into a lake and having to guess what your feet are feeling beneath you. Before this trip, telling Maddie how I feel has never even been a hint of an idea at the back of my mind. A secret I'd carry to my grave.

But I know time is running out.

I have to be smart. If I do tell her how I feel and she doesn't feel the same way, this whole trip becomes awkward and weird.

I still have at least six days. I'll take my time. See if anything between us shifts beyond what could easily be explained away.

I feel better for having let myself off the hook, but I still really want to reach over and take her hand. I want to hold it and show her that I'll be here, that she can take as long as she needs to work up the courage to tell me what's been bothering her. I want to tell her I can't stop thinking about her.

That I don't want our friendship to change, but I do want our relationship to deepen.

She scoots a little closer to me, shivering in the cool mountain air.

On instinct, I wrap an arm around her. "You're cold."

She leans into me, and I can almost imagine it different. *Us* different. "Who knew Arizona was this chilly at night?"

I'm not cold at all.

She's sitting right next to me, but she feels farther away than ever.

"You know, it's okay to ask for help," I say.

She laughs. "In all the years I've known you, I've never known *you* to ask anyone for help."

It's true. I don't like to rely on other people.

"So, the real question is, do *you* know it's okay to ask for help?" she asks.

"Oh, no. No, you don't. Don't turn this around on me," I say.

"It's a fair question," she says, sitting straighter.

I sigh. "If I ever need help, I'll let you know."

"But you won't," she says. "Need help, I mean." Then, after a pause, "You never do."

She sits, staring at the fire, almost resigned or transfixed, and repeats it. "You never need help. And I always do."

She scoots away from me a bit.

Is she embarrassed? Ashamed?

"Don't you think it's time I start taking care of myself?" She sounds sad when she says this, like the question is one she's been pondering. Like someone made her feel like something about her wasn't enough. Again.

She lets out a groan, pressing the heels of her hands to her eyes. "Ugh! I'm so depressing! This is *so* not me!"

I think for a split second about saying something, think for another second, *Eh, maybe I shouldn't,* and then think, *Oh, what the heck.*

"Yeah, but you're kind of hot when you get all angsty."

She turns, a bit slack-jawed and quietly laughing through her shocked face.

I did it again, I said the wrong thing, I've totally messed up the steps, and now she's. . .

"Not as hot as you were on that stage." She licks her finger and sticks it on my arm with a *Tssss!*

"You. . .wait. I. . .what?"

She's shaking her head. "I never thought I'd see you do something like that. Completely changed the way I see you, for sure."

I've changed the way she sees me.

"I thought those women at the end of the bar were going to throw their hotel keys at you."

I laugh, and thinking of those women actually makes me a little terrified.

"Wanna sing me an encore?" She indicates with open arms, inviting me to an imaginary stage.

I stretch my arms up over my head. "Oh no, I'm so tired all of a sudden."

"Simon."

I changed the way she sees me.

I stand, careful to keep the blanket on her and not on the ground. Comically flat, I say, "I can't even keep my eyes open. Oh my goodness. I'm going to bed."

She sighs, chuckling and shaking her head. "Fine. Go sleep, you weirdo."

I force myself to smile at her, even though what I really want to do is pull her into my arms and tell her that whatever it is, we can figure it out together. "Night, Mads."

I turn to go back to my tent, when her voice stops me.

"Hey."

"Yeah?"

She picks up a stick and turns it over in her hands.

"Thanks."

I'm confused. "I'm not sure what I did. . .but you're welcome. Always."

She turns to the fire, and I think. . .

I changed the way she sees me. Step one done.

Chapter Twenty-Four

Maddie

Road Trip Day Two

Before dawn, Lauren sits up and quietly shimmies her way out of her sleeping bag.

I lift my head. "Hey, sunshine."

"I didn't mean to wake you," she whispers, leaning over and putting a hand on my head. "Go back to sleep."

After my fireside chat with Simon, I didn't sleep. All I did was lie awake and think about how much I don't know about the guy I've called my friend for years. Where did he learn to play? How did his voice get so good?

And he flirted with me again.

It was. . .nice. And kind of familiar, like slipping on a favorite oversized college hoodie.

Different from when other guys "flirt." Simon's flirting comes with no expectations. Yesterday, I thought I knew Simon better than anyone, even Bea.

Now, I'm not so sure.

If my insides hadn't already been rewritten regarding my feelings for Simon, they certainly are now.

I blame his performance.

I sit up, stifling a yawn. "Are you sneaking off for some alone time with Will?"

Lauren laughs. "We're going to drive to the Painted Desert to watch the sunrise. And say the first of our vows."

"Oh my gosh! And you weren't going to wake me?" I kick myself out of the sleeping bag. "That's the whole reason I'm here." Then, affecting an Elvis accent I add, "to bear witness to your love."

She rolls her eyes, but she can't hide her smile. "I know, but you like your sleep."

"I like *you* more than sleep," I say, full body stretching in an X on the ground. "Let's do this!"

I jump up, aware I'm in a surprisingly good mood. We exit the tent to find Will and a sleepy-looking Simon standing by the remnant of the fire. At the sight of it, I recall the way I felt sitting there beside him, sharing a blanket and trying *not* to share the truth about why I'm acting so weird.

It had been nice not to feel so alone, even for a short while.

Normally, I'd spill everything. It's easy to vent when I'm the victim. But this? This is different. This is humiliating, and completely of my own doing. This is me being exactly the person I'm trying not to be anymore.

If I have any hope of growing up, I need to take responsibility for my own actions, and that means figuring my way out of this on my own.

As the thoughts swirl around my not-yet-awake mind, I glance up and find Simon smiling at me.

A friendly smile? A brotherly smile?

A flirty smile?

I feel like I should do something silly or at least smile

back at him, so I fake nodding off to sleep while I'm still standing and snore really loudly. After two snore-honks, I pop one eye open like a pirate and see Simon mouth the words, *Me too!*

"You two okay?" Lauren quips.

I snap out of my unspoken conversation with Simon and bounce up and down on the balls of my feet, rolling my head side to side, prize-fighter style. A few air punches, and I say, "Ready as I'll ever be." I do get a little strange when I feel awkward. It's a defense mechanism, I think.

Will looks at me and says, "Try not to think too much; it can only hurt the ball club." He holds up a fist to Simon, and he looks at it briefly and then high fives it.

He could never quite get the hang of that.

Will shifts his focus to Lauren, like she is his most prized possession, and at the sight of it, a surprise lump forms at the back of my throat.

Does she know how happy I am for them? Does she also know how scared I am that everything about our friendship is going to change? As Lauren joins the ranks of married, professional women, I'm still going to be floating around out here, her weird, single, broke friend.

Lauren steps into Will's arms, and as he pulls her close, my eyes drift over to Simon. He runs a hand through his sleep-styled hair and looks away. I wonder what he's thinking.

Before I can unpack my roaming thoughts, Simon says, "Sunrise is at 5:21 a.m., guys. We're cutting it close."

Out of nowhere, a pang of desire strikes me in the chest.

Actual, physical desire.

I can explain away being attracted to him last night when he was up on the stage, no problem. Me and every female with a pulse in that place. But being attracted to him now? When he's wearing a pair of Nike joggers and the glasses he'd long since traded in for contacts and he's spouting off facts about the time of the sunrise?

What is happening to me?

I clap my hands together, hoping the sound will snap my brain out of the gutter and into the moment. "Let's go, love-birds! Stop gawking, you're going to be late." I shove Will and Lauren toward the Jeep, and we all pile inside.

Simon and I are in the back seat, a fold-down seat divider and an unspoken world between us. It's the opposite of Will and Lauren, whose hands are intertwined constantly. If she were any closer to him, she'd be on the other side of him.

In the quiet hum of the sounds of the road, my thoughts run off track—and not in a good way. If anyone knew that I was having trouble keeping my hands to myself right now, life as I know it would end.

To fill the silence, I lean over and ask, "How'd you sleep?"

Simon pulls his gaze from the scene out the window and looks at me. "Not very long, honestly."

"Me neither," I say quietly.

A lull. A big, fat, horrible lull. The kind that makes your skin hurt.

"Hey, I read about the Painted Desert," Simon says, loud enough to include Will and Lauren. "I'm kind of jazzed I get to see it for myself."

"Did you just say *jazzed?*"

He looks at me.

"There's an old man trapped in your body."

I want to touch that body.

Bad, Maddie. Knock it off.

"You've never been?" Lauren asks, turning around to face us.

"Unfortunately, I've never really been anywhere," Simon says.

"No family vacations?" Lauren prods. "No long weekends?"

He shakes his head but doesn't say anything else.

I know very little about Simon's family. He doesn't talk about them. From what I've gathered, it was just him, Bea, and their mom. But in all the years I've known him, Simon has never gone home to visit, and his mother has never come out to spend time with him.

I always assumed it was a touchy subject, so I didn't dig deeper. Now, though, I'm curious.

My mind is full of ten years' worth of Simon taking care of me, but now I'm starting to wonder. . .what kind of friend have I been to him?

"Hey, you okay?"

I turn and find Simon watching me.

He points a finger to my forehead. "You've got a stress line. Is that what mine looks like?"

I laugh. "I'm fine."

I'm not fine.

Not only am I flat broke, I'm having *feelings*.

Unfamiliar feelings I'm sure I shouldn't be having.

We arrive at the Painted Desert with approximately five minutes to spare, and I'm thankful that I have something else to focus on besides what I've been desperately trying not to focus on.

We get out of the car and start walking toward a particular set of large rocks, overlooking the expanse.

"This spot wasn't on our first road trip," Lauren says as she walks around the car and slips her hand into Will's. "But on our way back, we stopped here, and. . ." she pauses. "I just can't wait for you guys to see it."

Simon is at my side, and he's fidgeting. The expression on

his face, one I haven't seen before, is. . .I think I'd call it. . .excitement?

"Oh my gosh, you really *are* jazzed about this," I say.

He looks at me like a kid who is next in line for Space Mountain. "I've read about this place, but I've only seen pictures. I can't believe I get to see it in real life."

I frown. "You know you can go see anything you want to see, right? Like, traveling could actually become part of your life."

"It's hard to get away." He shrugs and looks off in the distance. "Besides, I wouldn't want to travel by myself."

"I'd go with you!" I blurt, as if I actually have a dollar to my name.

"*You* would want to go on a vacation with *me?*"

"Sure," I say. "We'd have so much fun!"

"You and I don't have the same definition of that word."

A stark reminder of how very different we are, and exactly what I needed on this confusing morning.

"You guys!"

Lauren's voice pulls my attention, and I'm stunned silent as the sun breaks through, turning the rocks the color of fire. We're surrounded on all sides by small hills and valleys, varying shades of red and orange and brown. The dawn sky meets the earth as the moon goes to sleep, the twinkle of stars blown out like a candle.

"Wow," I whisper. "I've never seen anything like this."

Will and Lauren face each other, and I realize *this* is why I'm here—to witness moments like these.

We all shift our positions, and I pull out my phone so I can record the first of Will and Lauren's vows.

I glance at Simon, who is as taken with the whole scene in front of us as I am.

"Will," Lauren says, eyes focused on her soon-to-be-husband, "you already know I've had a crush on you since my Saddle Club days, and I'm so glad you came back into my life. I'm thankful that we were given a second chance to see what this was between us, because I can say without a doubt, you're the best thing that's ever happened to me."

My gaze drops to the red dirt beneath my feet and I shiver as a cool breeze goosebumps my arms.

Lauren stops talking and flashes Will a smile. "That's all for this stop."

"My turn?" He draws in a breath, and I can't be sure, but I think he's nervous. It's adorable how much he loves her. My soul aches at the thought. I want this. I feel wrong making this moment about me, but I can't keep the thought from entering my mind.

Nobody has ever looked at me the way Will is looking at Lauren right now.

But as Will pulls a piece of paper from his back pocket, my eyes float over to Simon's, and I see him watching me with a look that nearly stops my heart.

"I don't have mine memorized," Will says with a boyish smile. He clears his throat. "Lauren. I'm really thankful you have an irrational fear of flying."

She laughs, breaking the mood momentarily.

He smiles, and continues. "Because if you didn't, I would've missed out on the best thing that's ever happened to me. You put up with a lot. You forgave a lot. And I'm going to spend the rest of my life proving to you that you made the right choice."

The moment is sacred. I know Will and Lauren will have a traditional wedding once we get to Illinois, but somehow, it seems these moments mean more to them. And I get to be here for it. Simon and I are the sole witnesses, and that feels important.

Will goes silent, and Lauren wipes away a tear. He gives her arm a tug and kisses her. And kisses her. Simon and I both look away at the same time, and when we do, our gazes collide.

"Okay, okay. Good grief, you two look like two seals fighting over a grape," I call out—my attempt at lightening up the scene. "And the vows. . .can't you just say them all right here? It's so perfect."

"That would defeat the purpose," Lauren says. "Get over here so we can take a selfie!"

We do as we're told, all cramming together so we can mark the moment, then we take a few more minutes to admire the view before heading back to the car for the second day of our road trip.

"Do you get it now?" I ask Simon, who's lost in thought and staring out the window.

"Get what?"

"Why it's romantic," I say. "A wedding on the road."

Lauren spins around and faces him. "Wait. You don't think it's romantic?"

Simon looks caught. "No, I wasn't. . .I mean, it's really. . ." He flounders out a "I don't really think about romance," then fishes out a, "that much."

Lauren raises a brow. "Hmm. Maybe you should."

He frowns and something silent passes between them. Then Lauren says, "So, what do you think now?"

He looks away. "It was. . .nice."

Lauren tosses me a look as if to say *He's hopeless*. She turns back around, and we all go quiet again. I glance down and see that Simon and I are only inches apart. If I shifted a little, we'd be touching. There's a barrel roll in my stomach thinking about it, so I scoot two inches toward the door.

Why did I do that? What am I so afraid of here?

I know exactly what I'm afraid of here.

168

My track record with relationships leaves a whole lot to be desired. I don't speak to a single one of my ex-boyfriends, and some I hide from, like a steak knife salesman is knocking at my door.

I know that if things between Simon and me get even remotely romantic, everything will change. Things will be intense for two weeks, I'll mess up, he'll see me for who I really am, I'll fall too deep, he'll lose interest, and so goes the circle of my dating life.

I need to focus on the reasons Simon and I are a wrong fit. That's what I need to be filling my mind with right now. I should make myself a list and read it every morning to keep myself from making a terrible mistake.

I open the Notes app on my phone and type:

Reasons Simon and I are Better Off as Friends.

I capitalize it to make it look more official, and therefore, more set in stone.

1. Simon is passive. I like a man who's confident and knows when to take charge.

I think about how he packed my things, about his snack cooler, his itinerary, and his timeline. Shoot. He kind of does take charge. But not *all* the time, right? And definitely not romantically I'll bet.

2. Simon is predictable. I like being surprised.

I think about him singing, and chalk that up as a fluke.

He surprised me once, so what?

I think about his voice, about how he looks, about how the crowd reacted, about. . .

Stop it.

3. Simon works too much. Money is not important to me.

I think about how I felt at the register, looking for buried change in an empty purse while people waited in line behind me.

It's not a very good list.

Three imperfect reasons that I can try to convince myself are valid.

Then, a thought hits me—and I tenderly tap it on my phone.

4. Simon needs someone better than me.

I blink at the screen.

That's it. That's the reason. He needs—no, deserves—someone better than me.

I try to sneak a glance at him, and he's seemingly preoccupied in thought, looking out the window. I look down to see his fingers tapping a rhythm on his lap, almost like he's playing something in his head.

A part of me really wants to hear that song.

I shake myself out of it, and hope these reasons will keep me from doing or saying something really, really stupid. Like *I don't know when it happened, but I'm starting to feel tingly when I'm around you.*

I lean forward in my seat, sticking my face between Will and Lauren and praying for a distraction. I need to get Simon out of my line of sight. Even my periphery.

"What's on the agenda for today?" I ask.

"We're going to go back to the campsite and cook a big breakfast over the campfire," Lauren says. "Will is a master at bacon and eggs."

"I love bacon and eggs!" I say, with a little more enthusiasm than I should. Mostly, I'm just thankful I don't have to figure out how to pay for at least one meal today.

"Then on to New Mexico," Will says. "I have a player who lives in a little town called El Muérdago, and they want to have a big wedding dinner for us."

Yes! Two meals covered!

"It's a little off the beaten path," Will goes on, "but the town and this family are really important to us."

"And one thing we've learned along the way," Lauren says, putting a hand on Will's, "is that sometimes you find the most magical things when you ditch your plan and leave your route."

I shake my head. No matter how many times Lauren says this, it will always surprise me, coming from her. "Will, I don't know what you've done with my best friend, but she's not the same girl I've known for over a decade."

Lauren grins. "I'm learning to chill out."

I lean back in my seat. "Maybe you can teach Simon." I grin over at him.

"I can hear you, you know," he says.

I glance down, seeing that his fingers are still playing unseen chords. "You have nice hands."

The words are out before I can stop them. Lauren turns around, a quizzical look on her face.

"Nice hands?" Simon asks.

"Uhh. . ." My throat is dry. I'm usually quick on my feet, and I have no problem being the butt of any joke that makes people laugh, but at the moment, I'm frozen.

"Yeah," I say, "you know. It looks like you've been. . .playing something. On your lap. For a while."

Simon turns a bit, and I feel like I just tried to scale the wall at Shawshank and a spotlight on a tower has pivoted to encircle me in hot white light.

"Have you been just sitting there watching my hands?"

Now, Lauren raises a brow.

"No!" I blurt, playing it off and failing. "Like, I just noticed, and I thought I'd pay you a compliment. Nice for playing the piano, and, you know. . ." I make rubbing motions with my hands (*what am I doing?!*), "other things."

Abort! Abort!

"Other things?" Lauren asks, leaning farther into the back seat. "Like *what*, Maddie?"

"Like. . .designing websites and. . .computer. . .stuff," I mumble.

My side of that whole encounter was the equivalent of someone falling down a flight of stairs.

I don't have to look at Simon to know he's trying to figure out if aliens have taken control of my body.

"And you call me a weirdo," Simon says, then goes back to staring out the window.

When I glance back, I find Lauren, still watching me, eyes wide as if to ask, *What was that?!*

In response to her unasked question, I shake my head and give a little shrug.

She scrunches a grin, I stick out my tongue, and she turns back to face the front.

Mentally kicking myself and still feeling flushed with embarrassment, I tap my phone to life, hoping for some kind of distraction.

The Notes app is still pulled up, and reluctantly, I read the last thing I typed.

Chapter Twenty-Five

Simon

Apparently, I have nice hands.

Who knew?

After breakfast, we pack up and hit the road toward New Mexico and El Muérdago. A couple of hours into our drive, my phone rings.

"I need to take this."

Maddie turns off the music, and I answer the phone. It's a new client, and after only a few seconds, I wish I could pull over. I find myself repeating the phrase, "I'm not in front of a computer right now, but I can look at it when I stop."

Working on the road is proving to be more complicated than I thought it would be.

I'm a creature of habit, and I don't like to be out of my element, especially when I'm trying to make a good impression. Maddie must sense my uneasiness, because she picks up her giant tote and pulls out a notebook, taking notes as I talk.

Instantly, something inside me settles.

It's a good twenty-minute phone call. Maddie has a page and a half of notes, some shorthand, some circled, some starred.

When I hang up, I glance over at her. "Thank you for doing that."

She waves me off like it's no big deal, but the way she anticipated what I needed in the moment is no small thing to me. This is what Bea doesn't see. Maddie settles me. She always has.

And that's hard to do.

"I don't want it to be difficult for you to work. You can totally pull over if you need to," she says. But then, she gets quiet again. She's been quiet the entire time we've been in the car, and I'm not sure what to make of it.

After a while, I notice that Maddie's eyes are closed. Even though it won't make a difference on an interstate, I try to drive softer.

Around lunchtime, I follow Will's Jeep off the highway to a place called Pop's Diner. As I bring the car to a stop, Maddie stirs. I pull into the parking lot, and she sits up, looking sleepy and confused.

"I fell asleep?" she asks.

"For almost two hours," I say, stopping myself from adding, "*And you looked adorable.*"

"Wow." She runs a hand through her hair. "I didn't realize I was that tired."

"Yeah, sleeping on the ground isn't exactly restful." I put the car in park next to Will's.

She flips down the visor and opens the mirror. "'Raccoon' is sexy, right?" She rubs at a black smudge under her eye.

Step Three: Flirt.

My mouth goes dry. "I think you look fine."

Fail.

She tosses me an eye-roll, and the conversation dies, much like I wish I could, given the fact that flirting is going to be harder than I thought.

174

"Hey, um. . ." I try to change the subject, "I was hoping the timing would've worked out better, but unfortunately I've got a meeting in an hour."

She snaps the mirror shut and flicks the visor back up. "Work?"

"Yeah," I say. "I'm sorry."

"Don't apologize." She tilts her head. "But you know you deserve a vacation, right?"

"I don't have time."

She laughs. "You work for yourself now, remember? You can make your own hours."

I work for myself. Exactly. Which is why I can't afford to take any chances. I have to land this client.

I cannot fail again.

"I think being an adult is bad for your health."

My laugh is unamused. "I think not being able to pay my rent would be bad for my health."

At that, Maddie snaps her jaw shut and looks away.

"I know this is inconvenient," I say. "But I've got to take the meeting."

"Okay," she sighs.

"Why do you seem upset?"

"I'm not upset," she says. "I'm just sad for you."

I frown. "Because I have a job?"

She looks at me. "Because your job takes so much of your time."

I look away. "Most people's jobs take up a lot of their time."

"Mine doesn't," she says.

"Well, I can't make a living as a barista, Maddie."

I should not have said that.

I fumble a recovery. "I didn't mean—"

"It's fine." She cuts me off. "I know you think my job is silly."

"I don't, I just. . ."

She cuts me off again. "You do. I get it. But I can leave it behind when I want to."

I desperately search for a way to salvage this. I'm not saying what I mean.

"I know." Leave it to me to sound like a condescending jerk. "I know that's important to you."

"It is." She steels her jaw. "I did that on purpose."

Maddie has always had an aversion to the idea of working the kind of job that could be called "a career." I have theories on why, but nothing concrete.

I've never pushed her on it because I never want her to think she needs to change herself to be "good enough." But I do wonder why she sells herself short.

"You wouldn't get it," she says.

"I wouldn't get what?"

"Why work isn't the most important thing in my life," she says.

At that, she opens the car door and gets out, leaving me with the stark reminder of just how different Maddie and I are.

Did we just fight?

I pull the handle on the door and open it, getting out slowly, wondering how to re-engage with her without being. . .well. . .me.

I don't have the luxury of being a free spirit. I have a business. And responsibilities. And if I don't land a few more clients, LUNA is going to die before she ever has a chance to breathe.

The thought sends my pulse racing, and it must show on my face because Lauren and Will are both frowning at me.

"Everything okay, you two?" Will asks.

"With us?" Maddie laughs. "Of course."

I force a smile. "Yeah, just. . .work stuff."

"Thankfully I was there to take notes." Maddie nudges me with her elbow.

"A godsend. If I took notes, I'd have driven off the road," I say, silently grateful for Maddie's ability to think on her feet.

Will and Lauren exchange a glance.

"Okay. . ." Lauren says. "Well, can you take a picture with us? We want to get one with the Pop's Diner sign in the background."

"Of course," Maddie says.

Will asks a passer-by to snap a few photos, and Maddie and I slip into place next to the happy couple.

The person holding Lauren's phone, a large woman with a sleeve of washed-out tattoos, points at me. "Can we get that one to smile?"

I feel everyone stifle a laugh and look at me, and I do as I'm told. She takes the pictures, then hands the phone back. "Y'all on a trip or something?"

Will smiles, everyone's friend. "We are!" He puts an arm around Lauren. "We're getting married, doing our vows on the road, where we first fell in love."

She guffaws one loud "Ha!" and says, "That's cute!" She turns to me and Maddie. "And what, you're the best man and bridesmaid? You two hookin' up too?" She points between the two of us, expectantly.

Maddie and I both look at one another, then back to her, and overlapping, say:

"What?! Oh, no way, we're just. . ."

"We're friends, have been for a long. . ."

"We could never, we have. . ."

"Just along for the . . ."

We both peter out, and I nod through the lull.

Confused glances criss-cross from the woman to Lauren to Will, and the woman says, "Uh-huh. Well, I hope things work out for ya. Been married goin' on twenty-four years now," she waggles a ringed finger, "'cause he knows he can't find anything better'n this." She slaps a hand on her rear end.

Maddie says, "Oh my gosh, I love you."

She raises a hand in a wave goodbye and says, "Best ah luck!"

We all exchange pleasant goodbyes and waves, and are left shaking our collective heads at the encounter.

"And that," Will says, "is why you always take detours."

Chapter Twenty-Six

Simon

"All right," Maddie says. "What's the story with this place?"

Lauren grins. "Will did the first road trip in honor of his grandpa—Pops."

"I was recreating one we did when I was a kid," Will says.

"He had a whole slide show that he shared when we got back to his house for Christmas," Lauren says. "It was really special." Then, she looks at us. "So, if you guys are okay with it, we want to say our next vows here, in this parking lot."

Maddie brings her hands to a prayer position in front of her mouth. "You guys! This is so sweet."

"Are you going to cry again?" Lauren asks.

Maddie sniffs. "Probably. But I'm not apologizing for it."

My first reaction to Maddie getting emotional is that I don't get it. But then, seeing how Lauren and Will look at one another, I think I'm starting to understand.

Will and Lauren aren't exactly like other couples I've seen. They have something pure, something enviable. That morning, the vows they'd said to each other were surprisingly moving—

and I'm not usually moved. I didn't expect to be invested in the wedding part of this trip—because I thought I would focus on Maddie—but I've never seen a couple whose love seemed so genuine before.

So different from how I grew up.

I never knew my father and watched the revolving door of men in and out of my mother's life. Hardly a picture of true love.

Will and Lauren turn to each other, and I try to concentrate on what they're saying—something about not being able to imagine a single second without the other one—but I struggle to pay attention. My eyes dip to Maddie, standing proudly at Lauren's side. And all I can think is *I could love her like that.*

If only she would let me.

After the vows, Will and Lauren embrace, leaving Maddie and me standing awkwardly beside them.

She wipes her cheeks dry, and I shake my head. "Get it together, will you?"

She bumps her shoulder into mine. "Shut your face."

We take a few steps away, giving Will and Lauren a moment to bask in their glow. I lean toward her and say quietly, "Thanks for saving me back there."

She tosses me an amused look. "Don't underestimate me just because I'm a barista."

I stop moving and wait until she looks at me. "Maddie. I would never underestimate you. And I'm sorry if what I said before made you think—"

She cuts me off with an upheld hand. "I'm just giving you grief. Don't worry about it."

"I do worry about it," I say. "The last thing in the world I want is to make you think you're not enough when you absolutely are."

She holds onto eye contact for longer than I expect.

The air between us changes, and I can practically feel her *wanting* to believe me. My nerves start to buzz in a low-grade panic. If she looks too hard, she'll see that there's a whole lot more than friendship on my mind.

"Let's go eat!" Lauren calls over.

I barely hear her.

Maddie pulls her gaze from mine, and I struggle to unplug from the electricity of that moment. We follow Will and Lauren toward the diner, and I wish I could take her hand.

She looks up at me. "That was a nice story about Will's grandpa."

I nod. "Yeah, it was." I'm feeling that familiar feeling of not knowing what to say.

"Are you close with your grandparents?"

"Uh, no," I say. "I never really knew them."

I glance over to find her frowning at me. "None of them?"

I shake my head.

She seems surprised by this, and it's probably because I don't talk about my family. To her credit, she doesn't usually ask.

"Are you close with your grandparents?" I try to get the focus off of me.

She nods. "My grandma. We're close. She's a lot like me."

I think of something and decide to say it, hoping it's not too much.

"So, she's got nice curves, then?"

Her shocked laugh lets me know I'm in the clear. I think I'm getting the hang of this—and it's rapidly becoming my favorite reaction of hers.

"Kind of gross that you're thinking of my Gran that way, but it was funny so I'll allow it." She's still giggling to herself.

I love it.

"I'd like to meet her someday."

"She'd eat you alive." She grins. "Hey, what if I drive and you turn on your hotspot? You know, so you can work? Might be easier?" Maddie asks as we approach the entrance of the diner.

"It's unreliable," I say. "I can't risk the call dropping. You could go ahead with Will and Lauren? I know you don't want to miss anything, and I don't mind driving alone."

She stops moving. "Are you trying to get rid of me?"

"I mean. . ." I say, feeling a bit bolder after my last successful comment. "You snore."

"I do not!" She gives me a push, then, after a beat, "Oh my gosh. Do I?"

I laugh. "No. Actually you're so much more bearable when you're asleep."

She mock gasps. "Rude!"

"I'm kidding."

"You better be."

"I just don't want my work to interfere with your plans."

"No, it's okay," she says. "I'll stay with you."

Relief washes over me. I want her to stay with me.

Forever, if I'm honest.

"So, what, we meet them wherever they're stopping for the night?" Maddie asks.

"If you're okay with that," I say.

She nods as I pull the door open and let her pass through. "Sorry I keep pushing you about work." She looks at me. "I just think you deserve a break."

"It's nice of you to worry about me," I say. "But I promise I'm okay."

We sit in the booth across from Will and Lauren, and I hand Maddie a menu. She sets it down without opening it.

"Don't tell me you're not eating again," I say.

"Did you see how much I ate at breakfast? I'm still totally full."

"You said that yesterday, and then you ate half my food."

"And mine," Lauren adds.

"I won't eat your food," she promises. "I'm genuinely stuffed to the gills."

But when my meal arrives, it takes all of three minutes before Maddie is pulling french fries off of my plate.

Not only mine, though—everyone's. She eats my discarded coleslaw, at least a quarter of Lauren's uneaten burger, and when Will doesn't finish his avocado toast, Maddie eats that too. I think I've figured it out. And now I understand why she won't confess what's been wrong.

During the meal, Maddie explains our plan to stay behind so I can have my meeting.

"This one didn't fall at the best time," I say, apologetically.

Lauren takes a drink of her Coke, then smiles at me. "We know how important your business is, Simon. Do what you need to do."

"Yeah, she'd never tell you this, but Lauren's been working all morning," Will says.

"You what?" Maddie's eyes are wide. "Why? This is your wedding trip!"

Lauren shrugs. "I'm taking all of next week off for the honeymoon, and I don't want to be too far behind when we get back. Besides," she looks down, a bit coy, "I've been asked to submit set decoration ideas. . .for a Shonda Rhimes pilot." She looks up, grinning, her face lighting up.

Maddie slams her hands on the table. "Wait, *what?* Seriously!? That's amazing!"

Lauren laughs, and Will slings an arm around her shoulder. "I'm riding her coattails all the way to the top."

"Oh my gosh! That's. . .I'm so happy for you!" Maddie is giddy.

"Thanks," Lauren says. "It's not '*official*' official yet, but all signs point to it happening. If I don't land it, it won't be for lack of trying." To Simon, "So, I understand why you'd need to power through, even on vacation. Some opportunities only come along once—make the most of it."

"Thanks for understanding."

After we eat and pay, Will and Lauren scoot out of the booth and stand next to the table.

"We'll text the address of the motel in El Muérdago," Will says. "And just let us know when you get in."

"Sounds good," I say.

Maddie jumps up and pulls Lauren into a hug, as if we aren't going to see her in a few hours. As she does, Lauren leans in and whispers something.

Maddie shoves her away and shakes her head, her cheeks uncharacteristically pink.

We say our goodbyes, and then she sits in the booth across from me.

She smiles at me. "Looks like it's just me and you."

Yep.

Exhilarating and terrifying, all at once.

Chapter Twenty-Seven

Simon

Seven-and-a-half years ago

Working at Mo's isn't all bad.

With a little math figuring out the ratios, I'd learned how to make a perfect caramel Americano. I also developed a taste for espresso, forcing myself past the initial revulsion I assume all coffee drinkers experience.

And I had a built-in excuse to see Maddie almost every day.

Thankfully, Logan got a new job at a sporting goods store a few months after I started, and Maddie and I had become a good team. She handled all customer interaction, and I made most of the drinks.

It worked.

We worked.

Never mind that this job also gave me a front row seat to her dating life, or that I got to watch her prove she's not a serious relationship kind of girl.

Sometimes she'd try to set me up with her friends. Always,

I made it clear I'm not interested—while not letting on that they all pale in comparison to her.

None of these things deterred me from imagining things could be different.

In the fantasy, she'd look at me and realize, "Hey, what I really need in my life is a nice guy like you, Simon."

In the fantasy, I'm also taller.

This, I do know, makes me a first-class fool. As does the fact that Maddie is the only reason I stayed in this job for two years. But now that I've graduated, I can hardly justify it. Surely, she'll be moving on too.

On my last day at Mo's, I walk in with a sense of foreboding. Maddie and I are real friends now, but without the connection of work, would we still see each other?

Would I ever find the courage to tell her how I feel?

I come in through the back and punch my time card, same as always. I tie the apron around my waist and fix the black baseball cap on my head.

I'll miss this job, but I won't miss the cap.

I push the kitchen door open and search the space for Maddie. I find her, standing off to the side, talking to an older guy in a suit.

I busy myself behind the counter, keeping a close eye on Maddie and the guy—who is becoming increasingly more intense in his gesturing.

At one point, the man grabs her by the arm, and I flinch, instinctively moving toward them to intervene—but after a few seconds, the guy lets her go and storms out the door.

Maddie stands there, staring at the door, hugging herself.

"Can I get a vanilla latte?" A girl's voice pulls my attention.

I want to tell her, *No. Can't you see I'm trying to make sense of what's happening over there with the girl I'm hopelessly in love with?* But instead I say, "Of course." I ring her up, then move down the counter to make the drink, and when I look up again, Maddie is gone.

I rarely see Maddie upset. She's a wellspring of emotion, but the most prominent one on the surface is always happiness. Maddie is joy personified.

Knowing something is wrong instantly sets me on edge.

An influx of customers keeps me busy for the next fifteen minutes or so, and I do the work of two employees, taking orders, swiping cards, making drinks. I'm covering for her, and I know that will help her, but all I really want to do is go find out if she's okay.

Finally, there's a lull. I know it'll be short, so I hurry through the door to the kitchen and find Maddie sitting on the floor, knees pulled to her chest, head resting on them.

"Maddie?"

She quickly looks up, wiping her face with the back of her hands. "Sorry, Simon, I didn't mean to leave you alone out there. I'll be out in a minute."

"I don't care about that," I say, kneeling down in front of her. "Are you okay?"

"Totally fine," she says, putting on a sad smile. "I just need a minute."

"Okay." That's my cue to leave her alone, but I ignore it. "Who was that guy?"

She shakes her head. "It doesn't matter."

"It does matter," I say. "He upset you." A pause. "New boyfriend?"

She laughs. "Okay, I'm not so desperate to date someone *that* age, buddy." She sniffs and looks away, almost ashamed. "That was my father."

"Oh." I sit back on my heels.

"The one and only." Maddie makes a *ta-da* face and shifts, and I reach over to help her stand. When she slips her hand into mine, I squeeze it, trying to communicate *I'm here for you.*

But as soon as she's upright, she lets go.

"Your father." I cross my arms over my chest and wait for her to go on. When she doesn't, I ask the obvious, "You were fighting?"

"He doesn't approve of my *life choices*," she says, sarcastically. "Normally it doesn't bother me. I've accidentally made it my life's goal to disappoint him. But today. . .I don't know." She brings her eyes to mine. "I was already feeling sad."

I stick my hands in my pockets to keep myself from reaching over and swiping the last of the tears from her cheeks with my thumb. "Why?"

"Because you're leaving." Her face crumples, but she quickly recovers.

The words are like a pinprick to my heart. A tiny drop of hope seeps in. "You're sad about me leaving?"

"Duh!" She shrugs. "I don't have. . ." she stops herself. "I don't have many real friends, Simon."

That tiny drop of hope dries right up. *Friends.* Of course.

Maddie gives my arm a playful punch. "How many other people would let me crash on their couch after I get dumped? With no expectations? Do you know how rare that is, to find an actual guy friend who isn't mentally undressing you the whole time?"

As attractive as Maddie is, in this moment, I just really want to hold her hand and tell her everything is going to be okay.

Being there for Maddie has had the exact opposite effect I was hoping for—not showing that I'm excellent boyfriend material, but solidifying my friend status.

Still, I'm not going to stop being there for her. Not ever. "You know none of that is going to change, right?"

She looks up at me.

"I got a new job," I say. "I'm not going off to war."

"Good." She throws her arms around me, pressing her cheek into my chest. I inhale the sweet fruity smell of her shampoo and hold her, imagining for the briefest moment that this hug isn't completely platonic.

The bell on the counter rings, and Maddie blinks. "Customer."

"Right," I say, resigned that this moment I wanted to last forever has lasted only a few seconds. "Customer."

I watch her go. The second she pushes the door open, her face lights up like Christmas morning.

And for the first time since I'd met her, I saw that those twinkle lights flicker off when no one is looking.

And *that* is the version of Maddie I want to know most of all.

Chapter Twenty-Eight

Maddie

"I'm sensing serious sexual tension."

That's what Lauren had whispered to me before I pushed her away and my face flushed red.

I'd wanted to set her straight, but with Simon sitting right there, what was I going to do, shout "No sexy time with Simon today"?

And Lauren took my silence as agreement. Perfect. The list in my Notes app would beg to differ.

It's a list I need to keep at the forefront of my mind. Simon is too important to me to risk messing up our friendship. And if I were to ever even hint at the thoughts I've been wet-blanketing since last night, I would *definitely* mess up our friendship.

Simon pulls out his laptop, getting ready for the meeting, and that gives me a secret chance to add to that very list. I tap open the Notes app and, again, my eyes fall on the last item on the list.

4. *Simon needs someone better than me.*

I make a face and mentally decide to deal with that one later.

5. Our priorities are out of whack. Simon values work. I value fun.

But that's not quite right, is it? It's not that I don't want to be an adult. . .it's that I don't really know how.

And who would ever take me seriously anyway?

6. I cannot lose Simon as a friend.

I sit with this one for a moment, just like number four.

He's my best friend.

And I don't have many. Or any. Simon and Lauren. Those are my people.

It's hard when you finally, and honestly, take stock of where you are, only to find out that you've been socially treading water for the better part of your adult life. Or that the relationship you've claimed has been the best thing ever hasn't exactly been reciprocal on your part.

For other women who have a best friend of the opposite sex, this may be a cop-out. But for me? This is a genuine concern. And a critical point. I was right all those years ago when we first met. He is a serious relationship person.

I am the girl guys date right before they find "the one."

But what if I'm ready for something more?

My knee starts bouncing nervously at the thought. It's not like me to think deeply about things.

I glance up at him and note his intensity and focus—and think maybe I have the stress line completely wrong. I study him for a long moment as my gaze falls to his hands, moving across the keyboard as he prepares for what I'm gathering is a very important meeting.

Simon's seriousness has driven me crazy in the past—but it's also part of his charm.

I don't know that I've ever really paid much attention to Simon's looks. Not in *that* way, anyway. But now. . .with all these thoughts colliding like Lotto balls in my mind, it's *all* I can think about.

His dark, wavy hair is longer on the top these days than it used to be, and his neatly groomed facial hair makes him look more distinguished. This is perhaps the biggest change to his appearance in recent months, and I notice now that it hides his baby face. It hides the fact that inside this grown man is a hint of the gawky, nerdy boy I'd met over ten years ago.

His eyes are a bright blue and full of kindness and—

"Are you okay?" Simon says this without looking up.

I scoff. "Uh, *yeah*. Of course."

"Okay, because I can feel you staring at me."

"No, I'm not either staring." My cheeks are hot. *Not either staring? What language is that?*

He frowns, but an amused expression washes over his face.

Oh, Lord, help me. Does he know what I'm thinking?

"Sorry," I stammer as he meets my eyes. "I'm just. . .trying to figure out what to do when, you know, you're on your call and everything. Should I just maybe leave? Sit here? Make faces?"

I slowly tilt my head and cross my eyes—and Simon laughs, a genuine one.

True feelings successfully dodged.

"You're so weird," he says. "I promise I'll try to be quick."

"Oh, no, take your time, I don't mind sitting here watching. . .I mean. . .I'll just. . ." but I'm out of words. I search my mind but all I'm getting is *hands* and *hot*. I shake the thoughts away, draw in a breath and lift my water glass. *"To your health."*

"Thanks. I think." He smiles, then goes back to his computer.

Thank God.

What is *happening* to me? This is *not* how I behave around Simon. If he knew any of the thoughts I'm entertaining, he'd be appalled. *I'm* appalled.

And intrigued.

Stop. IT.

Desperately in need of a distraction, I open my phone. I go to my photos and start scrolling.

Sandwiched between blurry images from nights out with friends, there are countless shots of the many pieces of pottery I have back home.

Photo after photo of the passion I don't tell people about.

It's part of me. Important in ways I can't explain. I know it's frivolous to some, one in particular, because my father told me.

I was still in college, and I went home for spring break. I brought each of my parents a gift—a bowl for my father and a mug for my mother. I thought if they saw what I was making, they'd be supportive.

The conversation completely backfired. My father made it clear that pottery isn't a "real profession." That nobody "makes any real money by selling coffee mugs."

I should've known better than to tell him I'd been thinking about pursuing it. I should've known that anything other than his plan for me wasn't going to be good enough. I was young and naive and maybe a little too idealistic. I still am, come to think of it.

That's why I keep it to myself. Keep it *for* myself. If no one knows, no one can criticize.

Because while I pride myself on living my life differently than my parents, the sad truth is, I still want their approval.

In this moment, this unplanned deep dive into my life, I realize that I want *everyone's* approval.

And maybe because I never got it as a kid, I'm convinced I can never, ever earn it from anyone else.

Wow, I should charge myself therapist fees, I sarcastically think. *Such discovery and breakthrough.*

Looking through the photos now, though, I'm not filled with the normal thoughts that this is something I should hide. I'm proud of these pieces. I'm proud of how far I've come.

I scroll through a series of mugs without handles. All different colors, all bright and happy. I remember how I felt creating them. I remember putting my signature on the bottom. I remember loving every second of it. I was so proud of how they turned out that I took staged, well-lit photos of every single one.

I slide through the images, one by one, and happiness bubbles up inside me. I've ignored that feeling for a very long time.

I glance up and see a flicker of intensity in Simon's eyes as they dart back and forth, studying his computer screen in anticipation of the meeting. He comes alive when he works in a way that I never have.

Except when I'm at the wheel.

I know I never want to be a person who prioritizes work over people, like my father. I know that in my soul.

But I do want more for myself.

I freeze at the thought.

I want more.

And then a simple, singular thought.

Maddie Made.

The name of a business. My business.

The name of a shop. Online.

I can see the logo in my mind. Two handwritten capital letter M's, overlapped and intertwined.

My pieces. My creativity. My vulnerability. My choice. My risk.

My nerves are dancing like water in a hot pan.

What am I thinking?

I'm not ready. I don't even have a savings account. I have a whole pile of unpaid bills. I'm not going to make my rent.

I'm not going to make my rent.

The hot flash of creativity is washing over all of the negative thoughts. In this moment, I can put a positive spin on anything.

I can do anything.

I've had fleeting thoughts like this before, but never this strong. Or clear.

I've always pushed them off for "someday."

Apparently, *someday* is today.

The idea makes my palms sweat. I take a quick drink of water because my mouth has gone completely dry.

What if I fail?

That thought pops in my mind, followed by a rush of positivity.

Yeah, but what if I succeed?

I only get one chance to launch my brand. I have a whole notebook of ideas of things I want to do, but I don't have the means to build a whole website and open a store. I only have a few tools in front of me—my social media account being the biggest.

I could start anonymously? A secret account with my brand name? Or I could put myself out there, and the critics and my father can just stick it.

I already have a pricing chart and a catalog of the pieces I have available. I've even named each piece. I do some quick calculations to figure out roughly how many I'll need to sell to buy myself a couple of meals and a night in a reasonably priced hotel.

The number feels doable. Maybe? I really have no idea, but in the euphoria of this moment, I don't really care. I'll figure all of that out later.

"You're smiling," Simon says from across the table.

I look up, feeling a strange mix of excitement and fear and ideas and potential. I want to tell him everything, but not yet.

"I am smiling."

I can do this, and I can show him that I'm actually an adult who can do adult things. Not just a barista—although I know he didn't mean that the way I took it.

Maybe I can change the way he sees me.

Am I caring about that now? Is that something I care about? Apparently so.

His eyebrows are raised, as if he's expecting me to explain *why* I'm smiling, but I'm not going to just yet. I'm going to do this one on my own—like Jake in *Sweet Home Alabama* with his high-end glass shop on the water. Nobody took him seriously either.

"Just a funny video," I lie. "It's these talking huskies, howling, and. . ." I wave him off. "It's ridiculous. Go back to work."

I'm not sure he buys it, but he gives me a quick eye roll and goes back to his computer. My eyes linger on him for a few seconds. He *is* handsome. Boyishly so. But more than that, Simon is just so *good*. I'm lucky to have him in my life, and I know it.

Don't screw that up, Maddie.

"Is it going to bother you if I'm sitting here while you're on your call?" I ask.

He doesn't look up. "No, but it's pretty boring stuff. Somewhere between dryer lint and turtles."

I laugh. "Fair enough."

His meeting starts, and I get to work creating a new Instagram account for my new pottery business.

My new pottery business. The words sizzle inside me. I've got my mind made up. I'm going to go for it. And if I fail, well, nobody will know.

I'm not going to put my name on it. Just the logo.

A part of me really wants to stand in front of everyone and show them what I can do—but the one part of me that has always hedged my bets when it comes to success speaks pretty loudly.

I'll jump in. Headfirst. Like always.

And when I'm ready, when it's successful, I'll let everyone know it was me the whole time.

It's crazy how much time I'd already subconsciously put into this idea. Lists, photos, descriptions, even prices. I have been building to this moment on this trip in this diner and I didn't even know it.

I'll start small, using social media. Over the years, I've built quite a following—people who are oddly interested in my weekend exploits and my stories from the coffee shop.

I'm not sure how the people who follow me will respond to a post about a coffee mug—or how they're not going to find out it's me—but one thing at a time.

I pull out my iPad and open Procreate. I like to sketch my pottery ideas sometimes, and I'm shocked to see just how many sketches there are. Using the stylus, I script out the logo, in my own handwriting, and play with the size and edges.

After a few minutes, I think, *There. Perfect.*

I bump out the image and send it to my phone. From there, I use it to complete the new Instagram account. I add pictures of pieces, making sure to align the color—so they look pleasing on the grid.

I'm having way too much fun right now. It feels so new, so fresh, so. . .alive.

Next, I set up an Etsy shop, linking it in the bio of the new Instagram account. I upload several photos of the pieces I have on my shelves back home. I copy the descriptions I wrote previously, adding some fun and snarky lines to give my shop a little personality, and a note that shipping won't happen until I'm back home next week.

Finally, I open the photo of myself curled up in my bohemian bedroom with one of my mugs. When I post it on my *own* Instagram account, I'll tag the new, *anonymous* account and pray it helps me sell a few mugs.

Across the table, Simon is now actively engaged in his Zoom meeting—and since he's wearing headphones, I only hear his side of it. While I wait for photos to upload, I tune in to what he's saying, and I marvel at the cool, confident demeanor he takes on as he engages in this conversation.

"I have no doubt we can take your business to the next level by building a web presence. You guys are so unique. I think that's something we can capitalize on."

I listen, not to be nosy but because—and I would *never* say this out loud—I want to learn.

Knowing how to make the art is one thing. Knowing how to sell it is something else entirely.

If this is going to work, I'll have to figure out the latter.

And at this moment, I believe I can do anything.

I don't even hesitate and hit *share*.

Chapter Twenty-Nine

Maddie

I'm staring again.

Simon's explaining why every business needs to highlight their "story." He details brand framework, content creation, and explains ways to reach the people they want over branded streams—traditional, digital, and mobile. He says that LUNA can "create an app, partner with influencers, and determine the most effective way to specifically and uniquely brand your story—because marketing is basically storytelling."

There's a pause as the client says something, and Simon leans off camera and looks at me with a pained expression. He leans back into frame and says, "Yes, totally, if you want to add on a newsletter service, we can handle that too."

I'm impressed not only by the things he knows, but also by how personable and confident he is when he speaks. He's funny and charming and witty, and it's obvious whoever is on the other line is buying what he's selling.

I can't blame them. I'm buying, too.

Simon looks up from his computer.

Crap! I'm staring again.

He frowns and leans out of the frame of his camera, mouthing the words, "What's wrong?"

I brighten and shake my head, waving a hand in the air as if to say *oh, nothing*, and look down to find my photos have finished uploading.

I pull up the image of me with my mug (*I actually look kind of cute in this one*) and load it onto my main account, tagging the new, anonymous account, then freezing to stare at the "share" button for a three-count.

My heart is racing.

It's a big first step toward a dream I've been carrying around with me for years.

A dream that was foolish and frivolous and unrealistic and. . .*mine*.

It's a big first step.

My finger still hovers.

I draw in a breath, and without another thought, I hit the "share" button and set the phone down.

Fireworks go off inside of me. Succeed or fail, this one is all mine.

There's a buoyant, giddy feeling inside of me. I try to tamp it down, but I want to run laps around Pop's Diner and tell everyone what I just did.

My phone buzzes, which is probably a good thing because I'm *thisclose* to blabbing it all to Simon.

I pick it up and see that my new anonymous account has a notification. *Already?*

I open the app and navigate to the inbox on Instagram as two more messages come in.

These are so cute! How do I order a blue mug?

I want to get a whole set of these for my parents—the perfect birthday gift for my coffee-loving mom!

This bowl! Take all my money.

"You're smiling again."

My phone buzzes. And buzzes again.

I look up and find Simon watching me. I want to tell him *so bad*. I know he'll cheer me on. After all, he's been telling me to do this for years.

"You're popular all of a sudden," he notices.

"Ha. Ha. Yeah." I clamp a hand over my phone and it buzzes in my palm.

"Is your meeting over?" I try to divert the attention off of me, and I click the side switch to mute my phone.

"Don't change the subject." He sets his phone down and gives me his full attention. "What's going on?"

"I told you—funny video, and I commented on it, and now people are. . .commenting back? I guess?"

He squints over at me, as if trying to determine whether or not I'm telling the truth. "I love husky videos. Show me."

I glance down at my phone. Eight more sales have come through.

More than enough for two meals. And if I'm lucky, I'll make enough for tonight's room, too. I know I'm going to have to sell a *lot* more to afford the rest of the trip, but I'm focused on today. Today, I'll celebrate the fact that at least a few people out there are willing to pay me to make art.

"Oh, I lost the link," I say, shutting off my phone.

"Ah. I see." He doesn't believe me for a second. I know it.

He picks up his phone, clicks it to life, then turns it around to reveal the image I'd just posted on my public account. "Does it have anything to do with this?"

My jaw goes slack as I study my own post on his phone. "Since when do you pay attention to my social media?"

"Since always," he says.

"You *hate* social media. You said you're never on any of—and I quote—'those time-sucking sites.'"

"It's kind of my job now," he says, flipping his phone back around and looking closer at it. "Who's going to trust me to build their web presence if I don't have one of my own?"

"True," I say. "But you never post."

He looks up and smiles. "You follow me?"

Caught, I say, "Well. . .yeah, I do, just to, you know. . .stay in the know."

He clicks around on his phone for a few seconds, then slides it across the table. "That's my new business account. I created it right before we left."

I pick up the phone and scroll through the images, pretending I haven't seen it already. There aren't many because LUNA isn't very old, but each one is loaded with smart business tips. Simon's personal account has three photos posted, and the most recent one is at least two years old.

He looks expectant. "Not the greatest, huh?"

"This is a great start!" I'm actually a bit proud of him for stepping out of his comfort zone—these kinds of things are *so* not Simon.

Then again, I'm learning about quite a few things on this trip that I also thought were *so* not Simon

He smiles and takes his phone back.

"I knew you followed me," I admit, "but I didn't think you ever paid attention."

"I do," he says.

"But you've never even liked or commented on any of my posts," I say.

"I like and comment in person."

My eyes find his, and I'm shocked when I'm the first one to look away.

"You must think it's all incredibly juvenile," I say. "Me posting about the coffee shop or my weekends out."

His scrunched-nose expression makes me laugh. "Your

202

posts are entertaining, but it is a little exhausting. Don't you ever want to just stay home?"

An image of me at my potter's wheel floats through my mind. Yes. I love being at home. I love sitting there on my sun porch, sunlight pouring in from all sides, working the clay between my fingers. But I go out almost every night.

That's who I've always been.

And most nights, I hate to be alone.

"You know me. I like to go where the action is."

He closes his laptop and scoots it to the side. "Yeah, I know. We're different that way."

I make a mental note to add that to my list.

"For the record, I like the photos of you—" he clicks around on his phone, and when he finds what he's looking for, he turns it around to face me, "like this."

I stare back at the image of myself, sitting in the shadow of the morning sun, on my sunporch, holding a cup of coffee in a mug I'd made a few weeks before. You can't tell from the photo that I'd just finished making a vase—all you can see is that my hair is piled in a messy bun. I'm not wearing makeup, and one shoulder is exposed by an oversized shirt with a wide neckline. And there is a dreamy, faraway look in my eye.

"My Flashdance look!" I joke because the moment is feeling a little too heavy. Not heavy, exactly. . .maybe. . .intimate? Personal.

How can I be uncomfortable with it and long for it at the same time?

"I don't know what that means." He looks at it again. "But it's nice." He turns his phone off and flips it over on the table, avoiding my eyes. "One question," he asks. "Why don't you tell people this is your pottery? Why make a fake account instead of claiming it as your own?"

Darn it.

Although, if there's anyone in the world who might understand, it's him. He's seen me at my very worst.

Many times. So. Many. Times.

He's never made me feel ashamed before, so why am I being weird about letting him see this?

Because I know that if he finds out how bad my financial situation is, he's going to try and save me. He's going to jump in and pay my rent for six months or hire me to do some made-up job for his business or something.

Simon is in the habit of saving me, and it's not fair to him.

It's time for me to make it on my own.

"It's. . .an experiment," I say, looking away. "Just to gauge people's responses."

"You could've posted that this was your pottery and people would've bought it just because it's yours."

"You think so?"

"Yes. Definitely." He's so certain.

Why is he so certain?

"I bought this one." He flips over to my pottery page and pulls up the image of a very masculine speckled clay bowl I'd made.

"Simon! What?! You didn't have to do that!"

"I wanted to," he says. "It's really cool, and I love the colors. I'm going to put it in my entryway and use it for my keys and wallet."

I smile. "Thanks."

After a pause, I say, "You're different when you're working."

He looks curious. "I am?"

"Yes," I say. "You're. . .confident. And sort of. . .charming."

He scoffs. "Well, let's hope it worked on this guy."

It's working on me.

For the love, *stop, Maddie.*

"How is it that confidence doesn't spill over into your personal life?"

He turns shy at the mention of his "personal life," and something inside me squeezes.

"Okay, let's not go there."

"Why not?"

He looks uncomfortable. "I. . .don't like talking about myself. Plus, women make far less sense to me than computers," he says.

"Right." I smile at him. "Computers don't have boobs."

He looks shocked, and I love it. "Okay, *not* what I meant."

I grin. Simon says I have no filter. I say he's a prude. But now I see it's not a bad thing—it's one of his greatest strengths.

"I'm not. . .great. . .with women." He runs a hand through his hair, leaving it messier than before. "Let's just say I make a great *friend*."

"Okay, that's not true," I argue. "You've had girlfriends."

He sighs. "And most of them soon realized I made a better friend." He shrugs as he says this, as if this is simply his lot in life. "I mean, you did."

"But we never dated," I say, confused.

"Because I make a better friend." He watches me, as if waiting for me to contradict him. When I don't say anything, he gives a perfunctory nod. "Like I said."

"But. . ." I search for a way to argue with him. The truth is he *is* a great friend. The best, in fact.

"I'm sure there's someone out there that won't think of you as just that. You're so smart and successful. Any girl would be lucky to have you."

I have a strange sensation, like what I'm saying runs parallel to how I'm feeling.

"Yeah, they're beating down my door."

"You just don't put yourself out there."

"I do, actually," he says, then after pausing, adds, "Okay, maybe not a ton," and then another pause, and finally adds, "Sometimes."

"It's been months since you and Hannah broke up, and as far as I know, your Lakers date is the only one you've been on."

He looks away. He doesn't talk about Hannah. At one point, I thought he was going to marry her, but then, he announced that she broke up with him, and he never really told me why.

Thinking back on it now, I realize I'd been relieved when they broke up. Relieved he didn't propose to Hannah. Relieved I didn't have to let go of him yet.

"Even though it's a really small sample size, I've discovered that women don't want 'the nice guy,'" he says.

"Simon, that's not true."

"Maddie, in all the years I've known you, you've never once gone out with a guy I'd describe as 'nice.'"

I open my mouth to protest, but stop because I know he has a point.

Lauren had said the same thing after my last semi-serious boyfriend, Dylan, had broken up with me. I'd stupidly thought maybe, just maybe, he was the one, but then he met a law student named Rebecca and our relationship ended.

Apparently, Rebecca was the kind of girl Dylan was looking for. Smart and studious and serious and basically everything I'm not.

I spent the next four days on Simon's couch drowning my sorrows in Oreos, mint chocolate chip ice cream, and a days-long binge of *New Girl*.

Simon brought me dinner every night and made me breakfast every morning. He picked up my mail and even covered two of my shifts at the coffee shop.

Simon saved me.

Simon is in the habit of saving me.

"We're not talking about me," I say. "We're talking about you. And if you can do *that*—" I wave a hand in the direction of his phone and computer—"you can handle a date with a beautiful woman. Just pretend it's me on the other side of the table."

His eyes widen, almost imperceptibly, then he shakes his head.

He looks at me and says, "None of them are you, Maddie." His face is as earnest and honest and pleading as I've ever seen.

The words make me catch my breath. My teasing smile fades, and I search his eyes for a clue on how I should interpret that.

Possibly the most concerning revelation I have is that I *want* him to mean more than he probably does.

His phone buzzes on the table, a loud assault in the quiet of the diner.

He glances down, and I instantly want his attention back on me.

He straightens slowly in his seat, a smile spreading across his face—and I feel it all the way to my toes. Unlike me, Simon never smiles unless he means it. Witnessing a genuine Simon Collier smile is a little like winning the lottery.

"You closed the deal, didn't you?" I ask.

He nods. "I gotta text Bea." His thumbs fly across his phone's screen.

"We should celebrate!"

"One new client isn't something to celebrate." He sets the phone back down on the table.

When he looks up, I make sure he finds me frowning. "Yes, it is, Simon. You have to celebrate every victory, no matter how small it seems. You landed a client. *You* did that! That's a great reason to order a round of milkshakes if I ever heard one."

"Okay, but only if we can also celebrate the fact that you're officially selling your pottery."

"Oh, but that's—"

"Every victory," he says, "is something to celebrate."

Touché.

Chapter Thirty

Simon

After our celebratory milkshakes, Maddie and I walk out into the parking lot, but before we reach my car, Maddie races over to the driver's side door. "I'll drive."

I stop moving. "Uhh. . .no. I've got it."

"Come on, I know you're tired," she says. "I know you didn't sleep, and that meeting probably took a lot out of you. Let me carry some of the load."

She knows what I need without me saying it.

"Please? I want to help."

After a pause, I look away, knowing it's pointless to argue with Maddie anyway.

She must sense my resignation because her face lights up. "Okay, so let me drive for a little while. You can sleep or work or maybe *sing* or, you know, whatever."

She looks at me with a fun, trying-to-hold-it-back smile on her face.

"You forget I only seem to be popular with unhappily married women in their late 40s," I joke.

"I can guarantee every single woman in that place thought you were hot."

Without thinking, I say, "*Every* single woman there?" and look right at her.

She stammers a bit. "I. . .can't deny that it was. . .I mean. . ."

It's nice to turn the tables once in a while.

I pause. "I'll let you drive on one condition."

She folds her arms over her chest.

"I pick the music."

She throws her head back with a groan. "Nooo. . .!" But she laughs as she says it. It's my favorite sound.

When she brings her gaze back to mine, her face changes. Softens, somehow. I can see a struggle on her face, like she's deciding something. She draws in a breath and holds it. Then, she lets it out, and she says something that completely catches me off guard.

"I really want to tell you something, but I feel stupid saying it out loud."

Genuine moments with Maddie are hard to come by, and if I'm about to have one, I'm going to pay very close attention.

"Are. . .are we still talking about me picking the music?"

She makes a face. "No, Simon. We're not. Now just shut up and let me get this out."

I shut up.

She opens her mouth like she's going to speak, but then quickly closes it.

She takes a breath. "You know I've been making pottery for a long time," she says.

I nod.

She chuckles a little to herself, then turns serious again. "But I've never tried selling it."

"I know," I say. "I've been telling you you should for years."

"Yeah." She looks up at me, as if finally realizing something.

"Yeah, you have." She chews the inside of her cheek, something she only does when she's nervous. She sighs. Then, she lifts her face to the sky, closes her eyes and blurts, "I'm afraid that if people know it's me, trying to, I don't know, start a business or something, then they'll take bets on how long it'll be before I mess it all up."

She looks around at everything but me—ashamed and embarrassed.

I frown. "Maddie. . ."

She cuts me off. "I get it, you know. I get why everyone thinks that." She is getting more and more bothered as she talks. "I don't have a job that will turn into a career. I've made some questionable decisions in my life. I've never taken anything seriously." She kicks at a rock on the pavement. I can see this is hard for her to talk about.

"I'm not exactly the kind of person people think of when they think of success. Or. . .business. Or grown-up anything."

Her gaze falls to her feet.

I stare for a moment, and then suddenly I see things from her perspective. I've always been really pragmatic, setting goals and assigning steps to get there. She's not wired that way. She's a super spontaneous, figure-it-out-in-the-moment person who gets caught up in waves of creativity.

The thought of trying something—in her mind—"legitimate," almost certainly terrifies her.

And just as I can clearly see how she must feel, I know exactly what to say.

I move toward her. "I don't know who told you that you wouldn't be good at running your own business, but they were wrong." I make sure she looks at me before I go on. "The pressure you feel is you trying to live up to other people's expectations of you. *None* of that is important. Do you love making pottery?"

She sniffs. "Yes."

"Do you lose track of time when you're creating?"

"Yes. I do."

"And how did you feel when your phone was buzzing like crazy with comments from people wanting to buy your stuff?"

A pause. "Freakin' amazing."

I hold up both hands in a silent, *You see?*

"Nothing else matters. No other opinion matters. It's yours. Win or lose."

"It sounds easy. And it probably *is* easy for someone like you." Her eyes are locked onto mine. "You probably had people telling you your whole life that you were going to be a huge success."

I scoff. "Maddie, you really need to stop assuming things about me. It's astounding how little you actually know about me considering how long we've been friends."

She goes quiet. "I know. I was thinking that, too. You're kind of hard to know." Then, she glances up. "Or maybe I just haven't asked?"

I wish she would. I want to tell her all kinds of things.

She shakes her head, tensing up her body and then letting it go with a groan. "Ugh. . .why are you friends with me?"

"I honestly have no idea," I say, straight-faced.

She opens her mouth in feigned shock. "You jerk!"

The moment turns serious again, and I ask, "What are you so afraid of?"

"I heard you on the phone. There are websites and brands and a platform, not to mention taxes and shipping and permits and budgets. I don't know anything about any of that."

"And there are people out there to help with that stuff," I say.

"People I can't pay."

"People who would totally help you for free." I hold my arms out wide, indicating that I would be that person.

"And *that's* why I didn't tell you," she says. "I knew you'd try to fix it."

I hold my hands up in front of me. "Whoa. Hang on. I said I can *help*. That's what friends do. *You* have to make the pottery. *You* have to create the brand. But the tech stuff? Let me handle that."

"I need to do this myself, Simon."

"Why?"

She shakes her head but doesn't answer.

"Maddie, I get wanting to do something on your own. I do. Probably more than anyone else on the planet. But. . .if you want help, I'm offering."

Selfishly, I want to help because it will mean spending more time with her than just this trip.

She sighs and looks at me.

"I'll. . .think about it."

"That's all I ask."

She holds up her hand. "Can I have the keys now?"

"You've got to be the most stubborn person on the planet," I say as I fish the metal ring from my pocket. I press them into her palm, letting my fingers close around hers as I do.

"I think your pottery is amazing," I say. "And I don't have a single doubt in my mind that you can make this a huge success."

Her face softens. "Thanks, Simon."

I nod. "You're welcome. Now, don't crash my car."

Chapter Thirty-One

Maddie

Simon's words lift me up.

They always do.

I know he's the epitome of a nice guy, and he could just be trying to make me feel good about this crazy thing I've just done—but that's not how the conversation felt.

It felt like he believes in me.

Nobody besides Lauren has ever really done that before.

For the next few hours, my mind wanders. I don't dwell on all the doubts or the reasons to think I might fail. Instead, I wonder how to harness just a sliver of Simon's confidence in me.

What if my father was wrong?

What if I could turn this thing I'm so passionate about into a thriving business?

I let myself daydream, maybe for the first time ever, about how I could do that. I look over at Simon. His eyes are closed, and he's breathing deeply. I'm glad he's resting—and I know taking a shift driving isn't payback enough for everything he's done for me.

But it's a start.

I pull out my phone and talk into the Notes app, recording my ideas.

"Farmer's market every Saturday. Find out how to get a booth. Ask Will if he knows anyone that could build a booth. Check out Tootsie's to see if they'll carry my work. Order a stamp. Have the logo made. Every order will get a personal touch so when it arrives, it feels like a gift from a friend."

My mind races with possibilities, and I talk for a good forty-five minutes straight. Now that I have gotten the mental ball rolling, I can't stop seeing new ideas, plans, pictures. I haven't felt this energized in. . .maybe ever, and I fall into that zone where I lose track of time.

It's wonderful.

Is this work? On vacation? I'm starting to understand why Simon and Lauren like it. And maybe that's the key—finding something that doesn't actually feel like work.

Tonight, I'll list more pieces, and when I get back home, I'll pack up all of the orders and send them off to their new homes.

My art is going to be living in *other people's* houses. What a surreal thought. Not just people who know me, either—perfect strangers.

Beside me, Simon stirs and stretches. He sits up and pushes a hand through his hair. "I fell asleep."

"You did, like ten minutes after we got on the road," I say, eyes forward. "You slept hard. I knew you needed it."

He scrubs a hand down his face with a groan. "Yeah, I don't do well out of my routine."

"Shocker," I say. "You seem so spontaneous."

"Funny." He rolls his eyes. "How long was I out?"

"A couple of hours," I say. "Maybe three?"

"Three hours?" He sits up and looks out the window. "Where are we?"

"Um. . ." I glance over at my dark phone and realize I haven't been paying close attention to the GPS. "I'm not sure."

His forehead wrinkles in concern.

"I'm still on the route," I say. "Don't worry."

"But we're going off the route to that little town in New Mexico, remember?" He picks up his phone, clearly trying to get his bearings.

"I'm sure we're close. We've been driving forever."

The frown lines in his forehead deepen as he studies the map on his phone. "No, we're not close, Maddie. We're almost to Amarillo."

"Is that bad? Is that on the way?"

"We need to exit." He points toward the side of the road.

"Here?"

"Yes, get off here." His tone is clipped.

I do as I'm told. "I had the speaker on for the GPS," I say. "It didn't tell me to exit."

He picks up my phone. "I think you turned the volume down or something."

I had turned off the music to record my thoughts. Maybe when I did that, the phone disconnected?

Oh, no. This is bad. I can tell by the look on his face that I really messed up.

I bring the car to a stop at a gas station and turn off the engine. If Simon didn't think I was a total screw-up before, he definitely will now.

"I think you should call Lauren," he says. "Let her know we aren't going to make it tonight." He shows me the map. In the time he'd been sleeping, I'd blown right past my exit, which would've taken me into the mountains in New Mexico, to the little town Lauren had told me about a million times.

I know the story. I know how special El Muérdago, a town whose name means "mistletoe," is to my friends. They'll say the next part of their vows there with the mountains in the background, and I'm going to miss it.

I click my phone on, but quickly shut it off. "I don't know what to say."

"Just tell her we missed a turn?"

My laugh holds no amusement. "You are too nice, Simon. *We* didn't miss anything. This was all me."

A horrible, unwanted reminder that I have a knack for screwing things up. Hot tears burn my eyes, and I quickly look away. "I feel like such an idiot."

He reaches across the seat and sets his hand on mine. "Mistakes happen, Maddie."

My insides burn. I feel so stupid. It solidifies everything that I know people think of me.

"In my case," I admit, "lots and lots of mistakes."

He takes his hand off, and sits back. "Hey. We missed a turn, no big deal, okay? We'll find somewhere to stay tonight and catch up with Will and Lauren as soon as we can tomorrow."

"It is a big deal, Simon. We stay the night somewhere here, and the vows in El Muérdago will be over." I look away, talking with my hands. "I had one job on this trip. Be there for Lauren. And I didn't even get that right."

"Maddie—"

"You wanted to know why I didn't put my name on my pottery? This. This right here. I can't even get directions right, literally with a GPS talking to me. How am I supposed to run a whole business?"

He watches me for a second, and I can see that he's looking for a way to help.

That's what he does.

I'm starting to think, though, that no matter how hard you try, you can't change who you are.

Chapter Thirty-Two

Text exchange between Maddie and Lauren

MADDIE

I have bad news.

Simon let me drive and I missed our exit.

LAUREN

Oh no!

MADDIE

Oh yes.

LAUREN

Where are you?

MADDIE

Amarillo. <cringe face emoji>

LAUREN

As in Texas?

You're in the wrong state! LOL

MADDIE

I'm the worst.

LAUREN

No, it's fine! We can meet back up tomorrow!

MADDIE

I'm so sorry!! I guess I shouldn't be allowed to drive.

LAUREN

Maybe it's good. This will give you time alone with Simon.

<dancing woman emoji>

Are you sure you didn't do it on purpose?

MADDIE

STOP. IT.

LAUREN

You watch him when he's not looking.

MADDIE

I'm blocking you.

LAUREN

You do. But it's okay, he watches you too.

<heart eyes emoji>

MADDIE

He's a very good FRIEND.

LAUREN

You're so stubborn.

I'll have Will call Simon tomorrow and figure out the best way to meet up.

Have a fun night with YOUR FRIEND!

MADDIE

Thanks for being so cool about this.

I'm so sad to miss El Muérdago.

LAUREN

It's OK. I'll send a video!

xoxo

MADDIE

Love you!

Chapter Thirty-Three

Simon

I'm not mad.

I'm not sure what I am. We're at least two-and-a-half hours in the wrong direction, we're totally off schedule, *someone* has raided my snacks, I slept weird in the car, and I can't find a place to stay.

All of this would normally irritate me, almost to the point of walking away and figuring things out by myself.

But I'm not irritated. I'm not mad. I'm not even a little upset.

As I peek over at Maddie, I know why.

"Found one!" Maddie perks up from her phone. "It's perfect!"

I glance down at my own phone. All of the rooms at a nearby Holiday Inn are booked—apparently there's a big soccer tournament nearby, so it's the same with most places.

Maddie flips her phone around to reveal a series of photos of one of the strangest places I've ever seen.

"Okay, stay with me on this one. I know it's not *exactly* what you'd pick. . .but it's cute, right? Totally kitschy, and this

Alice in Wonderland courtyard is adorable." She scrolls through a few more photos. "It's a little cottage, out of the way, and how lucky are we that it's available for the night?"

Sometimes you find the most magical things when you ditch your plan and leave your route.

Lauren's words float back to me, calming my instinct to immediately find seventy-two things wrong with this place.

"Lucky."

She glances down at the phone in my hand. "Oh my gosh, you were going to put us up in a boring Holiday Inn? Where's the fun in that?"

I click the phone off. "It's booked anyway. I was trying to find somewhere comfortable. Thought we could both use a good night's sleep."

"Are you kidding? We're in a new place—we should go out!" She's back on her phone. "Want me to find another karaoke bar?"

I chuckle to myself.

"What?" She innocently looks at me, her eyes wide.

Her innocence is fake. I shake my head. "You're just dying to hear me sing again, aren't you?" I start the car.

"No!" She holds her phone close to her face, then side eyes me for a split second and adds, "*Maybe.*"

"It was a one-time thing."

She lets out an exasperated groan. "One-time thing? Are you kidding? We could probably stay somewhere for free if you'd sing to a group of fifty-five-year-old women."

I make a face.

"I mean," she continues, "you might have to do some immoral things, but. . ."

I turn and glare my best *stop-while-you're-ahead* face. "You're the worst."

"Really? Is that why you've been hanging around me for

ten years?" She does that thing with her face where she puts on a serious expression, but it's loaded with amusement.

"You better be nice or I'll return all three of the mugs I bought from your new shop."

"Wait." Her expression changes. "Three?" Her eyes go wide.

"Going to give them to new clients as part of my 'Welcome to LUNA' baskets."

"You are?"

I nod. "I want to make them special, you know, add a personal touch. Plus, most of my clients are small business owners. And they'll love to support another small business."

"Simon."

I can feel her staring at me.

"You didn't have to do that."

"I know," I say. "And I'm not treating you like some charity case. You know me, I would tell you if they were ugly."

She nods slightly. "Yeah, you actually would."

"I wanted to buy them. They're really cool. And I'm going to need a new piece for every new client I sign."

"That's going to be a lot of pieces," she says.

"Let's hope." I look at her with a chagrined smile. "Now, I'm about to ask you the most important question anyone has ever asked you."

She turns full in her seat, hands clasped on her lap. "Go for it."

I take a deep breath for added anticipation.

"Can you navigate or are you going to get us lost again?"

She hits me on the arm, mildly offended and laughing.

"Too soon!" she protests. "But very funny."

I hand over my credit card to pay for the room.

She looks at it. "I can write you a check for my half or. . .?"

"Just let me pay it," I say. "Don't make it a thing."

Her jaw goes slack like she has a comeback, but she snaps it shut, books the weird little cottage, then plugs the address into her phone.

It isn't until we arrive that either of us realize the cottage that claimed to sleep four is really more of a studio. From the door, I can see into every room except the bathroom—which is actually just a box on one side of the room, and the walls don't go all the way to the ceiling.

The place is, as Maddie said, *kitschy*, which to me just translates to *cheap* and *gaudy*. She's totally enamored with it, gawking at the interior and squealing at the framed pictures of gnomes.

All I can think is: *There's only one bed.*

"Isn't this place *great*?" Maddie drops her bag at the door and goes off to explore, which is really just walking around a 400-square-foot room.

I feel personally assaulted by the mismatched patterns and colors in the small space.

The floor is busy, with a diagonal pattern of various colored wood planks, and none of the furniture seems to go together. At the center of the kitchen is a bright turquoise island with a wood counter, and a small green table sits off to the side. That space flows into a living area with two floral sofas and an armchair.

Some drunk designer has taken an axe to *feng shui*.

"I can take the couch tonight," she says. "Remember, I can sleep anywhere, and we both know you're a little. . ." she gives me a once-over, "fussier."

I frown. "Fussier?"

"Yeah, like, more fastidious. It's fine." She says this nonchalantly, opening a door in the kitchen. "Ooh, I found the court-yard! Whoever painted these *Alice in Wonderland* scenes on the fence is incredible!"

I'm stuck on her words. "Fastidious?"

She turns and looks at me. "Yeah. Finicky. Everything in its place, you know? Don't pretend you don't know what a fussbudget you are."

I count out the words on my fingers. "Fussy. Fastidious. Finicky. *Fussbudget*? This is what you think of me? And where are you getting these words?"

She closes the door and steps back inside. "Simon. This is what everyone thinks of you."

I'm about to be offended when she smiles at me and adds, "It's part of your charm."

"Sure it is," I say with a groan.

She walks around the space, opening drawers, flipping through books, like a kid exploring Disneyland for the first time. Everything is an adventure.

And for me, nothing is.

She's not wrong about me. I like things the way I like them, which I'm guessing is the definition of all those F-words she just threw out at me.

She leans against the counter and pulls out her phone. "Let's go get dinner. I'm starving."

"Yeah, that happens when you skip lunch."

She ignores me, walking over to her bag and hitching it up on her shoulder. "I found a pub. Let me change, and we'll go."

I look down at my khaki shorts and plain black T-shirt. "Should I change?"

She shrugs. "Up to you. If you like the 'dad on vacation' look, you're more than welcome to wear that." She flashes me a smile and disappears behind the only door in the entire place.

"Wait. Dad on vacation?"

She doesn't respond.

"I know you can hear me in there. The walls don't go all the way to the ceiling."

There's a thump from inside the room, and I try not to imagine her changing in there.

"Yeah," she says, "should be fun when we have to go to the bathroom."

I didn't think of that.

When she emerges a few minutes later, her hair hangs in loose waves past her shoulders, and she's wearing a blue dress with thin straps.

And she is maddeningly beautiful.

She notices me looking, and gives a little runway spin. "Well?"

"You look. . .really. . ." I look away. "Uh. . .you look nice."

There's nothing on Will's list to combat this—the fact that she's gorgeous and I, apparently, look like a dad on vacation.

I finally dare to look her way, and when I do I find her smiling mouth-wide, chugging her shoulders with her palms up, waggling her eyebrows.

I laugh. She's nuts.

"Thanks," she says. "I was hoping for that kind of response."

And I wonder if she knows what seeing her like this does to me.

What it does is transport me right back to the first day I saw her. What it does is turn me into that gangly kid who could barely carry on a conversation. She's so far out of my league. She was then, and she is now.

"Should we go?" Maddie asks.

"Uh, yeah," I say, rubbing my hands awkwardly on my shorts, as if that would magically transform them into something else.

My phone buzzes in my pocket, and I immediately grab it and look.

She crosses the room, puts herself right in front of me, and places a hand on my phone. "No work. Not tonight."

At her nearness, I go silent. I'm not thinking about work. I'm thinking about the way the thin straps of her dress hug her collarbone.

"I know LUNA is important to you. *So* important. But if you don't take time for yourself once in a while, you're going to implode." A pause. "Explode?" She waves a hand with a quick shake of her head. "One of those two."

"I'm fine, I just—"

She cuts me off with an upheld hand. "I know you, maybe better than anyone, right?"

I love that I can answer yes to that question.

"Yes. You do."

"Every once in a while, you need a break." When she looks at me, I swear she can see a part of my soul that nobody else can. "And this is one of those times."

Change the way she sees me.

Change the way I see myself.

"Okay," I say, relenting. I don't want to be her uptight friend. I want to prove that I can let loose sometimes, too. Whatever she suggests tonight, I'll go along with it just to prove to her that I can.

"Great." She grins. "And before you say anything, no, I'm not anti-work or anything. I'm starting to understand how your job makes you feel."

I follow her outside, locking the door to the little cottage as I say, "Oh? How's that?"

She shrugs as I fall into step next to her. "I don't know —excited."

I give her a side-eye. "You know this because. . .?"

She bumps her shoulder with mine. "Because while I was missing our exit, I was daydreaming."

"About your business."

"It's not a business, Simon," she says. "It's just an Etsy shop."

"Maddie, people start businesses this way all the time."

"Really?" She stops on the opposite side of the car and looks at me over the roof.

"Really."

At that, her expression shifts, but I can't tell what she's thinking. The memory of Seattle, of my plan, of the steps I need to connect her heart with mine, reenters my mind and I'm struck with a fresh zing of nervousness.

I open the door and get in the car, wondering if tonight will be the night I come clean about the way I feel. The way I've felt for so many years.

She gets in, and I start the engine. The car fills with her familiar scent—citrus and sunshine. That's how I'd come to think of it. I inhale the fragrance as her GPS tells me to take a right. I take a left.

"You're going the wrong way."

"I have a surprise."

She turns to face me. "*You* have a surprise? You hate surprises!"

"I do," I say. "I hate them a lot." I look at her. "But you love them."

She smiles at me. "I *do* love them." She pulls on her seatbelt. "What is it?"

I laugh. "If I told you, it wouldn't be a surprise."

Her knee bounces. "But can you give me a hint?"

"Nope."

She leans in closer, the smell of oranges and grapefruit and sunshine and clean skin tingling my nose. "Si-mon," she sing-songs, putting a hand on my knee. Every muscle in my body tightens.

She touches me like this all the time. That's her way. She's like this with everyone. But tonight, for some reason, I let myself think this is different. That I'm different. That this maybe isn't platonic anymore.

"Forget it. Your charms won't work. I'm a steel trap," I say, hoping my voice is steadier than my nerves.

"I think you want to tell me."

My phone tells me to turn left again.

She inches closer. "Come on. . .! *Pleeeeeeease?*"

I glance over and find her face is dangerously close to mine, the phrase *just friends* shooting straight out of my mind and tumbling backward on the road in the rearview mirror.

"This is killing you, isn't it?" I ask. *I know it's killing me.*

"Yes!" She goes back to her side of the car.

I shudder a thankful laugh, now that I'm less electrified by her closeness. "Well, you're in luck because we're here."

"Already?" She looks out the window as I pull the car to a stop. "What is this place?"

"Cadillac Ranch," I say. "I thought you'd like it."

"How did you even know this was here?"

"Before we left California, I researched some of the different stops we could make on our route to Illinois," I say.

"Of course you did." She smiles, shaking her head and looking out the window.

"Thanks to your poor navigational skills. . ."

"Shut it."

I continue like I didn't hear her, ". . .we get to stop at one I hadn't planned on." I turn the engine off.

She turns to me. "Are you deviating from your pre-scheduled plan?"

"I'm. . ." I tilt my head back and forth, "adapting."

"That's so unlike you." She leans forward in her seat, hands on the dashboard, looking at the scene in front of us with the wonder I'd come to expect from her.

"It is." I cringe a bit, hoping that this is an opening. "But. . .I'm trying to change."

She looks quizzically at me. "You are? Why?"

Not the right time. . .

"Well, I mean, you said it yourself—fussy, finicky, particular. . .right?"

She softens a bit. "Simon, I didn't mean those in a mean way. I like that you have everything put together. It's exactly the opposite of me."

She's right. But maybe I can swing it positively? "Maybe we just fill in each other's holes."

She whips her head around at me, stifling a laugh.

"What?" I ask, taken aback. "What did I say?"

She bursts out laughing. "The fact that you don't know, Simon, is another thing I adore about you."

I have no idea what just happened.

She adores me?

"Well, I guess I'm trying to. . .take a page from your book. 'Loosen up.'"

She smiles at me. "*Finally.*"

"And I'm working on not being so cynical."

"Just cynical about romance, then, huh?" She chuckles.

I hold eye contact for about three seconds, then I have to look away. "Maybe not about romance either."

I feel—not see—her eyes go wide. "Maybe *not* about romance? Who even are you?"

Okay, that's about far enough.

I change the subject. "Do. . . you want to go look?"

She sits for a minute. "Let me sum it up here. You are working on loosening up—because of me—and you're changing your plans to take me somewhere that you thought I'd like, even though it might mess up your own plans."

I frown. "Yeah, that's about it."

She leans in and kisses my cheek. "It's exactly what I need. You're amazing!"

She does this so quickly it doesn't register until she opens the car door and jumps out. She shuts the door, and muffled, from outside, she exclaims, "This is amazing! Are you coming?!"

A kiss on the cheek should not have this effect on me, but I'm frozen in my seat.

It's like hearing your name called for winning an award you thought you were never in the running for, and you sit until they call it again.

She turns around and knocks on the window, comically motioning for me to get out. I draw in a deep breath, open the car door, and follow her. We walk around, and Maddie marvels at the row of Cadillacs nose-down in the dirt. The graffitied fins of the cars stick out of the ground, neatly (and oddly) balanced. She races around the strange phenomenon like a child seeing the ocean for the first time.

I stand back and watch her.

This is what Bea doesn't see. This is what Maddie's boyfriends never appreciate. Her unadulterated love for life, the sense of wonder that follows her everywhere she goes.

She never lets a moment go by without properly celebrating it or giving it the appropriate amount of attention.

She's the walking embodiment of stopping to smell roses, and I've been the definition of letting it all fly by me, barely looking up to notice.

Not anymore.

"This is *so cool!*" She reaches out and touches one of the cars. "Where did they come from?"

"It's an art installation," I tell her.

"What? No way! You know this from your research?" The wind blows through her hair, making her look like something out of a movie.

"Yeah, a group from San Francisco created it in this cow pasture. People add their own designs to the old cars as they pass through."

"Next time, we'll have to bring some spray paint." Then, she frowns. "What are you thinking about?"

How beautiful you look right now.

I stuff my hands in the pockets of my *dad on vacation* shorts. "I'm just trying to be in the moment."

At that, she mock-gasps. "*You!?* In the moment?"

I pull a wry smile. "I'm learning."

She crosses her hands over her chest. "Look at us. Me changing my view on work and you changing your view on life. Maybe we're rubbing off on each other."

"Yeah, we're quite the pair."

She takes a step toward me. "We are quite the pair."

I nod. *Is this it?* "I think so."

We stand like that, looking at each other. *Quite the pair.*

This might be the perfect moment? Should I. . .

The breeze messes up Maddie's hair, moving a long strand in front of her face. Instinctively, I reach over and tuck it behind her ear. At my touch, Maddie freezes, her eyes still focused on mine. My hand lingers at the back of her neck, sending quiet zaps of energy through my entire body.

She shifts, then brightens, pulling away. "Uh. . .let's take a selfie!"

I step back, feeling a little dazed. "Right."

She moves next to me, situating herself at my side. I look up at the phone poised in her outstretched hand.

She grins at the camera, then looks at me through the image on the screen. "Holy cow, you're smiling."

And *she* is the reason why.

A couple walks by, and the woman stops. "Do you want me to take one of the two of you?"

"Would you?" Maddie rushes toward her, handing over her phone. "That would be amazing."

She comes back to my side as the woman holds up her phone.

"You're still smiling, right?"

"I'm smiling," I say.

I turn to look at Maddie, not quite believing I'm here. And all it took was a nap and a wrong turn.

I put the jumble of thoughts out of my head, posing as the woman counts to three, then snaps a photo.

When she's done, the woman smiles at us. "I took a bunch! You two are such an adorable couple."

We look at each other.

"Oh, we're not—" I start.

"Thanks!" Maddie walks over and takes the phone from her. "He's a keeper."

At that, my skin flames.

Maddie looks down at the photos on her phone. "Oh my gosh, she's right, Simon. We *are* a cute couple." Then, she holds the phone out to show me one of the photos. Maddie, looking straight at the camera.

Me, looking straight at Maddie.

"Did I have something on my face?" she teases.

My mouth goes dry.

"Lauren's going to love it." She opens a new text message and sends the photo to Lauren.

"Can you, um, send it to me too?"

She looks up. "You're not getting sentimental on me, are you?"

Deadpan. "It's for my scrapbook."

She grins. "Very funny."

She sends the image to my phone, and I save it to my photos as Maddie lets out an "Awww."

She flips her phone around to show me a photo of Will and Lauren, standing in front of the mountains, facing each other.

"It looks perfect." Maddie stares at the photo for a few long seconds, and the smile fades from her face. "Simon. I really messed up. I can't believe I missed that."

"Hey. Stop beating yourself up," I say. "Lauren is fine. They're fine."

She closes the photo and nods. "I know."

But I know her. She's not going to stop feeling badly about this for a while. It's the kind of friend she is—fierce. She loves her people the same way she loves everything—with her whole heart. And even though she puts on a happy face, I know the thought that she let Lauren down is torture.

I wrap an arm around her. "It's okay."

She nestles in closer, and I press a kiss to the top of her head. It's a friendly gesture, but it makes me want more.

"I still feel so stupid," she says quietly. "Typical Maddie."

I inch back, forcing her gaze. "Typical Maddie?"

"Yeah, I mean, come on. It's me. Not exactly the poster child for responsibility over here."

I face her, both hands on her arms. "You know you don't have the monopoly on screw-ups, right? We all make mistakes."

She watches me, a hopeful look in her eyes. "You don't."

"Yeah, I do."

"I don't believe you," she says. "You're too smart to do stupid things."

I sigh. "I promise I'm not."

"Fine, tell me about the last time you screwed up."

I pull my hands away. "I. . .will. But not here." I look away for a brief moment, embarrassed. "Okay?"

She takes a step back, eyeing me. "More mystery, huh? Okay. I'm game. You already surprised me once. . .let's see if you can keep up the trend."

And then, as if on cue, her face lights into a bright smile as she races off toward the car. "Let's go eat!"

Chapter Thirty-Four

Simon

We arrive at the pub, which is definitely just a regular bar with regular bar food.

There's no karaoke, thank goodness. I'm not sure I would remember any of the words to even the most popular songs, the way the evening is going.

This new "go-with-the-flow" version of me is difficult. I'm trying to find enjoyment in a place like this, but it's loud. And crowded.

"This place is awesome!" Maddie leads me over to a high-top table against the back wall.

We sit, and she looks around, no trace of sadness anywhere on her pretty face. "It's awesome, right?"

"It'll grow on me," I say. "It's pretty noisy, isn't it? Do you like noisy bars that are full of strangers?"

She smiles. "I do, sometimes. It's fun!"

I shake my head. "I think you like the attention."

"What attention?" she asks. "I'm just sitting here."

"You didn't notice all the heads you turned on the way back here?"

She frowns. "No! You're crazy. No one did that."

I give her a look that says *I'm not buying it.* "Every guy in here is trying to figure out how to get your number."

She almost looks embarrassed. "That's not true."

I glance over to a couple of guys sitting at the bar. One of them hasn't taken his eyes off of Maddie since we walked in. "That guy, for instance—" I say with a nod—"is not admiring *me.*"

"Well, too bad for him," she says. "Because I'm here with you."

She's here with me. Maybe at the same table. . .but *with* me?

I shrug. "I don't think he cares," I say.

Maddie tosses a glance over to the bar, and the guy lifts his chin and his glass in her direction.

"Told ya," I say.

"Ugh. That's so rude," she says.

"Why? You and I are just friends." Not exactly the thing I was dying to say.

"But he doesn't know that." She glances toward the bar again, then back to me. The guy smacks his friend on the arm and then points in our direction. "You know what would totally put him off?"

"What?"

"If you were to lean over and kiss me. That'd prove the point."

"I'm sorry, what?" My heart sputters, and I look around, hoping someone in this bar knows CPR.

"I know, it's a totally crazy idea, but man, I hate it when guys do this. Gawking at a woman is *not* flattering. Like we don't know what they're thinking. . ."

I can feel the sweat on the back of my neck—and it's not because it's hot in here.

Is it suddenly hot in here?

"Yeah," I stammer, "that would be. . .totally crazy. But, I wouldn't want it to be like this."

She looks at me as if trying to figure something out.

"Like what?"

Uh oh.

I backpedal a bit. "Uh. . .I mean, if we, you know, kissed. . .I would want it to be. . .not like this." I'm failing and flailing.

"Wait. Did you think. . ." Her face opens up in realization. "Simon! Oh my goodness, I didn't mean. . ."

I try to brush it off, with a *no-big-deal* shrug of my shoulders. "Yeah, I didn't think you meant. . ."

"No! I only wanted to. . ." She vaguely gestures to the guy at the bar, who waves back, and starts to get up and make his way over to us.

"I get it, I get it. . ." I trail off.

She stops. "Simon. Did you. . .have you thought about. . .kissing me?"

I'm waist deep in this conversation, might as well sink a bit deeper. Here's hoping I don't drown.

I take a breath. This is it. I'm going to say what I've been wanting to say since I met her. That yes, I want to kiss her, and yes, that I've wanted to kiss her for nearly a decade. I want her to be mine. I want her to know me. I want every moment from this point on to be us. Together.

I lean in. She does the same.

"Maddie, I. . ."

"Hey, *darlin'*," the guy leans in toward her side of the table.

Maddie sits back and mutters, "Oh, lord," under her breath before begrudgingly saying, "Oh, hey! How's it, uh, goin'?"

"See my friend over there? He's embarrassed, but he wants your number." He inches closer to Maddie.

I can see she's hiding her disgust, trying to play it off,

though I'm not sure why she's concerned with niceties. My hand slowly closes into a fist.

"My number?"

"Yeah, he wants to know how to get ahold of me in the morning." He looks at her with a crooked smile.

Maddie looks at me, widens her eyes, and looks down.

"Do lines like that actually work?" I ask.

He looks at me, laughing. "Sometimes. But only," he leans toward Maddie, "with the *really* hot ones."

She straightens uncomfortably. "Okay, buddy. Thanks, but," she shrugs, "I'm not interested."

I shift in my seat as I rise up inside, shaking but feeling boldly protective. "Yeah," I say, "it's pretty clear you've had too much to drink, so why don't you just. . ."

The guy stands tall and faces me. "Sorry, man, I was talking to the pretty lady."

I stare at him—like watching a movie. It feels like this is happening to someone else, not to me.

"Maybe *you* should mind your own business. . ." He points a finger in my face.

"She *is* my business."

Now, he's leaning in to my side of the table. "Then we can settle this another way."

I've never been in this situation before—but for some reason I stop shaking and become ultra focused. I relax my hand from a balled-up fist and start to stand.

"Simon, don't. . ." Maddie pleads for a split second, but I hold up a hand to stop her mid-sentence.

There is no plan here. No step-by-step procedure. No spreadsheet. I'm moving on instinct, and all I think about is protecting Maddie.

I stand, and rise up a good four inches taller than this guy. I narrow my eyes and step forward, and he shrinks just a bit. I can see in his face he didn't think I was going to face him like this.

Heck, *I* didn't even know I was going to face him like this.

I take another step and he backs up, starting to raise his fists.

I walk right past him, around the table, pull Maddie up by her waist, tilt her back slightly, and kiss her.

I kiss her well.

I can feel her shock, through her lips, because the kiss is definitely one-sided for a moment—but then she softens, loosens, and wraps her arms around my neck and kisses me back.

I have dreamed of this moment for years, and all of those dreams pale in comparison to how this feels in this moment. I have no idea how I'm doing this, but it's happening, all the same.

I barely hear the whoops and hollers of "Get it!" and "Woo, go for it!" in the background. My whole world is washed over, and I'm drowning in the sweetness of her.

After what seems like half an hour, I pull back. Maddie's eyes are half-closed, glazed over and dreamy. I'm still holding her in my arms as the whole place erupts in cheers and applause.

"Is he gone yet?" I ask, hoping what I did worked.

Maddie's eyes change from half-closed dreamy to wide-open shock. She looks left, then right, eyes still wide, and I straighten her back upright to standing. The guy left, hopefully getting the clearest of pictures about whose girl she is.

She brushes her hands slowly on the front of her dress, offering half-smiles and nods to the people around her clapping the both of us on the back.

"S. . .Simon, maybe we should. . ."

"Yeah, I think we. . ."

A Cross-Country Wedding

We look at one another for a long moment, and I can't quite read her. Is it a look that she wants to do it again? Or that I've crossed over some unspoken line?

In the pandemonium of the bar, we silently grab our things and leave.

I'm desperately hoping that I didn't just ruin everything.

Chapter Thirty-Five

Maddie

Six years ago

What can I say, I'm good with coffee. And people.

When I moved to L.A., I immediately found a job co-managing a coffee shop, not unlike the one I'd worked at all through college. The job suits me—it's like I was built for changing people's moods from grumpy and sullen to energetic and happy. Plus, I'm content, even though a lot of my college friends, Lauren and Simon included, had found jobs in their respective fields.

My generic Communications degree qualifies me for a number of jobs, but nothing that interests me.

So, for now, I'm content to stay where I am.

I'm not one for huge life goals.

What I really want to do won't pay the bills anyway—a fact my father was quick to point out, repeatedly. And while he'd accused me of moving here to spite him, throwing his job offer back in his face, the truth was, I moved here because I wanted to. And because Lauren was moving here.

And Simon. To be honest, that makes this move a whole heck of a lot easier.

Now, I avoid my father's calls and texts because I can't stand having to justify my choices over and over again. I'm happy here.

And I know if I tell him what I really want to do, he'll remind me again of all the reasons it's a dumb idea. *"Art doesn't pay the bills."*

Apparently, neither does he anymore, a fact he made very clear when I turned down his job offer.

But it's better this way. I have something to prove, namely that I don't have to live my life *his* way.

I'm wiping down the counter when my eyes fall to the tumbler-turned-pen holder I'd made in my very first ceramics class. It's wonky and misshapen, but I love seeing it next to the register, half-full of coffee beans and pens.

I brought it with me when I moved. It's ugly, but I love it. Maybe because it's something that *I* did, that *I* created—or maybe it's more than that.

When I look at it now, it reminds me of the joy I felt creating it; and it's almost enough to banish my father's words.

When are you going to grow up, Madeline? When are you going to stop wasting everyone's time?

My leaning mug of Pisa retorts, *I don't have to. I'm fine where I am.*

There is a small fear that he might be right about all of it.

Someday, I think, *I'll figure it all out and then you'll see.*

I hope.

The bell above the door pulls me from the daydream. I look up to find Simon strolling through. "Oh, thank God you're here, I need a distrac—" but I snap my mouth shut when I realize he's not alone.

A petite brunette follows him inside. He flashes me a quick

smile, a little embarrassed, then leads her over to a quiet table in the corner.

Is Simon on a date?

Who is this woman?

And why do I feel weirdly possessive? I give her a quick once-over, understanding why Simon has always said no whenever I've tried to set him up with someone. I was picking girls who might make him laugh. Girls who were fun, because let's be real—Simon needs to have more fun.

Clearly, he's not in the market for laughter. The brunette wears a serious expression and an even more serious power suit. Together, she and Simon look like they could take over the world—or at least the five businesses leasing this building.

I busy myself behind the counter, feeling oddly drawn to the scene playing out in front of me. I clean the machines. I straighten the utensils. I load dishes into the sink. I straighten the utensils again.

And all the while, Simon seems to make easy conversation with the girl sitting across from him.

I watch as he casually reaches over and takes her hand—a move I'd coached him through just a few weeks ago. At the time, I had no idea Simon was actually looking to date someone.

After a few minutes, he stands up and walks over to the counter.

I flash him the biggest grin I can find, but it feels phony on my face. I lean toward him and hiss, "Simon Collier! You're on a date?"

Simon turns shy. "Don't make this into a thing."

"It *is* a thing." I lean in closer. "You *never* go on dates! Who is she? Where is she from? Where did you meet? Tell me everything!"

"Her name is Aspen." He tosses a glance over his shoulder.

"Aspen?" I repeat, thinking I heard him wrong. "Like the tree?"

"Like the city."

"Ah. Probably conceived there," I say.

"Maddie." He gives me a stern look.

"You never told me you were asking someone out," I say.

"I didn't ask her out," he says. "She asked me."

I widen my eyes on an exaggerated "Okaaaay! Go Simon!" I hold up a high-five hand and he hesitates, then fist bumps it.

He has never really gotten the hang of that.

His ears go red. "Please don't embarrass me."

I stick my hands on my hips and stare him down. "Fine. I won't. But only because I'm the best friend ever. But if I don't get a full report, we're going to have words."

"Noted."

"I mean it."

"I know."

"You're not going to tell me anything, are you?"

"Nope."

"Simon! I tell you about all my dates."

He groans. "I don't remember asking you to do that." He glances over at Aspen, who is now watching us from the table across the room. "I should get back. Bring us a vanilla latte and my usual, okay?"

I give him a mock New York accent. "Go get 'er, tigah."

He rolls his eyes, then makes his way back to the table, where he spends the next two hours seemingly engrossed in a girl named after a tree.

I spend the whole of that time trying not to be engrossed in the two of them. But I am. I can't help it. It's a different side of Simon—a side I never get to see.

I've always thought he'd make a great boyfriend for someone, but now that I'm witnessing him on a date, all I can think is. . .*Is she good enough for him?*

I'm fully staring when one of my co-workers, a college sophomore who calls herself Kismet (yes, for real), catches me staring at Simon and Tree Girl.

"Hey, stalker," she pokes at me.

I recoil a bit. "I'm not stalking!"

"What are you, jealous?"

I scoff. "No! Just. . .intrigued. Curious."

Kismet grabs a stack of cups. "Uh-huh."

I barely hear her. "He's so attentive. And like, chivalrous. He stood when she got up to go to the bathroom. And that look on his face—I think he really likes her. I've never seen him like this."

Kismet muses, "Yeah. You're not jealous at *all*."

I fold my arms, still watching them from behind the espresso machine. "I've just never seen him with a woman before."

"Maddie. Are you blind? That's how he is with you."

I shoot her a look. "What?! No, he's not," I say. "He's clearly on a date right now, totally into this girl. Simon and I are just friends."

"Yeah, okay." Kismet rolls her eyes. "You might've missed your chance, and I gotta say, that was a huge mistake."

What is she even talking about?

She walks away, and I glance back to his table just as he looks up. He smiles, and I lift my hand in a wave.

There. See? Perfectly normal.

Friends.

Right?

Chapter Thirty-Six

Maddie

Present day

My feet take me to the car and my hand pulls open the door and I feel my body get in and sit in the passenger side.

But my mind is buzzing and my hands are sweating and my lips are tingling and—*what in the world just happened?*

Simon gets in and closes the door.

The interior lights slowly dim until we're in the dark, lit only by the flashing neon of the pub sign.

It's quiet.

I can feel the awkwardness in here like a heavy backpack, mostly because I'm contributing fifty percent to it.

I turn and try to talk, but Simon does the same at the same time.

Me: "So, maybe we should. . ."

Him: "I'm really sorry about. . ."

We both stop, and surprisingly, we both laugh. It's an odd feeling, being comfortable and uncomfortable at the same time.

He says, "You first."

I pause. I go to speak, but I pause again. I try a third time.

"Simon?" I clear my throat, hoping the words coming out of my mouth make sense. "What. . .what was that?"

He sits, looking pensive.

"I don't exactly know," he half-whispers. "I've never been in that situation before. I. . .I just really wanted him to go away."

"And you thought kissing me was the way to do that?"

"Was it bad?"

No it was amazing, and soft, but firm, and I want to do it again and. . .

"That's not the point. I just. . .wasn't expecting. . ."

He cuts me off. "When you brought it up as something that might make that guy go away, I guess I took that literally."

Oh crap. I did. I said exactly that.

He goes on, "And I didn't have a plan, I just did what I thought you. . .wanted me to. . .do." He looks down.

I'm trying to wrap my head around it.

"So. . .you just did it to get rid of the guy? To avoid a fight?" I look at him. "Just for show?"

And for no other reason?

A pause, then Simon replies, "Yep. Just for show. He was drunk and super pushy, and I thought it would help. What a jerk, right?"

For a split second I thought I saw his face betray him, telling me he doesn't believe what he's saying—but then it goes back to normal, straight forward, black and white Simon face.

I relax a bit, but still can't push away how I felt with his lips on mine, my body pressed to his. It was exhilarating.

I'm so conflicted. He's a friend. I'm a mess. I can't ruin him, ruin our friendship.

"Yeah, he *was*! What a jerk!" I go along to get along.

He chuckles to himself. "And that pick-up line." He shakes his head.

I nod. "S*o* lame. I'd never fall for something so ridiculous."

A few half-hearted laughs, then a lull.

"Sorry for making you go out, Simon," I say. "I know it's not exactly your idea of fun."

He glances at me. "No, it's fine. It was—" he makes a face— "interesting."

I smile. "Yeah, that's one word for it."

"But look." He takes my hand. "Let's just maybe look at what happened as just, you know, me helping you out of an uncomfortable situation. Like, you know, if you came over after getting hurt by some random relationship. Like usual."

"Right. Of course." I try to ignore the fact that I want him to pull me into another kiss. "Like usual."

That was definitely not usual.

"So," he lets go of my hand. "What now?"

"What now?" I desperately need to take what just happened and put it in a box and pack it up for later. I do what I normally do and switch gears, push the difficult feelings away, and fill the space.

"We need a do-over on this night. A rewind. A fresh start." I'm starting to come off the high of that kiss, but I'm still not thinking *exactly* clearly. "Let's start by going back to the cottage. On the way we can grab pizza. Pajamas. Food. Relaxation."

He nods. "That sounds perfect." He looks at me as he turns the key to start the car.

"A do-over."

"Yep." And we'll figure out what just happened later.

Simon

Car. Cuppini's Pizza. Cottage.

Confusion.

"We'll make our own fun! Who needs to go out?" We're back at the cottage, and Maddie lifts the lid to the pizza box, deep dish, thick, cheesy and sauce-covered perfection, and inhales before setting it down on the table. "We'll have a pizza party."

Regret twists in my stomach. I think I messed up. I can't read her.

Even my own book is in a foreign language lately.

"Are we going to paint each other's nails too?" I ask, trying to figure out how to relax.

"I mean, if you *want* me to paint your nails, big guy, I can do that." She giggles.

She seems totally at ease now, as if what just happened an hour ago never happened.

I wish I could be like that sometimes.

She grabs a steaming slice, holding it with both hands and cramming the front third of it in her mouth.

"Are you afraid it's going to run away, or do you want a plate?" I ask.

She nods as the cheese stretches from the slice to her mouth. She pulls on it, only making it longer, and then with a mouthful, says, "Dhish ish mot gooingh wellph!"

I can't help but smile. She's such a nutcase.

Never mind that I can still taste her strawberry lip gloss.

I pull a plate down from a cabinet and hand it to her, and she tries to grab it and set the piece down at the same time—and promptly drops all of it on the floor.

"Oh no!! Mah pissha!!"

I sigh. This is a perfect metaphor of how I'm feeling about

this whole night. It seems like a great thing, exactly what you want, and then it all comes crashing down in a messy pile.

I'm appalled—but not surprised—when Maddie picks up the plate and the piece and continues eating it.

"Disgusting."

She smiles a cheesy grin. "You love it. Going to change into pajamas!"

She sets the plate down, but keeps the pizza, and races off into the bathroom where she'd left her bag. When she emerges two minutes later, she's wearing a pair of plaid shorts and a loose white T-shirt, and she has half a crust of pizza hanging out of her mouth. She pulls her hair up into a messy bun.

She looked amazing in her dress, but I prefer her like this. Natural. Relaxed. Comfortable. Unguarded.

Maddie.

"You okay?" she asks.

I realize I'm staring. Again.

"I mean. . .kind of an eventful night. Lots to process."

She pauses. "That is the elephant in the room, isn't it?"

"It is," I agree.

She changes the subject. "Did you get some pizza?" She grabs the box and brings it into the living room, where she throws it back open. She plops down on the floor on one side of the coffee table, then pulls out another piece of pizza, holding it out to me.

I sit on the opposite side of the table, only now realizing we hadn't turned on the overhead light—only the soft glow of a single lamp fills the space, making the whole scene feel a little too much like a date.

"So," she says.

"So," I say.

"What should we do now?"

My mind is assaulted by a thousand ideas, none of them appropriate, and I force myself not to entertain a single one. "I have no idea."

Chapter Thirty-Seven

Maddie

I'm good at boxing up unwanted feelings, but this is really putting me to the test.

Never mind that when I joked about him kissing me, I thought the whole situation would go very differently.

And never mind that I really, really want him to kiss me again. With slow motion and swelling music.

But this isn't a movie. And it isn't right. If I pursue this, any of it, Simon will become just another guy I dated. And I can see how that would play out. Of course, we'd both swear it wouldn't change our friendship, but we'd both be lying.

And I'll lose my best friend.

I try to start up a normal conversation. Change the vibe. Lighten the mood.

"Why'd you name your business LUNA?" I take a bite of pizza.

He laughs. "That's what you want to know?"

I shrug.

"Okay, I'll play along." He pulls out a bottle of water and unscrews the cap. "It's named after a cat."

I swallow. "A *what*?"

He nods. "It's true. When I was a kid, there was this stray cat named Luna that would come around our house sometimes."

"Did the cat tell you its name was Luna?" I smirk at him.

"I named her Luna, smart aleck."

I laugh. "Smart aleck. Classic insult." I take another bite. "But really, why name your whole business after a cat?" I'd rather talk about this cat than the elephant sitting between us.

He draws in a breath and lets it out. Then, seriously, he says, "Because Luna understood eleven-year-old me. That cat was sort of this. . .happy thing in my life at the time." He plays with the cap on his water bottle. "We looked out for each other, and I guess that meant a lot to me."

He's so sincere. I want to ask him more about his childhood—which he never talks about—but I don't press my luck.

"My turn," he says.

"We're taking turns now? What is this, Truth or Dare?"

I dare you to kiss me again.

I scold my brain.

"No, more like Truth or Truth."

This whole game is only going to raise more questions.

"Okay," I say, getting up on my knees. "I'm an open book. Shoot."

He seems to be contemplating his options as he quietly chews. "Do you like working at the coffee shop?"

I laugh.

"What?" he says. "It's as good as your LUNA question."

"Fair enough, fair enough." I look at him. "I like my job fine. It doesn't exactly pay the bills, but I like the people I work with, and the customers are mostly okay."

"Maddie."

"What?"

He looks at me. "It's Truth or *Truth*."

I make a face. I really thought I could skate through this impromptu game.

I set my slice down. Maybe it's the dim light of the room, or maybe it's the way he's looking at me, or maybe it's the way I feel right now—which is the way I *always* feel with Simon around.

Safe.

"I want more," I say, suddenly nervous saying it out loud. "I think I deserve more. I don't know what that is, if it's the pottery, or something else. . .but, yeah."

He smiles softly. "More."

I smile back. "More."

There's a moment that passes between us, and I *have* to lighten this mood.

"My turn!" I climb up onto one of the mismatched chairs, feet underneath me, like a thirteen-year-old at a slumber party. "Okay." I think for a moment. "Describe your first kiss."

His cheeks flush, and he tries—fails—to conceal a smile. "You're really going to make me relive this, aren't you?"

"Why, was it bad?"

"So bad." He groans. "Epically bad."

"Oh good!" I sit up straighter. "I want details."

He leans against the loveseat and smiles shyly. It's adorable.

"Her name was Arianna. She was my chemistry partner," Simon says.

"Chemistry? So, what, like tenth grade?"

"Eleventh." He groans.

"Eleventh?" I giggle.

"I was a late bloomer." He shakes his head, laughing at the admission. I would've expected it to make him less appealing somehow, but it only makes me like him more.

"I guess she had this big crush on me, but I had no clue."

"Your inability to see that kind of thing hasn't changed."

He frowns at me.

"Remember Kailey, that girl I worked with and that horrible crush she had on you? You were completely oblivious."

He shakes his head. "I don't know who that is."

I laugh. "You just proved my point."

He shrugs.

"Okay, on with your story."

"Okay, so one day, in class, we were doing a lab—I think it was trying to create certain smells by mixing certain chemicals. . ." He gets a far-off look, like he's trying to remember it.

"Those are not the details I care about," I say.

I can practically see him wipe the thought away and move on. "Well, she just went for it—planted one on me right there in the classroom."

"Whoa! Bold move, Arianna. In front of your teacher?"

"No, he'd stepped out," he says. "I think there were donuts in the teachers' lounge or something. . .?" Again with the far-off look in his eyes.

"The donuts don't matter." I laugh as I say this, then frown. "That doesn't sound so bad."

"Arianna wasn't very experienced either, and when she stuck her tongue in my mouth. . ."

"Okay, *ew*, that sounds so weird you saying that," I laugh.

"Right? It was sudden and wet and I was so caught off-guard, I backed into the lab table and knocked all of the beakers onto the floor."

"Oh no," I say on an exhale, picturing the scene he's describing.

"And the beakers were full of chemicals you aren't supposed to mix together."

"So, literal fireworks," I say with a laugh.

"More like a poisonous gas cloud. We had to evacuate the

school." He laughs behind a hand that covers his mouth—and it's the most genuine sound I've ever heard. I doubt he's ever told this story to anyone, and that realization makes me feel special.

"Our teacher gave us both a D on that project because of our 'obvious carelessness' and 'lack of self-control.'"

"Aw, *lame*. He should've pinned a medal on you both. It takes guts to make out in a chemistry lab." I smile. "But hey, at least it's memorable. My first kiss was behind the bleachers at an eighth-grade basketball game, and I don't even remember the boy's name." I take another bite of pizza, and talk while chewing. "Actually, that's not true. I think his name was John. Or Jack? Jackson?" I shake the thought away. "Anyway, your turn. I gave you my first kiss story for free."

"That seems a little unfair, but I'll roll with it." He thinks for a minute, then smiles. It looks like he's hatching some kind of plan.

"What is *that* look for? What are you concocting in that Simon brain of yours?"

"Show me a picture on your phone of your favorite piece of art that you've created."

Suddenly, I don't want to play anymore.

Why? Why am I so protective of this? It's Simon! He's my biggest fan! He's seen my work a million times. But never in this context. Always with me shooing him away, telling him it's *just a hobby*. Now that he knows it's more, I feel exposed.

"Um. . .maybe pick a different truth? I feel. . .weird talking about it."

He folds his arms and waits.

"This is a dumb game."

He shrugs, as if ten-year-old me just dropped my ice cream cone on the ground, and he's saying, "Oh well, should've been more careful."

"You're the one who wanted to play it," he says.

I pull out my phone, tap it to life, unlock it, and start scrolling.

As I scroll, I realize this is an impossible question.

I love them all. Each one. And I can remember creating each individual piece, even down to the feel of the clay between my fingers.

He holds out his hand and says, "Here. I'll make it easier. I'll pick the one *I* like the most."

After a few minutes of his scrolling, chuckling, and generally ignoring me, I hold my hand back out toward him. "There has to be a time limit on this."

"Sorry, I was distracted by this picture." He turns it around and there's me, in a full bee costume, complete with a yellow tutu and a dangly spring-mounted antennae headband.

"That is *not* pottery!"

"Was this for Halloween?"

I frown. "No, that was a night out with work friends."

"You wore that out? Like on a normal day?"

I grab my phone back. "Yes, I did, and I had a blast. It was fun. Have you ever heard of fun, Simon?"

"No, but this annoying girl I know won't shut up about it."

"Ha ha."

He pauses, then says, "For someone who didn't have a pottery business until today, you sure do have a lot of photos of your work."

He noticed.

"Those are nothing," I say.

He watches me for too many seconds.

"What? They're nothing." I try to ignore his stare. "And I already told you. An Etsy shop is not a business. And I don't even know if I'll keep it after this trip is over. It's an experiment."

"An experiment you won't put your name on," he says.

"Moving on," I groan.

He eyes me for a long moment, then gives in. "Last one. Make it good."

I latch onto his gaze. "I joked about kissing me tonight at the bar."

He matches my eyes. "I remember. I was there."

I press, "And you said something like, 'if we kissed you would want it to be not like this.'"

His face is steady. "Yes."

I get out of the chair and kneel back at the coffee table, closer to where Simon is sitting. I'm trying not to shake, like I've had a cold drink and I'm freezing from the inside.

"What did you mean by that?"

Simon's eyes flicker something unreadable. Something new. And I feel my heart turn over in my chest.

"Ask me something else," he says. "Please."

I shake my head. I'm holding my breath, but this is the question I want answered.

"Simon. What did you—"

"I wanted our first kiss to be different." He almost looks pained saying it.

A first kiss. *Our* first kiss.

I put two and two together.

"You've thought about this?"

"It's fine." He's suddenly defensive, embarrassed even. "It was just to save you from that guy, and it worked, and it's done. We're friends, really great friends, and. . .and I don't want. . ."

I finish his sentence. ". . .and you don't want to screw that up."

He looks at me. "Right."

I smile at him, choosing again to lock the elephant back

outside the room. "Oh, thank goodness. Simon, I don't either. You're too good of a friend."

He nods. "Yeah. And. . .you're a good friend, too." He sits back on the loveseat and runs a hand through his hair. "Wow, kind of dodged a bullet there, huh? We would be so wrong for one another."

"Yeah, totally," I half laugh, trying to decide if I fully believe him or not. "Hey, I have to go to the bathroom, can you. . .um. . .put on headphones, or. . ."

"Oh, yeah, for sure. I can step outside for a minute?"

"Thanks, I won't be long!"

He steps outside, and I walk into the changing stall masquerading as a bathroom.

I look in the mushroom-bordered mirror.

I don't believe what I'm saying. I don't want to say what I'm saying. I felt something in that kiss. Something I want to explore.

But I can't. I simply can't.

I like Simon too much as a friend to love him.

Simon

I step outside after completely ruining my chance to tell Maddie how I really feel.

I don't believe what I said. I didn't want to say what I was saying. I felt something in that kiss, something I want to explore.

But I can't—because she won't.

She likes me too much as a friend to love me.

Chapter Thirty-Eight

Maddie

Bathrooms with ceilings are underrated. You never realize what you have until it's gone.

I open the outside door to let Simon back in, and he seems to be back to his normal, predictable self.

"Everything. . .uh. . .come out okay? In there?" he asks awkwardly.

I muse, thankful for the change in emotion and mood. "Yes, Simon. My bowel movements are regular, thanks for your concern. I even lit the complimentary candle." Never mind that all I did in that bathroom was stare at myself in the mirror. It was a much-needed break from everything going on out here.

"Yeah, I didn't think you ate anything that smelled like pine," he says.

I laugh at that, and he joins in.

Whew. Maybe we're past it. Maybe we're okay. Friendship intact.

My eyes drift to the one bed and I think, *well, shoot.*

"We should probably get some sleep, huh?" I grab the pizza box.

"There's only one bed." Leave it to Simon to say the quiet thing out loud.

I wave him off. "I already said I'd take the couch." I point the pizza box to the loveseat, not looking forward to the pain I'll be in after folding myself in half to sleep on it. "And you can have the bed. You're driving, so you'll need a better night's sleep."

I want to prefer him. He prefers me all of the time.

"You sure? I don't mind, I can even sleep on the floor."

"Simon. You're not sleeping on the floor. The gnomes will carry you away in the middle of the night."

He makes a face.

"Maddie. Take the bed. And stop arguing with me."

And here I didn't think Simon was a take charge kind of guy.

I like Simon. Of course I do. Technically, I love him. He's one of my very best friends. But I've never thought of him as anything more than that.

But now?

Because I get dumped every three months? Because I'm alone? Because Lauren thinks we're perfect together?

I watch as he sets, and then opens, his small suitcase on the couch.

His clothes are all rolled up, perfect and neat.

I recoil. I know he deserves better than me. He deserves someone without a negative balance in her bank account. Someone with a life plan and goals and a real job.

Maybe not someone named Hannah or whatever that basketball girl's name was, but someone. . .who isn't me. Someone who won't screw it up the second it gets too real.

That thought stops me. I'm standing in the kitchen, holding the pizza box, and I freeze.

I don't like my relationships to get too real. How am I just now realizing this?

"You need a moment alone with the pizza, or. . .?"

I turn and see him standing there, looking nothing like a dad on vacation, and I can see the concern etched into his forehead.

For me.

Just like always.

"I'm good." I force a smile, glancing at the box. "We came to an understanding, the pizza and me." I set the box in the fridge, then turn and look at him.

Phrases like "not my type" and "just a friend" and "he deserves better" bounce around in my mind.

He pushes a hand through his messy hair and comes out looking a little more rumpled—and a little more attractive.

How did he do that?

I want to mess up his hair. At my sides, my fingers twitch. "I'm going to go to sleep now," I announce to the room for some reason.

He looks around, as if looking for other people—probably because I said what I just said so loudly.

"Okay—" I hear the confusion in his voice. "Um. . .good night?"

I give a definitive nod, but don't move. My legs aren't working.

I'm thinking about his lips. And his hands. And how nice it would feel to curl up next to him and let him hold me like we're not just friends.

The mind is an amazing thing. When you're screaming at it to not think of something, it casually puts up the biggest picture of that very thing on a mental IMAX screen. In 3D. And slow motion. With a John Williams score.

I want to entertain these new feelings I'm having.

And that's a very scary thought.

"'Night, then!"

I quick-step over to the bed, aware that I look ridiculous and awkward and weird. How am I going to sleep tonight?

You're not, my brain answers in Dolby surround sound. Here's a scene from Pride and Prejudice starring you and Simon in the lead roles. At that, I picture Simon walking across a misty field at dawn, eyes trained on me, and my pulse quickens.

For the love.

Then another thought hits me.

Why not just talk about it? Why not just have an actual grown-up conversation? Simon is safe. I could confess all of these thoughts, and we could sort through them, like adults. He's so reasonable he'd probably set me straight, and confirm what I've always known—we're not compatible. We don't go together. We're just too different.

I don't need a conversation to remind me of that. I know it all too well. I yank the covers back and slip underneath as Simon clicks off the light.

I then proceed to spend the next forty-five minutes staring at the ceiling.

In the living room, which is to say the bedroom/kitchen/living room, Simon is tossing and turning. I can hear him shifting every four minutes, trying to find a comfortable position.

This is dumb. I'm acting like a child. Simon is my best friend, and so what if I have a few stray *feelings*? I can set those aside long enough to be the bigger person and give up the bed. He *is* driving tomorrow.

I sit up in the dark. "You're not going to sleep well if you stay there."

"Sorry, did I wake you?"

"No, I haven't been asleep yet."

"Because of me?"

Yes, but not because you're tossing and turning. . .

I swing my legs over the edge of the bed. "I can take the couch."

"No, Maddie, I'm fine. I'll get settled, I promise."

A pause.

Then, "You aren't going to sleep if you stay out there, and then you're putting both of our lives in danger because I know you're not going to let me drive again."

"We'll end up in Canada if I do."

I stand, eyes adjusted to the darkness enough to where I can make out the shape of him. "I can sleep on the couch."

He shifts. "I'm not going to take the bed while you sleep on the couch. Call me old fashioned, but that's rude."

I'm going to prove to him, and myself, that nothing has changed. We're friends. Nothing more. I don't care if my stupid brain is on overdrive. This is dumb, and I'm being dumb.

Friends. Nothing more.

"Fine, then get in here with me." I blurt it out before I can stop my mouth.

Silence.

"I. . .uh. . .I'm fine, Maddie, I promise."

"Simon," I say, "we're friends. It's not a big deal. Plus, this bed is humungous, I won't even know you're here."

Oh yes you will! my brain announces, *and might I interest you in these quick clips from Shakespeare in Love and The Notebook and Titanic and Outlander and. . .*

SHUT UP! SHUT UP! SHUT UP!

"I can put a wall of pillows down the middle so we stay on our sides."

Silence in the darkness.

But then, he shifts, and I hear the padding of his feet across the hardwood floor.

"Promise me you're okay with this." I can practically hear the frown line on his forehead.

"I promise." I scoot over in the bed to make room for him. He's close enough now that I can see he's holding a pillow and looking rumpled and adorable.

I add, "This is necessary for both of us to get a good night's sleep."

"Yes. It's. . .necessary. Got it," he replies.

See? It's fine. We're fine.

Friends. That's it.

This isn't some trope-y rom-com where two people are forced into a small room with one bed and end up falling in love.

He lays down next to me, taking up as little space as possible.

There. Easy. No big deal.

"I just don't want you falling asleep at the wheel tomorrow," I say, trying to convince myself. "I have a wedding this weekend."

"So do I."

Perfectly platonic.

I close my eyes, allowing my brain to take over. This time, though, I do very little to stop it.

Do your worst, I think. *I've made my decision.*

And then, my mind takes me on a journey I wasn't exactly prepared for.

I think of the kiss in the bar.

I think of laughing with him over music preferences.

I think of how he bought my pottery.

I think of Cadillac Ranch and how he picked it because he thought it would be something I liked.

I think of his voice.

I think of his cooler of snacks and how he brought some of my favorites that I know he doesn't eat.

I think of him packing my suitcase.

I think of him having my coffee creamer in his fridge.

I think of the countless times I knocked on his door, and his face as he opened it to welcome me in.

I think of his first day on the job at the coffee shop.

I think of our blind date and how nervous he was to be there.

Then I think of how I feel around him. How he's my biggest fan, and it fills me up. How I can't stand to let a day go by without texting or calling him. About how he makes me laugh. About how he works hard to surprise me. How he cares about the details of me. He's welcoming and warm and thoughtful and stubborn and successful and focused and loyal and attractive and. . .

Oh my gosh.

It's him.

I think I'm in love with my best friend.

This revelation does the exact opposite of what I expect—it settles something deep within me, like cogs of a gear fitting into place, or an old couple finding their rhythm on a tandem bicycle.

After a few minutes, I feel Simon turn over on his side to face me. I tuck a hand under my cheek and open my eyes, hoping he can't see me well enough to know that I'm staring, my mind filling in the blanks when the darkness keeps me from making out his features.

I like his face. It's kind and familiar and so very *Simon*.

A peaceful thread continues to weave its way through me. I feel safe next to him. Calm. Secure.

Somehow, in this moment, I know that even if Simon and I

never become more than friends, he still might be the greatest love of my life.

Within minutes, Simon's breathing falls into a rhythmic pattern.

I move a little closer, as softly as I can.

He inhales as slowly as he exhales, the sound of it relaxing me.

Without thinking, I reach over and touch his forehead, moving his hair out of the way and letting my fingers glide lightly over his cheekbone.

At my touch, his breathing hitches, but I don't pull away.

His hand finds my elbow, then slides up my arm until it covers mine. His long fingers rest on my wrist bone, and his feet find mine under the covers.

I want to slide in closer, right in the crook of his body, to bring my breathing in time with his, like a metronome. I want to fall asleep wrapped in his arms.

"Good night, Mads." His whisper cuts through the darkness, pulling me back to reality.

"'Night, Simon."

I drift.

Maybe it's okay, just for tonight, in this one-room chalet with mismatched furniture, off the route and in the middle of nowhere, to let myself get a little lost.

Because tomorrow, we're back on the road again.

And now that I've finally found a direction, I have no idea where it will lead.

Chapter Thirty-Nine

Simon

Road trip—Day Three

C *offee.*
   The alarm.
   Maddie.

I open my eyes. *Maddie.*

I don't move. My arm is draped over her body, which is perfectly tucked next to mine. Our feet are intertwined. She's holding my hand. Her hair is splayed out over the pillow, and if I move just a little, I'll be close enough to inhale the citrusy scent of it.

I'm still groggy. Not fully awake. But I'm pretty sure I sleep better next to Maddie.

She breathes softly in my arms, and I wonder what it would be like to wake up with her like this every morning.

I should get up, run away from this compromising position.

I should—but I don't. Instead, I pull her closer, hold her tighter, inhale her deeper.

I imagine, just for a moment, that this is normal. And real.

Courtney Walsh

Entertaining this idea—getting my hopes up—it's not something I usually let myself do. I routinely take all romantic thoughts about me and Maddie and lock them away in the dusty room at the back of my mind.

But now that door has been unlocked and flung open. This is unexplored territory.

But this *is* what I want. I don't believe what I said yesterday for a second. I want her to know the truth before I make a final decision about Seattle. I want her to know by the end of this trip.

Beside me, she stirs. I freeze. I'm not even sure I'm breathing.

After a few seconds, Maddie's hand moves up my arm. Her touch sets off fireworks inside my body. I force myself to stay still. She presses herself into me, letting out a quiet hum that makes me wonder if she's still dreaming.

And then, she freezes.

Ah, so now *she's awake.*

Her body is locked up, and I prepare for her to bolt straight out of the bed.

The trouble is, I don't want her to. I want her to roll over, to wake up slowly, to look at me with sleepy eyes and tell me she had an amazing revelation where the two of us finally realized we're meant to be together.

But, reality is a cruel thing.

And today, it's back on the road again.

She slides slowly from my embrace, and I screw my eyes shut to preserve my dignity. She tiptoe races into the bathroom, and seconds later, the shower turns on.

I should've explained myself last night. When she asked what I meant when I fumbled my "Not like this. . ." I should've told her everything. It was the perfect opening, and I blew it.

Now, there's a risk that Maddie took that whole scene at

270

the bar as a rejection. Just a way to get that guy to leave her alone.

The thought makes my stomach roll. As if I could ever reject her.

I should just tell her.

And that thought makes my stomach roll again. I'm such a coward.

I get out of the bed and walk over to the coffee maker. I make a fresh pot, but quickly realize that while I can drink mine black, Maddie can't. And I need to busy myself, so I pull out a napkin, find a pen, and write her a note:

Went to get breakfast stuff. Back in a few.

—S <3

I write the heart without thinking. I decide to leave it. I'm on a deadline, after all.

I find the nearest market, go in for a few supplies, and when I return to the cottage, I find Maddie sitting on the couch, hair messy and damp.

She's glowing.

Is this what it would be like to come home to her every day?

"Hey," I say, forcing myself to act normal, even though I feel like someone rearranged my internal organs, leaving me dazed and confused. Nothing in my body wants to work properly.

She smiles brightly, just like always. "I'm ready to hit the road."

"Your hair is still wet." I close the door.

"I mean, I'm, you know, mentally ready. I do still need to make myself presentable."

"You look perfect," I say as I set the grocery bags on the counter. "I got some stuff for. . ."

I stop short because I notice the artwork above the bed for the first time.

271

It's three mischievous-looking gnomes, one who is pointing down at the bed with eyes wide, another doubled over in laughter, and the third with his hands over his mouth in frozen shame and horror.

I point. "Has that always been there?"

"Yep," she grins. "It even has a title."

I walk over to see a small brass plate grommeted to the woodsy frame.

"*We Won't Tell, We Promise,*" I read aloud.

"Classy, right? I already took a picture of it."

I hide a grin. Now the memory of waking up next to Maddie for the first time ever will be forever connected to three naughty gnomes.

"Sausage and eggs okay?" I pull out a small jug of her favorite caramel creamer. "And coffee, of course."

She smiles at me. An easy smile, not forced. Is she okay with last night?

We've disrupted the dynamic. But that's kind of what I wanted to do.

I tell myself this is a good thing. I don't want our friendship to stay like it is, but the fear that she'll run at the first sign of something real between us makes me want to hit the delete button.

She walks into the kitchen and pulls out two mugs, pouring coffee in both. She doctors hers with what has to be about half of the bottle of creamer and two heaping spoonfuls of sugar. When she finds me staring at her, she shrugs, self-aware.

"I love how you basically mask the taste of the coffee altogether." I find two small pans in a cupboard and set them on the stove, spraying them with cooking spray I'd discovered at the back of the pantry.

She sits down on one of the stools on the opposite side of the counter. "Sorry if I woke you. You. . .fell asleep pretty fast."

"Yeah, it was a good call to get me off that couch." This makes me think of the bed, which makes me think thoughts I have to quickly shut down.

She grins from behind the mug, and her eyes crinkle at the corners. "See? I knew you needed sleep. I'm smart."

I slide four slices of bread in the toaster. "I never thought otherwise."

I crack two eggs in one pan and spread the sausages in the other. They immediately start to sizzle against the heat.

The elephant is back, and I want to talk about it, but I don't.

Thankfully Maddie breaks the silence. "I still can't believe I missed El Muérdago," Maddie says, hugging knees up to her chest. "I know you said it's fine, and I know *she* said it's fine. . .but I messed up. And I *hate* messing up."

She reaches out, picks up her cup and holds it with both hands. "And you, Mr. Perfect," she makes a face at me, "you never mess up. Not like this. You would've been early to El Muérdago with pre-packaged gifts and a mariachi band you booked three weeks ago."

"Mariachi music is sorely underrated," I say. "Did you know that mariachi music was used by young men to express their love in a society where young people of opposite sexes were kept apart?"

"Oh my gosh, of *course* you know something like that," she laughs. "Don't tell me you are in some secret mariachi band and your name is Simón or something."

I laugh, keeping my eyes on the food cooking in front of me and say, "No, no secret mariachi band for me. And remember, I make plenty of mistakes."

She watches me.

I hesitate, then decide to open up. "I messed up at work."

"That's not really a mistake," she says. "I mess up at work

all the time."

"No, this was a big mess-up," I say.

The toast pops up, and Maddie moves around the island to take it out and butter it. Good. It will be easier to talk about this if she isn't looking at me.

I don't like failure. And I especially don't like admitting it.

This could change the way she sees me. Which was a napkin goal, but not like this. She's supposed to fall for me, not think I'm the town idiot.

Still, I don't want any more secrets between me and Maddie. The *I'm in love with you* one is killing me as it is.

"This was before I started LUNA. I was working for that big firm, remember?"

"Oh, I remember," she says. "It was a huge deal that you got a job there, I was so happy for you."

My spirit lifts another three feet when she says that. She'd shown up at my apartment with two gallons of ice cream, declaring she was there to celebrate. Took away some of the nervousness about starting the new job.

"Well, I was in charge of a pretty big client," I say. "I had to fight to take over the account, and it took a lot of time to convince my boss I was ready." I pour myself a small glass of orange juice. "But this client needed a lot of attention. A lot of hand-holding and reassurances. And as you know, human inter-action isn't my strong suit."

She moves back over to the seat at the counter and sits. "You don't say."

I look up, confused. "I just did."

She laughs. "You're such a dork."

I'm not sure why she's laughing.

Some of the *we woke up spooning* awkwardness leaves the room as the air between us relaxes.

"I started dodging the client's calls, mostly missing high

maintenance questions that would've driven anyone insane," I tell her. "But I also missed a very important one. His site had gone down on Black Friday, and he lost tens of thousands of dollars in revenue because of it." I swallow, still avoiding her eyes. "Because of me."

I slide the spatula under the eggs and then onto her plate.

"I'm sure there was an explanation—"

I cut her off with a look. "There wasn't. I screwed up. I lost my job."

She goes still. "You. . .what?"

"They fired me."

Saying it out loud taps into the helpless, fruitless, completely demoralizing feelings of that moment.

People can stereotypically say what they want about men and work, but nothing is worse than telling a guy, *"You're not good enough. Get out."*

"You think I started LUNA because it was my dream, because I wanted to be my own boss. Or because I'm some genius. But none of that is true. I started my business because I got fired. If I hadn't, I never would've had the guts to take that leap."

"Really?"

"Really," I say.

"Wow." She turns her coffee mug around in her hand.

The moment hangs between us.

"Yeah."

"Why didn't you say anything before?"

I shrug. "Work is everything to me, you know that. It was humiliating, and I was embarrassed. For a long time, I couldn't even say the word 'fired.'"

She levels a gaze at me. "You could have told me."

"Yeah, maybe I should've."

I finish making the breakfast and load the rest of the food

onto her plate and mine. Then, I put the pans in the sink and move around to sit beside her.

"Although, I seem to remember *you* starting a business," I say, "and you were sitting across the table from me and didn't say a word."

The trace of a smile flits across her face.

"I'm sorry, Simon," she says. "I'm sorry you went through that."

"It's for the best," I say. "But that's why LUNA is so important. I can't fail again."

"There's no way you will. I heard you on the phone yesterday. You were born to do this." Then, after a minute, she asks, "Why'd you decide to tell me now?"

I shrug. "It felt like the right time."

"I don't think any less of you, for the record," she says. "I think you losing that job was the best thing that could've happened to you."

I laugh to myself. "Really?"

"Absolutely," she says. "You wouldn't be here with me right now if you were still there. You never had any time off, and your boss really, really abused your loyalty."

I sit with that. I'd never considered that maybe getting fired was a good thing.

"Anyway," I say, "I just wanted you to know I *do* make mistakes."

She watches me for a moment, then nods. "Thanks, Simon."

"You're welcome, Maddie. And you should eat before it gets cold."

She stuffs the whole slice of toast in her mouth and chews with her mouth open.

It's disgusting.

And I love it.

Chapter Forty

Text Exchange between Maddie and Lauren

MADDIE

Help.

LAUREN

Uh-oh. What's wrong??

MADDIE

I did another bad thing.

LAUREN

Are you in Florida now?

MADDIE

No. We're still in Texas. . .packing up now.

And I'm so, so sorry I missed you in El Muérdago.

I still feel really bad.

LAUREN

It's totally okay. . .but it was amazing!

<bride emoji> <groom emoji> <heart eyes emoji>

MADDIE

<crying emoji>

LAUREN

Sorry. I'm a little wedding-obsessed.

MADDIE

You deserve to be.

LAUREN

What's the bad thing??

MADDIE

. . .

LAUREN

Uh-oh.

I can see the three dots.

That means you're thinking.

MADDIE

I don't even want to type it.

LAUREN

It can't be that bad.

MADDIE

It is that bad.

I think I like Simon.

LAUREN

<scratching chin emoji>

I don't see the problem.

MADDIE

LAUREN

He is all wrong for me.

LAUREN

Still waiting for a legit reason this is a bad idea.

MADDIE

I have a literal list in my Notes app.

LAUREN

You're going to sabotage this before it even happens, aren't you?

MADDIE

Probably.

LAUREN

You run away when you get too close. You're finally starting to see what the rest of us have known for a very long time. . .You and Simon are great together.

MADDIE

I can't lose him as a friend.

LAUREN

You won't.

MADDIE

I don't want to love Simon.

LAUREN

Maddie.

MADDIE

Yeah?

LAUREN

I think you already do.

Chapter Forty-One

Maddie

Two years ago

I'm standing in front of a familiar door.

I raise my hand to knock, and I stop, thinking of the past hour and a half.

Dylan's text came in in the middle of a shift.

DYLAN

> Hey, I've got something to talk to you about. Are you free tonight?

My first thought was "princess-cut diamond."

I texted back:

> Heck yes I'm free.

After our hugely successful Christmas together (despite his mother's under-her-breath comments about me being "a little immature") I felt like this is where we were headed.

I thought Dylan might be my person.

I showed up, giddy with excitement, only to have him figuratively drain my swimming pool while simultaneously popping my balloon and letting the wind out of my sails.

Pick a trite saying. It all sucked.

The *something* he wanted to talk about turned out to be a list of reasons he didn't see our relationship working.

Is there anything worse than feeling like a complete fool?

Dylan wanted someone more serious. Someone with *goals*.

Like someone who plays hide-and-seek in the aisles of Target doesn't have goals. Whatever.

That *someone*, for him, wasn't me.

And now I'm heartbroken. Again. Not because I'm *so in love* with Dylan or anything, but because I got all wrapped up in yet another guy.

This is getting old. Not old. . .just futile.

My dating life feels like it's the same soup, just reheated.

And so, here I stand in front of a familiar door.

Simon's.

And no matter what he's doing, he never seems to mind setting it aside to give me his undivided attention.

Nobody else in my life does that.

Instead of knocking out of the blue, I step down the hall a bit and pull out my phone to shoot him a text.

MADDIE

> Hey, Simon. I'm sorry to bug you, but can I come over? I really need to talk.

I tap send, and wait.

Two minutes. Three minutes. No response.

He's probably asleep already—I mean, it is 12:30 a.m., but I don't think he'll mind if I wake him up. We're due for a late-night ice cream binge anyway. It's been weeks.

I walk back down the hall to his door and knock. I wait for a few long seconds, but there's no answer.

"Simon! Hey, are you home? I'm so sorry it's late, can you talk?"

I hear movement inside the apartment, and then finally, he pulls the door open slightly.

He looks rumpled in his jeans and sweater and his hair is messy. "That's what you were sleeping in?"

He blocks the door. "I wasn't sleeping."

"You weren't?" I frown. "It's like, after midnight, what were you. . .?" My voice trails off as realization hits. "Are you on a date?" Then, quieter and a bit mortified, "Oh no. I'm so sorry. Is Hannah in there?"

A few months ago, Simon had started dating a woman named Hannah. I don't know much about her, but I do know she's been keeping Simon all to herself.

It must be getting serious if she was keeping him awake past midnight. His patterns and schedules and routines are hard to overcome.

"I'll leave. Oh my gosh, I'm sorry," I say. "I texted you but. . ." I look around, feeling trapped like a rat in a cage. Who did I think I was, barging in on him like this? Did I just expect him to be alone? To be there any time I came calling?

Oh, gosh. I did.

"I'm a horrible friend," I say, fighting back tears.

"What's going on, Mads?"

Something inside me breaks. I'd lost Dylan. Lauren has Will. And now, Simon has Hannah. I'm completely alone. Tears brim and spill down my cheeks, clouding my view of him. "I'm. . .so sorry I bothered you."

I start to back away, but he reaches out and gently takes my hand, holding me in place.

"No. It's fine. You're upset," he says. "What happened?" The kindness on his face shames me.

This is so unfair of me to even be here.

I lower my voice to a whisper. "I'll be okay," I tremble. "I don't want to interrupt your date."

"Maddie, you're more important." His voice is so earnest, so genuine, so *Simon*.

There's a soft *slam* from inside the apartment.

"I never would've come here if I'd known you had company."

He sighs, pushing a hand through his messy hair, responding with a pleading look. "You're upset. Let me help."

At that moment, the door swings open to reveal Hannah, an accusing expression on her face.

Simon backs away from me. "Hannah, hey, you remember Maddie."

"I'm so sorry. I was just going," I say, wiping my tear-stained cheek with the back of my hand.

"No," Hannah says, pertly. "*You* stay. *I'm* just going." She looks at Simon. "I guess you made your choice."

She shoves a bag into his chest, which he instinctively grabs, and she brushes past me.

"Hannah, wait." Simon's attempt to stop her is half-hearted at best, and, not surprisingly, it does nothing to stop her.

Her footsteps echo loudly on the wood floors of the hallway.

I look at Simon. "You should probably go after her."

He stares down the hallway and slowly shakes his head.

"Simon, go," I say. "This is not what I wanted. I did not mean to cause trouble in your relationship."

"It's probably for the best."

I stop.

"Why?"

He takes my hand, gently again, and pulls me inside the apartment, closing the door behind me. "Forget it, it's not important. Tell me what's going on."

"No," I say. "You tell me what's going on. What was she talking about?"

He runs a hand across the back of his neck on a slow exhale. He's still holding the bag she shoved at him, and he looks at it pathetically then tosses it on the entryway table.

"It's nothing. I mean, it's not *nothing*, it's that she wants a lot of my attention, and with work and everything, it's just. . .not really working. We've been arguing about it most of the night."

I tuck my hair behind my ears and pace. "This is my fault. I can go to her—tell her she'd be a total fool to let you get away."

He shakes his head. "Yeah, that might not be the best idea."

"Why?"

"She's convinced that you and I are. . ."

"What?"

He winces. "More than just friends."

"Me and you?" I scoff. "Is she nuts?"

He says, almost to himself, "I will try not to be offended by that."

"No, I just mean, we've been friends forever, and—" I pause, realizing. "Simon, I. . .wait, is this why you've been MIA?"

"I haven't been MIA."

"You have, actually," I say. "For like two-and-a-half months."

He moves to the couch and sits down. "Maybe. I guess. I was trying to prove I could give her more attention or whatever."

I sit down next to him. "So it is my fault. I just didn't know it."

"No, it's fine," he says. "I tried to make it work, but honestly, everything about it felt wrong."

"What do you mean?"

His smile is sad. "Turns out I don't want to be with someone if I have to give up our friendship."

"You know this isn't going to get better. Whoever we date, they aren't going to understand—" I flick a hand between us— "this. Or like it."

"I know." He leans back into the couch and stretches his arm behind me.

I shift, sinking my body into his, pressing my cheek into his chest.

"Now," he says, "tell me what happened and who I need to throttle for making you cry."

Chapter Forty-Two

Maddie

I think you already do.

Lauren's last text to me is still lit up on my screen.

I glance sideways at Simon, making sure he isn't seeing my text conversation—and he's not. He's tapping the steering wheel to the music, in a zone, driving this stretch to Oklahoma City.

I click out of messages and open my Notes app.

After my revelation about how I feel—which I'm still wrestling with—I feel I have to amend this list.

Or change it from a *con* list to a *pro* list.

I drag my finger and highlight the whole list. . .then hit delete.

I replace it with one sentence that's been on repeat in my mind since the cottage.

I think I'm in love with my best friend.

I stare at the words, rolling them over in my mind. They're truer than anything I just deleted off this list.

Shoot.

I set my phone on my lap and close my eyes. *What now?*

"You good?"

His voice startles my eyes open, and I quick flip my phone over on my lap. "Yep. All good."

"You're acting weird again," he says.

"I think it's pretty established that I *am* weird."

"Not this weird." Then, after a beat, he asks, "Did you check your sales today?"

"No, actually. I probably should, huh?" *I've been a little preoccupied trying not to imagine what it would be like to kiss you again.*

I open my email and discover eighteen sales have come in. "Whoa. That's a lot of sales."

He glances over. "I'm not surprised. Be ready for more."

I can't lie, the feeling is a mixture of surreal and exciting and scary. And Simon is in the front row, as usual, cheering me on, lifting me up, giving me hope.

Do I even have that many pieces? Wait. Did I put a cap on how many can be ordered? Do I have time to make more?

"Is tonight Oklahoma City?" I ask.

"Yep," he says. "Unless your GPS lands us in Pennsylvania or something."

"Har, har. And, I'll remind you that if it weren't for that little detour we never would've landed in. . ."

BED.

I cough. ". . .in a strange magical cottage."

"*Definitely* a memory I'll want to keep," he says with a more serious tone.

Me too.

He nods at my phone. "Ready to put your name on it yet?" he asks. "Bet your sales will triple."

"I don't even know if I can handle the ones coming in now." I click back and scroll through what are now pages of comments on the post.

"You'll get there. I know it."

There he goes, believing in me again.

"Hey, I found a small-town coffee shop with Wi-Fi and sandwiches," I say, anxious to get the focus *off* of me. "We can stop there for your meeting."

"Sounds good," he says.

Simon hasn't told me anything about his meeting today, but after his confession, I know there's pressure on him that I didn't understand before.

The admission shocked me. It seems that all of the sides of Simon that I thought I knew were doing a complete one-eighty.

Him opening up to me made me feel closer to him. It's like he knew I needed proof that I don't have to have everything figured out. That I can make mistakes and keep going.

There's comfort in that.

He parks the car, and we go inside.

"I can order us lunch if you want to go find a table," I tell him. "Get yourself all set up."

"Okay, my treat." He pulls out his wallet and hands me his credit card. There's a knowing look on his face as he nods it into my hand. "It's a business expense."

"No, I can—"

"Maddie. My treat." He says this more pointedly, with a kind of authority he doesn't usually employ.

Simon knows.

And here I thought I'd kept my secret so well hidden, but in the silence, something passes between us, and it's clear.

He knows that I'm broke.

I glance down at our hands, still pressed together. He pulls his away, leaving the card, then walks off toward a booth near the back of the little café.

Without me having to say a word, he still knows the truth.

Of course Simon knows. He's the smartest, most observant person I know; how did I think I'd hide this from him?

I place our lunch order, the heat of humiliation rising to my cheeks.

I wait by the counter for someone to bring us our food, trying not to overanalyze the fact that he'd figured this out. It's fine. Lots of people have money trouble. What's the big deal?

He's my best friend. I *should* confide in him.

More so now.

But I don't want him to know this about me.

I care *so much* about what Simon thinks, and not in a superficial way. He's the only one who's ever seen the potential in me, and I can't stand the thought that this could change that.

The girl behind the counter slides me a tray with our food on it. I pick it up and walk toward Simon.

When I reach him, I stand dumbly beside the table, looking at him.

He glances up at me.

"You know."

A frown.

"You know I'm broke."

His shoulders drop, and he looks down at his computer. "I made an educated guess."

I sit, eyes focused on the turkey, bacon, and cheese sandwich waiting to be eaten.

"How bad is it?" he asks.

I shrug. "It's bad. I'm probably going to have to find a new apartment. Or a second job. Or a sugar daddy." I try to laugh, but it sounds hollow in my own ears.

"I can help—"

"No." My eyes lock on his. "This is why I didn't tell you in the first place. It's my problem, Simon. Not yours."

"I have savings," he says.

"Absolutely not."

And the fact that you'd give it up without hesitation for me makes me love you a little bit more, if that were possible.

His gaze falls to the table—then he looks up, eyes a bit more intense. "Wait. Maybe there's another way I can help."

I shake my head. "I don't want you to feel like you have to fix it."

"And I don't want you to feel like you have to handle everything all on your own all the time." He reaches across the table and takes my hand. "You've been doing that for as long as I've known you, you know—pushing everyone away, keeping everyone at an arm's length."

"I don't keep you at an arm's length."

"Which is why I'm going to help," he says. "And why I think you're going to let me."

"I'm horribly stubborn."

"Yes." He pauses, as if thinking for a second, then says, "And you have horrible taste in men."

"Hey!"

He holds up his hands in a *just kidding* gesture. "I also think I know why you're setting yourself up for failure even before you try to succeed."

"What does that even—"

"Lauren told me about your dad."

I'm taken aback. He's focusing on me, eyes intent.

"Don't be mad at her. I asked. I know he doesn't approve of your choices, and you decided to do your own thing instead of taking the easy way."

"There's nothing easy about my father."

"But his money could've been," Simon says. "That was brave, Maddie."

"And look at what a bang-up job I'm doing," I scoff. "All I've done is prove him right."

"No," he says. "You started a business yesterday. A *business*. That's huge."

I bite the inside of my lip, choosing not to correct him this time. "But what if it fails? I mean, you said so yourself, failure isn't an option—but what if I can't make it work?"

He shrugs. "What if. . .?"

I sigh.

"If you fail, then you pivot," he says.

"Is that what you'll do?" I ask. "If you fail?"

"Yes," he says.

"It's so simple for you," I protest.

"It's not," he counters. "It's hard. And the work is hard. And dealing with people is hard. But at the end of the day, it's all yours. Pass or fail, win or lose. . ."

I jump in without thinking, "For better or worse?"

He squeezes my hand.

"Yes."

Forget my revelation about my feelings at the cottage with the three gnomes watching over us as we slept, forget how I'm feeling right now—Simon is proving once again just how *good* he is.

It's something I've always known—but took for granted.

Am I really willing to risk that? To risk adding him to my long list of romantic failures?

"And you're not going to fail either," he says. "No matter how proud and stubborn you are about the whole thing."

He opens his laptop. "I've been working on something. For a while, actually, and this trip gave me the last few pieces I needed to finish." He clicks a few keys, then spins the computer around to face me.

The *Flashdance* photo of me in my apartment, hair messy, mug of coffee in hand, fresh off of a session at my wheel, stares back at me.

At the top of the screen, in big, bold letters, are the words *Maddie Made,* and then underneath, in a smaller, scripty font, it says: *by Madeline Rogers.*

"Simon. . ." I frown.

"I have a confession to make," Simon says. "When I had your phone at the cottage, I sent all of your pottery photos to myself." He scrolls down to show how he'd set up an actual website to easily sell the pieces I've created.

"All you have to do is add pricing and details," he says. "But the bones are there."

"You built me a website?"

His ears turn red, and he looks away. "I'll make sure it's just how you want it before we make it live."

"Simon, when did you have time to do all this?"

"I've thought for a long time that you should be selling those pieces you make," he says. "So, I. . .may have. . .built the site, um, a while ago."

My heart is bursting.

"And then, when I saw you took the step to start your shop, I thought. . ." he trails off.

"Thought what?" I ask.

"Finally."

I burst out laughing, then look at his laptop. "Simon. You. . ." But I don't have the words. And it's clear that I don't deserve this. Or him.

He looks endearingly proud, like a kid who built an erupting volcano for fifth-grade science fair all by himself. "There were placeholder photos on it until yesterday."

I scroll through the homepage, in awe of his kindness. "I don't know what to say."

"Say you love it."

"Simon, I love it." *I love* you.

"Say you'll let me help. This is what I do, Maddie. I build

the frame and you make it come alive." He waits until I look up at him before adding, "And say you're ready to put your name on your work because you're one-of-a-kind."

I blink back fresh tears. "Nobody has ever done anything like this for me."

"I'm not trying to take over or butt in or fix it or anything," he says.

"No, no, I get that now," I say.

"I'm not trying to solve your problems. Just trying to help you solve them on your own."

"But not alone."

"Right." He smiles.

"What did I ever do to deserve you, Simon Collier?" I ask, meaning it with my whole heart.

He shrugs. "I have no idea. I really am too good for you."

I laugh. "You *are!*" And I believe it.

"No way, Mads. You're the best, and I love your work. I just wanted you to feel like you've got someone here, cheering you on."

"Thank you," I say. "I don't know how it's possible for me to love you more than I did before, but I do."

I said it.

At that, his eyes flash, and I know I should add "as a friend," but I don't. Because I'm not sure that's accurate anymore. Was Lauren right? And if she was, how had I been so blind that I'd missed it all this time?

I'd withheld a huge part of myself from Simon, but somehow, he still saw it. Maybe even before I saw it. He believes in me. And I just don't want to hold back anymore.

Maybe it's time to let Simon see the part of me that I keep hidden.

Finally.

Chapter Forty-Three

Maddie

I know we don't have long before his meeting starts, but I'm a shaken bottle of Diet Coke and there's a pack of Mentos hovering over the opening.

There are things I want to say, and I feel like I'll burst if I don't.

I want Simon to know me. Not just the surfacey, happy, fun-loving, laid-back version of me. And not the overly dramatic, emotional, *I can't believe I'm going to get old and have a thousand cats and die alone and miserable* side of me either.

The real me.

I'm not even sure I know who that is. But I know there are things about myself I don't usually share. Anything that matters, really.

"Lauren told you about my father, huh?"

He frowns softly. "Yeah. She did. I'm really sorry for asking about him, but. . .I was curious. And you never talk about him."

I laugh to myself. "I don't like to talk about things that make me upset."

Simon stops what he's doing and focuses on me.

I find his eyes. "I didn't take anything seriously unless it was fun, and my father didn't have the patience for it. He spoke my shortcomings into existence. Told me I'd never amount to anything. That I'd wasted all the money *he'd* spent on *my* college."

He listens.

I hate being this serious, and part of me wants to push it all aside. I have a hard time feeling like I'm burdening others with my problems, and the problems aren't that big of a deal anyway.

"So, I never really tried for anything. Had fun with everything. Which is stupid, because I was simultaneously trying to prove to everyone that I'm *not* a failure, that I'm an actual adult who can do actual adult things." I huff a breath. "I just didn't want to do them his way."

"I get that," he says.

I go on. "Work was all he cared about, really. His priorities were so out of whack—his whole life is about money and power and status. I suppose I rebelled against all of that."

"I'm sorry." I groan. "Blech, I don't mean to be a downer."

"Stop," he says. "Not with me, Mads. Never with me."

Translation: *You don't have to perform.* I hear the words he didn't say. "I know."

"I don't think you do," he says. "I think you've spent your whole life believing a lie. That you're not capable, or smart, or savvy, or talented." His laugh is soft. "You know me, I'm not one to make up stuff or say things I don't believe."

"I absolutely know that about you."

"Then believe me when I tell you that you're all of those things."

I'm not used to compliments like this. Sincere ones that have nothing to do with how fun I am. It feels weird, and I don't know how exactly to take it.

"You really believe that?" And if he says yes, can I keep myself from crying?

He reaches his hand out across the table, palm up. He uses his fingers to motion for me to slide mine into his, as if to say *It's safe here.*

I do, and when his fingers wrap around mine, something inside me goes still.

"Whatever message you've been getting all this time, it's the wrong one." He squeezes my hand. "You're more than enough."

I look down at our hands. *More than enough.*

"Secondly, I don't think that's what you have to do to be successful," he says, letting go and tapping a few keys on his laptop.

"But," I protest, "isn't that what you do? Push everything aside so you can focus on work?"

"Oh, for sure," he says. "I'm totally guilty of that."

Fundamental difference.

"But I want to change," he says. "You make me want to change."

Oh.

"You just have to take the first step," he says.

His phone buzzes on the table. He looks at it, then back at me.

"Get it," I say.

"I can postpone it," he says.

I shake my head. "I'm good. I promise."

Another buzz.

"Pick it up, Simon. Make magic."

He smiles at me, and I feel it all the way to my toes. I don't even try to make sense of it, and I don't pretend something isn't happening between us anymore.

I'm not exactly sure how to process it, but I do know it's there. And it's real. And I like it.

He slips into professional mode, and I pull out my phone. I navigate to my anonymous account and stare at all the images I'd posted. Not a single one gives me away.

I find the image Simon had used on my website, the one of me looking perfectly happy after creating a piece I was especially proud of. I move to the caption and start to type:

MEET THE ARTIST

I've been obsessed with pottery since my days at Berkeley when I was first introduced to the clay and the wheel. The process calms me, and at the same time, it energizes me. I never feel more myself than when I'm in my studio.

I look up at Simon and think, *Except when I'm with him.*

His eyes meet mine, and I smile. A real, honest, genuine smile.

I can't believe the perfect guy for me has been right here this whole time. And that terrifies me as much as it excites me.

He listens to his client, eyes still watching me.

I post my photo and smile, turning the phone around to face him. I mouth the words, *"OH MY GOSH. LOOK!"* completely overexaggerated. I start to shimmy my shoulders at him, as if to some unseen salsa music.

He tries not to laugh into his phone, and I'm not sure I've ever seen a better view than that smile.

Chapter Forty-Four

Simon

Six months ago

I'd been working at Smith and Beatty for five years, and only now just begun to prove that I could take the lead with clients, on my own and without oversight.

I have a tendency to hang around in the background, a fact I've always known on some level, but never confronted until Maddie pointed it out.

Of course, she wasn't talking about my work when she mentioned it—she was talking about my love life. Per usual.

She would bring it up every time she started dating someone new, and this current conversation is no different. She loves the beginning stages of a relationship, so of course she wants everyone to feel the same way she does.

Especially me.

"You're always on the sidelines," she says. "You've got to get yourself in the game."

"It's not a game I want to play," I say.

She shoots me a look like she knows better. "I know you don't want to end up alone."

She's right. I don't.

I want to end up with her.

"There's a new girl who just started at the coffee shop. Her name's Annika. She's gorgeous. You guys would be super cute together. Want me to set you up?"

I groan. "Absolutely not."

"What if she's the great love of your life?"

"She's not," I say.

"How do you know?" She stares at me, eyebrows raised.

I stew. I can't say "Because she's not you," now can I?

Still, the conversation wasn't for nothing because her advice was good—for my professional life. I find I *am* tired of always being on the sidelines. I want in the game.

Inspired, the following day, I walk into my boss's office and give my pitch. I should be the one to handle the McAvoy account. It's a big online retailer, and they need a complete rebrand. New website, logo, app design, brand, story, integration—the works.

I have a plan. I have a lot of plans, actually. I want to succeed, and I know this is how I can do it.

My boss goes for it, impressed by the thought I've put into it.

But McAvoy is harder than I anticipated. They want changes I think are unnecessary. They micromanage every decision I make. Constant phone calls, email, texts—about font color, photo placement, colors. It's never-ending.

I grow frustrated, because I think I know better than the client. I think I know what they need, instead of giving them what they want. Plus, it's a *lot* of talking. And meeting. And video calls.

It requires interpersonal skills that I lack.

Four weeks later, I'm asked to pack up my personal effects while being escorted from the building.

I bet on myself, and I lost.

And now, I'm sitting in my car while two security personnel are standing outside of it, making sure I exit the outdoor parking garage.

But I just sit. Let them wait.

In a daze, focus still deadened from what just happened, I look up to see nature's irony.

It's raining.

Fitting.

My phone vibrates.

MADDIE
I'm bored. Let's go out!

Normally my heart buzzes like my phone when seeing her name. Today, though, my feelings are thick and numb.

SIMON
I really don't feel like it tonight, Mads.

MADDIE
Why not? It'll be fun!

My shaking thumbs are hovering over my phone. I don't even know where to start or what to write. All I can manage is:

Simon

Bad day.

MADDIE
I'm sorry. Can I do anything?

Simon

No, I'll be okay.

I toss my phone in the passenger seat and hold my head in my hands.

There's a *tap tap tap* on my window, and it's one of the security personnel mouthing an *I'm sorry* and holding a thumb toward the exit.

An hour later, I'm sitting in my apartment, still feeling stunned after life just sucker punched me in the gut. I've never felt like this in my whole life.

There's a knock on my door. I ignore it. I don't want to see anyone right now.

More knocking. Then, "Simon?"

I close my eyes. *Of course.*

It's Maddie. And I know she's not going away.

I trudge over to the door and let her in without a word. She's wearing jean shorts and a frilly white sleeveless top that shows off her arms. Her wet and wild blond hair drips onto her shoulders.

Just by standing there, her light cracks a small sliver through my crusty, crestfallen mood.

I want to feel better, but I also don't want to feel better.

She's just inside the entryway, hopping from one foot to another, dripping a small puddle onto my floor.

"Hi," she says, shivering just a bit.

"Hi. You're dripping," I say.

"Duh," she says. "It's raining."

"Do you want a towel?"

She shakes her head. "I want you to come with me."

"Mads. I'm not good company right now." I frown and turn

away, stubbornly trying to resist the brightness of her personality.

"No. You aren't," she says, grabbing my hand. "But I will be."

Another piece of the darkness I feel cracks open and falls away.

"Can I get my umbrella?" I ask, but she gives my hand a tug.

"That would defeat the purpose."

I frown. "Maddie, what—"

"Will you just come on?" She faces me. "Don't you trust me?"

Maybe it's stupid, but I trust her more than just about anyone in the world. "I trust you," I say, quietly.

"Then come on!"

I'm barely able to grab my keys as she pulls me out the door and into the elevator. She's so close, just a shoulder away.

Same elevator, different moods.

Same planet, different worlds.

I know I need to move on. To accept, once and for all, that Maddie will only ever see me as a friend. But I'm not ready to do that yet. Not when she can change everything, simply by knocking on my door.

She smirks over at me.

"Can I at least get a hint?" I ask.

"You'll see," she says.

The elevator doors open, and we walk into the lobby. She takes my hand and pulls me into the vestibule, where we stop, looking through the glass doors as the rain pounds the sidewalk in front of my building.

"You should let me go get my umbrella," I say. "We don't want to spend the rest of the night soaking wet."

It hardly ever rains in L.A., evidenced by the confused people scurrying around to try and keep themselves dry.

Maddie grins, pushing open the door. "Don't we?" The sound of rain hitting the cement almost drowns out her laugh. Almost.

"*What* are you doing?"

She props the door open with her back and grabs my hand, tugging on it like she had upstairs. "Come on, Simon. . .live a little."

"You want me to go out in this?"

"No, I want you to *play* in it." Her grin widens, and she steps farther out into the downpour. "Haven't you ever played in the rain?"

She pulls my arm again. I'm still mostly covered, but the rain splashes on the concrete and up onto my pants.

Maddie drops my hand and moves out onto the sidewalk, and she's drenched in seconds.

"You're going to get sick," I call out, not sure she can even hear me over the sound of the deluge pounding on the cement.

She holds out her arms and spins in a circle, tossing her head back and letting the raindrops cover her face. She laughs again, the sound of it like a melody that drowns out every fear and feeling of failure that had gotten ahold of me that day.

The last bit of gloominess fades away, and I'm enraptured.

Maddie races over to a dip in the sidewalk, where a pool of water has collected. She takes off her shoes and jumps in the puddle, splashing water all over her bare legs. She's absolutely soaked, hair dripping wet and sticking to her face, and she's never looked more beautiful.

She looks up, joy radiating from somewhere deep inside of her, and when she motions for me to join her, I'm faced with a choice.

Stay dry or get soaked.

Be safe or take risks.

Miss out or jump in.

I take a breath and step out of the building and onto the sidewalk.

The rain is cold, shockingly so, but immediately I'm past the point of caring. The coldness doesn't matter. How I look doesn't matter.

I don't know how to play—it's not in my nature—so I mimic Maddie, who is more than happy to teach me. I stretch my hands out to the heavens, turn my face to the sky, and let the rain wash it all away. The stress. The worry. The feeling of failure.

I let it all go. And in its place, something new is born. An idea that, maybe, this is exactly what was supposed to happen all along.

Chapter Forty-Five

Maddie

I'm not fancy.

That's an understatement. I'd choose burgers and fries over filet mignon. Jeans over formal dresses. Sweats over swank.

Maybe this is part of my rebellion against my rich father? Probably need to dissect that, but I don't have time. I'm too busy gawking at the Grand Hotel in Oklahoma City.

We are a long way from the Days Inn.

"Are we sure this is the place?" I ask as we pull into a circle drive in front of the most expensive-looking hotel I've ever seen.

"This is the name and address they sent us," he says, craning his neck to look out the windshield at the palatial expanse, lit from the ground with soft flood lights.

"Sheesh. This is a huge hotel."

Simon gets a funny look on his face. "Or maybe it's a. . .*big bed and breakfast.*"

I see what he's doing. I'm not losing this time. "Huh. I would've pegged it for more of an immense inn."

"Not bad, not bad," he nods his approval. "But then again, it could just be a humongous hut."

I giggle as I repeat it. "Humongous hut." Then, without thinking, I blurt out, "Or a bulky brothel."

That gets him laughing. I shoot my hands up inside the car for the win.

I love that I can make him laugh.

"I guess they stayed here when they got a flat tire," I say. "Something about a Christmas ball they never got to go to."

Simon parks the car. "This is good. We could use a night of luxury."

"It's too much," I say.

I'd been so worried about paying for this place, but this morning, Lauren had texted to let me know she and Will were paying for our rooms tonight.

LAUREN
We all deserve a night of pampering.

Now, sitting in the parking lot, I pull my phone out and text her back:

MADDIE
This is too much!

You can't pay for this place!

I feel like I'm stealing!

LAUREN
Just stay out of the minibar <winking emoji>

As we grab our bags and head for the entrance of the hotel, Will and Lauren walk out to meet us—and I drop my bag and race over to her, throwing my arms around her in an apologetic hug.

"I'm so sorry I missed that exit," I say.

"Are you really though?" Lauren squeezes me, keeping her voice low. "Your texts didn't seem very sorry."

I pull back, confirming that Simon is, in fact, not within earshot (thank God Will is a talker.) "Lo, everything in the world is upside down. You need to stop me from making a giant mistake."

"Not a chance," Lauren says with a smile. "I think you're finally figuring things out."

"I should've known better than to count on you to talk me out of it," I groan.

"Why would I do that when I'm the one who's been trying to get you to see what everyone else has seen for months now?" She laughs as she says this. "Years, even."

I groan again, trying to punctuate my predicament.

"I don't think you should fight what you're feeling," she says.

I don't want to. But I know me. And I know Simon. It's great that I had some overnight revelation, but I never underestimate my ability to mess things up when it comes to guys.

"I. . .don't want to screw it all up," I whisper. "And that's what I do. All the time."

"I know you can talk yourself right out of this," she says. "But I think *that* would be the big screw-up. He's the best guy, Maddie. And you really do deserve the best."

"But am I the best for him?" I frown. "I think Simon deserves an amazing woman. Not someone who clearly doesn't have her life together."

Lauren takes a step back and studies me. "Funny, I thought you were a business owner now."

"You saw that?"

"Maddie, you started a shop! You did it!!" She leans in. "That is *not* something someone who doesn't have their life together does."

"Let's not get ahead of ourselves," I say. "It's an Instagram post and some pictures on Etsy."

"You're the one who *always* says we should celebrate the small things," she says.

She's got me there.

"Don't downplay your awesomeness," she says. "I'm so proud of you!"

Nerves bubble up inside of me. "Yeah?"

"Yes," Lauren says.

I look down, unsure how to take the compliment. I look back up, sheepishly. "You sound like Simon."

She laughs. "Well, then that tells me I'm right. If he's agreeing with me, then I'm also a genius."

I laugh. It's true. Both Lauren and Simon have been telling me to sell my pottery for years. I've been so convinced that other people wouldn't take me seriously—but now I understand that *I* didn't take me seriously.

Lauren holds up a key card. "I can't wait for you to see our room." She looks at Will. "You guys good?"

He smiles. "Never better."

"Okay, we'll see you down here in a few hours," Lauren says.

My eyes find Simon's. He picked up my backpack when I dropped it in the parking lot running over to Lauren.

I would've completely forgotten it.

I walk over to him and take it. "Thanks."

"'Course."

"I'm going to go make myself look beautiful," I say.

"You already are."

My hand tracing his cheek on his sleeping face floats back into my mind's eye, and I'm full of wanting to tell him about my revelation.

How do I do that?

I look away as Lauren loops her arm through mine.

"See you two in a little bit," she says, pulling me away.

Simon nods, a familiar shyness coming over him. "Can't wait," he calls after us.

Lauren leans in close as we walk into the hotel. "What was that?"

I look at her, face scrunched. "We have a lot to talk about."

Chapter Forty-Six

Maddie

We find our room and I drag my bag inside.

"This room is bigger than my apartment," I say.

Lauren laughs and tells me the story of the first time she and Will stayed in this hotel. It happened to be the night of a grand Christmas ball, but because Lauren was stubborn (her word), they never actually attended.

"So, tonight, you'll finally have your dance," I say.

She nods.

"And I get to tag along." I smile.

"I wouldn't have it any other way."

"Okay, but one question. There's no Christmas ball on the schedule tonight," I say. "Being summer and all."

Lauren pulls a beautiful black dress from the garment bag hanging in the closet. "We're suspending disbelief."

"When Will sees you in that dress, he's not going to know what hit him."

Lauren reaches into her bag and pulls out another dress. This one, bright red. "And when Simon sees you in *this*, we might have to have him resuscitated."

I gasp. "Lauren, that's gorgeous."

"I brought it for you."

"You did?"

She nods.

I'm overwhelmed in the moment. I'm not sure why my emotions are raw in this area, but acts of kindness touch my soul in a very specific way lately.

My bottom lip trembles.

"You're getting teary again, aren't you?" Lauren gives me wide, teasing eyes.

Several tears find their way down my cheek before I can wipe them away. "I just don't know what I did to deserve such a wonderful friend," I say. "Thank you. So, so much."

She makes an *aww* face and pulls me into a hug. "Hey. You deserve it. And you're going to look stunning."

I have such good, wonderful friends. I silently vow to be the same back to them.

"Don't get too sentimental," Lauren says. "I borrowed it from the costume department at the show."

I laugh. "Well, thank them for me."

We start the process of making ourselves look fancy, and I try not to think about how things are going to change after Lauren gets married.

I don't bring it up because I know she'll assure me that no matter what, we will always be close—but our lives will go down separate paths, and who knows if we can stay as close as we are now?

To avoid dwelling on this potentially depressing train of thought, I tell Lauren how Simon built me a website, how we played Truth or Truth, how he saved me from the guy in the bar, and how we fell asleep under the naughty gnomes.

I tell her when I discovered I have feelings for Simon, and then I tell her it was no big deal, and that it was nothing.

"It wasn't nothing!" Lauren grabs my arm. "We leave you two alone for one night and *this* is what happens? I feel like I'm watching an episode of Bridgerton with the long, lingering looks and the kissing and the spooning."

"Oh my *gosh*," I hit her side with the brush I'm holding. "You're imagining things. Heck, maybe *I'm* imagining things. This is Simon we're talking about. Me and Simon. It's never been like that between us." I open my mouth as I dab my mascara wand at my lower eyelashes.

"Your excuses aren't going to work anymore, Maddie," Lauren says. "If you don't do something about this, you're both going to. . ." she waves her hands around, looking for the right words, "spontaneously. . .erupt!"

I turn to her. "Okay, first, *ew*. And second, how am I supposed to tell him any of this? I mean, if I tell him I'm having. . .*feelings*, I could mess everything up."

"That's lame," she says. "You guys are adults. If you tell him you're having feelings, he'll probably tell you he's been having feelings too, and then we can all get on with our lives."

"And say we date for a while," I say. "You know my track record. Guys think I'm great for almost exactly three months."

She faces me. "I know you've never dated anyone as good and wonderful as Simon."

I look away. That's true.

"And," she continues, "you already know he's a great kisser."

I gasp and chuck a lipstick at her.

Then, after a beat, I say, "You're not wrong."

We both pause for a split second before laughing together.

Lauren does my hair, and I do her makeup, and when we're

all finished, we stand next to each other, looking into the mirror.

I set the memory in my mind so I can hold onto it forever. Only a few nights before everything changes, so I'm going to treasure every moment.

I carry this sentiment out into the hallway. We step inside the elevator, and I turn to Lauren. "I want you to know that you mean the world to me, and I'm so, so happy you found the love of your life. Will is a very lucky guy."

Lauren's eyes fill with tears, and she hugs me, sniffling.

"You're going to ruin your makeup," I say. "And I worked hard on that."

She pulls back and dabs under her eyes. "Okay, okay." She draws in a deep breath and waves both hands at her face. "Better?"

I nod. I can only assume she senses the change in the air too, and I think on the injustice that beginnings, even good ones, are accompanied by endings. Our friendship will change, whether we want it to or not. Time and life demand it to be so.

And maybe that's true of every relationship—even mine and Simon's. It's going to change, whether we want it to or not.

Which maybe makes my feelings a little less terrifying.

I feel a mix of emotions at that thought. Scared. Excited. Nervous. Changing my relationship with Simon could be the best idea in the world. Or the worst one.

Do I have the courage to try?

I catch my reflection in the shiny elevator doors.

Heck yeah, I do.

"Ready?" Lauren asks, thankfully interrupting my thoughts.

"Let's go knock your groom off his feet," I say with a smile.

The elevator dings, and the doors slide open.

"We're meeting Will in the bar," Lauren says. "Just like last time."

"The time you saw him sitting with some random woman and decided to get all stupid about it?" I tease.

Lauren shoots me a look. "Let's not relive it again."

We find the bar. It's a dimly lit space with only a handful of people, but even if it'd been crowded, my eyes would've zeroed in on Simon.

He and Will are standing by the long counter, each holding a drink. I am one hundred percent sure Simon's is a Diet Coke.

The thought makes me smile. I love that he doesn't drink. He never has. And he makes no apologies for it. I'm not sure why I love it, maybe because it's just so *Simon*, and I'm starting to appreciate almost every little quirk about him.

He's wearing a pair of gray dress pants with a blue button-down and a darker blue tie. The shirt is neatly tailored and fits him perfectly.

Which I notice.

"I bet he ironed that shirt in the hotel room," I say as we start walking toward them.

Simon looks up, and the expression on his face shifts. Even from a few yards away, I can see his eyebrows raise, and his body freeze.

"I hope the paramedics are close by," Lauren says. "Because Simon looks like he's about to pass out."

I might not be far behind.

"Told you he was hot," Lauren says.

I laugh because I'm nervous and if I don't, I might, as Lauren said, spontaneously. . .erupt.

We reach the bar, and Will takes his time admiring Lauren. "This is the woman I get to spend the rest of my life with."

Lauren's face flushes, and I try to focus. I dare a glance at

Simon and find he hasn't stopped staring at me. I also find I don't mind that one little bit.

Lauren takes Will's hands. "I think I'm the lucky one."

"You look beautiful," Will says. "Worth the two-year wait."

I step away, giving Will and Lauren a moment of mushy private time. I walk around to the other side of Simon. "Hey."

He shakes his head, a smile slowly forming on his lips. He tries to say something, then stops. He starts again, and shakes his head.

"I got ya speechless," I say, turning a coy shoulder at him.

He finally gets out, "You have no idea how beautiful you are, do you?"

"No, I don't." I smile back. "Why don't you tell me?"

His smile holds.

He's never been one to comment on my looks. Never said anything to indicate he sees me as anything more than what I am—his friend. So, this is uncharted territory between us. Even though I know him so well, there is still so much to discover.

"I don't know what to say," he says. "Words are failing me."

I look away, feeling shy for maybe the first time because of Simon. "Well, *sir. . .*" I put a hand up on his arm, and slide it down to his elbow, giving it a shake, "you aren't so bad yourself."

This is an understatement. Once I let myself see it, I can't un-see it. Simon Collier is a beautiful human.

With a big, kind, wonderful heart.

"We're going into the ballroom," Lauren says, interrupting my thoughts. "Will apparently has a surprise."

Simon looks at me, and after a pause, offers me his arm.

I take it with both of my hands.

As we walk through the bar, I notice that I like to be near him. I like the way it makes me feel.

I don't like that I'm not sure what to do with those feelings, but part of me just wants to stop thinking about it, to let whatever happens, happen.

Maybe we don't need a big, intense conversation. Maybe it will all work out. Maybe he's feeling the same way I am, and like Lauren said, we can all get on with our lives.

Or maybe this is all wedding magic casting a spell on me too.

We walk through a door and into a ballroom, decked out in Christmas decorations.

"What in the world. . .?" Lauren says on an exhale. "How did you. . .?"

"I called ahead and sweet-talked one of the managers," Will says. "I told her our story, and it turns out, she's a budding romance novelist."

I turn to Will. "Shut *up*. You're kidding!"

"Nope. Said I gave her a great idea for her next book."

"They decorated the ballroom? For us?" Lauren asks.

"For you," he says.

Lauren squeals and hugs Will. "This is incredible."

At the center of the sectioned-off space is a tall Christmas tree, decorated with giant red and silver ornaments. Thick, glittery ribbon had been wound from the top of the tree to the bottom, and white twinkling lights make the whole thing look like magic.

Soft Christmas music plays in the background—Bing Crosby singing about being home for Christmas. And while it might be sunny and warm outside, in here, it's as cozy as a cold day in December.

I glance at Simon. He's standing off to the side, looking around the space. His hands are stuffed in his pockets, and there's an expression of wonder on his face.

"Worried the gnomes are watching?" I say.

He chuckles and looks at me. Then, more serious as he

looks back at the décor. "I was just thinking how special this whole experience is. And I'm glad you asked me to come along."

"Yeah?"

"It's made me realize something." He looks away. "I want what they have."

I widen my eyes and tease, "Oh? Is Mr. Cynic coming around to the whole icky idea of romance?"

He turns to face me, and without even a second of hesitation he says, "Yes."

I go still, looking into his eyes. They're intense and soft and beautiful. "I. . .think we all want this, Simon."

He shakes his head. "I honestly didn't think this kind of love existed."

In a moment of either vulnerability or boldness, I reach down and take his hand. I've done it before, but with the way I think about him now, his hand feels different in mine.

"It does."

He looks down at our hands, then at me. "But you fall in love every other week," he says.

I nod toward Will and Lauren. "Not like that."

Not like this.

He clears his throat, then frowns, as if he's about to say something important. I feel my muscles tighten in anticipation.

"Maddie, I—"

"If you guys are up for it, we're going to say our vows," Lauren cuts in.

I take a step away from Simon and let go of the breath in a hot stream. "Of course."

He nods dutifully, and we move over to where Will and Lauren stand, facing each other just like they'd done on each stop of this trip.

As they speak, I try to listen, but my thoughts wander.

What would Simon have said if Lauren hadn't interrupted?

Would he have spoken my thoughts aloud? Should I speak them aloud? What am I waiting for?

After the vows, there isn't another moment to even consider opening up.

We're treated to a big, festive Christmas dinner, and I try to focus on the *whole* conversation and not just the unspoken one going on between Simon and me.

Once we finish the meal, Lauren and Will stand and move to the dance floor, leaving Simon and me sitting at the table alone.

"Do you want to dance?" he asks.

"You hate dancing," I say.

He stands. "I'll make an exception." He reaches a hand toward me, and I look at it, then at him.

This is a snapshot of who Simon is and what he does for me every single day. He always puts aside his preferences for mine. Always.

"Are you sure?" I ask.

He nods. "But I'm not doing the Macarena or anything."

I laugh as I slip my hand into his. He leads me with strong confidence onto the dance floor, then takes me in his arms with surprising firmness. His one hand is at my waist, and when he pulls my body to his, my breath catches in my throat.

This is a different side of Simon than the one I've seen before. The one I've grown so used to. The one I've taken for granted.

There are so many layers to this man, and I want to peel them all back until I've memorized them all.

We sway softly to the music, and I force myself not to shy away from the thoughts racing through my mind. I look up into his eyes and wonder. . .has he always looked at me like this?

Like I'm special?

It's a silly thought, but one I can't stop thinking.

Maybe now is the perfect time. Maybe I should just blurt out how I'm feeling, how I don't know how it will all work out, but I just want to let him know that he's amazing and beautiful and perfect for me.

I don't want to run anymore. I don't want surface relationships that mean nothing. I want the real thing. What Will and Lauren have.

And I want it with Simon.

Before I can start, he gently leans away from me. "Hey, do you want to go for a walk?" he asks. "I know you love exploring."

"I *do* love exploring," I say, grinning. "Can I change my shoes? They're in my room."

"Of course," he says. "I'll meet you outside in ten minutes?"

This is it. Ten minutes to prepare what I'm going to say.

Ten more minutes before everything changes.

Chapter Forty-Seven

Maddie

I hop into the elevator after changing from heels to a pair of tennis shoes, owning my new look like a teenager at the homecoming dance.

In the quiet of the enclosed space, I pull out my phone. I haven't even checked it in favor of being in the moment for the Christmas ball do-over.

It's only been hours since I claimed the anonymous pottery account as my own, but as I unlock my phone, I discover that I've made more sales.

I scroll.

I scroll some more.

I swallow.

Lots of sales.

If these numbers are right, I won't have any problem paying for the rest of this trip. Or my rent.

But that realization is secondary to the realization that Simon was right.

The sales have tripled in twenty-four hours because I put my name on it.

Why had I waited so long? Why had I let my fear get in the way?

The meaning behind the question shifts, and I start to wonder if I'll have the same sentiment after this conversation with Simon. . .

The elevator doors open, and I see him standing outside, wearing the heck out of that suit. I can hardly wait to tell him about my sales. My feelings. *I can hardly wait to tell him everything.*

But as I approach, I notice he's on the phone. And he's pacing. I don't have to hear either side of the conversation to know that something is wrong.

I push through the doors and come up alongside him.

"I'm out of town, sir, but I can certainly have that for you in just a couple days." A pause. "No, I understand you're looking for someone motivated, sir, and I can assure you I am." Another pause. "By tomorrow?" He sighs.

I see the stress on his face. I've seen this look many times before, but knowing what I know now, all the reasons this business is important, I feel my body take on his stress as my own.

If he were home right now, he'd pull an all-nighter to deliver whatever he had to.

But he's not home. He's here.

Because of me.

Crap.

I can't be the reason he fails.

I put a hand on his arm. I have no idea what it will take to accomplish whatever the person on the other end of this phone call is asking of him, but I know we have to try. And if I can only help by going on coffee runs and driving the car tomorrow, I'll do it.

He needs to know he's not alone in this.

"Tell him you'll do it," I whisper.

"One moment, sir," Simon says, then mutes the phone. "Maddie, there's no way."

"Is there really no way?" I squeeze his arm and level his gaze. "Because I think you can do anything."

The weight of those words hangs in the space between us. He's been my cheerleader so many times, and now it's time for me to return the favor. I can tell, when his eyes search mine, that he wants to believe me.

"It's after nine," he says. "And we're back on the road in the morning."

"This is when creativity wakes up," I say. "I'll help. Come on—we can do this!"

He ponders, unsure.

"Simon, how many times have you stayed up with me? How many times have you saved me, helped me, built me back up when I needed you most?" I swell up with sudden emotion. "How many times was my heart broken only to be put back together? By *you*? You always answer when I knock. You're always there for me, *always*." I start hitting him on the arm with every word, "Let. Me. Return. The. Favor!"

"Ow, ow! Fine! Geez," he starts laughing, then shakes his head. "This is crazy."

I raise my eyebrows and grin. "Tell him yes."

He hesitates another moment, then unmutes the phone. "Sir, are you still there?" A pause. "Yes, I'll have it for you by tomorrow."

He ends the call, then turns toward me, the worry line in his forehead even deeper than before.

I throw a fist in the air. "Let's do this!"

"This is nuts," he says, slipping the phone into his pocket. "It's at least twelve hours of work, Mads. I'm going to be up all night."

"We," I say. "*We* are going to be up all night." I pause. "And we're going to need coffee."

He reaches out and puts a hand on my cheek, stopping my heart like my life line had been severed. "You're amazing, you know that?"

I want to kiss him. I want to tell him all of my thoughts, even the iMax ones that are a little bit naughty. Instead, I simply whisper, "Thank you." Because as much as I want to correct him, for some unknown reason, Simon actually believes it.

He thinks I'm amazing.

And that makes me feel like maybe, just maybe, I really am.

Simon

I stare at the screen of my laptop.

This is insane.

Even in the best of circumstances, creating this website in one evening would be nearly impossible. And being on the road, out of my comfort zone—well, it isn't the best of circumstances.

Somehow, Maddie had convinced me I'm invincible. And with her, maybe I am. Because I was ready to tell this potential client—JB Manning—no, there's no way to deliver what he's asking.

But then Maddie punched me. And I saw the light. She makes me feel like I can do anything.

We're in the sitting area of Maddie and Lauren's hotel suite, and I'm saying a silent prayer of thanks that the bedroom is hidden behind a door. No way I'd be able to concentrate on work with images of waking up with Maddie in my arms still rolling through my mind.

The afterimage of her body, collapsed into mine, had kept me company all day long—and it was good company.

And then she took my hand, and it was the perfect time to tell her everything I was feeling. . .until Lauren interrupted us.

Downstairs, after I hung up the phone, I thought about kissing her again, right there, standing in the dim light of the hotel awning.

And it's odd, but I feel like there's been a shift with her, too. She's. . .more open, maybe a bit more serious? Her touches don't feel like friend touches anymore.

Doesn't matter. Right now, I can't analyze it. I have to focus.

"Okay, put me to work," Maddie says.

"Promise not to hit me anymore," I weakly joke, "that's a good start."

"Can't make any promises," she says, pretending to roll up imaginary sleeves. Then, affecting the gravelly voice of the old coach from *Rocky*, she closes one eye, points a crooked finger at me and rasps, "*Get up, Rock! Ya gonna eat lightning, and ya gonna crap thundah!*"

"Will you get out of my face?" I can't help but laugh, it's just so ridiculous. And immediately, I'm more relaxed. I feel more creative. Her personality just might be the catalyst I need to get this huge project done.

She sits on the couch, feet underneath her, full of energy. "Do you already have a concept for the design?"

JB Manning is a wealthy man with a new start-up. His regular web design firm isn't meeting his needs, and I know that landing Manning means landing multiple accounts, and that would mean really, really good things for LUNA.

But now, faced with the horror of a blank page, I let out a sigh. "I've got nothing." I look at her. "This was a mistake."

Maddie stands and moves into the space behind me. She

puts her hands on my shoulders and we both stare at the blank screen of my laptop.

"I mean, it's minimalistic, but it could work," she cracks.

There's no way I'm concentrating with her this close to me. No way I'm forming a coherent thought or having a creative idea.

"You're trying to think of all of the things all at once. It's piling up, and you can't start," Maddie says, hands on my shoulders. "Forget all that mess. Think simple. What's step one?"

I don't want to think about step one. I want to chuck all my responsibilities and take step one with her.

Get it together, man.

"Step one. Yes." I navigate to my email. "That would be the client's wishes." I pull up the email with everything the team at JB Manning requires.

"Okay," Maddie says. "Let's brainstorm."

When I look at her, I can see that same earnest *I believe in you* expression on her face.

It's exactly what I need.

About an hour later, the door to the suite opens, and Lauren steps inside. At the sight of us, she freezes. "Why do I feel like I just stepped back in time? Is this a tutoring session? Maddie, is Simon going to help you pass Econ again?"

"No," Maddie says. "We're going to help Simon catch a whale."

"Land a whale," I say absently.

Behind me, she throws up her arms. "Let me be right!"

I look at her, confused. "But you're wrong."

She takes a pillow off of the couch and throws it, but totally misses.

I grin, eyes still focused on the computer. "I think I've bitten off more than I can chew, but Maddie seems to think I'm a superhero."

Lauren smiles. "There's nothing quite like Maddie believing in you, is there?"

No. There's not. It's like I've gone through invincibility training.

Lauren raises a brow at me, but I say nothing.

"You're going to help, right, Lauren?"

Lauren sets her purse down and kicks off her shoes. "Of course I am. Just let me change and call Will to tell him goodight."

"You just left him," Maddie says.

Lauren responds with a smile.

"Okay, hurry up!" Maddie claps her hands in front of her. "We've got work to do, people!"

I know before we even start that Lauren and Maddie can't help me with the programming, but they turn out to be great brainstormers. Both creative people, Maddie and Lauren buzz with energy, and at one point, I feel like a scribe, trying to capture all the ideas they have to create a truly unique user experience for JB Manning's thriving business. Maddie practically turns the whole project into a game, bringing the kind of fun to work that only she can.

They're quiet when I need them to be, and a great sounding board when I get stuck. Maddie keeps me caffeinated with hotel coffee, and makes a run to the front desk when we exhaust our supply. She also brings in a giant bag of candy, which she calls "brain food" even though I'm pretty certain it's the exact opposite of that.

After several hours, the room goes quiet, save for the sound of my clicking on the keyboard. I review my work just to be sure, but. . .yes. . .I did it. I finished.

I stretch, now aware of the stiffness of my whole body, being locked in one position.

How long have I been sitting here?

I look at the clock. It's 3:42 a.m.

I have completely finished twelve hours of work in four hours and forty-two minutes.

I've heard about a mental state people get in when they're at their most creative—the "flow state." The melting together of action and consciousness, the tightrope balance of skill and strength.

For the first time in my entire professional life, this didn't feel like work. It felt like. . .like play.

I turn toward the couch and look at Maddie.

She's sleeping soundly, hugging her arms and legs to her chest. Her hair falls in long waves around her, and her jaw is slightly slack as the peace of sleep settles on her.

She's beautiful.

"Are you ever going to tell her?" Lauren's voice pulls my attention.

I turn and find her balled up in a chair, blanket up to her chin, watching me.

"Maybe she's ready to hear it now?" Lauren keeps her voice low. "Things seem different between you two."

I glance back at Maddie. "I thought I was imagining it."

"I don't think so."

"What if I spook her?" I ask. "You know how she is."

"You know in horror movies when the girl hears a noise and she goes to investigate it by herself?"

I frown. "Yeah."

"And the audience is all like 'Don't do it! Don't go in there!'?"

I chuckle. "Yeah. . .?"

"That's how I've felt for the last ten years, watching you come so close to confessing your true feelings and then chickening out at the last minute. Only in reverse. Every time I've been cheering you on, like 'Yes! Tell her! It's time!'"

"In my defense, I've been right to keep it to myself."

"Why?"

"She wasn't ready," I say. "There were things she needed to figure out, and no amount of anyone telling her was going to do it."

"Things like. . .?"

"Like she deserves a guy who'll treat her right," I say. "Not some idiot who tells her she isn't serious enough."

"Dylan." Lauren rolls her eyes. "What a moron."

"And Austin," I say.

"Another moron."

"Or how about the guy who only called her after midnight?" I really, really hated that guy.

"Oh yeah, and he had a ridiculous name?"

"It was Street."

Lauren laughs, then catches herself for almost being too loud. "They've all been so wrong for her." She shakes her head. "And you've been there the whole time, patiently waiting for her to figure it out."

I shrug.

"It's time, Simon." She stands and stretches, then walks over to me. "It's been ten years. This isn't some little crush. It's not going to go away."

"And if she rejects me?" My eyes fall to Maddie. "Again?"

She squeezes my shoulder. "Then you can finally move on."

I sigh, but don't respond. What can I say? I know she's right. It's time to put it all on the line and tell Maddie the truth.

And if it's the end of everything, at least I can move on.

To Seattle.

Without her.

Chapter Forty-Eight

Maddie

Road Trip—Day four

Morning comes fast, as it always does when I stay up for most of the night.

This time, instead of being out with friends, though, I'd been here, in this hotel room, with Simon, watching him work his magic and marveling at how truly incredible he is.

I'd dozed off on the couch, which is where I find myself now, under a blanket that wasn't there when I fell asleep.

I sit up and look around the room. There's a pain in my neck I'm afraid may not go away.

And no sign of Simon.

On the desk next to me, I find a note:

Thanks for everything last night. If I 'catch the whale,' I'll have you to thank.

xo,

Simon

I smile. I really did think the phrase was *catch a whale*. Huh.

When I click my phone open, I'm reminded I have a shop now. And it's doing well.

Plus, I never thanked him for the nudge. Because of him, my numbers keep climbing, doubling again overnight.

It's surreal.

I'm not sure how I'm going to manage everything—the shipping, the advertising, the creating—by myself. But after last night, I'm starting to realize maybe I don't have to. Maybe I was never supposed to.

Simon was right. It's okay to ask for help.

After all, Lauren and I helped him last night, and it didn't make me think any less of him as a business owner. It just made me happy to be a part of it.

Also, in the madness of last night, I never told Simon how I feel about him.

Lauren stumbles out of the bedroom, makeup streaked across her sleepy face.

"Whoa," I say. "You look hungover."

"And I didn't even drink!"

"You've got a little something—" I point to my own cheek, and Lauren scrubs a hand across her own. I shake my head. Lauren tries again, and succeeds in smearing it worse. "You should've been cast in Les Mis."

"I hated that movie," Lauren says. "Everyone was so dirty."

I gesture to her face.

"Shut up," she grins.

"I wonder if he got everything done," I say.

"He did." Lauren starts the single cup coffee maker brewing. "He didn't want to wake you."

I smile.

"What's that look for?"

I shrug. "I don't know. I kind of feel like we helped him. It feels nice—he's always the one helping me. Like, *always* helping me."

The coffee maker hisses, and Lauren opens a few small containers of creamer and pours it in. "And that's all?"

"What do you mean 'that's all'?"

"Nothing. Things seem different with you guys. And the way you were dancing last night. . ." Lauren fans herself.

"I'm surprised you noticed, given how wrapped up in your fiancé you were."

"He did look good in that suit, didn't he?"

I laugh. "I'm not commenting on his hotness now that he's going to be your husband. That's weird."

"But he looked good, right?"

A slow smile spreads across my face. "So good."

Lauren plops down on the armchair across from me. "I get to marry that man."

"You guys are so lucky you found each other. He chills you out, and you push him—he said he never would've gotten the job as head coach if it weren't for you."

Lauren's eyes flick to mine. "You know you just basically described you and Simon, but in reverse, right?"

I frown. "No, I didn't."

Oh my gosh. I did.

I go still, quietly happy that these feelings are becoming more. . .real. That the doubt and fear are drifting away.

"We talked about this. I know your feelings for him have changed, so what's holding you back?"

"I was so ready to tell him everything last night in the Christmas room." I look out the window.

Lauren sits forward. "And?"

I laugh to myself. "You interrupted me."

Her jaw drops, and she says, "No I did *not!* Oh no, I'm so sorry, Maddie! What were you going to say?!"

I look back at her. "I have no idea."

We both laugh.

"But seriously," I continue, "it's great that I've figured it out, it's great that it's finally clear. . .but you know how bad I am with relationships."

"Yeah. But you aren't bad with Simon." She stands to get the coffee, which is done brewing. "Stop overthinking. Just start talking. . ." She grabs a cup and starts to pour. "You'll get around to the right words eventually."

Yeah. Hopefully the words *love, I,* and *you* come out in the right order.

———

I hurry to get ready because all I can think about is how much I want to see Simon. I want to hear about his project and tell him about my sales—but mostly, I just want to see him.

I want to give the green light on the website he'd created for me and commit—finally—to making a real go of this pottery thing.

Maybe I'll have to keep my job at the coffee shop a little while longer, or maybe I'll always have a second job, but the idea that I can potentially make any income with something I love so much thrills me in a way nothing ever has before.

I'm not used to being professionally stimulated.

And yeah, maybe I just want to see Simon because I like seeing Simon.

The thought doesn't terrify me.

I've just finished drying my hair when my phone vibrates.

SIMON

I'm downstairs getting breakfast.

Come down when you can, I want to show you the end result before I send it.

MADDIE

Just need to roll up my clothes and pack them back in my backpack.

SIMON

<eye roll emoji>

MADDIE

Be down soon!

I stop short of adding a heart emoji.

Then I impulsively tap it and hit send.

MADDIE

<heart emoji>

My mind's made up. It's him.

Yeah, we're different, but different can be good. It can be great. It can be everything. And I intend to find out. . .even if I'm scared.

When I finish packing, I tell Lauren I'll meet her in the lobby, and then I practically race to the elevator and, when it doesn't descend quickly enough, I hit the LL button fifteen times to make it go faster.

I spot him instantly. He's sitting at a table, alone, talking on the phone. Probably landing the deal with Mr. Big Time Client from last night. I don't want to interrupt, but I'm excited. And I can't wait to celebrate this success with him.

I'm a part of this now.

I walk over to Simon's table, coming up behind him. My

intention is to plop right down across from him and make goofy faces while he tries to hold a serious conversation, but as I get within earshot, Simon's side of the conversation stops me.

"Will you stop? Please?" His voice has a different tone. One I've never heard before.

"You've already told me all of this," he says. "She's too flighty. She doesn't respect the importance of my job. She takes advantage of me. I'm too nice. . .*I get it.*"

A pause. He hasn't seen me, and he doesn't know I'm behind him. I slowly, and carefully, take a few steps back.

He lowers his voice so as to not yell, but the force behind his tone is still there. "Yeah, I know. I know you think this is some huge mistake. I know you think she's not good enough for me. But I don't care, Bea, okay?" A sigh, hand through his hair.

Ah. His sister.

She's tapping into my greatest fear. That I'm not good enough for him.

And on some level, I believe it.

He's put together. I'm thrown together.

He's coffee table books and hung up keys. I'm karaoke bars and overdrawn bank accounts.

But things have changed. *I've* changed.

Right?

"No, I haven't made a decision about Seattle yet."

Wait. What?

"You know why I took this trip. I needed to figure things out, and. . .I just don't know if I have yet." Another pause. "You're being crazy. I'm not going to throw everything away for some girl. I'm not stupid."

I'm frozen in place, my feet two cinder blocks.

Some girl.

Is he just repeating what she called me? Or are those his words?

No. It's not him. It can't be.

But that's what he'd said, wasn't it? And that's definitely all I am to his sister. His protective, bossy, eighty-five-percent correct sister.

I turn a circle, feeling trapped. I want to walk away, but I want to hear what else he has to say.

Why is he talking about Seattle? My stomach drops.

Is he moving? Is Simon moving away? His business is totally mobile now—he can live anywhere.

My mind flashes back to his last day at the coffee shop in college. I'd been worried about losing him then too, and we'd kept in touch.

Still, this feels different. This feels final. If he moves to Seattle, there's no chance for us.

My mind spins. Maybe this can all be figured out with a simple conversation after he gets off the phone. I'm not going to sit here and assume everything just from his side of the conversation.

"She's not dragging me down, Bea, she helped me! I didn't think I could do something and it was. . ." She must have cut him off. "No, you don't understand, I finished it because. . ." He stops short again.

My heart squeezes. Simon is defending me.

But she's not hearing it. I'm praying he's not hearing *her*, either.

"Bea, I know where you stand, okay? You've made your point. Loud and clear."

He's about to wrap up the call, and I'm still frozen in the shadows.

He ends with: "I don't know. Yes. Fine. I'll talk to you later." He punches the phone and slams it down angrily on the table.

My heart races as I stand there, staring at the back of his

head. Only seconds ago, I'd been so certain of what I wanted to say to him. Certain these feelings were worth acting on. That it's time we took a risk and see if there's something between us.

And, of course, that's true for me. A relationship with Simon means I'd get to be with an attentive, smart, kind, handsome, wonderful, successful man.

But it's not exactly a fair trade, is it?

An Etsy shop and a few pictures doesn't exactly equate to "she's got it all together."

I take a deep breath and walk from the elevator as if I just got off.

"Hey!" I try to be as chipper as I can, not letting on that I overheard his conversation with Bea, whose concerns are valid, honestly.

He doesn't wave. He doesn't move. He just sits.

I blink back tears just as Lauren walks up behind me. She looks at me, then frowns. "You okay?"

"I'm great," I lie. No way I'm going to be a downer on Lauren's wedding trip.

She frowns just as Simon stands.

He takes a breath and looks away from me. "Hey, can we just. . ." He presses his lips together. "Do you care if I ride with Will for this last leg?"

I'm taken aback. "Uh. . .yeah. Sure. Is everything. . ."

He cuts me off. "I just. . .have to think. About things."

My heart sinks a little.

"Think?"

"Yeah. There's a lot."

In my mind, the practiced script I was going to say to him, about how I feel, about everything, slowly gets torn in half.

I offer a weak "Okay. . ." as he turns and walks away.

I know he's not mad at me. But what I don't know is if his

very practical and level-headed sister just invalidated my newfound feelings for Simon.

Feelings I'm suddenly thankful I kept to myself.

Chapter Forty-Nine

Maddie

The drive from Oklahoma City to St. Louis feels long. Time with Lauren and a happy playlist helps take my mind off thinking and caring and worrying about Simon.

But only a little.

If I have any fears that we're a wrong fit, it's because he's too good for me. It's the ongoing mental teeter-totter that just won't go away.

I want Simon to have the best of everything—and that, according to his sister, is not me.

After hours of driving, Lauren pulls off at a little roadside café in Missouri.

"This is the real gem on this trip."

I study the small restaurant, situated next to a fudge factory.

"The air here smells like chocolate," Lauren says. "You gain ten pounds just by breathing."

I chuckle. "Why is this 'the gem'?" I ask.

"This is where I finally told Will the truth." She gives me a pointed look. "Unloaded every single thing from our past right here in this parking lot."

I stare back. "You don't say."

"I do say," she retorts. "And this is where you're going to finally get the chance to talk to Simon." She holds her hands up and adds, "And I promise I won't interrupt this time."

I smile through my worry.

What if Bea finally convinced him what I've always feared —that he can do so much better?

I fix a bright smile on my face as I exit the car. I force that smile to hold as I wave at both Simon and Will, summoning every bit of my resolve to pretend everything is perfectly normal.

"This spot," Will says, wincing a little. "Not the greatest memory for me."

I know Will and Lauren's history. I know he broke her heart years ago, when they were kids, and he didn't even remember. I know they had a past to overcome in order to get to where they are now—preparing to commit themselves to each other for the rest of their lives.

And I also know it all started here, the moment Lauren was honest with Will.

The similarities aren't lost on me. My relationship with Simon is different, of course. But being honest about my feelings? Talking about my loves and fears? It's scary.

It's scary when I don't know if it will be reciprocated. It's scary when the question *Is Simon moving to Seattle?* is hanging around at the back of my mind.

"Then let's make a new memory," Lauren says.

They turn toward each other, and I step into place next to Lauren, finding Simon's eyes.

He's watching me. Just like always.

Simon deserves better than me.

It's not a thought I've let be loud enough to stop me from talking to him about how I feel—time and circumstances have done that—but now it's getting bigger.

Maybe Bea is right about me.

"Lauren." Will's voice pulls my attention back to the real reason we're here. "Thank you for being honest with me. For caring enough to relive a hurtful memory and to give me a chance to make it right."

My eyes drift from Will to Simon.

I don't *want* Bea to be right, but maybe she is. Maybe I have to be honest with myself.

Ugh. I *hate* self-doubt. It's just not me. Maybe it's having an effect on me because I know how high the stakes are.

Will goes on. "It's that kind of openness that's going to make our relationship stronger, because once it was out there, we could face it. *I* could face it."

I look down.

"It was here, standing in this very parking lot," Will smiles, "surrounded by the smell of fudge, that I realized just how much you mean to me. And I can't wait to spend the rest of my life with you."

My mind drifts while Lauren says her vows, desperately trying and failing to focus, and afterwards, when Will pulls her into his arms, I look away.

I look up at Simon, and I know how I feel. I knew that night in the cottage, and I still know now.

Maybe Bea is right about me.

For some reason I can't shake that thought.

I just don't know what will happen with us—and that terrifies me.

"Let's go get lunch," Lauren says.

I nod. "I'll be right there. I'm just going to—" What? What am I going to do? Go find a secluded place to scream? "I'm going to get some fudge. I'll be back." I rush off in the direction of the little fudge shop. Maybe chocolate is what I need right now.

But as soon as I reach the door, I feel a hand on my arm. "Maddie, stop."

I spin around and find Simon, his eyes desperate and fixed on me. I force a smile—one of my best ones yet—but it falters, and I have to look away. "I'm just really craving some chocolate."

He pulls me off to the side, to a surprisingly solitary spot around the corner of the building. And then, we're alone.

"I'm sorry about the way I acted back at the hotel."

I nod, not wanting to talk about it, really.

"You heard my phone call with Bea, didn't you?" he asks.

I look away. I don't want to run from this. I want to be honest. I want to face it, like an adult. And yet, I don't want to say anything I'm feeling out loud.

Why not? Why not just tell the truth? I do it all the time. Why is it so hard now?

"Maddie. . .?"

"Yeah, I did. I'm sorry, I should've—" I wave my hand in the air—"It's not a big deal."

"It *is* a big deal," he says. "She thinks there's more going on here, between you and I."

"Yeah, well. . ."

"She's right." His words stop me cold.

"What do you mean?"

He goes still. "I think you know."

I just stare. I feel like I'm in a dream. I want to spill it all, everything I'm feeling, but instead I say, "What's in Seattle?"

He sighs. "I wanted to be the one to talk to you about it."

My heart beats hard and fast. "Are you moving?"

"I was thinking about it."

"To Seattle?"

"Bea is moving there. And I told myself—" He looks at me then, but stops talking.

"Told yourself what?"

He shakes his head slightly. "That if nothing changed between you and me on this trip, if we stayed friends after spending all this time together, if I. . ." he works hard to get this next part out, "if I told you how I really feel about you and you didn't feel the same way, then I'd go with her." He holds eye contact, and my heart sputters to a halt. "It's the only way I'm going to be able to get on with my life, if I—" he awkwardly looks down to the ground—"if I'm not seeing you every day."

"What are you saying?"

And then, he lifts his chin and brings his eyes to mine. "Maddie, I have loved you since I first saw you."

I don't move.

"I can't keep doing this," he says. "It's torture for me to just be your friend—" he pauses— "when I want to be so much more." He takes another step closer. "So. . .?"

"So. . .?" I whisper.

"You need to tell me there's nothing between us if that's how you feel, because if you don't, then I'm always going to think I have a chance." He tucks my hair behind my ears. "And if I think there's a chance, I'm never going to get over you."

"I don't want you to get over me," I say in a whisper.

And I really, really don't.

Not when he's looking at me like that. Not when all I can think about is his hands on my body, his lips on my lips. Not when all I want in the world is Simon.

Sweet, boyish, boring, wonderful Simon.

"You don't?" He puts a hand on the wall behind me, pinning me in place with his eyes.

I've taken one step too far over the edge, and now I'm falling. There's no parachute. No soft landing. There is only Simon, and I can't think of anything else in the world I need.

I shake my head.

"But Bea is right," I say. "I'm not good enough for you."

"I don't want to talk about my sister." He reaches for me, his firm, strong hand at my hip, his finger connecting with a sliver of skin just above my waist.

"Okay," I say, so very unsure about any of what is happening right now. It's different than it was in the bar. There's no drunk cowboy. No honor to protect. There's only Simon and me.

And there's nothing *friendly* about the way he's looking at me or the way I'm thinking about him.

I move to him quickly, not caring about bystanders or politeness. I throw my arms around him and say one thing.

"It's you." My hands press into his back, pulling him closer.

"It is?" A mix of confusion and hopefulness mingle on his face.

"Yes. It's always been you." But even as I exhale the words, I pull his face toward mine. He's the oxygen and I'm drowning.

I press my lips together, impulsive—and I can't form a logical thought in my head.

We've already passed the point of no return. Everything between us has already changed. We've crossed a line, and there's no going back.

My hands slide up around his neck, and he inches even closer. The rest of the world falls away as finally—finally—I lift my chin. His lips find mine, and he kisses me.

Simon is kissing me.

And it's good. *Really* good. And more than that. . .it's *right*.

The kiss is soft and tender at first, laced with wonder and disbelief. Is he as much in shock as I am? He takes my face in his hands with such care I might as well have been made of glass.

But then, something shifts, and I feel his desire in the firmness of his kiss. He presses into me, and I want to pull him closer—even with our bodies touching, it's not close enough.

The kiss grows deeper, more intense, as if he's unleashing ten years of feelings right there in that secluded parking lot. Soft, but no longer gentle. He's not holding back as his lips find my neck, my collarbone, as if he wants to explore every inch of me right here in this exact moment.

My knees buckle, weak and spent, and I realize I've never in my life kissed someone I really, truly loved.

It's so much better than I could've ever imagined, and I decide in that moment, if he's the last person I ever kiss, I'll be happy.

He breaks away from me, out of breath, eyes searching mine with such an intensity, I can't process it. And that's when I see it.

The way he looks at me isn't *I want to take you out and have a good time*—it's *I want to love you for the rest of my life.* It's the very thing I've been searching for, and it was here all along.

There's no turning back now. We both know it. We can never go back to pretending. And I don't want to.

He leans in and kisses me again, mining feelings inside of me I never even knew I had. I love him.

I love Simon.

He presses his forehead to mine. "Maddie I—" But the buzz of his phone cuts him off.

He pulls the phone out of his pocket, and then looks at me. "It's Manning."

"You should get it."

"I'm out of breath."

I laugh. "So am I."

The buzzing pulls my attention from the rush of confusion. "It's okay, go ahead."

He hesitates, and the phone seems to grow louder in the silent space between us. Then, finally, he steps away and answers it.

I bring my fingers to my still-tingling lips.

I draw in a deep breath.

My mind is swirling, nerves overloaded and emotions over-flowing—and somewhere, among all of the giddiness, lies a singular thought.

Maybe Bea is right.

I shut my eyes and lean my head back against the wall.

I know I can do better, *be* better.

But there's just a small, needling sliver of doubt—that I'm not good enough for Simon, no matter how much I want to be.

And now that I'd tasted the sweetness of his kiss, I'm not sure how I'll ever survive without it.

Chapter Fifty

Simon

I'm seriously out of breath. Plus, my legs aren't working.
I try to listen to the voice on the other end of the line,
but my mind is reeling. I have to lean up against the side
of the building just to stay upright.

Did that really just happen?

I hobble a few steps away from Maddie, but keep her in my
view.

We kissed.

And...and just...*wow.*

"Mr. Collier?"

"Sorry, Janine," I say to Manning's assistant, who I don't
care about at all right now. "I'm listening." I turn away from
Maddie in an effort to focus.

"Mr. Manning loves what you've done. Loves it. Wouldn't
stop talking about it, in fact."

I refocus, unsure I've heard correctly. "He does?"

"He does. You knocked it out of the park. A few changes to
the color scheme by tomorrow, and you've got yourself a deal."

"Really?"

She laughs. "Yes, really. I don't know how you pulled it off, but Mr. Manning is impressed. With you *and* the work."

I did it.

No, that's not accurate. *We* did it—

I spin back around to bring Maddie into my excitement, but she's gone. I step out from around the corner of the building and see her walking toward the diner, where Will and Lauren are waiting for us.

"I'm on the road this afternoon," I say, starting off in the direction of the diner. "But I'll make the changes tonight and send them over." Assuming I don't collapse.

"Great," Janine says. "Looking forward to your email."

I hang up, tuck my phone in my pocket, and open the door to the diner. I spot Will, Lauren, and Maddie sitting at a booth near a window, looking over their menus.

I squeeze my hands into tight fists at my side, praying she doesn't try and pretend what happened outside never happened. That might kill me.

"So?" Lauren looks up at me, expectancy on her face. "Maddie said the client was on the phone?"

I glance at Maddie, whose cheeks are a little pinker than usual. She looks down, then back up at me with a knowing smile on her face.

Is she replaying it all in her mind like I am?

I'm not the most experienced guy in the world, but I'm no slouch either, and I can safely say it was the best kiss of my life.

I want to do it again.

Pretty much every day for the rest of my life.

"Simon!" Lauren snaps her fingers. "We're a part of this now—what did they say?"

I slide into the booth next to Maddie, keeping my face somber for a beat, then finally, breaking into a smile. "We caught the whale."

"We did?" Maddie bursts. "You got it?!"

"They requested a new color palette, but once I implement that, yeah. We got it." My smile widens. I can't help it—it's a huge deal for LUNA. A huge deal for me.

"I knew it! I knew you could do anything!" Maddie says, still facing me.

"I got it," I glance at her, "because of you."

She shakes her head. "I didn't do anything."

"Are you kidding? I wouldn't have even tried if it weren't for you."

She presses her lips together, a mix of pride and joy on her face. "I'm so proud of you."

"Thank you." I look at Lauren. "Both of you."

"This is awesome, man," Will says. "We need to celebrate."

"We *do* need to celebrate," Lauren says. "This is huge! Simon caught the whale, Maddie is selling her pottery. . ." Then, she gasps. "Wait, Maddie, did you tell him?"

"Tell me what?"

"Her sales did a triple-double," Lauren says.

"What's that?" I ask.

"They tripled. Then doubled again," Lauren says.

Maddie's smile is uncharacteristically shy. "Because of you."

"No, I didn't do anything."

She raises a brow. "We both know if it weren't for you, I never would've put my name on it."

"Actually, that's true."

She laughs.

"You guys are a good team," Lauren says.

Maddie and I share a glance. She crosses her eyes and I shake my head, laughing.

"So, how should we celebrate?" Will asks.

I glance at Maddie, and then, in unison, we both say, "Milkshakes."

There's no tension at the table. If Maddie is freaked out by our parking lot make-out session, she's doing a good job of hiding it.

I want to pull her back outside and let her verbally process everything, and by "verbally process everything" I mean kiss her again.

But she and I are not the reason we're here. And I know how important Lauren is to her. So, if I have to wait a little longer to say another word about it, I can do that too.

But it's going to be really, really difficult.

Two-and-a-half milkshakes later (one was a refill that we split), the waitress brings our checks.

Maddie grabs mine. "Yours is on me."

"No way." I try to snatch it from her, but she's too quick.

She stops me with a raised pointer finger. "I owe my positive bank balance to you, and I want to say thanks."

"You don't have to thank me," I say. "You know I'd do anything for you."

"Anything?" she grins. "Like, stand up in this diner and sing your guts out."

I frown. "Okay, almost anything."

"Okay," Will says, scooting out of the booth. "Back to the grind. Last leg of the trip!"

Lauren stands. "We're in the middle of a full Abba sing-through, so we've got to keep going." Then, to Will, "It'll give you time to miss me."

As Maddie gets out of the booth, she stands too close to me and brushes her hand purposefully on mine. I link our fingers behind her back, hidden from Will and Lauren.

Like two teenagers. It's exhilarating.

Will and Lauren walk off, leaving me to fall into step next to Maddie.

Our arms brush up against each another.

She looks at me, a half-smile on her beautiful, full lips. "So. . ."

"So. . ." I answer.

"That was. . .crazy."

"Yeah," I say. "That's one word for it."

She stops moving and faces me.

"Are you freaking out?"

I shake my head. "No. Not at all. You?"

She shakes her head, and we start walking again. "What are you thinking?" She leans into me.

"I'm thinking. . ." I blow a breath out slowly, "that was some kiss."

She smiles up at me with a scrunched nose. "It was, wasn't it? I couldn't even feel my legs."

"I thought I was going to pass out."

She takes my arm. "You know, that was just the first one."

"Second," I correct her.

"Yeah but that one in the bar didn't count," she quips. "It was not my best work."

I start to imagine what her "best work" would entail.

"Unfortunately, though, we may have to put a pin in this conversation," she says.

I understand immediately. "Will and Lauren."

"Yes. We're here for them. So, let's focus on the wedding," she says. "I really want to be here for Lauren."

I nod. "I know. And what, we'll talk about it later?"

"Definitely," she says. "But I can't guarantee much talking."

It takes every ounce of self-control not to kiss her again right there.

"Ready, guys?" Lauren calls from a few yards away.

Maddie gives my hand a squeeze, then lets it go.

I want it back.

We say a quick goodbye and get in separate cars.

Will drives the last leg so I can implement changes to the Manning website—while I'm simultaneously FaceTiming with Maddie about colors.

We finish about two hours into the four-hour drive, and Maddie and I say our goodbyes—while trying not to alert Will or Lauren. It's exciting, like we have some secret.

For the last two hours, Will and I small talk a bit, and then he flips on sports radio, and my mind wanders back to the parking lot of that fudge factory.

When we arrive at Will's parents' house, my work plate is clear. I'm done for the weekend, freeing me up to focus.

On Maddie.

But it's clear by the exhaustion in her sleepy face, that the pin is staying in our conversation a little while longer. She fell asleep after we hung up, is barely functional, and the imprint of the seatbelt is still hilariously indenting her cheek.

I grab her bag and follow them all inside the quiet house. It's dark, and Will's parents are sleeping, so we do our best not to make noise as we find the guest rooms his mom made up for us.

Maddie steps inside one of the rooms, which she'll be sharing with Lauren, and I set her bag down just inside the doorway.

She turns and looks at me. "Always taking care of me."

I take a step toward her and bring my hand to her cheek. "Always will."

She presses a soft kiss into my palm, then closes her eyes.

"Okay, bedtime." I walk over to the bed and pull back the covers.

"How are you not exhausted?" She sits on the end of the bed and takes her shoes off.

"Oh, I am. I'm running on pure adrenaline," I say.

She lays down, and I pull the covers over her. "So tired."

"Get some sleep, Mads," I say, brushing the hair back from her face.

And I'm pretty sure she's already out.

I make my way down the hall to a different room, this one with a frilly pink comforter and pale pink curtains.

I *am* exhausted, and I want to collapse. It's been a day. From Bea's warnings to wedding vows to Maddie's kisses to landing JB Manning for LUNA.

It's a lot to process.

I replay the kiss over and over, hoping it will lull me to sleep, but instead, it keeps me awake for another half hour.

The following morning, I wake up to the smell of bacon and the sound of chatter. I know from Lauren that Will's family is close, and only now does it occur to me I could feel slightly out of place here.

Fitting in with strangers isn't my strong suit.

But I want to see Maddie. I *need* to see her.

The knock on the door pulls my attention, and I sit up halfway. "Come in."

When it opens, Lauren steps inside. "Morning." She studies me. "You look like you need another eight hours of sleep."

I push a hand through my hair. "Gee, thanks."

She laughs. "We're going to do some last-minute shopping with Will's sisters before the rehearsal dinner tonight. Do you want to come?"

"Shopping with a bunch of women?" I smirk. "I'm good here, but thanks." But I'm wondering why Lauren is asking me and not Maddie.

"You sure?"

"I'm done with the big projects," I say. "But it'll be good for me to catch up on all of the other stuff I've put off for the week."

"Okay." She smiles. "You sure you're good?"

"Yep. I promise. Have fun."

It doesn't seem like Lauren knows what happened between me and Maddie, and I'm trying not to read into that. I know Maddie wants this weekend to be about Will and Lauren, but they drove hours together after our kiss.

Girls talk, I hear.

"There's breakfast and coffee on the counter downstairs," she says. "Help yourself, and make yourself at home." She slips away.

I head downstairs to get some food and meet Will's parents. They make it easy for me to feel welcome, and I'm amazed at how relaxed I feel here. No pressure, no fake small talk. It's like we're all old friends and I've come home for the holidays.

It's really nice.

I work a little, nap a little, but mostly try really hard not to think about Maddie.

That afternoon, Will's mom asks if I would be up for filling tiny white bags with bird seed, and I'm happy for the distraction. She grabs Will and steers him toward the table, parking him there to help, too.

As we're sitting, surrounded by white ribbons and sheer white bags, Maddie, Lauren, and Will's sisters, Nadia and Kayla, walk in. They're laughing and talking and then they see us and all four of them stop.

"This is something I never thought I'd see," one of Will's sisters says. "How dainty."

"Yeah, come over here and say that." Will holds up a small bag as if to throw it.

"It's a *beautiful* sight," Lauren lays it on thick. "My future husband, stuffing bird seed bags for our wedding."

"Yep," Will says. "Visual proof of how much I love you."

There's a choir of high-pitched "Awwws," and finally, Maddie looks at me. She smiles, and I can't tell if she's being polite or if she's spooked about everything that happened yesterday.

It's selfish of me to want to steal her away—just for a minute—but I can't help it. She's all I can think about.

"We have to get ready for the rehearsal dinner," Lauren says. "We'll leave you guys with your. . .crafts."

As they leave the room, Maddie stops beside me. "Did you have a good day?"

"Yeah," I say. *Would've been better if I could've spent it with you.* "You?"

She nods. "I did. I missed you!" She hits me on the arm. "But not that much."

I flick some bird seed at her—I like how we still feel like friends, but more.

"We'll be back in just a little bit," she says.

I watch her as she leaves down the hall and around the corner. After she's gone, I turn back to the bird seed and find Will looking at me.

"Did something happen?"

I take a deep breath.

"Yep."

"What step are you on?" he asks, calling back to our original napkin list.

I chuckle. "Well, I think I added a couple."

"Oh yeah?"

I nod. "Yeah. I'm on the step where I tell her exactly how I feel and she kisses me behind the fudge shop." I deadpan.

Will sets down the bag he's working on. He shakes his head in apparent disbelief. "You've surpassed my expectations."

I laugh. "Let's hope I surpassed hers. In the moment, she told me how she felt, but I have no idea what I'm doing. Where do we go from here?"

Will ties the last ribbon and tosses the bag into the box with the others. "Simon, my friend, I still have no idea what I'm doing. Or why Lauren decided to love me. All I know is that I love her like crazy, and I'll do whatever I can to hold on to that."

After we finish our "arts and crafts" project, we rush to get ready. The women have claimed the bathroom, and despite the fact they've been at it at least an hour longer than we have, we still end up waiting for them.

Turns out, it's worth the wait.

Maddie and the others (that's how I see the group, because nobody else really matters right now) walk down the stairs. I can't keep my eyes off of her. I can hardly believe how stunning she is. She walks into the room, which has started to get a little crowded, and finds my eyes. She smiles.

I move toward the back of the room, trying to stay out of the way. Will's parents are fussing over everyone, and Lauren's brother Spencer and his wife, Helen, are here. Kayla and Nadia's husbands and kids sit on the couch and chairs, and everyone is chattering on about the wedding.

It's a big, family affair, and for the first time, maybe in my life, I think maybe I could fit into something like this.

The crazy kids running around. The overlapping conversations. The subtle, loving teasing. The overly loud laughs.

It's chaos, and would normally send me packing.

But it doesn't. This is what's been missing from my life.

And I want it with Maddie.

She makes her way over to me, and I take a moment to admire the black dress. "You look amazing."

She lifts a brow. "You're looking pretty sharp yourself."

I give my suit coat a tug. "Oh, this old thing?"

"Thanks for doing all this, Simon," she says. "I know it's been hard with work and all these strangers and, just everything."

I shove my hands in my pockets and bring my eyes to hers. "Anything for you, Mads."

At that, a smile tips the corners of her mouth.

I resist the urge to explain that by "anything," I really do mean "anything." Because that's what I'd do to have her in my life.

No moving to Seattle.

No starting over.

I'm all in.

Chapter Fifty-One

Maddie

The Day of the Wedding

The sunlight filters in through the space between the curtains in the guest room, and the noise in the house pulls me from slumber.

I barely have time to wake up when the door to the room is flung open and Nadia and Kayla rush in.

"Today's the day!" Nadia says. "Get up, girls!"

"We brought Camille! And coffee!" Kayla adds.

Camille is from a salon downtown. The coffee is straight from heaven.

"We forced Will out of the house already," Kayla says. Then, she looks at me. "Simon too. We can spread out to get ready."

"Simon's gone?" I ask.

Both of Will's sisters stop moving and look at me.

"Yeah, sorry," Nadia says. "If it's any consolation, he didn't want to go until he talked to you, but we sort of forced him out."

I smile. "Of course." But my heart aches a little that it's going to most likely be hours before I see him.

Turns out, putting a pin in a conversation we really need to have wasn't the best idea. I've still got all kinds of *things* to say to him, and they're just sitting in my brain, taking up space.

Hanging on the closet door, still in a garment bag, is Lauren's dress. Nadia unzips it and we all pause for a long moment to admire it.

Tears spring to my eyes. "Lo, you're going to be so beautiful."

She gives me a quick hug. "Not if I don't get moving!"

We take over the kitchen and the large upstairs bathroom, all of us in various states of the "beautifying ourselves" process when the outside door to the kitchen opens to reveal Simon, standing there, with a large bouquet of flowers in his hand.

I'm standing at the counter with curlers in my hair, sporting a pair of gray joggers and a white camisole.

He freezes. "Oh. . .I should've knocked."

"Don't be silly," I say. "It's not like *I'm* the bride or something."

I glance down at the flowers.

"Uh, Will sent me in with these," he says. "They're for Lauren."

"Right," I say.

A lull.

I can't stand it anymore. "Stop it. This is awkward."

"What is?"

"You and me," I say. "It's weird."

His face falls. "I don't want it to be weird."

He closes the door. He's also wearing joggers, but his are black, and his white Nike T-shirt somehow makes him look like he just got home from the gym. "It's only weird because we haven't had a chance to talk."

He's right.

He takes a step toward me. "We just have other things to focus on right now."

"I know, but we need to talk about—"

Lauren walks in. "Oh, hey, Loverboy!"

Simon's eyes dart to her, then back to me. I look away.

"Oh yeah. I know," Lauren says, raising her eyebrows.

"You know what?" Simon asks.

Lauren leans in and whispers, "*Everything*."

He stammers. "You. . .know?. . .Everything?"

"Will sent Simon in with flowers," I say, enjoying Simon floundering like a newborn giraffe.

Simon gathers himself enough to hand the bouquet to Lauren. "He knows he's not allowed in here today, but he said, 'Tell her I'm counting down the minutes.'"

Lauren takes the flowers and inhales the scent of them as I steal another look at Simon.

He gives me a once-over, as if just now realizing the state of my hair and clothing. He smiles. "Nice hair."

"Cute, right?" I say, touching the curlers.

He hands me two bags, one long and thin, the other from what looks like a bakery. "Got you these."

I take them from him, but don't open them right away. We both start talking at the same time.

"Thanks, I'll, um. . ."

"Yeah, they're for. . ."

We laugh clumsily.

Then look at each other for a weighted moment.

"I'll, uh, see you at the church," he says finally. "Hopefully without the—" he points to his own head—"curlers." And then, he leaves.

"He's adorably awkward," Nadia says.

"And cute," Kayla adds.

I nod. "Yes. He is both of those things."

"What did he give you?" Camille asks, tugging one of the curlers from the back of my hair.

I open the long thin bag. It's a small bouquet of wildflowers. I set them down on the counter and open the other bag. Inside, there are two chocolate croissants.

For a moment I'm confused, but then it dawns on me.

I said something, in passing, about my perfect date.

My perfect first date. *The flower market. The chocolate croissants. Talking straight through lunch. . .knowing everything about each other.*

My eyes well with fresh tears. I'm standing in the kitchen and I'm crying over croissants.

I sniff and glance up and find Lauren, Nadia, Kayla, and Camille all staring at me.

"Guys," I say. "He got me croissants."

Lauren looks at the others and walks over to me, as the depth of this love I have for Simon washes over me. It's a love I've dreamed of, but never thought could really be mine. And I still haven't told him how I feel. . .

"We have no idea what that means. . .but it seems to mean something to you?"

I grab the flowers by the stems and thrust them out to Lauren, who flinches back.

"And he got me flowers! It's my perfect date! *Don't you see?!*"

I settle back into a full-body sigh. "He *remembered. . .*"

"So what the heck are you still doing in here?"

I sniff and look at Lauren, who is staring at me. ". . .What?"

"Are you going to just let him go?" Lauren swoons, gently lowering the flowers I'm holding out of her face.

I look at the door and wipe my nose with my free hand. "I'm wearing curlers."

"So what?" Kayla says.

"Maddie. Go!" Lauren says.

I stand and move toward the front door, racing outside just as Simon is walking around to the driver's side of his car. At the sight of me, standing on the porch, he stops.

"Is everything okay?"

"No!" I yell at him. "Nothing is okay!"

He moves toward me, instant concern on his face. "What's wrong?"

"This—" I motion to the space between us. "We need to do something about this."

He stops. "What do you mean?"

"I've been thinking about us," I say, trying not to lose my courage. Because even though I know how he feels, and even though I hinted at how I feel, there is more to be said.

Out loud.

"I've been thinking about all the ways you've shown up for me over the years. Ten years of you bending over backward to make sure I'm happy."

He watches me, but says nothing.

"I took it for granted."

He shakes his head.

I come down the steps and stand right in front of him. "Simon, I took advantage of your kindness, and I'm really sorry. I never meant to."

He reaches for me. "You never did that."

"I did," I say. "Between the two of us, you bring a lot more to this friendship than I do."

"I don't believe that for a second." He wraps his hands around mine, staring straight at me, confident in a way I haven't seen before.

"I can't stop thinking about kissing you," I say. "I've

replayed it to death." I take a step closer. "It's not the craziest idea in the world, right? You and me?"

"You know how I feel about you. What do you think?"

"I think your sister is probably right," I confess. "She makes a great case. I'm probably all wrong for you, and you can do better and all of those things, and—" I draw in a breath.

He cuts me off. "Do you remember the day you made me go out and run around in the rain?"

I stop.

"That's random." I smile. "But I do. I didn't think you were going to actually do it."

"I didn't think I was going to, either." He smiles. "That was the day I lost my job."

I frown. "It was?"

"Yeah, it was."

"You never said anything," I say.

"I didn't need to. I didn't have to say a word and still you knew exactly what I needed. You knew I needed to play in the rain like everything was going to work out fine."

"I had no idea." I can still picture him, soaking wet, face up, stress free.

"You have every idea, Maddie. It's like you have this sixth sense about me." He takes my face in his hands and smiles, gaze dipping to my lips, then back to my eyes. "You keep me sane. You remind me there's more to life than work. You watch out for me."

"I do?" I want it to be true. I want to believe that I can be as good for him as he is for me.

"But you are just so good, Simon, and I'm such a screw-up," I say. "You deserve so much better."

He scoffs. "There's no better."

"There could be. Someone smart and steady, not someone

who is overly emotional or who cries when she kills her houseplants."

"I love that you were so heartbroken over Prickles."

A soft laugh escapes. "I miss that cactus."

"No," Simon says. "There is no 'better.' Not for me. There's only you. There's only ever been you."

"So, what you're saying is. . ."

He wraps his arms around my waist and pulls my body to his. "What I'm saying is it might not make the most sense, but you and I belong together. We make each other better." He draws in a breath. "I love that you have a goofy side. I love that you're emotional. I love that you're extra sometimes, and that I'm one of the few people who knows there's a quiet, pensive side to you. I love it because all of these things are *you*." He presses a soft kiss to my forehead. "And I love you, Maddie. For ten years, I've loved you. And *not* as a friend."

"You *love* me." I can't keep myself from smiling.

He playfully scolds me. "Quit making that face. This is serious business."

"Oh. Yes. You're right." I stifle a giggle. "Go on."

"I think there is something legitimately wrong with you," he says, shaking his head. "But I love it. And you. More than anything," he says. "More than everything."

"Even though I'm a mess?"

"Yes," he says.

I smile as his face dips toward mine. "You love me."

"I love you."

My eyes search his, and there it is, as plain as day. How I'd missed it all this time, I have no idea. "Simon?"

His lips barely graze mine, a touch as gentle as a feather. "Yeah?"

"I love you too." And then finally, he kisses me, lips moving over mine with a quiet desperation. Behind me, the sound of cheering pulls me from my euphoria, and I realize that we have an audience on the porch.

A very invested, very noisy, very nosy romance-craved audience.

And I have no problem giving them exactly the show they're here to see.

Simon grins down at me. "I'm going to spend the rest of my life loving you, Madeline Rogers."

"And I'll happily return the favor."

Epilogue

Maddie

The Wedding

The wedding of Will Sinclair and Lauren Richmond will go down in history as one of the most beautiful, joyous weddings that has ever been.

Not because anyone had spent thousands of dollars or because it had the trendiest things, but because the two people standing at the altar loved each other so purely and so wholly that it was like watching something magical unfold right in front of our eyes.

I stand at the front of the small church beside Lauren, holding her bouquet and trying not to cry.

It's hard to hold it in because *that look* on Will's face tells me everything I need to know. This man loves my best friend more than anything else in the world.

And when I dare a glance to the third row, I find Simon looking at me the same way.

The thought that someone could cherish me like that stuns me. I've spent a good portion of my adult life thinking I was destined for three-month relationships that barely scratched the surface. That I had to change who I am if I had any hope of ever being enough.

But the truth is, for Simon, I *am* enough.

Simon knows all my faults, and he loves me anyway. And now that I know that, I'll never take it for granted again.

While driving to the church, I daydreamed about what it would be like for Lauren and me to be two married women with kids and dogs and jobs and husbands and backyard grills and houses right next door to each other.

And I found myself liking that daydream a lot.

"Will and Lauren have written their own vows," the pastor says, with a nod at the couple.

I listen as Will and Lauren repeat their vows from the cross-country trip, each taking turns the way they had on the road. The words are so full of promise.

And I'm so filled with hope.

Once the ceremony is over, Will takes Lauren in his arms and kisses her so sweetly, I start crying again. Then, they turn to their guests and are met with more applause. They walk back down the aisle toward the back of the church, stopping in the lobby for another kiss.

I turn toward Spencer, and he offers me his arm, leading me down the aisle toward Will and Lauren. As I pass by Simon, he smiles at me, and my heart leaps.

I mouth "You love me" in an over-exaggerated fashion, giving a little sway of my hips down the aisle.

He responds with pointing at me and then taking the same finger and twirling it next to his temple.

Yep, I think. *One hundred percent crazy for you.*

I wait outside as the guests are released pew by pew, watching the door with the kind of anticipation I haven't felt since I was a kid on Christmas morning.

When he finally appears at the back of the church, he scans the crowd, looking slightly out of place in a way that only endears me to him even more.

I stand off to the side, watching as he searches, and when his eyes finally land on me, he stops moving, lifting a brow so slightly I almost miss it.

He stands, unmoving, and while I can't be sure, I have the distinct impression I'm being admired.

I like it.

I like knowing that he doesn't need me to entertain him. How many quiet nights had we spent on his couch? How many times had he let me be still, giving me space to recharge? He doesn't expect me to be anything but who I am—who I *really* am.

And he challenges me to be better in a way that has never made me feel like I'm not good enough.

When he starts toward me, I realize that I've also been admiring him. He looks pretty darn handsome in his dark gray suit and teal tie, clean shaven and neatly coiffed.

He must feel self-conscious at me openly ogling him like this, because he laughs a little to himself and looks away.

Good grief, I'm in trouble. Adorable and sexy at the same time.

He sticks a hand in his pocket and walks toward me, navigating through the crowd of people and straight to where I stand.

When he reaches me, he stops, taking me in in a way that makes me feel seen. And *loved*.

He reaches out and tucks an unruly curl behind my ear.

"She looked amazing, and everything went off without a hitch. Wasn't it a beautiful ceremony?" I ask, trying not to pay attention to my body responding to his touch.

"It was a marvelous marriage."

I look at him with knowing eyes.

"Yes, yes," I wave my hand around like I'm the Queen of England, complete with a posh accent, "a wonderful wedding."

He grins. The challenge is on.

"Nice nuptials."

I laugh, "Okay, that sounds dirty."

He smiles. "I didn't even know there was a ceremony," he says. "All I really saw up there was you." A slow smile creeps across his lips. He reaches out and takes my hand, giving me a little tug toward him.

"Oh, great. You're going to be a sappy boyfriend, aren't you?" I ask.

"I might have trouble keeping my thoughts to myself," he says. "Now that I can speak freely."

"I can't believe you've been holding out on me." I settle into his embrace and wrap my arms up around his neck. "I'm sorry it took me so long, Simon. I think maybe I wasn't ready to be loved."

"And now?"

"Now, I'm ready." I inch up on my tiptoes and kiss him gently. "Now I can't wait."

He smiles, our lips still pressed together. "Finally."

***

Simon

I'm grateful this isn't one of those weddings where the bridal party sits separately from everyone else during dinner. I don't want to be away from Maddie for another second.

I take my seat next to her, perfectly content to serve no function other than being her date. I'd admired her quietly, secretly, for so long, I thought it might be a struggle to make my feelings public, but it wasn't.

She's here, at my side, and while she'll probably try and find a way to talk me out of loving her when the dust of this day settles, I'm armed and ready with a whole list of reasons why I'm set on this.

Why I've always been set on this.

She thinks she's bad for me, but I'm pretty sure she saved me. Over and over again. From being too withdrawn. Too serious. Too stressed out. From letting work take over and become the only thing in my life.

When it's time for her to give her toast, she actually looks a little nervous, which is not an emotion I'm used to seeing on her.

She stands and takes the microphone from Lauren's brother with a smile, then turns all of her attention to the bride.

"Lauren. I have so much dirt on you." The crowd laughs. "Will, do you have any idea what you're getting into?"

Scattered laughs as Will calls out, "You know I'm the lucky one here!"

"I think you're both lucky." She smiles and clears her throat. "I first met Lauren back in college," Maddie begins. "We were fast friends, even though we couldn't be more different. She loved to work. I loved to play. She loved checklists, and I loved no lists. Maybe our friendship didn't make sense, but it didn't take long before Lauren became my family."

Maddie pauses, then looks at Will. "And boy, did she have a crush on you. She'd sleep with your picture."

"I did not!" Lauren protests.

"Yes, she did. She drooled whenever she talked about you, which was disgusting, by the way."

"Oh my gosh, you're the worst. You're fired as my maid of honor," Lauren laughs.

Maddie shakes the mic at her. "Too late!"

Will laughs as Lauren covers her face with her hands. He leans in and kisses her.

"Friends, I'm talking a bad, bad crush," Maddie says. "She didn't tell me much, just that she liked this boy back home. If I'd known what you looked like I definitely would not have questioned this torch she carried one little bit."

More laughter, and someone in the back cheers.

"But it's more than that, isn't it?" Maddie says. "It isn't just that you're two beautiful people. It's that you were drawn together. Destined. Connected, body and soul." Maddie glances at me.

It's exactly how I feel about her.

"It's no secret that I didn't really believe that kind of love existed," Maddie says. "My track record with relationships has been, well. . .not great. I honestly believed that when it came to romance, the only good part of a relationship was right at the beginning. The *falling* part."

Her eyes smile as she looks back and forth between the bride and the groom. "But then, I watched you two. I was there when you found each other again. And the beginning was, in fact, beautiful. But what's more beautiful is what's happened in the two years since that first cross-country road trip."

She moves a bit closer to them. "You became each other's best friends." Her gaze wanders over to me again. "And there's just something wonderful about being in love with your best friend."

I don't hear much after that. It's hard to concentrate when all I want to do is find somewhere private so I can show Maddie just how wonderful it is.

She finishes her speech. Will and Lauren kiss. There are other things happening, I'm sure of it, but everything that isn't Maddie falls away.

"You okay?" She sits down beside me.

"Better than okay," I say.

"Will you do me a favor?"

I smile. "Anything."

"Sing."

I look around the room. "Here?"

She nods.

I shake my head. "I don't sing in public unless there's a girl I'm trying to impress."

"It can be your wedding gift to Will and Lauren."

"But I got them a toaster."

She leans over and whispers in my ear, "Then it can be just for me."

Moments later, I'm on the small stage, playing piano and singing "To Make You Feel My Love" while Will and Lauren have their first dance. I zero in on Maddie, standing off to the side, and pretend there's nobody else in the room—only her—and that's all I need to do to give the performance of my life.

The song ends, and I hand the microphone over to the DJ and step off the stage, straight into Maddie's arms.

"You should do that every single day for the rest of your life," she says.

I take her face in my hands and kiss her, right there on the dance floor for God and everyone to see. "As long as you promise to be there, I will."

She wraps her arms around me and kisses me back. For a second, I wonder if I'm dreaming, but no, my hands are touching her soft skin. My lips are kissing her sweet, strawberry flavored lips. My heart is beating in time with hers.

She pulls back and lifts her chin to look straight into my eyes. "I promise."

"Good enough for me."

A Love Letter

From the Author

Every book I write is a completely different experience.

Some books are easy. They come together without a ton of angst. They're fun. The characters are alive from the first page. They make me happy.

This book was not one of those books.

This book took its time. And no amount of me willing it into existence seemed to do the trick.

It made me work for THE END.

And in some ways, maybe that makes releasing it a little sweeter. (Even though, a part of me is still a little angry with it for being more stubborn than all three of my children combined...and that's saying something. I raised three VERY stubborn children!)

When I wrote *A Cross-Country Christmas*, I needed a creative break. I needed to rediscover the joy of writing. I gave no thought to sales or reviews or anything having to do with the business of writing. I just wrote it for fun.

And that book brought joy to a lot of readers in a way I'd always dreamed.

I never planned on writing a sequel.

And then one of my sweet readers told me I should. (Krysten Kruse, I'm looking at you.) She even had a title and everything. And from the second I saw the words *A Cross-Country Wedding*, I knew I wanted to make this book happen.

Lauren's friend, Maddie was an obvious heroine (and honestly, the only other character in the first book that wasn't married!) but finding her perfect hero took some doing.

In the end, I've fallen in love with Simon just as much as Maddie has, and I hope you love him too.

As always, I hope this book brings you JOY, more than anything. Because I believe that life is heavy. . .but your books don't have to be.

Thank you for reading this book. I hope you'll check out more of my work and please don't hesitate to catch up with me via email: courtney@courtneywalshwrites.com I love to chat with my readers & make new friends!

With gratitude,

Courtney

Acknowledgments

Adam—For all the ways you help me. On the page and off. Always and forever. Me + you.

Mom—Thanks for always being my first reader. And for still buying a paperback copy. I'm so thankful for you. You're a good one!

Sophia—Turns out you're a pretty fabulous co-worker. Thanks for making me laugh with your editorial comments. I think you're pretty awesome.

Ethan—Thank you for always reminding me that my phone camera is dirty. And for being a genuinely good human. I see so much good in you.

Sam—Thank you for making me laugh. And for being one of the most authentic souls I know.

Becky Wade & Katie Ganshert—For helping to get me through the angst of this book. With every single rewrite...and there were many!

Melissa Tagg—Always such a good friend. I'm so very grateful for you.

Krysten Kruse—Thank you for suggesting this book in the first place, and for giving it a title. You are a gem!

Our Studio Kids & Families—Do you have any idea how special you are? You make my "day job" nothing but pure joy. I'm so thankful for each one of you!

Denise Harmer—Thank you for once again being an awesome copyeditor. I'm so thankful for you!

About the Author

Courtney Walsh is the Carol award-winning author of eighteen novels and two novellas. Her debut novel, *A Sweethaven Summer*, was a *New York Times* and *USA Today* e-book bestseller and a Carol Award finalist in the debut author category. In addition, she has written two craft books and several full-length musicals. Courtney lives with her husband and three children in Illinois, where she co-owns a performing arts studio and youth theatre with her business partner and best friend—her husband.

Visit her online at www.courtneywalshwrites.com

Printed in Dunstable, United Kingdom